Comments on

I loved this book. I like good hist
smart female characters, if the
patriarchy, so much the bette
awareness of the land, its medi
put down. This story is replete with insight, and char...
things like 'Who would speak for the wild?'

The women in *The Swan-Bone Flute* cope with change and challenge, faced with dilemmas that countless women have known, in feudalizing and colonizing societies, that continue in our own times. The transformations they go through, and the subtle teachings of the wandering bard Hilda, speak to the lives of women today, and what we are reaching back to recover.

Max Dashu, Director of the Suppressed Histories Archive and author of *Witches and Pagans, Women in European Folk Religion, 700–1100*

We all half-remember the stories of *The Swan-Bone Flute*. We have inherited them in our DNA. Meg, Hilda and all the others are strangely familiar; we catch sight of them with the corner of an eye or dance with them in our dreams. Reading *The Swan-Bone Flute* is like sleep-walking in our mothers' memories or overhearing whispered gossip about nearly-forgotten neighbours.

The characters Rachel O'Leary has conjured are well rounded and colourful, jumping off the page and into the imagination. This is a book you will want to savour. It will enthrall and enchant you and fill you with righteous indignation. Travel with Hilda as she battles to raise the consciousness of the women who have had their ancient status and rights stripped from them and cheer for Meg as she steps into her female power.

Maddie McMahon, *Author of Why Doulas Matter and Why Mothering Matters*

THE SWAN-BONE FLUTE

BOOK ONE
OF
THE STORYTELLERS TRILOGY

RACHEL O'LEARY

BOG
OAK

Published 2019
Bog Oak Publishing

British Library Cataloguing-in-Publication Data
A catalogue record for this book is available from the British Library

Paperback ISBN 978-1-9160738-0-7
Ebook ISBN 978-1-9160738-1-4

Bog Oak Publishing
https://racheloleary.co.uk/bog-oak-publishing

'... those of us who dream
with and of the land
can believe that ... there is hope
that a different way
of seeing the world
may emerge;
that we could learn from
who we were
and so change
who we might be ...
It is not too late to go forward
differently.'

Manda Scott
Boudica: Dreaming the Serpent Spear

From **Boudica:Dreaming The Serpent Spear by Manda Scott**
Published by **Bantam Press**
Reprinted by permission of The Random House Group Limited. © 2006

Excerpt from
DREAMING THE SERPENT SPEAR: A NOVEL OF BOUDICA, THE WARRIOR QUEEN
by Manda Scott, Copyright © 2006 Manda Scott.
Reprinted by permission of Alfred A. Knopf Canada, a division of
Penguin Random House Canada Limited.
All rights reserved.

Excerpt from
DREAMING THE SERPENT-SPEAR: A NOVEL OF BOUDICA, THE WARRIOR QUEEN
by Manda Scott, copyright © 2007 by Manda Scott.
Used by permission of Dell Publishing, an imprint of Random House,
a division of Penguin Random House LLC.
All rights reserved.

For Corrie, Fran (who would only respond to the playgroup register if addressed as Little Snow White) and Nick – and all the world's children.

Contents

CHAPTER 1

AT THE CROSSROADS

URSEL

Ursel held her breath. She slid her feet up onto the oak branch so she lay hidden. The red deer calf from last year trotted at the heels of its mother. They drifted from clump to clump of grass and curled their tongues around the stalks, searching out juicy shoots. The mother hind's flanks were rounded out with the new little one growing inside.

Their pungent scent on the breeze tickled Ursel's nostrils. They couldn't smell her, upwind – or the hunters.

A twig cracked and Ursel inched her head round. A man's beard bristled in the cover of a holly bush. Low sun glinted on a steel arrowhead – pointed straight at the hind. Her mother's words buzzed in her head – something about not upsetting her uncle, how they depended on him now. Behind those words lay blackness and a cramp in her heart. She brushed the thought away as if it was a beetle in her ear.

Ursel swung down and waved her arms. The hind's brown eye met Ursel's and she barked to her calf.

'Run!' Ursel shouted, 'Get out of here!' She turned to face the arrow on the taut bowstring. 'Don't shoot! Can't you see she's pregnant?'

Her uncle's scowl told her he didn't care. Men cursed, hounds bayed, but the hind got clear.

'You witless girl! That's our feast gone crashing away. What can we serve when Thane Roger comes?'

'Get a stag – an old one – don't kill next year's herd! It's not right to target females.' Ursel stood her ground, fists clenched.

'How dare you!' Her Uncle Kedric swung his fist at her. She ducked under his arm and dived into a thicket of thorn and hazel so dense the horses couldn't follow. The wildwood wrapped itself round her.

MEG

Cold shocked Meg's body as she eased her head under water *as cold as Headman's narrowed eyes before he hits you.* She pursed her lips round the hollow reed in her mouth. She learned long ago not to let the chill make her gasp. The shelduck's legs were just out of reach. She waited, hoping it would paddle nearer. A fish silvered past – she met its glance. Nobody to shout at her down here. *What do clouds look like from under the water's skin? Which way is up? Which clouds are real?*

Her breath, in through the reed, stirred the reflected clouds; her fingertip shattered the shine above her head to make a run of ripples. *What if I could push through the fluff of clouds inside the sky, what would I touch above them? Would I prick my finger on a star, smooth it on the cool moon …?* The ducks clattered away and she bobbed up with a gasp.

May, her little sister, hopped up and down on the bank, 'Come on Meg, there's a tune coming from our meeting place!'

Meg pushed her feet down into sludge, reached up to grab a willow root and hauled herself out. *I've only caught three small ducks! That won't go far between everybody for the feast. Mother will frown.* She wrung out her hair and the drops splattered the downy breast of the cloud in the water. Everything was slippery since her friends Ursel and Winfrith had gone cold on her, three months ago now, soon after Yule. *Why? Just because May and I are slaves, and they're free? Because they're a bit older? None of that used to matter! Is there more?*

She shook water out of her ears – yes, a thread of music rose from the top of the chalk scarp. She pulled on her tunic, tied her belt with the three teal swinging from it, slung on her quiver …

'Wait, May. That's not one of our elder pipes. It might not be safe.' Her little sister scrambled up the slope, ignoring bramble scratches in her eagerness. Meg slithered on the steep bit, climbed and panted up after her. At the top, she squeezed May's hand and drew her close. Together they stared between white blackthorn spikes at the tall woman playing a flute in the clearing.

Music rose and tumbled out of the sky like lapwings. Notes dived and swirled around. Low tones called to Meg and reeled her in.

'How do you do that?' she wondered aloud.

The lanky stranger strode over to them, lifting one eyebrow higher than the other as if she wanted to find out everything about them. 'Aha, what have we here? Could be a buttercup, this small one with the golden head and mud on its roots. What's the big one? Otter? Been swimming, by the drips coming off it!'

Meg stepped closer, sniffing wild thyme in the folds of the stranger's faded cloak. *So! She came down the trackway along the chalk ridge. She's from outside, not from any of our settlements … from some place nobody knows about.*

'By the size of your eyes,' the stranger went on, 'I'd say you're hungry for stories. Any more of you youngsters about? This looks like a good place to tell you about the queen who went off in search of a wise woman …' She swept her arms round, pointing to the circle of logs in the clearing.

'This is where we meet up around sunset, to chat before we go down to the settlement. Us girls, I mean.'

'There's a bunch of you, then? Good!' The stranger smiled. 'Do you like stories?'

Meg ran to the edge of the slope that she and May had just climbed. Hanging onto a hawthorn trunk and leaning out over the drop, she yelled down the chalk scarp to the water meadow: 'Winfrith, Roslinda! Herd the geese together and come up here! There's a storyteller!'

It feels good to be the one shouting the news; like when we were small and all played together. Meg squinted against the gleam of low sunlight. Twenty geese grazed rich grass and flocked around Winfrith's tall figure, spear-straight, her white-blond head catching the light. Roslinda's copper hair shone as she waved up to Meg with a grin. *At least the little ones still talk to me. I know Winfrith gets bored looking after the geese every day, but she could be more friendly, like she used to be.*

Beyond the water meadows the river snaked and looped. The fringes of the mere and pools were pale with last year's dry reeds – all the way to the curve of Eel Island on the skyline. Whooper swans circled down to roost in the reed beds. The marsh breathed out a wisp of mist as it settled towards evening.

Winfrith swung up the scarp to join them, whistling, the old goose tucked under one arm so the others would follow. She pushed aside the blackthorn spikes at the top of the slope to help Roslinda, her young niece, get through. Winfrith looked past Meg as if she wasn't there. Roslinda danced over to her friend May.

'Look, I've got a wobbly tooth!' Roslinda showed May, baring neat teeth amongst her freckles. May's snub nose came close as she admired it. 'Come on!' The two friends ran around the meeting place. They hopped from log to log in the circle of rough-cut seats, making the geese squawk.

Snorts and shouts caught Meg's ear, from the beech woods on the other side of the clearing. Ursel and her brother must be driving the pigs towards the sitting circle. *For how much longer can we meet up like this? Surely Headman Kedric must be planning a marriage for Ursel, and Winfrith too. Their days of freedom will soon be over, no more roaming forest and fen in charge of pigs and geese. But for me? I'm just a slave ...* Endless work stretched ahead of Meg.

'Watch out, the pigs are in a hurry!' Ursel shouted on the run, her bright brown curls flying loose, cheeks flushed. The geese flapped and honked as the boar, Yorfor, black and bristly, hurtled into the sitting-circle with all the settlement's swine following. 'Get out of the way, Meg, don't stand there being useless!'

Meg hid her scowl as she shuffled aside. The insult stung like a wasp.

Why does she hate me? We used to be friends. I may be a year or two younger than Ursel and Winfrith, but I was always the one to invent games. Let's be foxes, the fox cub's run off, we have to search ... now we're crows circling round, wheee ... the crows have spotted the cub, will the vixen get to it in time? Ursel and Winfrith would giggle and follow me, yelping like foxes, flapping like crows.

Is it just because we're older? They always have their heads together. The days of jumping in the river off a willow branch have gone. Now it's, 'Meg do this, you can't do that,' Ursel edging closer to Winfrith, no room for me. But never the chill and tight lips – that came after ... when? After Ursel's father died. It was Winfrith that Ursel turned to, Winfrith's arm round Ursel's shoulders for comfort, two pairs of eyes glaring at me with, 'Get on with your sweeping, Meg.' Meg bit her lip.

Ursel yelled to Otred, her younger brother: 'Tap his nose with your stick.' Yorfor the boar settled down among his wives and children to rootle for cowslips. He grunted his pride: he'd been chosen to live through the autumn killing in his home settlement and swapped to father this year's piglets! Otred stood tall, nearly reaching his sister's shoulder, in charge of the swine-stick now.

'Has my uncle been here?' Ursel looked over her shoulder, talking to Winfrith as if Meg wasn't there. 'You should've seen what happened on the ridge crest ...' Spotting the stranger at the edge of the clearing, she asked, 'Oh, who's this?'

The stranger tilted her head and looked round at all of them with a twisty smile. 'My name is Hilda. People call me a travelling bard, or Hilda Hedgebackwards, because that's the way I leave a place sometimes when my tales get up the nose of a headman.' The lines round her eyes and mouth twitched to show this was only half a joke. Meg drank in every ripple of Hilda's face as laughter chased pain across it.

Hilda smiled at Meg and put a hand on her shoulder. 'Your friend here has welcomed me warmly.' Meg's innards curled up with delight.

The storyteller, serious now, turned to Ursel. 'Sounds as if you have a story to tell yourself?'

Ursel poured it out. 'I left Otred to look after the pigs when they got sleepy in the sun. I'm the one who looks after the herd and takes them out to find acorns, but he's got to learn how, so I let him practise when they're quiet. I followed the track of the pregnant hind I've been watching, over into the oaks. I climbed high in a tree to watch her. I love the way she licks and nuzzles her calf even though it's half grown. I couldn't believe my eyes; the hunters from our settlement had got their bows trained on her. I didn't stop to think! I jumped straight down from the branch and scared the deer away. My uncle, leading the hunt, raged at me. I ran and hid, found my brother with the pigs and brought them over here. Where's the hunt now?' She shinned up a beech, one of the wide branching ones that fringe the forest where it thins out on the chalk. 'They're over on the heath, chasing a couple of hares – they're giving them a run for it! They'll be half way to – wherever the track goes to – soon. They're zigzagging way past the barrow, down the dip, up the long slope, across the ridge, everywhere. They won't get over this way for a while.' She dropped down from the tree.

'Now that you're all together, and the hunt is far away, shall I tell you a story?' the stranger asked. 'You are a young woman braving your uncle's fury, on a quest to protect tender new life,' she nodded at Ursel, 'The young queen in this tale has to stand up to her husband's anger, leave her comfortable halls and set out on her quest.' Meg settled on a log in their sitting-circle and gripped Hilda with her eyes, ready.

Winfrith sat down beside Ursel. 'Sounds like your Uncle Kedric was in one of his rages. Worse than when we tried to borrow his horse without asking, when we couldn't even reach up to Dragon's bridle?' Meg shuffled her feet, wanting Hilda's story. She could feel the storyteller's eyes flit over her and her friends. *What's she seeing?*

'Much worse.' Ursel wrapped her arms round her body. 'That time he only had a serious talk with Father. I think it's going to be different now.'

'No father to shield you.' Winfrith nodded, pulling her pale eyebrows together with worry. Meg knew to keep out of their way. There was lightning in the air between the two of them, no room for her. A pit opened in her stomach.

Hilda the storyteller stepped forward and opened her arms wide, so everybody looked at her. 'This is about a queen on a journey to find something she needs, all alone on a mountain. Do you want to hear it now?'

'What's a mountain?' May asked. She was sitting on the grass, leaning against her sister Meg's shins, and squirmed round to look up at Meg.

Hilda smiled, 'A big hill, so high it's got snow at the top all year round.'

'Bigger than this one we're sitting on?'

'Much bigger. If you were an ant and Meg was a mountain, and you walked over Meg's little toe, that would be the size of this one we're on. If Meg stood up, that ant would need to climb up and up.' May lay down in the grass and looked up at her sister. 'Meg's head would be lost in the clouds, eagles would fly past her ears, the wind would howl and loosen her plaits. Can you see dark hair blowing like trees in the wind?'

May's eyes were screwed shut, now busy imagining.

'A story, just for us?' Ursel sounded doubtful. 'Usually they only tell stories in the Great Hall, for the men.'

'Yes! Tell us a story!' Meg shouted then looked around, her face hot.

'Meg, be quiet, it's not for slaves to say what happens here.' Ursel glared at Meg. Her finely shaped nose seemed to stab, those level grey eyes held thunder.

Outrage bubbled up in Meg's chest. *Am I less than nothing? I don't want this storyteller to think I am nobody.* 'We used to be friends, Ursel! Only last harvest we jumped off the roof together and got told off by our mothers –' *and giggled all night,* she thought. 'Now you're Headman's niece and I'm –'

Ursel leapt up and her palm slapped down on Meg's cheek hard enough to leave a red mark. 'Don't you talk about sliding down the roof!'

A quick stride and the storyteller was so close, they felt her eyes blaze. Her eyebrows shot up, then down. She spoke to Ursel, then Meg, then Winfrith. Every one of them heard each word, though she spoke softly. 'My stories are for everyone – bond and free, young and old.'

When her eyes met Meg's, there was such warmth in their fire that Meg looked round to see if someone more important was behind her. No, the light was for her. The tightness in her throat eased.

The lines around Hilda's eyes deepened. 'The ones who told these stories first are here with us now, rustling in last year's beech leaves. My tongue's a track they tread along, if the way is clear. Talk of slave and free trips us up like clods in the path. Sweep it away. Warm up your hearts. Open your ears. There's nourishment in the tales for you, and maybe they'll shake up your thinking. We need these stories and you are the ones who can learn to tell them – this year, next year, until the green shoots come.'

Hilda took a step back and looked round all of them with a half-smile. The sun slipped out below a bar of cloud over the mere and lit the tips of willow wands bronze bright.

Hilda's kind look salved the pain in Meg's heart. *What green shoots? Who will tell stories? Us?* The tale began to step along Hilda's tongue-path and Meg relished every word.

'This is the tale of …

The Queen's Quest, Alone in a Blizzard

All the young queen could see as she woke up was – what? A star, melting?

Hilda looked up and Meg saw the star, if it was a star, in the air just above their heads. How did Hilda do that? Meg could still see Hilda but pictures shimmered in the space between them.

Queen Marelda blinked. Everything hurt. As soon as her head touched the fur rug, dreams crashed through again. 'Still barren, you useless sow!' – the thump of her husband's knuckles – pain, and bitter tears as she huddled in shame in the corner.

She must have cried out, because arms held her, knotted strong as roots. She tasted a brew of heady vervaine, sun-dusty chamomile, and slept.

When she woke again, the star still dripped. It was the smoke-hole in the turf roof of a round hut. Ice glittered and drops hissed as they fell onto embers below.

A woman's face wrinkled with concern. Those tough arms lifted her up to give her broth. Meat and herbs made her mouth water. 'Who are you?' she asked.

She looked around at neat stacks of pots and jars, bunches of herbs hanging from the rafters to dry, a carved wooden chest.

The healer's gear appeared as Hilda pointed to it – reminding Meg of her mother's corner of the sleeping house.

Hilda's voice changed – deep and soft with an edge of danger, like a rosemary bush humming with bees.

Tell me first who you are. Why are you out on this mountain, alone, in a blizzard?'

Meg shivered with delight. This was not an ordinary healer. Hilda continued:

Guarded, the bright eyes studied the younger woman as she replied.

'I'm the Queen of Peony Valley. That's my title, anyway. I don't feel like a queen ... not even like a woman. Bors, my husband, says I'm shrivelled up like a sour apple – stick-thin, no juice in me. What's a woman who can't have a child? Nothing.'

Queen Marelda's voice trailed away, Hilda catching it tight in her throat, and then she became the healer again.

'Ah! So you are the one I've been waiting for. Who told you to come here?'

'My old nurse, Piroshka. Are you the wise woman she told me about?'

'Yes, I am Huldran. What's troubling you?'

Marelda hugged her knees, gazing into the fire. 'Every month it's the same: blood on my cloths, cramps in my belly. I cradle myself with empty arms and cry myself to sleep. At last, Piroshka told me about you, and I begged Bors to let me come.'

Hilda's voice changed. With a rasp, she shouted.

'But he said, "What, is that old troublemaker still alive?" Bors called you ugly names: witch, outlaw, mad. Why does he hate you so much?'

'He thinks I'll put ideas into your head – and I might do too!'

Huldran's mischievous chuckle intrigued Marelda.

'He said "No" again and again. But I kept on. I even saddled up my mare.

'I told him, "This is our last chance to have a baby, Bors – the son and heir you want to show to all your friends. We've tried all the healers for miles around. Nothing has worked. This old one might have a secret remedy."

'So he said: "Go then! Don't bother coming back until you're able to have a baby – or die on the mountain! There are plenty of young women here for me to choose from."

'He complained, but sent servants with me. Ha! They didn't stay long. Happy enough while the sun shone. When we rode into the dark under the pines, they were scared. They muttered and ran off.

'I didn't like it either – all shadows and spikes. When the snow started, I was on my own. My mare slipped and stumbled on the steep scree, so I clapped her on the rump and sent her home. I clambered up through the rocks. Piroshka told me to follow the sound of the river on my right and climb until I got to a crag shaped like a raven. Snowflakes whirled around and dazzled me. My feet went numb. I fell – I screamed. That's all I remember. If you hadn't found me, I'd be dead.'

Hilda called up a snowstorm with a twist of her wrist and became Huldran the healer again.

'I heard that cry between rolls of thunder and came looking for you. I found you half frozen and dragged you back to my hut on a sledge.'

The old woman looked kindly at the girl. 'Tell me, do you want a child?"

The young queen looked into the flames. When she met the wise woman's eyes, her voice was clear. 'I want a daughter as strong as a blizzard, as deep as shadow, her blood dancing with life. She will unite my husband's tribe and mine with her joy and the beauty of her spirit. We will have peace in the land at last. Can you help me?'

Hilda became Huldran again and spoke slowly, sounding out every word.

'Yes I can help you step forward into your life as a strong woman who stands alone or a strong woman carrying a child. But first, we must talk about what you will give me in exchange.'

Hilda the storyteller stopped and looked up at the sky. A kestrel hovered overhead. For now, the story was finished.

Bit by bit Meg came back to the clearing and blinked. She ran her palms over moss that covered the log she was sitting on, stood up and gave May a hug.

Ursel gathered the pigs together. 'Otred, help me move them down the track.' They set off towards the settlement. Ursel turned to Hilda. 'I want to hear what happened next. Are you staying in Wellstowe for a while?'

Hilda replied, 'If I can. I'll ask when we get there.'

Winfrith counted the geese and led them alongside the herd of swine, with a quick grin to thank Hilda. May and Roslinda shooed geese that wandered off the path.

Hilda walked next to Meg. 'You drank that down like a cold drink on a hot day. Do you hear many stories?' Hilda was talking to her, Meg.

'Never enough. Everyone's too busy or tired or they can't remember. Somebody came by last year, but I only heard part of it while we were clearing up – swords and monsters and knee-deep in blood and all that.'

'If your wits are as sharp as your knees, you'll have this one now and you can tell it again yourself.' Hilda's eyes glinted green edged with bronze, like a hazel leaf in autumn.

'Me?' *How long is it since somebody spoke to me – especially to me? Usually it's: 'Meg, hurry up!' or May buzzing round or Mother calling instructions.* She moved closer to the storyteller. Something smelled fresh and earthy – a sprig of ground ivy was tucked into Hilda's foxy-brown plait.

Hilda smiled and handed it to her. 'This is always the first to come up when summer's on its way. It's all purple, the first leaves as well as the little flowers. They look like mouths talking, don't they?'

May and Roslinda asked questions and jumped up and down as Hilda played her flute to speed their tired feet. They were nearly at the hedge around the cultivated strips, when hooves drummed on the turf.

CHAPTER 2

SPEAR-BUTT
SPITS BLOWS

HILDA

Hilda the storyteller thought about today as they walked down towards the settlement. *My calf muscles ache! Will they have enough food to share with me tonight? Will they let me stay? At least I've given these young people one story.*

She looked again at Meg. *Otter-girl, I called her, when she was dripping. Now she's dried out, the name still fits. She's lithe as an otter, although her knees and elbows stick out.* Meg trudged alone, winding strands of dark hair in her fingers. She was whispering something to herself. Hilda drifted closer, to hear without seeming to listen. '… strong as a blizzard, deep as shadow, her blood dancing with life …'

Hilda's heart thumped in her chest. *She's mulling over the story I just told, fixing it in her memory! Her mind is as nimble as an otter in water … Her wide forehead could be the shining brow of a bard … Stop, don't get excited,* she scolded herself. *I'll only be disappointed – again. Yes, I yearn for an apprentice to tell all my stories to, who'll remember and understand them and tell them after I'm gone. I've looked all over – north to south, west to east – and any time I see somebody who might do it and say, 'Will you be my apprentice?' they look at me as if I'm a pig doing handstands. What if I don't ever find my apprentice, and the tales I've found, and given my whole self to, vanish when I die … curdled air,*

21

blown away on the wind? I'm not young any more. Despair welled up inside her. *This girl – she's different, isn't she?* Hope wiggled in front of Hilda like a worm on a hook. *I'll just … see what happens –*

A flash of blue shot past with a screech. *A jay!* What had startled it?

Down the trackway towards them thundered four hunters, turf flying from their horses' hooves. Three looked like each other: two young men, tall and blond, and a bald one trailing behind. In the lead, a dark-haired rider pierced the air with a face as sharp as a jackdaw's beak.

This must be Kedric, the aggrieved uncle. He was mounted on a glossy black stallion that reared as he hauled on the reins.

'Ah, there you are, disobedient girl! It's your fault, Ursel! We could've got a good beast to roast if you hadn't interfered!' He wheeled his mount round towards his niece.

Ursel dodged the hooves and jumped back amongst the pigs. They ran everywhere, squealing. Yorfor the boar lowered his head and swung his tusks, looking for something to attack. Geese honked and hissed, scattered across the track and out among the hazel coppices.

Hilda looked round to make sure the children were safe.

'There now, don't fret …' Ursel turned her back to calm the boar, so she didn't see Kedric's spear-butt raised to strike her.

He whacked the blunt end down on her head. Blow after blow rained on her shoulders, back, face. She threw up her arms to protect herself.

Open-mouthed, the others froze. Winfrith shouted: 'Stop! Help!'

When he made to hit her again, Ursel grabbed the spear-shaft and pulled. Her jaw was tensed so hard against the pain she couldn't even yell. Caught off balance, Kedric wobbled and almost fell from his horse.

'Easy, Dragon, easy!' He had to clutch the horse's mane to regain control. 'You're no good to anyone and never will be, girl!' Roaring, Kedric tried to beat her harder, but Ursel slipped on pig dung and fell to the ground.

Hilda took a deep breath, stepped forward and grasped the stallion's bridle. She knew the first words that rushed towards her mouth would make him even angrier, so her tongue stepped over those. Many a hedge held shreds of her cloak because of words like those. *I've learned what not to say – but what can I say? Let's try for a calm tone.*

'Good evening, sir. You must be Kedric, Headman and Farmer at Wellstowe. I'd like to introduce myself and offer my services.' He was surprised. *Good!* 'I hear you are the host of a feast tomorrow so you may be in need of entertainment. I'll tell you stories you've never heard before. I juggle too.' To distract him from his anger, she fished out leather balls from her pack, saying, 'Let me show you.' She began to toss the balls into the air, three at a time, round and round.

The hunters' horses shied and shifted uneasily as Kedric called out, 'Who are you? Where have you come from, in Woden's name?'

Woden, eh? Trying to join the thane class even when he swears, using the name of the all-father god. Most farmers swear by Ing, god of the fields and herds, but this one's got his eye on feasts in the thane's mead-hall. Named his horse for fire-snorting power, he's dreaming of being a warrior. No wonder entertaining his thane at this feast is so important to him. Aloud, she introduced herself, 'I'm Hilda the bard. I travel all over the land. I tell legends and myths for thanes and freemen in their mead-halls, play my harp, and sing the songs that give men renown. Everywhere I hear about your hospitality and the honour of your Hall.' She directed a quick glance to Meg, raising her eyebrows ever so slightly, and bowed again to Headman Kedric. Unnoticed, Ursel got up and brushed herself down. Winfrith dabbed at her friend's face with the hem of her tunic, muttering under her breath, as Ursel winced.

Dragon pranced sideways. Headman Kedric patted him, shushing him.

When Headman Kedric straightened up, his beard bristled with decision. To Meg, he growled, 'Slave, take this stranger to your mother. Get these geese and swine out of my way! Don't just stand there gawping, girl! Ursel, I'll deal with you later,' he threatened as he dug his heels into his horse's flanks.

Hilda breathed a small sigh of relief.

Ursel bit her lip until it bled to stop the tears coming, then snapped, 'Meg, get on with your work. You heard what he said! May, get out of my way!'

Meg swallowed hard and raised her hand to her cheek. It was red from Ursel's slap.

It must still sting, Hilda thought.

May whimpered.

Hilda seethed inside, but set aside her feelings for later. She studied Ursel's face as if she had not heard what she had said. 'Your skin's broken. There'll be bruising. How does your back feel? Sounds as if your heart's hurt worse than your body; it's making you lash out at the ones who care about you. Meg and May, where can we find some herbs? A healer will need them to make a poultice for Ursel. I hope you can forgive Ursel for speaking to you that way – it's the blunt end of a spear talking through her.' She made her voice light, while making sure everyone heard every syllable.

Winfrith put her arm round Ursel. 'Come and find your mother. Otred, you take the swine back to the sty.'

'The healer is our Mam,' announced May, brightening. 'People come from all over to see her.' Hilda watched Meg as she slouched, shoulders folded in like a sparrow in a storm. Could she put an arm round her? *No, not for me to do. Nobody's mother, me.* A bitter taste was in her mouth. She straightened up. *Do it with words. That's how you do it.*

'Which of you is older, May, you or the boy with the grasshopper legs? He's grown a foot taller now he's got the pig-staff in his hand and the whole herd's following him.'

'Otred's a bit older than me and Roslinda.' May replied. 'He usually just helps …' She brightened up as she spoke, but Meg was still grinding her teeth.

'Is that true, Meg, is your mother a famous wise woman?' Hilda sent Meg a smile. 'I'd like to meet her. Please will you introduce us?' Meg's speedwell blue eyes brightened – just a little.

Hilda's thigh muscles ached more, demanding her attention. She strode down the slope with as much of a swing as she could muster. How much longer could she keep going? Last night she dined on nothing at all, and slept in a pile of dead beech leaves. A savoury cooking smell quickened her pace.

Otred worked hard to keep the pigs out of the hawthorn hedges round the strips of cultivated land as everyone veered left off the trackway and down into the settlement.

A sea of bleating wool surged around them. Sheep were coming down off the heath, lambs hopping by their sides.

The old boar led his wives through the flock to their sty and Otred shut the gate.

A tall youth with tight curls guided the sheep towards their shed, and turned to congratulate Otred. 'Yes, Aikin,' said grasshopper legs Otred, grinning. 'I'm in charge today. Look, we've got a storyteller.' Aikin looked as hungry as Hilda, so didn't stop to chat, just smiled and headed towards the scent of soup.

From a hall on their right, a rant blistered the air. A dark woman glared out of the doorway, her mouth clamped. *Taking a short break from her fury to check why the dogs are barking,* Hilda thought, nodding to her.

It wasn't a grand hall like the one beyond it, but it was solidly made with plank walls and deep thatch, and well cared for. The new patch on the roof and the stack of peat under the eaves told her that. Inside, she could make out curtained-off living quarters, a bed beside a fire, people moving about … *That woman with white-blonde hair must be Winfrith – washing Ursel's face with a cloth.*

'Who's the crow woman in a rage?' Hilda asked Meg quietly. 'She reminds me of your Headman.'

'That's Ragnild, Ursel's mother.' Meg whispered. 'Yes, she is Headman Kedric's sister. Crow woman! Yes, her face is pointy like his, and they're both dark.'

'Ursel must look more like her father who died. Whose is the calm voice?'

'Elder Edith, Ragnild's aunt, who lives with them. She's so old her hair has turned grey all over!' Meg replied quietly.

Ragnild dived back into the hall and took up where she'd left off, her voice rising to a screech.

'What kind of Elder is Edith?' Hilda wondered aloud. 'Does she gather everyone together to make decisions, in the old way? Or does she issue commands?'

Meg hesitated. 'Kedric is Headman Farmer, but Elder Edith sits on the carved chair. You'd better ask Mother.'

'Are Ursel and Winfrith sisters?' Hilda asked.

'Not really, but Winfrith lived there with Ursel and her family for a while, after her own mother died,' Meg explained. 'Winfrith's family live over there. Can you see that hall with the huts round it?' She pointed to where the land rose gently on the other side of the settlement. Beyond the buildings were vegetable strips protected by a thick hedge, and woodland outside it.

Hilda looked round. The chalk ridge was behind them, covered in beech and elm trees. Hazel coppices fringed the settlement. Wellstowe was built on a curve of land looking out across the fen.

Hilda knew she'd need to remember it for her story tomorrow.

'Is our settlement like the others you've seen?' Meg asked.

'They're all different,' Hilda said. 'Yours is thriving, with all these people and sheep and pigs and geese and chickens.'

They walked on. 'That's the weaving-house,' Meg gestured to a building on their left. 'That's Headman Farmer Kedric's family house,' to their right. 'And here's the Great Hall!' The path ended at the largest building in the settlement. Its gable end must be visible from far away across the fen, Hilda realised, as the sunset lit it. A wide door faced them in the long south side.

Hilda craned her head back to look at a carving over the doorway. 'Is that the prow of a boat above the lintel?' She admired the ancient wood, weathered almost past recognition. 'Whose is it?" She guessed it was Angry Uncle's hall, but she liked hearing Meg describe things.

'It's from the ship that brought Headman Kedric's grandfather's grandfather and his family here, all the way over the sea and up the rivers. They call it the Crossing, but Mother calls it – er, something else.'

'May I have a look inside the Great Hall?' Hilda asked.

Meg checked quickly at the window of Headman Kedric's family house next to the hall, through the open shutters. 'Headman Kedric's not in his house, he's probably giving Dragon a rub down in the stables, at the back of the men's sleeping house over there.'

Meg turned back to the Great Hall and beckoned Hilda to look. 'Tomorrow they'll have trestle tables out for the men and the important ladies.' A tapestry, fine but faded, hung on the wall behind the space for the high table. 'They'll light the fire in the central hearth and we'll hang a big pot over it, from that rafter.' Hilda smelled the ash of many fires and looked up. In the shadows she could make out adze marks on the great central beam, cut from a whole oak trunk. Above it, the thatch was blackened with smoke. Meg showed her the eastward end of the hall. 'We girls and women will be squashed in the corner by the cooking door, behind those willow screens, getting the food ready.'

'Thanks,' Hilda nodded. 'It helps to see the space where I'll be entertaining everyone.' She paced out the length of the Great Hall.

Meg jigged with impatience. 'Come and meet Mother. She's by the cooking-fire, just outside.' Hilda blinked as they stepped out of the side door into the light of an open area in the centre of the settlement.

May whirled past, arms outstretched, round and round. 'I'm a snowflake, look at me!'

'Me too!' Roslinda followed.

'Stop that, May! You're upsetting the chickens. Meg, catch her before she falls in the fire-pit.' This voice spoke Anglish with a depth of tiredness that dragged the lilt out of it.

That must be Meg and May's mother, who can help or stop me, Hilda thought.

There she was, with her feet planted wide on the ground in the outdoor kitchen area at the heart of the settlement. With a wooden spoon, she stirred stew in a huge pot that hung from a tripod over the cooking-fire – the source of the mouth-watering smell.

'Is that all you've got, Meg – three scrawny teal? Let's hope the hunters got a good haunch of venison.' She pushed dark hair back from her wide brow.

Hilda flicked her eyes over Meg's mother in search of telling details: heavy under the eyes from not enough sleep; a fine herringbone weave overdress frayed round the hem and tattered at the knee … it must have been made for somebody else and handed down; a Breejsh cross of rowan twigs bound with woollen thread on a thong at her neck …

So she's British like me. Her back aches, from the way she's rubbing it, and she hasn't had a chance all day to tame that heavy braid of hair that's snaking loose all round her neck. Meg's mother feeds the whole settlement, by the looks of things. If I want to nourish the whole group of them with my stories, I need Meg's mother's help.

Meg's shoulders hunched. Her chin tucked in. Eyes narrowed, mouth drawn down. *Meg's hiding inside herself because of her mother's scolding.*

She looked around. Nobody was helping Meg's mother with the cooking. Nothing was roasting for the feast.

No wonder she's stressed.

Meg was clenching her knuckles so hard, they were white.

This matters to her, introducing me to her mother. Hope kicked Hilda in the chest again with the thought: *Meg needs her mother to approve of me. If she doesn't, I'll lose this chance of an apprentice and there aren't many. Never met one as promising as this otter-girl.* She swirled her old cloak dramatically. *Swirls nicely now that it's worn so thin. Not too much. Just to catch the eye of this heavily burdened mother and the others coming to look.*

Hilda turned to Meg and made her voice carry: 'Is this your mother, the healer skilled in herb-lore I've heard so much about?'

Meg straightened up and coughed.

She's found her voice, even though she had to dredge for it – good! She cares what her mother thinks of her, but she's not squashed by her.

'Mother, this is Hilda. She's a storyteller and Headman Kedric says she can stay for the Feast. Hilda, this is my Mother, Seren.'

Hilda bowed. Aloud she said in Anglish, 'It's an honour to meet you, Seren.' In a low tone, she added another greeting in her own language, the one flavoured like heather-honey from the moors of her home. *Am I guessing right that Seren's language is the same, or nearly?*

Seren's eyes widened. Then lightning struck through the cloud of them – a warning as she looked past Hilda's shoulder.

A woman was bustling towards them. She wore a blue woven belt with a leather bag hanging from it.

Full of important things, I'm sure, Hilda thought. The way she moved left no doubt. *First owner of Seren's dress,* Hilda guessed. *She's carrying a weight of worry – good thing her shoulders are broad!*

A two-year old boy rode on the woman's hip without slowing her down. She balanced a basket of dough on the other side.

'Who's this, Meg? A trader? What have you got in your pack?' she snapped, setting down the toddler and the basket, and put her hands on her hips.

'Ma'am, Headman Kedric said she could –' Meg started.

Hilda stepped forward and bowed so as to put herself between Meg and the snapping.

'My name is Hilda.' She switched easily back to the Anglish language to introduce herself. 'I travel with stories and music, which I offer in exchange for a meal and a corner to sleep in. They tell me you're hostess for a feast tomorrow. When there isn't too much to eat – and it's the hungry time of year – it can help if there are songs and tales to season the food.'

'I'm the Headman's wife, Oswynne.' She offered a brisk handshake. 'Can you tell legends, how our people came to this place, that sort of thing?'

'Of course,' Hilda replied.

'Good, good, just what we need for our Feast. Seren, show the bard where to put her things, but don't be slow or the stew will stick. May and Roslinda, hurry up and get these chickens in their coop. They're pecking my dough and we've got little enough of it to go round – shoo!'

Another person who can lift the latch and let me into this community! This burdened Headman Farmer's wife needs to lose herself and find herself, stronger, more aware, in a good story. It's a small place, everybody's important. They rely on each other. I wonder how they all get along? How can I help them get closer, warmer, so they can work together to stand against their bully Headman? First, they've got to let me stay! She smiled and made a little bow to Oswynne, who nodded in response.

Seren clicked the wooden latch shut behind them. The women's sleeping house was dark, lit only by a glow from the firebox in the middle. Peat smoke mingled with an earthy smell. Grunts from the other side of the wall told Hilda they were next to the pigsty.

'Don't let the Angles hear you speak in British; we'll all get beaten. They don't like it. Do you understand?' Seren hissed, her face thrust close to Hilda's.

'Yes, I see,' Hilda nodded.

Seren gave her a level look.

Sizing me up, thought Hilda. *I must have passed a test.* Seren slid back into British. The accent and some of the words were unfamiliar, but Hilda understood well enough.

'You can put your things here, on the sleeping platform. I have the corner by the door, with my daughters Meg and May.'

Meg sat on a pile of worn blankets, hugging her knees. She followed the talk with bright eyes.

Seren went on, 'There are ten or twelve of us in here at nights, women and children and us slaves. Headman's wife Oswynne and her children have the bed where it's warmest, next to the pigsty wall. The swine sleep in a heap on the other side of the planks so they keep the draughts out. This nice bed in the middle,' she straightened the furs that covered springy hazel wands and a thick straw mattress, 'is for Elder Edith, and her niece Ragnild, and Ragnild's daughter Ursel, when they choose to sleep here instead of Edith's hall.'

Hilda laid her blanket and cloak on the sleeping platform next to her bundle.

Seren turned to study Hilda, folding a woven bedcover as she spoke in a low voice. 'What have you come for? To tell legends about how the Anglish came here?' Seren shook out a deerskin.

'I have to earn my keep when I stay in a place. I'll need help from somebody later, to get the history – from not just the Anglish, but the Britons' side as well, so I can make a tale for this settlement. The tales I tell when I can are the ones that wake up women.'

'What do you mean? Are you going to get us into trouble?' Seren folded a rug and smacked it flat.

As Hilda gathered her words, Meg broke in, 'Mam, she told us about a queen who goes off by herself up a hillside in the snow, to find a healer!'

Seren put her hand on her daughter's shoulder.

'Not now, Meg. The stew will stick if we hear it all. Queens, snow, what's it about?'

Hilda spoke softly, but made each word hum. 'In my stories, it's long ago and far away. In them we can see habit-patterns sharply – as if through the eyes of a circling raven. Our own lives are too close. We can't see the weave of them. We think problems are all our own fault or somebody else is to blame and nothing can be done. My tales are about a past time when everything hung on the brink, like our times, when people struggle to grip hands with each other and hold onto what's good. The folk in my stories aim to forge new ways, using the best of the old. They get discouraged and fall out, as we do. When I open the door to the Cave of Dreams, people listening see characters who find strength and wisdom, which they never knew they had – as we can. Even when this isn't seen, the tang of the wood-smoke in the cave lingers, like the knowledge of power.'

'What do you mean, we struggle to grip hands with each other?' Seren asked, straightening blankets.

Hilda sat on the sleeping platform. 'Some places I go, the men have started making all the decisions. The women run about after them, cook the food and sew the clothes, and never make their voices heard. They sleepwalk through their lives, with their freedoms being taken away right under their noses. They start hating the men and feeling useless. Women who own horses and houses look down their noses at the women who cook and dig for them. The ones who work hard snarl at those who swan about pouring mead at the feast. They're afraid to reach out to each other and celebrate the rituals of birth and death and blood that used to bring women together. Disgust grows in the dark places like toadstools, for our bodies and our feelings, for each other and ourselves.' She breathed in deeply and sighed.

'In one place, men were chopping down forest and ploughing the claimed land. The women twisted their aprons in their hands and muttered as they watched finches and foxes fleeing for their lives. One fondled a squirrel kit that had lost its mother. The girls cried out but the grown women were too scared to shout, "Stop the axe blades." That fear smells bad. It's everywhere.

'When the whiff of self-loathing reaches my nostrils, or hate and fear stink the place out,' she held her nose to make her point and Meg giggled, 'I dig around a bit. There are so many ways women get trampled and men have their tenderness stamped out! When these come to light, I cough gently and say, "Have you noticed this midden in your midst?" Usually they chuck me out, arse over tip, backwards through the hedge. That's why I call myself Hilda Hedgebackwards. But it isn't me that puts the trouble there; I don't carry it in my pack – only stories. The mess is still there when I've gone – unless I drew attention to it and somebody decides to clean it up.' She rolled her eyes and waved a hand in mock daintiness, and Meg chuckled more.

Seren poked the fire so it flared. 'This gentle cough you're talking about – do you mean the tales you tell to wake up women?'

Hilda blinked. *I'll lose her if I go on mucking about. Is she confused – or exasperated with me?* She sat down and rested her chin on one hand while tugging at her hair with the other one, to help her think.

Seren frowned. 'What if we know very well how much strength and wisdom we have, but – things stop us from using them? If we choose to stay quiet, who are you to judge us? You can scarper, maybe with bruises, but we must stay and live through the rows and beatings and see our children suffer.'

'It sounds as if you've considered making some changes yourself and thought better of it, Seren. You've got your eyes wide open, with the honesty to stare down the sun. When I find a woman with courage like yours, I stand with her and see whether I can help. Sometimes she starts to make small changes, though always with an eye on the safety of her family. Sometimes she slips the leash entirely. Nobody wants their children to live crushed lives. I don't blame any woman who chooses to live a quiet life for the sake of her loved ones. We do what we can. Sometimes all we can manage is to make a meal for a sister in trouble, to warm her heart. That's a fine thing. Every small action counts.'

'Have you ever really changed a place, made a big difference?' Seren asked.

'I don't know,' Hilda sighed. 'We don't always choose our path. This path chose me. So I walk it. If they come after me with a big stick next time I pass by, I will take that as a good sign. Sometimes a woman tugs at my sleeve and tells me how much I've helped her and my heart glows. I dream about a place to stay put, feet by the fire, where I can watch girls grow into women and women into themselves. And maybe a cat would sit on my lap sometimes.'

'There's a blue line round your mouth. When did you last eat?' Seren sounded almost tender. Hilda was about to reply when May burst in.

'Mam, come quick!' She tugged at Seren's arm. 'Ragnild's shouting at Headman Kedric and now Oswynne's joining in and the dogs are barking, and I can't find all the chickens and if they roost up in the trees, the fox'll get them and then we won't have eggs, and I'll be whipped ...'

CHAPTER 3

HOT RAGE

SEREN

'Nobody shall hurt you, cushla, beat of my heart.' Seren laid her arm round her little daughter's shoulders, and wished she could make it true. *When they beat us – the ones who are supposed to protect us – who can we turn to?* 'Meg, help your sister catch the chickens.'

Hilda asked how to help.

'Put them in the wicker coop on stilts, over by the pigsty.' She gestured to where the after-glow of sunset lit the thatch, wattle and daub and planks that made up their settlement, and the smooth beech boles beyond.

May raced, laughing again, to grab the squawk and flutter of the hens.

Seren couldn't help watching her youngest with a soft heart, before she turned and strode towards the cooking-fire and raised voices, keeping her head down.

She wrapped her hand in a rag to pull the lid off the cauldron, then slipped the rag to her other hand to steady the pot. It swung from chains that hung from a tripod taller than her, while she wielded a spoon as big as a paddle. *The stew's catching at the bottom!* She scraped, added water from a jug and stirred again. She caught snatches of the argument, between plumes of smoke and the hiss of steam round her ears.

'Scumbag! How could you? You're supposed to be our protector, now that my husband's gone, and what do you do?' Ragnild faced Headman Kedric by the door to his house, hands on hips, thin face alight with fury. 'You beat my daughter Ursel black and blue and bleeding, down her back! Her poor shoulders! She's a free woman, not a slave, not a dog! You split her face. Come here and I'll break yours for you, see how you like it.' She wagged her finger at him. 'Where's your respect for me, your older sister? I demand an apology!'

People hurried to the cooking area to see what was going on.

Seren didn't dare look, as she didn't want to be noticed. She knelt to test the heat of the bread-oven with a hand on its clay wall. *Hot enough.* She raked out the smoking ashes and blinked as they swirled in the wind.

'Don't shout at me, Ragnild!' Kedric yelled, pushing down his sister's pointing finger. 'If you can't teach your children sense, somebody's got to. Do you know what she did? Did she tell you? No?' He spluttered. 'You tell them, Bertold.' A vein stood out on his forehead and he mopped the sweat that ran down the black bristles on his throat. He pushed Bertold forward into the light of the cooking-fire.

'Who's this poor fellow swinging his big pale head like a bullock for the slaughter?' Hilda asked quietly as she loaded six small loaves onto a greased skillet. Seren took the long handle and opened her mouth to reply – but Meg jumped in, whispering back.

'That's Bertold, Winfrith's father. He was hunting with Headman Kedric earlier, we met them on the track, remember?'

Seren slid the loaves into the oven, jiggled them off the blade and came back for more. Hilda was ready to load again. Seren was surprised – help was an unexpected treat.

'Headman's friend since they were boys.' Seren added. She had not much breath for talk, as she slid another batch off the shovel. Hot air blasted out of the oven. They kept working.

Meg gestured with her head, hands shaping loaves. 'Those are Bertold's daughters-in-law with the little children, coming over from their hall. His sons, the other hunters, will be rubbing down the horses.'

'So the bee and the beanpole are the wives of the two blond giants.' Hilda replied. 'Why's the tall stringy one with frizzy hair hanging onto the rounded blonde one?'

'Keenbur needs help because she can't see well,' Meg told her. 'She's nervous about falling. Nelda looks after her; they've been friends since they grew up together.'

'The short one with a bright face – Nelda, you said – wants to be darting after the toddler. Oh, she's got a baby on her hip as well. Busy as a bee! But she's slowed down by the beanpole leaning on her arm – Keenbur. Is it a child each?'

Meg giggled. 'No, they're both Nelda's – baby bees! Keenbur's baby is due in the summer.' Meg's eyes shone like sloes, sharing talk with this stranger.

Seren felt a pang – *Who is this woman, taking my place with my daughter?* She slapped some more dough.

'Bertold looks uncomfortable. Who's he worried about?' Hilda whispered.

Meg replied, 'He's looking round for Winfrith – she won't like him siding with her friend Ursel's uncle.'

Bertold cleared his throat, spread his big hands wide and looked around. He told them how Ursel scared away the deer. 'That was it, then – no meat,' he finished.

'What are we going to cook for the Feast then?' The words burst out of Seren's mouth before she could stop them. Horrified, as many eyes looked at her, she clapped a hand over her mouth.

'Mind your pot and keep out of our business, slave!' Ragnild snapped.

Seren shrank her head down into her shoulders. She wished she'd bitten her tongue rather than say that. She didn't want to line up with the Headman when he hit people. *It's true – wishing doesn't put meat in the pot. But Ragnild will be trotting round to see me soon enough, wanting a poultice for Ursel, a charm and a chant and a potion, and never a word of thanks, that's for certain. Where's Wulf when I need him?*

'Seren's right, if there's no venison to roast in the fire-pit, we'll be very short of food tomorrow.' Oswynne fretted. 'We have to honour the goddess at her Feast, or she'll turn away from us and we'll starve – hungrier even than now. There's all thirty of us in Wellstowe, and Thane Roger will bring his sons and servants ... they'll get here tomorrow and be hungry ....'

'We can't give them bean soup. How will I dare show my face again in Thane Roger's hall?' Kedric snapped. 'I can see it now – I'll walk into the mead-hall, they'll all be pointing and whispering. They'll put bean soup in front of me while they all feast on roast swan! Thane will say – come and get a gold ring, my good friend. Come and I'll give you an arm ring, treasured shoulder-to-shoulder man, but you, Kedric, you treated me worse than a dog when I came to your hall. Even a dog gets a bone – and you gave me what? Bean soup! No rings for you. Go down to the end of the bench, with the boys! And they'll all throw their heads back and roar with laughter – at me.'

A tiny sigh slipped from Hilda's lips. Seren looked a question in her direction. 'So it unfolds. Sometimes I don't even have to wiggle my toe under a rock. Out it comes crawling, all by itself.'

Meg murmured, 'the midden in our midst' and her mouth twitched at one corner, threatening a smile.

Seren wiped her hands briskly, as if she could wipe away the storyteller. *Hilda will be gone in a couple of days.*

'Get ready, Meg, they'll be hot.' Seren tapped her daughter on the shoulder. She wrenched aside the oven door and reached in with the long-handled bread shovel, hauled out a batch of loaves, tipped them into the basket Meg set ready, pushed her hair out of her eyes when the heat made it writhe, and checked for the last bannocks from the back of the oven. She wiped the skillet, covered it with balls of dough, shoved it in, pulled it out, refilled, until a heap of barley loaves steamed on the trestle table. She wiped ash from her face – and realised a respectful hush had fallen. *Our Elder is here!*

Elder Edith came over from her hall, her weight on Winfrith's arm. The coil of hair that circled her head gleamed silver in the moonlight. The growing moon looked like a face watching them as it swung up over the trees. 'Hold the horn lantern up, Winfrith,' Edith commanded.

'Kedric, I have come to shine some light on this situation.' Behind them, Ursel hung back, her head turned aside. 'Step forward, Ursel. Take the lamp,' Elder Edith said. *What's Ursel trying to hide?*

Reluctantly, Ursel did as Elder Edith, her great-aunt, asked. Gasps ran round the groups gathered by the cooking-fire. They muttered comments and tut-tutted. Ursel banged down the lantern on the table and turned, tears sparkling over her fingers as she tried to hide behind her hand. She had the makings of a black eye, a crust of dried blood on her forehead, and her tunic seemed to be sticking to her back – *she must have wounds there too.*

Seren's own resentment stepped back a pace as she churned with fury on Ursel's behalf and warmed to her embarrassment and pain. Floating above these feelings, a calm voice inside Seren assessed the damage and mentally checked her stock of herbs.

Ragnild put an arm around Ursel, steering her back to the light, shouting. 'Look! Just see what he has done!'

Kedric roared with anger.

Elder Edith interrupted with a hand held up. 'Not now, Ragnild. Stop, Kedric. That's enough shouting, both of you. This will take some deep thought and much talk to put right. We've seen, and we have heard. As Elder, I shall make a judgment, but not until everyone has been heard and had a chance to talk. This is not the time. Now we shall eat.'

Seren nodded to herself as she filled a big crock with stew. *Elder Edith will sort this out, if she still holds power enough. If they will all let her.* Oswynne ladled the steaming mix into wooden bowls and passed them round. Some sat on benches, some on rugs by the fire. They tore into the crusts and caught every crumb, and there was silence.

Quietly, Hilda asked, 'What's in the broth, Seren? It's good.'

'Dried split peas and oatmeal, mostly; a ham-bone with not a shred of meat left on it – it's been used a dozen times already – a few onions and carrots. We're running out of everything.'

They used the bread to scrape out the last morsels of food. Not everyone was eating. Seren could see strings pulled taut in Ragnild's neck – she was only picking at her dish.

Ragnild muttered to Winfrith, 'Aunt Edith always thinks she's in charge, but I'm sick of her whining about the old days. I have to run after her all day long and she's so tetchy.'

Ragnild put her bread down and Otred devoured it.

'I want an apology from you, Kedric.' Ragnild began.

'Don't start again,' Kedric banged down his empty bowl. 'Ursel's brought shame on us and defied my authority. I will not put up with it!'

'The old ways provide guidance to settle disputes without violence,' Elder Edith's voice wavered a little. 'We need to bring the people together …'

Seren thought, *Kedric daren't shout at Elder Edith, but his anger's curdling in his throat. He doesn't know yet if he's in charge, or her. They should all listen to her, she knows so much!*

'Excuse me, Headman.' It was Wulf, with a frown, who approached Kedric with his head down. 'I'm worried about Dragon. I think he's got a stone in his foot and I can't seem to work it out. He won't stand still for me. Would you come to the stable and hold his head? You're the only one he trusts when he's upset.'

Always keeping out of it, when there's a quarrel. When will he stand up for what's right? Seren thought. *He's hunched his shoulders to hold in whatever he's feeling. He wants to stay out of trouble.* But the line of his back reminded her of the dunes by the sea, back home.

Kedric turned and followed Wulf down to the stables.

Like a little lamb! Seren thought, and wondered, *Did Wulf interrupt on purpose? He never likes a ruction. Or is he just concerned about the horse?*

An owl drifted past on ash-white wings. Seren watched her and allowed the feathers to sweep clear her mind, for the healing.

CHAPTER 4

HEAL SKIN, CATCH SOUL, KEEP THE HEART ALIVE

URSEL

Ursel trailed behind her Aunt Oswynne as they headed for the women's sleeping house. Pain thudded at the back of her skull and the ground tilted under her feet. Winfrith's arm steadied her, muscles from her spear-throwing practice moving under the cloth of her sleeve. Ursel remembered snuggling with her friend after Winfrith's mother died, how frail her little frame was then – now tall as a pine, and just as prickly.

'My father didn't stop him! My brothers just watched when he hit you.' Winfrith's bitter tone warmed her. Her friend had anger churning in her stomach just as Ursel did. Not like her mother. *Do as you're told, bend with every breeze like a rustling reed, eat dirt if that's your dinner – that was Ragnild, her mother.*

Through a tight jaw, Ursel forced out, 'Only slaves get beaten. Headman can't hurt a free woman. Or can he now? Is this how it's going to be?' She felt Winfrith's shudder through her own body.

'He's always been a bully, the big man shouting at us, ordering us to look after geese, go off with pigs, cook this, butcher that, without asking anybody. Why does everybody let him? Look where it's got us – what next?' They clung together for a moment before stepping over the threshold.

Oswynne held the door open for them. 'Come on in, girls.'

Ursel winced as Oswynne's voice cut through the dark of the women's sleeping house. She could tell Oswynne's teeth were clenched, by the rasp of her tone. *I'm a nuisance for her,* she realised.

'Seren? I've brought Ursel for healing. Ah, you've got the herbs boiling already. Good.' Fragrant steam rose from a pot on the peat fire, adding to the fug in their sleeping house.

Seren probed Ursel's cheek-bone with gentle fingers. 'Wait here on the bench while I prepare a poultice,' the healer instructed.

She leaned against Winfrith's shoulder, to stop herself from slumping as they sat.

Winfrith whispered, 'Why won't you let me get him? I could push him in the mud and make it look like an accident. I'd like to bash him like he whacked you. That's how I stopped my brothers teasing me when we were little – I got stronger and jabbed them back.'

'That'd only make it worse, bring them all down on our heads, Thane Roger and his thane friends from all around.' Ursel shivered. She loved the blaze of her friend's protective spirit, but an icy wind from the outside world made her skin prickle. Some new danger was stirring amongst thanes and headmen and she didn't understand it. She wriggled closer to Winfrith.

Seren brought a pot of warm water and dabbed Ursel's face. 'Why didn't Ragnild bring you?' the healer asked.

Ursel tasted salt blood as she bit her lip. 'Mother's still angry with me. She says I shouldn't have upset Uncle Kedric. She's helping Great-Aunt Edith get to bed.'

Seren's face went blank, the way slaves do when they know they could get into trouble for a wrong look.

Ursel felt a surge of heat – was it shame or anger? She tried to pull her tunic over her head, but it was stuck to her shoulders and her scabs stung as she tugged.

'I'll soak it off, dear.' Seren's hands were deft. Nelda gasped and described the damage on Ursel's back to Keenbur. Oswynne sucked her teeth. Ursel's eyes filled. She didn't want them all looking at her – and at

41

the same time it was comforting to feel their outrage. She held her damp tunic to her chest.

'Let me see the cut under your eye. Meg, bring the light here.' Seren put a damp cloth with rosemary in it on the bruise, which made Ursel's eyes water. 'You'll have a black eye, but there's no bones broken.'

Meg glared at Ursel, adding to her discomfort. Meg whispered to her mother, but Ursel heard: 'Have I got to sit here all night holding the candle, for her? Nobody makes a fuss of me when I'm hit.'

The tallow dip sputtered and smoked as the storyteller Hilda took the light and Seren drew Meg away to tend the peat fire in the middle of the sleeping house.

So, I smacked her – she deserved more! Ursel grimaced, remembering. *It wasn't much, just a tap. I should've hit her harder. Disrespecting my father like that, when it was our fault that he died, hers and mine. She acts as if she doesn't realise what we did. Of course she knows – she just doesn't care, the little brat.* Playing with Meg seemed a lifetime ago, not just last summer. Memories blurred in her mind: their 'let's pretend' games; Winfrith with a glint of mischief in her eye; the three of them blowing grass leaves and laughing at the noise. *But Meg's not my friend any more. She can't be if she's so selfish, if she can't take responsibility for the tragedy we caused.*

Again she felt thatch slip under her feet – as she did in all her nightmares now. She scrabbled and giggled and clung on and slid and jumped down with Meg. They dared each other again and again, and their laughter echoed away into blackness.

She lay awake and heard the winter wind howl away a swathe of thatch where her and Meg's feet had dislodged it. She relived the time when she saw her father on the roof.

His breath's making clouds in the cold. He's working a bundle of rushes into the loose patch. Me and Meg made that hole, now he's got to mend it.

Her stomach clenched. Father's lost his footing on the thatch slick with frost. His hands clutch at rush stalks, his eyes stare as he slithers and falls – right onto the sharpened adze blade in his leather bag of tools. It was open on the ground, as he'd left it when he rummaged through the chisels and knives to find the seax he wanted for this job. He always kept his tools keen.

42

Meg softened a little to see her mother flush pink with pleasure, like a wild rose petal.

Seren sang softly into Ursel's ear, then stronger across her back and gently close to her bruised nose. Her mother the healer! Seren seemed to grow taller as she stepped back and repeated the words louder. She beat time with the wooden spoon on the rim of the pot.

Meg dug under rugs to find her mother's frame drum and handed it to her. Seren continued the rhythm without missing a beat.

Meg looked round at the faces alight in the glow of the peat fire. They were all joining in, those who were still awake. The spell thrummed round the sleeping house and grew stronger as the voices joined together. It echoed in her bones as Seren packed away her herbs and settled Ursel next to Winfrith on the sleeping platform with plenty of rugs.

In the silence after it died away, Oswynne hung her head. *This is Oswynne, Headman's Wife, who usually forges ahead like a boat on rough water! Now she's twiddling a blanket fringe through her fingers.*

'I see,' said Oswynne. 'You're using the herbs to soothe the hurt inside, as well as the broken skin. I wish there was a remedy to help me. My husband will want to come to my bed tonight. He's furious with his sister and niece, and Elder Edith, annoying him with her endless talk of the old ways. It's up to me to bring him some peace, so we can all work together tomorrow.' She set her jaw in the tense line that always made Meg cringe. 'Seren, take Hubert for me tonight. I can't cope with him as well.' Oswynne dumped the sleepy toddler on Seren's lap.

As the door shut behind her, Seren sighed. She tried putting little Hubert into bed with his sister. Adela grumbled, Hubert grizzled. So she took him back and nursed him.

'Meg, cushla, beat of my heart, tell us a story so this little one will settle down. Anything ...'

Hilda whispered in Meg's ear. 'Tell them the tale I told you at the crossroads. Your mother hasn't heard it yet and I'd like her to – about Marelda going to visit the Wise Woman of Raven Crag.' Hilda yawned, a huge yawn with her teeth showing.

When Meg started, she wasn't sure she could remember it, but then that poor sad queen started talking through her. She climbed and slithered on the icy hillside with her. Her own troubles disappeared as Marelda's longing roared through Meg, as strong as a storm. Icy fear settled like snowflakes when she told about the husband. The wind spoke through her voice.

All the while, Hilda was fast asleep under her cloak in a corner. Usually when people sleep, they snore or breathe deeply; sometimes they twitch and move around. Hilda didn't move a muscle, didn't make a sound. Maybe she was just very tired.

HILDA

Yes, this is the one I've been looking for.

Warmth flowed through her like a river as she realised. She heard Meg tasting the story as it flowed from her mouth. Words rushed out, slippery as snow; she paused to find the phrase she wanted, turned it over on her tongue and plunged on again. Her tone shook with desperation, tingled with icicles, lifted into hope. Meg hadn't just remembered the words. The story had sunk into her, taken root and grown up again with fresh leaves.

This is my apprentice. I've walked north to south, one side of this land to the other, searching. Oh yes, she'll need some teaching, I can do that.

Hilda lay rigid under her cloak, with past and future rattling round her ears.

What am I thinking? Hilda screwed up her face under the covers to stifle a groan. *Meg lives here. She's a slave – not free to wander.* The thought punched her in the gut. *The day will come when I have to leave. Maybe that will be a good thing for Meg, if I go. Already I can smell a gulf opening between Meg and her mother – a snap here, a grumble there. Meg's turning to me for sustenance, drawing stories out of me with her eyes. Better for her to forget about me and stay close to her family. Don't think about when the pitchforks come out. Don't think about waving goodbye to Meg.*

a good man and I love him, but when it's like that between us, I lose a piece of myself. What about him? He needed me to make his soul whole again. How can I do that when I shrink down inside and can't be my real self with him? Tears welled in her eyes.

'Meg, wake up. Come and get water,' Seren whispered. Her daughter pulled the blanket over her ears.

'I'll come.' It was Hilda.

Seren narrowed her eyes. *I do need a hand,* she thought. She put a finger to her lips and whispered, 'Shush' as Hilda followed her out. *At least she knows how to set the wooden latch down silently. She copies the way I slide my feet so I don't clank the buckets. Even so, what'll I do when we get to the spring? It scratches to think of a stranger peering into my secrets.*

They passed Headman's house in silence and crossed the track down from the ridge. Tussocks drenched with dew chilled the soles of her feet. Hazel roots twisted through the track where it sloped down to the water meadow. Squelching here, the fresh smell of water-mint.

Hilda's voice startled Seren, 'May your path be warm with joy as the sun turns back to the earth.' In Seren's own language, with an accent, but close enough to her dear ones' way of talking to make hairs rise on the back of her neck.

'How do you know those words?' *Is this a trick to make me say things I shouldn't even think?* Seren hid her thoughts behind her eyes.

'We said the same, back home. We had a response to give. Do you?'

The words slipped over Seren's tongue like water. 'When ice comes again, may your cellars be full with harvest.'

'And your deep heart remember the day of melting.' Hilda replied.

How long had it been since she'd been blessed in the old way? Seren leaned over to smell a spray of wild plum blossom, afraid for the stranger to see her so soft. 'Who are you? One of us or one of – them?'

'My mother was a Pict, from the north. My father was British, like you. My second mother was a Saxon, so what does that make me? A weed in the crop maybe.' Hilda had a lop-sided grin on her face.

53

'Where are you from?'

'We lived where hills bite the sky.' Hilda turned aside abruptly. 'I've walked all over this land, but I spent mud-month with the shepherd tribes on the chalk ridges south of here. It's a long walk from there with only hares for company. By 'them', do you mean the Saxons?'

'That's what they call themselves: "Knifers". They worship their knives. Ugh!' Cold slid down her spine. 'That long scramasax, the one-bladed knife, that's how they get their name – Saxons. And the Anglish are no different, I can't tell them apart. They'll do their knife ritual today – they call it the Day of Hretha, Glory-Dawn Day.'

'I've heard their dawn goddess called Estre in some places,' Hilda nodded. 'What do they do here?'

'They bring out all their blades – flash them in the sunlight and sing to Hretha. They bang their weapons against their shields and shout a lot. Everyone dances – except me, of course. I'll be cooking for the feast afterwards.'

'Are there any more of your people in the settlement?'

'Only me, Meg and May. Wulf's mother was one of us. He came here when his wife died, from Eel Island, to join his twin brother, Kenelm.'

'Kenelm was Ursel's father, wasn't he? She and her mother Ragnild are full of grief for him.'

'He died last Yuletide. I couldn't do anything for him.' A familiar stone of misery dragged in her stomach.

'You've got so much healing skill, Seren,' Hilda's hand touched Seren's arm. 'I saw that last night. You've got herb-knowledge, but, more than that, you're a wind-walker – you can see deep into the heart and take people on a journey to heal themselves. That's rare. I saw how everybody got in your way, bringing their own struggles into the space you held for Ursel. I'm sure if you couldn't heal Kenelm, it wasn't for want of work or skill.'

Seren felt the weight lift a little. She eased her shoulders.

A heron flapped up from the edge of the pool, gobbling a frog in its beak. Where the spring bubbled up from underground between ash roots, the chalk scarp reared up against the eastern sky, making a hollow to cradle the last of the night. The big grey bird folded its long neck and flew away downstream, trailing its feet in its reflection. In elder and hawthorn, warblers, great tits and chaffinches lit the sky with song. Seren tucked the skirts of her tunic and overdress into her belt and stepped onto a flat chalky clunch rock at the edge of the water, bucket in hand.

'Seren,' Hilda grasped her elbow. 'I need your help.' Seren sighed. *Earth Mother is calling me to be alone with her, but here's this Hilda needing me. Everybody wants me to give …* She set aside her own needs and turned to the storyteller. Hilda went on, 'I want to be here longer, to give you all my stories – the ones to shake up women's thinking – so I need to tell my way into Headman Kedric's favour.'

'Ah, you want to turn the founding of Wellstowe into a legend, is that it?'

'A bard at a feast should repay hospitality. If I make them cheer and bang their ale-mugs, perhaps they'll let me stay.'

Seren felt a niggle of doubt, imagining Meg turning away from her, admiring Hilda … She spoke sharply, 'Will you cover the knifers in golden glory and make us British into wild savages in the woods?'

'I try to speak truth, with a swish of glamour. I'll honour your people, Seren. Around the fire at lambing time, the shepherds told me what happened when the Anglish and the Saxons came in over the North Sea. They told me how in some places they settled quietly and mingled with the British who lived there. In other places there were battles, where the land was best, or there was a good harbour that the incomers wanted to control. How did they get to Wellstowe?'

'The Saxons came in their ships one bright day in the spring.' Seren felt the pull of the old tale drawing her in. She put her bucket down on the grass. 'My grandmother told me. I called her Nana. Everybody calls their grandmother Nana, don't they? My Nana's grandmother was a little girl at the time. The people went down to the shore to welcome the newcomers. Sharp prows crunched onto shingle and out they jumped – wave after wave of fighting-men, spears at the ready. They butchered our heroes and tore off their torcs – and put them round their own necks. That night they feasted in our Great Hall, with dead bodies strewn on the floor instead of rushes.' Seren's hands made the same gestures that Nana used to make: they thumped together as the ships rode up on the beach; clutched her throat when the torcs were stolen.

'What happened then?'

'They worked their way along the coast and took over Ousemouth Harbour and the salt pans there, put fire to thatch and our men to the sword, raped our women and made us slaves, stole our herds and our flocks. Then they rowed up the rivers, wriggling into the heart of our rich farmland like worms into a carcass.' Seren's voice carried an adder-hiss with a choke of tears behind it; she felt her grandmother speaking through her. In the singsong rhythm, all the tongues that had spoken those words echoed down the years. As the sun rose, red clouds bled into the shimmer of the pool.

'Tell me the names of the heroes who fell on the beach, and the names of the Saxon leaders. Who came here and founded Wellstowe?' Hilda leaned towards her, intent.

Seren spoke the names. A heron feather drifted down to float on the dark water.

'Now, Hilda Storyteller, make something out of this that won't shame us.'

'When I start work on a new tale, I make a gift for Neath – that's our river goddess back home. What is the great goddess called here?'

'My people call her Breejsh. The Angles and Saxons seem to have forgotten her.'

'Breejsh, Brigantia, Brid, Brighid … I've met her with many names up and down the land,' Hilda nodded. 'Will she mind if I draw my picture for Neath on a flat place by the edge of the stream?'

'If Neath is not one with her, they are sisters. There's a little beach beyond that willow,' Seren pointed. 'I have my own ritual to make here.' She allowed her eyes to carry a message to Hilda, *Go! I need to be alone here.*

Hilda pushed through a curtain of green-gold fronds with a smile over her shoulder for Seren. *Phew! Now I can listen to Earth …*

Seren waded into the deep eddies and pushed a bucket down so that water lapped over its iron rim. It was suddenly heavy and she hoisted it up onto the bank. Her legs were numb with cold, but she didn't want to step out of the stream. She scooped some water in her cupped hands and splashed it on her face, gasping. Breejsh was there, in the water. The breath of the goddess rose like mist from the surface. Seren threw off her clothes and slid into a smooth swirl that welled up from Earth's opening. She rested for a moment, floating. The glide of spring water filled her ears. She could hear the goddess singing now – a deep, slow note with a lilt of sadness – the land longing for her people.

She found a footing on mud at the edge. *There's only me to honour you, dear one.* Seren leaned forward to kiss the Breejsh stone where the carved goddess squatted by the spring, half-hidden by ivy trails. Some ancient hands had placed the stone with care, so the water bubbled up out of the earth just below it. *Her hair blazes out like glory, wild and thick like mine,* thought Seren. *Dear Breejsh's arms hold open her body to let the water rush through. What could be more sacred than this? The channel our Great Mother opens to bring forth all beings!* Seren sang softly, 'Thank you, dear Breejsh, for your cunt of compassion, through which love leaps into life. Gurgling streams gladden our hearts; we quench our thirst with clear water. Your generosity nurtures all living things; the flow of your love goes with us.'

The upwelling was like the moment when Hubert nuzzled Seren's chest. She'd try to pass him back to his mother, but when he looked up at her with big eyes, a current of Breejsh's power arose in her and swept away the tightness in her soul. When she suckled him, milk sprang from her breasts, eager to fill him with peace.

When she called Meg 'cushla, beat of my heart', the power flowed again. Last night, that's when Meg's voice was freed to find the story, Seren realised, and when something melted between them.

When Wulf called her 'honey-sweet', the wet came inside her if she wasn't aching for sleep. And she could rub his back and talk love to him and welcome him into her deep place.

More words overflowed from Seren's lips, with the low notes of running water – a chant her grandmother had taught her. There was a word in there that she could never turn into Saxon – a word with compassion, love and friendship in it, with a brightness about it like wings of cloud arching across the sky.

She stepped out onto the bank, pulled on her tunic and began to dance. Was that another voice, humming along with her? Seren's feet beat the ground at the centre of a spiral that only she could see. She threw back her wet hair from her face, arms wide to greet the sun, eyes half-closed as she traced wider loops. Fire spread from the palms of her hands through her body and met with the pulse of the earth at her root.

Seren's eyes snagged on Hilda, pushing aside the willow curtain. Her feet lost their pattern. Hilda threw her arms up and sang along out loud. She danced down to Seren's side. Seren faltered, fearing a joke – but Hilda kept going, panting a little. Seren began again. Hilda watched her feet and followed her lead. The dance was stately at first, then fast and wild. They kept the rhythm as they leapt and kicked and whirled, arm in arm, following the twists of a spiral, from outside to in, and back out again. When it was done, each of them scooped a handful of water from the shallows and sprinkled it over the other's head with a blessing. They picked up the heavy buckets and hauled them back towards the settlement.

'Where did you learn our stepping-into-larksong reel?' Seren asked.

'Back home,' Hilda replied. 'I haven't had a chance to do it for a long time.'

'They can wave their knives as much as they like. At least we've thanked Breejsh for the flow of love,' Seren said.

Hilda grinned. 'These buckets are heavy! Do you bring water every morning?'

Seren shrugged. 'Through the day as well. We all do. Not the men, of course; they take the animals down to the stream to drink, a bit lower down.' She cleared her throat. 'Thanks for coming, Hilda. Meg should have done it. She's getting so lazy these days; I don't know why.' Hilda was listening. Seren sighed and went on, 'Yes, I do. She'll be starting her moon-bleeding soon. Her breasts are just budding and she's got that sulky, dreamy look. I want to tell her what to expect, how to cope, what it means to be a woman – but I'm running to serve Oswynne, Headman's Wife, all day.'

'Meg told the story so well!' Hilda said. 'I really saw the queen seeking out the wise woman. She has natural skill, and you've taught her well.'

'I want to tell Meg all my grandmother's legends,' Seren exclaimed, 'But it's always "Seren do this", "Seren haven't you finished that"… They will crumble into dust with me if I don't pass them on. I used to sing the old songs to get her to sleep, the ones with stories hidden in them, and tell her tales when she was little. Now she's thirsting for the old strong stories. She can understand the meanings at their roots.'

Hilda nodded. 'We all need those stories, Seren, and Meg could pass them on with beauty and depth.' Hilda seemed to be biting her lip, then she shook her head as if to clear it and said, 'Meg's having a hard time, I think. When Ursel smacked her yesterday, it seemed to really hurt her. Weren't they good friends not long ago?'

Seren's insides twisted up. 'What, Ursel hit her? If I'd known that, I could never have given Ursel healing last night; it wouldn't have worked. No wonder poor Meg was upset.' She put a bucket down outside Headman Kedric's house just as he banged the door behind him. He glowered at them and stamped off towards the stables.

'Looks as if Oswynne's efforts didn't work,' Hilda murmured.

Seren groaned. 'We've got enough to do already to prepare for the feast. What next?'

CHAPTER 6

BLOOD, MILK AND FEAR

URSEL

Ursel tickled her pig's stomach with a hazel stick. 'Eh, my lovely, look at the size of you now!' she crooned. 'Your mam's fed you well and you're good at getting acorns for yourself now, aren't you? Your spots and stripes are fading – you're growing up. You survived the frost that killed your runty little brother and you're getting nice and fat. Delicious crackling we'll get from you – but not yet, pretty, not until you're bigger. Don't worry, you've got all the long summer to rummage for mushrooms and wallow in the mud.' The pig sprawled back, legs waving, and grunted with pleasure.

Otred opened the gate and all the other pigs jostled out into the sunshine. Ursel's pig snuffled contentedly as she pulled the gate to and fed him a handful of acorns – a treat just for him.

The pigsty door crashed open. Ursel straightened up. Her Uncle Kedric slammed the gate shut so that the pig couldn't escape, grabbed it by the ear and unsheathed his seax.

'Get out of my way, girl,' he shouted, as she lunged to free her pig.

'What are you doing?' she yelled. 'That's my pig!'

Meg looked away from the meat into the sky, reaching for beauty to hold onto. The sun dipped below a line of low cloud over the fen. As the light frayed like the hem of her worn-out tunic, the moon rose pale and huge above the trees on the ridge. *Like a brooch … or freshwater oyster shell …*

'Now!' Seren called.

Meg jumped to help her mother haul the piglet from the spit onto a platter and got splashed with hot fat. She quickly licked pork dripping off her burning hand, her mouth watering.

Seren arranged the sage leaves round the piglet. She looked up as Oswynne came out to the cooking area for another refill of the big ale jug. Oswynne signaled to her with a nod and Seren straightened her skirt, stood tall, lifted the platter of roast pig and walked into the Hall with it.

Meg slipped in after her and ducked into the women's corner behind the screen. She pushed between aprons and worktables to find a nook where she could peer at the feast through a crack between the woven hazel wands. Her nose wrinkled at the smell of smoke from the fire in the central hearth. Up the smoke drifted, past the long chains that held the cauldron. She watched it wreath round the massive rooftree beam and sift into the thatch.

Her mother laid the platter on the high table in front of Headman Kedric and Thane Roger. It looked so impressive, yet the two men ignored it and continuing lolling on their bench chatting.

'Ursel, ladle stew from the cauldron into this serving dish and start round with that,' Oswynne ordered. 'Kedric will carve the roast for the high table. There may be some small pieces for the other men, but not much. We don't want them to notice.'

'I can't!' Ursel was sitting hunched over on a stool and hung her head, covering the bruises on her face with her hands.

Oswynne sighed, 'Alright then,' and patted her on the shoulder. 'Winfrith, will you do it?' She looked around, but Winfrith was nowhere to be seen.

Nelda pushed her fair plait back, getting dough in her hair from her kneading. 'I asked Winfrith to look after the little ones because I'm busy.

She's their aunt after all, my husband's sister; it's about time she got used to looking after small ones. We'll have Keenbur's baby in our hall soon. Maybe Winfrith will have some of her own before too long, if we can find her a husband.' Nelda's bright face was wreathed in smiles.

'Meg!' It wasn't a question from Oswynne but a command. Meg slid along the edge of the worktable, picked up the dish and ladle and went round the screen with them into the Hall.

Pools of candlelight glowed on oak trestles worn smooth with use. Polished drinking horns gleamed. Bronze buckles glinted. Voices boomed with banter and laughter rang out.

Meg's breath caught in her throat. It felt as if hundreds of eyes stared at her as she walked into the centre of the Hall and dipped into the great cauldron. She had to take care that her skirt didn't catch fire.

Moving along the tables, she ladled stew into wooden bowls for the men, refilled the serving dish, then served the boys. The heat from the fire made sweat gather in her armpits.

Under the tables, hounds waited for scraps. Even they seemed to be watching her.

Ragnild, Headman Kedric's sister, called her over to the corner of the high table where the great ones sat. *Crow woman, Hilda had called her. Is her anger coming my way, am I going to get pecked?* Ragnild's face was calm. *Phew, she just wants help with Elder Edith!*

Ragnild and Elder Edith were the only women sitting at the Feast. *Elder Edith looks dignified in her special chair. I'm glad she sat still for me to braid her hair earlier, the plaits wound on top of her head look like a crown. Her arms are resting on carved dragons to show how important she is. Do the dragons talk to her? Silly idea! But the ancestors do, so maybe it's not so silly …* Ragnild was sitting very straight. Her smooth dark head bent over her aunt Edith's dish, as she diced the old lady's meat. Meg drizzled meaty juice onto bread, mashing it with the spoon.

Elder Edith gazed into the distance. *I know that look. It means she's listening intently.* Meg helped Edith eat while Ragnild exchanged polite words with the guests.

Headman Kedric carved slices of pork for the men at the high table. His face glowed. Was it because his cheeks were scraped bare of beard, leaving the length of it on his chin, or was his shining look caused by the gleam of the torc round his neck? The men at the high table commanded a view of the whole hall.

Thane Roger got the piglet's head. It looked tiny on a platter in front of his hefty shoulders. His son Grimbold sat next to him, his ratlike teeth showing as he talked. Redwald, Thane Roger's foster-son, was only half-listening to Grimbold. His eyes roamed round the Hall. *Who is he looking for?* The stranger they called 'Brother', though he wasn't anybody's brother, sat in a place of honour too.

Music made everybody look around. It came from outside. *Was it a breath of the fen?* The notes started far away, thin as smoke, then grew louder like bird cries. Everyone's feet began to tap. The lads sitting near the door peered out.

In came Hilda, her skirt swirling around her like flames, playing her swan-bone flute.

Only the Thane seemed unsurprised. 'Aha, you've got a bard for us, Kedric. Good, good. Never seen a woman one before. Funny kind of pipe she's got.' He tapped his knife on the table in time with the tune.

Hilda bowed, so elegant and graceful that Meg imagined gold adorning her. 'My name is Hilda, travelling storyteller, good sirs and ladies.' Out from nowhere came her coloured leather balls; they flew up into the air, round and round, fast. Mouths gaped and gasped. She winked at Meg briefly. 'Do you like riddles? I wonder if you know what this is?' She swept the Hall with her eyes, catching everybody's attention. 'A wonderful thing I am, a woman's delight: I stand up strong in the bed, rather hairy around my root. If a girl has the courage to grip me and stow me in her strongbox, she weeps at our wedding with a wet eye. What am I?'

There was a roar of laughter as men dug each other in the ribs. Meg grinned as Hilda gave them the answer – an onion – her mouth very prim, and they shouted with mirth.

'Down in the shed, she stood in a corner, along comes the young man and they begin to work away together, up and down and round and round with something stiff.' Hilda rolled her eyes. 'At last he grows tired but something precious thickens beneath her belt. What is that?'

They chuckled and scratched their heads and turned to ask each other. Hilda daintily took a piece of bread and a scrape of butter from the crock at the head table, showed it to the Thane Roger and Headman Kedric.

'Why are you showing me butter?' Thane Roger asked, puzzled. 'Oh … butter! Churning butter!' He banged the table and guffawed and all the rest told each other the riddle again, giggling as they got it. They had never thought of a butter-churn as 'she' – but now they would!

Hilda told more riddles – about storms at sea and fire, then one about a harp. She brought out her harp from a bag and struck a few chords. The men fell silent.

Meg set down her bowl and ladle without a sound and slid onto the bench behind the wicker hurdle. Hilda's voice swelled until her song rang out to the rafters.

KEEN WAS THE KEEL

Keen was the keel that skimmed over sea-foam,
Wave-weary warriors carried from far.
'Land!' called the look-out. They all crowded round him,
Staunch son of Saywynn, sharp was his sight.
On the low shore-line waited the war-band,
Sharp spears ready, skin blue with woad.
Shrill sang the war-axe as strong bones it shattered,
Red broke the billows with blood of the fallen,
Fierce was the fighting on that shingle spit.
So many strong men lay wounded, as sea birds
Shrieked in the storm-winds that blew over sand.
Life from limbs leaked, but comrades came running,
Bound up the gashes and helped their dear friends.

The guests looked at each other as Hilda praised the heroes of the British who fought on that day. Meg recognised the names that Seren always chanted in her singsong voice when hate filled her. Then Hilda turned it around, saying how mighty were the warriors of the Angles who overcame the British on that beach, to win against such noble enemies. She sang about the dangers they withstood in the Crossing of the North Sea, and how they made the royal family of the British into slaves to show how strong they were. When she told about the despair of the British, Seren narrowed her eyes to listen, intent.

The men were pleased to hear how clever their ancestors were to band together, Angles with Saxons, some already settled and some who came in their ships soon after. Hilda's verses about the strength of these Anglo-Saxon fighters had the men banging on the table with their drinking-cups and cheering. She told all the names of the ancestors of Kedric and their close friends, the great-grandfathers of Bertold. She sang about how faithful these elders were to the forefathers of Thane Roger, telling all the names of the men and women of each generation. She told how they carved up the land between them. Some took the salt pans at the coast and some the rich farmland.

Seren nudged Meg. 'Take this bread to the high table, and do another round of stew, but don't use it all up. Make sure there's some left for us.'

As Meg set a basket of bread on the high table, one of the strangers tapped her on the arm. It was Redwald, that foster-son of the Thane's, the one with the lovely hair. *I remember; he's somebody important. His own family is special; it's an honour for Thane Roger to foster him …* 'Yes, Sir?'

'Where's Ursel tonight?' he asked, and his smooth skin flushed pink to his thick, level eyebrows. 'I always talk to her when we come over … er, that is, um …'

Meg didn't know what to say. 'She's not very well tonight, Sir.' When she got back to the women's area behind the screen everyone wanted to know what he said. 'He asked where Ursel is. I said, not very well tonight.'

It was hard to tell what Ursel felt under the bruises, but she turned away and eased two split hazel wands apart to make a narrow peephole. Meg watched too, nearby.

'What else did he say, Redwald, the Thane's foster-son?' asked Ursel.

Meg told her and Ursel smiled behind her hand.

When will some young man want to talk to me? Meg wondered. *Never, of course. Slaves don't get noticed and I'm just the one with the bony elbows.* She turned back to watching through her peephole as Hilda entranced the men with their own story.

'How does she know all this?' Ursel asked. 'Is she making it up?'

Meg turned those words around in her head. They didn't sound big enough for what Hilda was doing.

Now Hilda told about the push upstream, how the bands of warriors divided up and each took a fork of the river. Her words took them through trackless forest where wild boar snorted and giant bears ranged. The heroes pushed on despite all danger. When they met with natives, first there was suspicion, then trading. Sometimes they made an alliance or agreed to settle on a separate stretch of land. Often there was treachery on one side or the other, with a knife to the throat in the night. At last Kedric's great-grandfather and his friends found a special place, a place blessed by the gods, where river and trackway meet, close to forest and fen, with the gift of fresh water always flowing and the sun's path broad across the wide sky. There was a silence as her voice died away.

Then the men shouted: 'That's our place, Wellstowe! This settlement here, where we are now! That's us she's singing about. Those heroes are our fathers and grandfathers.' They banged their mugs on the table and roared the words of the song over again, waved their arms in the air and chanted the names of their ancestral heroes.

'More drink!' Oswynne hurried to refill their cups with the best strong ale.

When the noise died down a little, Seren began a round of the tables with a dish of chopped dried apples, hazelnuts and walnuts, with cream for the head table. The lads by the door got porridge with their apples. Nobody seemed to mind too much, especially when Hilda juggled her leather balls again.

Two hounds growled and tussled over a bone. Hilda did not miss a ball, but nobody was watching her anymore. All eyes were on the hounds. Hilda put the balls away, bowed, and sat down behind the screen with the women. Somebody gave her a drink of everyday weak ale.

Redwald lunged for the fighting dogs and got hold of one collar while Headman Kedric grabbed the other. They pulled the hounds apart as they snarled and scrabbled with their claws. Kedric swore and cuffed them. He stood straight with pride as they obeyed him and retreated to whimper under the table. Redwald wiped his brow on his sleeve. The men cheered again.

Kedric and Redwald missed entirely what was happening at the head table. Seren leaned over to spoon cream into Thane Roger's dish. He grabbed her buttock and squeezed. She made a small, strangled noise and pushed his hand away, spilling cream on her arm. He kept his bloodshot eyes on her face and licked the cream off her arm, all the while clutching her skirt.

Seren raised her arm – *was that a knife she held?* Meg held her breath. *Is Mother going to stab him – what kind of trouble will that start?* Meg could almost smell his meaty breath. *Not a knife* – it was a heavy copper spoon in her hand. She was about to clang it on his head when Oswynne stepped close to Seren.

'Ah, Seren, I need you to tend to the ale-barrel,' she said calmly as she grabbed Seren's arm and knocked the spoon from her hand, at the same time deftly pushing off the man's grasping fingers. She hurried Seren out behind the screen with a protective arm around her waist. Meg breathed again, quietly, gratitude flooding her with warmth – Headman's Wife Oswynne had been so calm, so skillful.

Her mother was shaking. 'That man! He's always been slimy with his wandering hands, but he's getting worse! And the rest of them – they're all sitting there letting him grope! What's got into them? All quaffing strong ale as if there's a prize for falling down drunk. Ugh!'

Nelda shrugged, 'They work hard day after day. This is the only time they get to enjoy themselves.' She still had flour up to her elbows.

'Are they really having a good time? Looks to me as though they're little boys vying to make themselves look big to each other,' Oswynne frowned.

'So what's making them feel small?' Hilda put the question out there with a keen glance round.

She knows the answer, thought Meg. *She's up to something.*

'I don't want to hear excuses,' Seren hissed.

Meg put an arm round her mother.

Out in the Hall, Thane Roger thumped the table, his voice thick with drink. 'Glad to see you're a strong fellow, Kedric. You'll be useful when you come over to my place to take your turn on the earthworks. It's coming along nicely – at least it was last summer. Some of the rampart fell down in the icy weather at Yule time. We need lots of big lads to build it up again and start the next section. How many can you bring with you? I see a good half dozen here. Some of them a bit skinny though.'

Headman Kedric sat tall at the table. 'Yes, I can count on my friends: Bertold and his sons, Gaufrid and Evrard – always my trusty comrades. My son Edgar, young though he is, can help too.'

Edgar's pale cheeks went pink with pleasure at his father's recognition.

The men raised their mugs as their names were called, proud to be acknowledged in the feasting hall. Did they hear what they were being called to do?

'Young Aikin may be thin, but he's agile. Wulf, we'll need you for your strength.' Kedric said. Wulf looked down and shuffled his feet. Meg could see Aikin asking him something, but Wulf just muttered.

It was Aikin who spoke first: 'Headman Kedric, Sir, pardon my asking, but what is this rampart being built? Why do we need to help with it?'

Thane Roger scowled.

Then a thin old voice rang out, 'Well asked, young Aikin. Never be afraid to speak up if you need to know something.' It was Elder Edith, not napping in her chair after all.

Thane Roger's eyes flicked over the carved dragons on her chair, the embroidery on her dress, the double row of glass beads she wore hanging from long bronze brooches.

Meg could almost hear his thoughts: '*Must be worth twenty cows just for the beads. Chair's been in the family since the Crossing by the looks of it. She's one of the elders, only one left of that generation. Let me see, she's Kedric's aunt – of the founding family of Wellstowe, I think. I'd better be respectful.* None of this was voiced, of course.

Aloud, Thane Roger said, 'It's those wild Britons. We're always waiting for the next raid. Last time they came after cattle. Sometimes it's horses. It'll be women and children next. Once we've got the rampart up across the chalk ridge where the trackway goes, we will be much more secure. Right across from the deep forest in the east to the trackless fen on the west, that's where we need to build it. Our ancestors started it, but their mounds have slipped, we need to start again. We've only done a couple of miles so far. It's a huge work and there are not enough faithful men like you to stand by me and build it. They all witter on about harvest time and horse breeding – not like you, Kedric, my good companion! By Woden, we'll finish the rampart to make our lands safe for our children and our children's children!'

They all cheered him then. Even Wulf looked happier.

'You're doing well here, Kedric,' Thane Roger continued, 'Your settlement's growing. All through Hretha-month I've been travelling round my settlements, the ones I protect as Thane, so we can greet the Glory-Dawn together and they can give me their tribute. Yours is among the strongest. You'll soon be a Thane yourself at this rate, once you've taken in more of the wood for farmland and your children start their own families.'

Headman Kedric puffed out his chest like a cockerel about to crow.

Elder Edith's calm voice cut in – reedy, but loud enough for all to hear: 'There will be no going off to build ramparts until we have sorted out our problems, young Roger. There's a dispute between my nephew, Kedric, and his niece, Ursel. We need to bring all of the local elders and wise ones together to talk it through and advise me, before I make my judgment. I call a Moot!'

A hubbub of voices, all talking at once, filled the Hall.

Elder Edith struck her knife against a pot to interrupt. Her voice sliced through the noise. 'We need our men for ploughing and planting. We need their wisdom to decide our future ways. This Moot is not just about one young woman and her uncle, however important they may be.

79

What we decide will set a course for future generations. We need a steady hand on the tiller just as much as the first settlers did when they crossed the North Sea and came inland down the rivers.'

'What's going on?' Thane Roger said, caught by surprise.

Headman Kedric coughed and reddened.

Ragnild stood up, her eyes blazing. 'My brother, Kedric, beat Ursel, my daughter. That's why she's not here tonight.' *Brave crow woman!* Meg thought.

Elder Edith was clear. 'This needs talking through. Thoroughly. The girl must have her say and so must my nephew.' *Elder Edith's brave too!*

Redwald pushed his way quietly out of the Hall, as if he was just going out to water the trees, as men had been doing all evening. He stopped and peered into the gloom behind the wicker screen and called softly: 'Ursel? I need to talk to you.' Winfrith gave her a push and Ursel slipped out with him, through the cooking-fire doorway, into the moonlight.

Thane Roger scratched his head. Kedric's mouth hung open.

'Now take me to my bed, Ragnild dear, please.' Edith stood, leaning heavily on her stick. Ragnild helped her past the central hearth and slowly, with great dignity, out of the formal door.

'So, what's this, you let the women boss you around now, Kedric?' There was a sneer in Thane Roger's voice. 'You should be bringing disputes to me; I am your overlord. You hold your lands from me, under the king, or had you forgotten that?' Though he understood little of what Edith had said, he knew she had drawn all the talk towards her and his ramparts were vanishing in the distance. 'We'll have to show the women who's in charge here.'

CHAPTER 9

BOSS MEN

MEG

Headman Kedric opened his mouth to answer, but a burst of music interrupted the conversation. Hilda played harp tunes with such life, they set toes tapping and stilled chat. The feasters scraped their dessert dishes clean, licked their fingers then beat time on the tables.

'Are you ready for another story?' Hilda asked. Kedric nodded. The men leaned back and picked their teeth. Hilda stood up and looked round the Hall slowly.

How could she bear to take such a long time in silence? Meg tracked Hilda's eyes as they met those of every person there. The Hall fell quiet as Hilda began.

'There's a shout in this story –

WE RIDE WITH VARAGAN!

The chieftain's son threw a stick into the fire. 'I'm sick of this,' he complained. The circle of young men and girls nodded in agreement. 'We're sitting here waiting for the old women to tell us off. All we did was race the horses, and alright some barley got trampled, but we've got plenty. I want more from life!'

His friend asked, 'What's your idea this time, Varagan? You always have great ideas!'

'I rode up into the mountains last month. The foothills are full of marmot, fat and juicy. Higher up I saw ibex and a wolf howled.' His face lit up with excitement.

'Yes, let's hunt!' his friend exclaimed. 'But aren't the mountains too far away? We'd have to ride all day across the steppe to get there.'

'We can take horse-hide tents and camp,' Varagan grinned. 'That's not all though. Why don't we just take off? We'll leave this place and get up high where the air blows fresh. Who knows what's on the other side of the range?'

The lads looked at each other. 'Leave our families?' some asked. 'When would we get back?'

'Never!' Varagan warmed to his plan. 'We'll live like our fore-fathers did, riding wild, catching our meat.' He jumped up and mimed loosing an arrow from a bow. 'You'll have to be strong, whoever comes with me. No whining when it's tough.'

Two of them started arm-wrestling to show how tough they were.

Varagan went on, 'Think of what we'll get! Bearskin cloaks – only warriors have those. Vulture feathers to hang from our headbands. Pretty women looking up to us, because we've seen things nobody can dream of …'

His father the chieftain interrupted them, leaning on his staff. 'Come over to the Elders' fire, Varagan, all of you. They have decided how you can make good the damage you've done.' A severe look over his long nose nudged Varagan into an old habit of obedience.

He was too restless to listen. '… months of shocking behaviour … fighting with your cousins … serious injury …

now this disregard for our shared food supply ... you must help with the harvest! ... no more racing, horses only to be used for ploughing ... hand in your best arrows to your father ... give your belt-buckle to your uncle ... If you fail to comply, you could be thrown out of this community ...'

Varagan turned on his heel. 'Don't worry, I'm not staying.' He spat on the ground. 'This is no life for a man, scratching in the soil, being told off by old women! We're off to start again, somewhere new. Who's with me?'

A party of young riders, men and women, gathered. Brandishing their spears in the air, they shouted, 'We ride with Varagan!'

The old chieftain stood, stern and upright, to watch the group set off. 'When the wind howls cold, don't come back here snivelling. We are well rid of you!' He stamped his staff on the ground and turned away, sighing to his tribe's elders: 'When we were young, hunters got killed or wounded going after wild oxen on the plains. Now that we grow crops and stay in one place, our boys grow fat on corn and scrap with each other instead. Hah, I'd go with them if I didn't have this knee.'

There was good hunting on the plains and foothills: lynx and wild goats. Up into the mountain range they rode. They wrapped their cloaks round their heads and pressed on over scree and crag, leading the horses into the high snows. Varagan's friend fell into a crevasse and they couldn't save him. Building a cairn for his memory, Varagan did not weep. 'I've got to stay strong, or look it – they all rely on me now,' he thought. The hunters' custom was not to cry out if they got hurt, they had to pretend to have thick hide. The girl who had loved his friend didn't utter a sound. That night in fitful sleep Varagan dreamed of his mother's arms, groaned and cursed his weakness. Unshed tears congealed into a lump in his belly.

As the days went by, fever gripped them. They made camp and waited for the shivering to pass, with only bark and lichen to eat. Their heads throbbed as snow-light scoured their eyes. 'Don't even say the names of the ones we have lost. We can't go back, never,' declared Varagan. 'Too many harsh words have been spoken. We have to go onward.'

The elders' words rattled in his head, '... will be thrown out of the community ...' Bitterness scoured his heart, leaving no trace of kindness.

The riders muttered amongst themselves, blaming Varagan. He pretended not to hear. There was not one he could talk to now, they all turned aside. His mouth drew into a hard line and his jaw ached from clenching back the terror and grief that rushed into his throat. He shouted curses to make them move on. Cold gripped his heart, too numb to thaw. He threw rocks at the fleeing rump of a mountain hare.

At the pass they caught their breath, leaning on their spears. The land tumbled in valleys and ridges down to another great plain. An eagle soared and slid on the wind, away over the land, and their eyes followed it across waves of grass, golden with sunlight and green with new growth. 'The sky god is smiling on us!' shouted Varagan. Gaunt riders streamed down the valleys, onto the plain.

A wide river meandered through the flat land, and on either side of it lay settlements rich with cream and corn. Such easeful living! They ground their teeth. Death and despair, unspoken, clung to them like leeches and sucked the warmth out of their hearts.

The famished riders came down into low hills. Where a waterfall poured into a water-lily lake, they stopped to drink. A strange old woman spoke to them in a language they'd never heard before. People from her settlement crowded round to look at them. The riders were jumpy, suspecting an ambush. Fearing attack, Varagan ordered his riders to shoot arrows into the crowd. In the skirmish, Varagan captured a woman with eyes as deep as the lake. He tied her onto his horse. These people

they meshed their fingers over their bellies and leaned back, Hilda caught the sticks deftly, replaced them in the fire, and began to tell the rest of the story. She didn't use her usual voice though – she dragged the words out and droned on the same note.

Men's heads rested on their friends' shoulders. Thane Roger started to snore. Kedric's head lolled into his empty dish. The Brother slid down onto the rushes on the floor and slept neatly, his cheek on his hand. Only Wulf was half dozing.

Seren gently shook him awake as she took away his ale-mug and spilled its contents on the floor. The quarrelsome hounds lapped it up and flopped down, closing their eyes, noses on paws, ribcages rising and falling gently.

Carefully, Seren, Wulf and Meg removed mugs and dishes. They wiped knives and sheathed them at their owners' sides. Nelda crept out from behind the screen, brushing flour off her arms.

One of the men rolled onto the floor yet stayed asleep. Meg was overcome by giggles until Seren wrapped her in a shawl and sat her down by the fire. Nelda fetched bolsters and blankets to make the men comfortable where they lay.

Oswynne slid Kedric and Thane Roger down to lie prone on their benches and Ragnild covered them with their cloaks, looking confused. 'Strong ale,' Oswynne remarked.

Seren pressed her lips together.

They dragged more blankets from the women's sleeping house, pulled over an empty bench, and made seats around the central hearth. Girls and women made themselves comfortable by the fire. Winfrith, with her little niece Elvie in her shawl, came over from the sleeping-hut and passed the baby to Nelda. Nelda undid a brooch so her overdress folded down and she tucked Elvie under her unlaced shift to nurse. Keenbur carried Nelda's toddler Leofric, with Roslinda's hand in hers to help her find firm footing in the dark. May staggered a little as she carried Hubert, floppy with sleep, and laid him on Oswynne's lap. Oswynne stroked her little son's pink cheek.

Redwald, Thane Roger's foster-son, tried to slip back unnoticed into the hall. After a short while, Ursel came in. They pretended not to be together, but their eyes crept back to each other's faces when they thought no one was looking.

'There's room for you here,' Hilda told them, patting a rug.

One of the men snored loudly. Everybody chuckled.

After everyone was settled, Seren raked through the embers and brought out the three teal that Meg had caught. She had baked them in clay in the embers of the hearth fire. She broke them open and a savoury smell made Meg's mouth water. Everybody got a piece – small but delicious. They shared the remains of the stew and bread. Leofric snuggled close to Nelda, sighed deeply and surrendered to sleep. The women brought out their hand spindles and yarn grew longer as the flames flickered.

Meg asked, 'If the queen's baby was called Marelda, did she grow up to be the queen in the story with the wise woman?'

Hilda smiled. 'That's right, Meg.'

'I'll tell you that story another time,' Ursel whispered to Redwald. His hair flowed loose over his shoulders, less tidy than when he went out. Their fingers were laced together, Meg noticed.

Last year, it would've been me sitting next to Ursel and Winfrith, the three of us. All that's gone. Not because of this handsome boy, even though he's some kind of noble. I thought Ursel would come back after she'd grieved for her father for a while, but no, I'm alone. The stab of loss caught her by surprise and she blinked away tears.

Wulf leaned forward to listen to the story and Seren slid onto the bench beside him, up close, holding his big hand. Hilda's voice caught their ears and her face drew their eyes.

'Now I can tell you how ...

THE WISE WOMAN AND THE QUEEN MAKE A BARGAIN

The young queen Marelda and the wise woman Huldran sat spinning in a hut high up on the mountainside. Huldran raked embers from the fire into an earthenware bowl and stood up. 'Bring our spindles, a bundle of sticks, and some food for later. Come with me,' she said, her voice serious, 'we'll strike our bargain in my Cave of Dreams, where the deep mysteries happen.'

Their boots slipped as they edged, step by step, up the snowy slope towards the crag on the other side of the clearing. Marelda looked up – the jagged rock was the shape of a raven just as Piroshka had told her. Clouds raced high above. They scrambled up onto a rocky shelf and perched on stones.

Marelda panted, 'I can see the whole valley! There's the waterfall – catching the sunset light. There are the fields of our settlement. I can't see the houses; the oaks are too thick. Do you watch everything from up here?'

Huldran smiled and beckoned. She pushed open a weathered wooden door – into the mountainside. Marelda paused to run her fingers over the carvings on the lintel and doorframe. Sinuous shapes curved and twined around each other, seeming to slither with life in the slanting light. Were they beasts, or plant-stems? She took a breath, and stepped into the dark.

It was not cold or damp. As Huldran kindled a fire from the embers in the pot, Marelda sat down to spin. Shadows danced over smooth walls. 'Did you level the floor, Huldran, or was it always like this?'

'I made it homely, with the help of some friends, bit by bit over the years.' There were rugs and furs, a wooden chest, a tall drum made from a tree trunk. 'Now, Marelda, we must talk about your child, and what you would give to have her.'

Hilda's voice changed. Meg could hear the echo of the cave as words rose up from deep in her chest.

Marelda felt the power of the old woman's eyes melting her bones. 'Tell me what I must do,' she whispered.

'First, I want to know why you want this baby so much. You said your husband is not good to you, hard to love. So why have a child with him?'

'It's not just for me!' Marelda said.

Huldran nodded, listening, so Marelda drew breath and went on. 'It's to bring our two peoples together. Bors, my husband, he's one of the horse-riders from the plains. I am from Peony Valley. The different groups have been living together for a long time now but they keep quarrelling and scuffles break out all the time. Sometimes it's "they stole our something" and sometimes it's "we didn't get our share of something", but it's always "them" and "us" and nobody wants to make it work. A child who was one of "them" and one of "us" would make them all see sense and bring peace. Only our child can do that; only I can make it happen. If you help me.'

'What about when people from different groups marry and have children together?' Huldran asked.

'Those children don't fit in anywhere. I've even seen somebody spit on a mixed-blood child. The horse-people call us "mud-slugs" and my people call them "dung-tramplers". They have even worse names for the mixed children. So, I am going to have my child, and she, or he, will stand up proudly and say, "I am Plains and I am Valley, I am a child of Earth and nobody can shame me!" That's what I want, a daughter who can do that.' Her eyes were filled with tears, her fists clenched.

Huldran was silent for a time, thinking. 'I can help you to grow strong in yourself, Marelda, my dear. Then it depends what the fates are weaving. You may become a strong woman who stands alone, or a strong woman carrying a child. This is what I ask.

'If I help you, and you have your baby, and it's a girl, send her to me in the month she becomes a woman. I will help her learn the skills she needs and find the path that belongs to her.' The wise woman leaned forward, intent. Her brown eyes gazed into Marelda's dark ones.

'Will she come back to me?' Marelda's voice caught in her throat.

'I don't know. It depends where her path takes her, and where you are on your journey through life.'

'How could you do that – to take a daughter away from her mother?' Marelda wrapped her arms round her thin body and rocked herself. 'My only child – if I ever get her!'

'My dear,' the warmth in Huldran's voice pulled Marelda to look up out of her misery. 'I will never hurt her, or you. I can't foretell what will happen in her life, I can only give her the skills that belong to her by right: the long-held wisdom of our people that links women and men in friendship. I'll walk beside her as she sets out on her path. A child of yours will be a special child, one so deeply wanted, so hoped for, so dreamed about.'

'Hmm. I'll think about it.' But, there was nothing to think about, Marelda knew. Huldran was her only hope. She blinked back tears while her spindle whirled and the thread grew longer.

'Did you know my mother?' Marelda asked. 'You said something before, as if you did. What was she like?'

Huldran sighed. 'Your mother was my dear friend.' Her voice closed off any further talk.

Marelda could not let it go. Breathless, she insisted, 'Piroshka told me that Mother had a dress with felt flowers sewn onto it – I asked when Mother wore that lovely thing, but Piroshka just put her lips like this' – Marelda made a thin line with her mouth – 'and told me to take more care with my sewing, my stitches were too clumsy. Once she said the oak chair with a carved back was Mother's, but when I asked her where Mother sat in it, she said, "Oh, the Queen presided at the feast, with us women all around her" and then clapped her hand over her mouth and wouldn't say any more. That's the chair Bors, my husband, sits on when he gives out arm-rings to his fighters. It's only men at the high table now, we women wait on them and then go back to our own rooms to the side of the hall.'

Huldran sighed. 'She has reasons to watch what she says, my dear. She's protected you, all these years. When you were a child, your life hung by a thread.'

'What?'

Huldran leaned back, eyes closed, seeing into the past. 'You knew Varagan, your husband's father. When he and his riders conquered Peony Valley, young Bors rode by his side on a pony. After the fighting, they settled in. Servants heard Varagan swearing about some girl who'd left him. She was no good anyway, he cursed, and they were well rid of her, but his foul temper got worse.

'Varagan sent out his troop to show all the people of the valley he was king now. The riders clattered through the summer heat, hooves thumping on the ground, making people's throats jump with fear. The smell of sweat brought flies and the glint of their weapons made people run and hide. The riders worked their way down through the terraced fields, stopping at every hut and hamlet and demanding a tribute. In some they got grain, others brought out baskets of ripe peaches and cherries, or beer, cider and mead they'd brewed. Farmers mopped their brows when the soldiers rode away.

Wives folded their arms and demanded, 'What are we going to eat all winter?'

'At least we've got our heads still on our shoulders,' the men replied. 'They know they need farmers to work the land.'

Higher up where the river cascades down from the peaks, the troop found the fishing settlement. They took dried and smoked fish and fat fresh river fish with shimmering scales. Up on the mountainside, they threatened goatherds and stuffed their saddlebags with cheeses, hides and leather and drove away with cartloads of charcoal and firewood.

'What did they trade for all that?' Marelda asked, wide-eyed.

'Trade!' Huldran laughed bitterly. 'They took it all! One farmer stood up to them. He climbed up on top of his haystack and roared defiance and brandished his scythe – daring them to come and take his grain. An arrow got him in the throat and his blood soaked into the hay. Children and hens scattered, screeching, and his widow sobbed over his body. Everyone got to hear about it so the people stayed quiet after that, stone-faced as the fighters took their plunder. Tax, they called it, for the King.

Varagan tore down the queens' roundhouse and scattered the timbers. He ordered his men to hack down ancient stands of oak and ash and used that to build his great hall, the doors bolted with tree trunks. You know it, Marelda – that's your home!'

'Oh!' Marelda started. 'Our women's rooms are a fine place to live. They lined the walls with planks to keep us warm in winter, cool in summer. We can sit and look out over the valley, right to the far ridge, and watch eagles circle in the summer heat. But they never told me about the queens' roundhouse. Please go on, Huldran, tell me more. Why didn't people get together and fight back?'

'It wasn't so easy for them. They are farming people. They didn't have any weapons, or know how to use them, though I suppose they could have used a boar-spear or their hunting-arrows. Maybe Varagan was wary of that. He called the people together and stood in the doorway of his great hall while they clustered in the dusty courtyard in front. He told them he was their king now, ruling the whole valley from the high clearings and cultivated lands right down to the marsh where the river begins to wander over the plain. They listened, tight-lipped. One man shouted – "You're not welcome here. We never asked you to come. Give us back our meat and grain!" Varagan spoke to one of his men and three soldiers dragged the rebel out of the crowd and pushed him down on the ground before him. Without a word, King Varagan split his head with his war-axe. The people groaned as his soldiers advanced towards them, knives at the ready. "Anybody else have something to say?" roared Varagan, blood dripping from his blade. The people scrambled and ran, shocked into silence.'

'Were you there in the crowd?' Marelda asked. 'You sound as if you saw it all.'

'No, I wasn't there.' Huldran went quiet for a few moments, wondering how much to tell the young woman. 'I heard it from Piroshka and my other friends in the settlement. They told me over and over again. It's the kind of story that shapes what people do for years to come – and keeps them frozen with fear.' Huldran sighed.

'You still haven't told me about my mother,' said Marelda.

'She was killed in the invasion.'

'I know that! That's all they ever tell me, whenever I ask: she died – as if I hadn't noticed! Other girls grow up with a mother to braid their hair. Not me. Piroshka is kind to me, but it's not the same.'

'Piroshka nursed and fed you and held you and picked you up when you fell. That was the easy part. It was harder for her when you asked questions, because she knew that if she told you too much, you could be killed – like the rest of your family. You were the only one of the royal house that they spared, when Varagan and his men invaded Peony Valley. You were a little girl, and Varagan planned for you to marry his son, Bors, to get the people to accept him as their king. If you had grown up to lead a rebellion against him – your life would have ended suddenly with a knife in the night. Piroshka thought that if you didn't know too much, she could keep you safe. She loves you.'

With a strained voice, Marelda said, 'Sometimes I lie awake at night, longing for my mother to touch me. I bury my nose in the fur rug and think – was this hers? Does it smell of her? What did she smell like? How did she wear her hair? Did she wash me when I was little? Did she love me?'

'Yes, she washed you, she fed you and she loved you.'

Marelda thought about this for a while. 'I still can't see her or smell her, or remember the touch of her hands.' A great sigh shuddered through the young queen. 'You haven't told me about the dress. What was it like?'

Huldran looked far away, into the dark at the back of the cave. 'Red and white peonies, stitched onto a dark background. Beautiful work. She made it herself when the old one wore out. Some of the women helped. I hemmed a bit myself, I think. It opened at the front so she could feed you. I remember one day when two brothers came to see her, to ask her to judge which one of them should get a bearskin. They had gone hunting together. One shot arrows, the other threw his spear and together they killed the bear. They shared out the meat amongst all their settlement – they were from up the valley where the forest is thick. One brother cured the hide, but the other one claimed he'd killed the animal. There was a lot of showing your mother the Queen exactly where the spear had struck, where the arrows had broken the skin and arguing about who gave the fatal blow. Your mother yawned. You toddled over and climbed up on her lap. It was obvious she relished being close to you, stroking your hair and crooning to you. The men gradually stopped arguing as they realised she wasn't listening. You slid down and played at her feet and she smiled at the men and said, "It's clear to me that you are both strong, skilful hunters. I shall ask the harper to create a song about the way you worked together to catch this bear. Please go and see her when we've finished here, to make sure she gets all the details right. Now, what to do with the skin? It's a fine hide, big and warm. I know someone who needs one like this, an old man who's suffering from aching bones. I'll ask my steward to take you down to his hut by the river after you've talked with the harper. You will give the bearskin to him – and ask if there's anything else you can do for him. He might tell you about his hunting days, when he was fast of foot and sharp-eyed – not so very long ago. Then come back here. If the new song is ready, we'll hear it in the roundhouse this evening!"

'Oh, she was a fine judge, your mother. She understood people and what warms their hearts. You helped there too, of course. When you nursed, you made the juices of kindness flow in her heart.'

'I can't remember that far back.' Marelda shook her head. 'How old was I?'

'Little, dear. Very little. I remember the night you spilled honey on that dress – not so long after. We were preparing for a feast. The queen from the plain at the foot of our valley travelled up to our roundhouse to talk with your mother and celebrate the Peony Festival with us. Your mother was busy, arranging everything for the festival, making sure there would be enough food for everybody. You sat on her hip as she moved around the courtyard and checked the baskets of fruit, counted eggs, admired the dancers' new costumes. She talked with you and the other queen as she worked.'

'You were there too?'

'I helped your mother when she sat in judgment or spoke for the people. I was the wind-walker for her.' Marelda looked puzzled. Huldran explained, ' As her wind-walker, I spoke with the spirits when she needed help from them. Later, your mother asked Piroshka to take you and all the other children out to the orchards where the women were picking fruit. The queens and their advisors got down to the difficult talk then, about trade and

'Of course! It's the one that points towards the North Star. Why did Huldran start showing stars to Marelda, Hilda? And all that talk about nuts and twigs – what was that for?'

Hilda explained, 'She wanted to help Marelda move her thoughts out of the pain and back into everyday time, where Marelda was loved and they were together.'

Meg thought about this for a while. 'But she sat there with Marelda while she cried, for ages, just patting her hand. It sounded as if she was encouraging her to cry!'

'Yes, that's right. Huldran knows how good it is to let sharp pain flood through us, while tears are hot. She watched Marelda's fierce weeping with her warm heart as well as her eyes, listening, feeling it too, not saying much, letting it flow. Once it's out, there's some kind of magic that heals the hurt place. Seren did the same thing with Ursel last night. She's a skilful woman, your mother.'

'But Marelda wanted to stop.'

'Yes, she got stuck in cold misery, after the hot tears were all wept out. She was struggling like a fly in a spider's web. She trusted Huldran enough to ask her for help.'

Meg asked, 'What about the nuts and twigs?'

'Huldran wanted to give Marelda a pathway back into everyday awareness, back to the safe place. She asked her some questions about their work that day to make her think about earth and water. She pointed out beautiful things around them, like that group of stars up there.'

'You're talking about Huldran as if you know her, Hilda. Is she real? Have you met her?'

'Ha! Kind of. You get to know someone when you tell their story. You melt into them and they into you. Be careful who you tell stories about in the Great Hall, Meg. They get into your insides.'

'Me, tell stories in the Great Hall?'

In a gleam of firelight from the Hall, Meg caught a sideways look from her. There was a twist of her mouth that wasn't a smile, but wasn't a frown either, one eyebrow lifted and a brightness in her eye.

'Of course!' Hilda seemed to hurry past this delicious thought. 'Now look where the Bear's paw points – to the North Star. Did you know that's the only star that never moves? All the others turn around it like a cartwheel. Inside you there's a place that stays calm and quiet all the time too, like the North Star. Sometimes it's hard to find it, but it's still there, deep inside. The way to get there is by riding on the river of tears or laughter.'

They turned back towards the hall where the others were sleeping.

Meg's chest glowed with Hilda's words. She hugged them to her. *Me, tell stories in the Great Hall?' 'Of course!'*

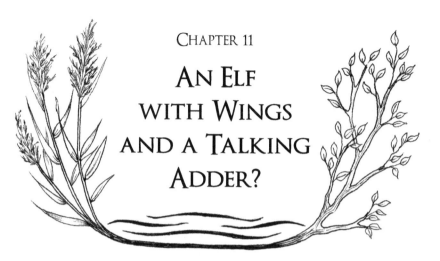

CHAPTER 11

AN ELF
WITH WINGS
AND A TALKING
ADDER?

SEREN

'Help me lift the top off this trestle table, Hilda, please. We're piling them by the wall,' Seren asked. She swept the space where it had stood.

'Meg, I'm tripping over you, cushla. Will you look if the feverfew tea's steeped enough yet?' Seren tried not to snap.

Meg chewed her lip as she stirred the steaming jug. 'I had a dreadful dream, Mother, eyes jabbing me like fire-sticks ...'

'Not now, Meg, we've got to take this over to Headman's house. They'll be wanting their morning drink after a night of strong ale. I put willow bark in it too. Will you take the jug? No, thought not.' Seren sighed and looked around.

'What's worrying you, Seren?' Nelda asked, hoisting baby Elvie higher on her rounded hip. 'Elvie, don't chew my hair!' She pushed her yellow plait over her shoulder.

She doesn't usually notice me, Seren thought. *Today she does, because of how I protected Meg.* Aloud she said, 'I wonder if they know what we did last night. What they'll do if they realise ...'

'We?' Nelda remarked with a dry tone.

'Everyone helped,' Hilda put in, leaning on her broom. 'I drew their eyes away. Oswynne served the potent drink, not asking what was in it, knowing something was, trusting Seren that it was enough but not too much. It could have killed them all if Seren lost count of the drops! Nelda, you watched and said nothing. I think we'll all be seen as part of the plan, if they understand why they slept so soundly.'

Nelda gulped as the words sank in. 'I'll finish up here,' she said, 'Elvie, go to Aunty Keenbur. She likes it when you sing to her, Keenbur.' She took Seren's broom and tutted and clucked as her dirt-pile built up: a broken dish, dog vomit, spilled crumbs, chewed bones.

Seren stepped out of the Hall, steadying the hot jug with both hands. It was only a few steps to Headman Kedric's house, but it gave her a chance to look across the shine of the fen. A cloud scudded closer, trailing a fringe of rain. She breathed deeply. Words leapt into her head from the story last night: *wind-walker, speaking with the spirits. I could do that! If only they'd let me …* Her heart rushed with longing as sudden as a gust of wind. *I could be a truly skilful healer, using all of my grandmother's teachings. I could walk between the worlds like Huldran, if I didn't have to sweep dirt all the time.*

Oswynne let her in just as the rain started. Seren served tea for Thane Roger and Headman Kedric. Oswynne gave the men newly-made bread.

I wonder if anyone's thought to pull the cover over the bread-oven? Seren wondered. She ducked out and the squall buffeted her. *I'll just shelter under the eaves at the back until the worst of it blows over, then run across to the cooking place.*

She could hear Thane Roger and Headman Kedric groaning and grumbling about their headaches. *Oh! There's a crack between the planks of the wall, I can see through.* She peered in, hardly daring to breathe.

'Must've been a good night – can't remember a thing!' they said. They slapped each other on the back and laughed.

Phew! Seren turned to go, but Headman Kedric asked Thane Roger, 'What's so special about this story the Brother wants to tell us? Why do you want everyone to hear it?' Seren leaned towards the crack. *They mustn't see me!*

Thane Roger said: 'This god he talks about, I like the sound of him. Brother Michael calls him "Lord" and he's very respectful when he says that word.'

Headman Kedric looked puzzled. 'A lord is a just loaf-ward, the man whose duty it is to feed the people and look after the grain-store, isn't it?'

Thane Roger replied, 'The way he says it, he makes "lord" sound more like a king or a king's companion. He's keen on getting all the people to follow this "lord". It would be good if all the people looked up to us that way, Kedric old chap, and were more obedient, don't you think?'

Headman Kedric nodded, 'I know what you mean.'

Thane Roger said, 'As soon as the rain stops, we'll get him over to the Hall to tell the story about the beginning of the world. That's a good one – especially if you're having trouble with your women-folk, Kedric, old boy.' And he laughed! Headman Kedric didn't laugh.

Seren slipped back to the Hall fast. She told the women who were still working there every word of what she'd heard. 'I felt chilled to the bone, not just from the eaves dripping down my back. The way they said it!' She shivered. 'And now they're all coming in here for the Brother to tell his story.'

Meg and Seren hustled to sweep out the last corners of the Hall – just before Brother Michael appeared in the doorway.

Headman's Wife Oswynne hurried in and snapped instructions about benches in a square, but the Brother contradicted her. He wanted benches in rows, all looking at him. He made himself as tall as he could – not very.

URSEL

'We can get a bit of time together,' Ursel whispered. 'Come away to the weaving-house.' *Can I say 'my love'? I'm not sure if he'd like that.* Redwald's face pointed towards the Great Hall, wooden like the prow of a ship, and she trailed in his wake. They stood near the cooking door in the Great Hall. He squeezed her hand, and she felt warmth rush up her neck.

'I want to hear these myths my uncles argue about,' he explained. 'I haven't heard them told properly, just snatches here and there. I think I should know about them.'

She got a seasick feeling of lands and people she didn't know sliding between them. His voice went hard and cold when he mentioned those distant uncles. *Redwald doesn't belong here*, she remembered. *He'll only be with his foster family until his own people call him back. Not yet, please!* 'We've got our own myths,' she tried.

'The Brother's not staying long in these parts. He's off to Kent soon, so this is my chance.' Redwald was intent.

Ursel turned to look for Winfrith. Where could she be? She spied her by the wall, next to Nelda, and beckoned her. Winfrith slid away from her family to stand beside her friend.

'What's Kent?' Ursel whispered into Winfrith's ear, putting a little space between Redwald and herself so he couldn't hear.

'Um, I think it's a place. South of here. I heard your uncle and my Father talking about it once. There's a big king there. They were talking about how many fighting men he can call up.'

'I thought the king lived at Rendlesham?'

'Our king's at Rendlesham, but this is a bigger king, Headman Kedric said. The great king's got a scabbard with garnets on it, and he drinks mead out of a cup made of glass. Wouldn't it be grand to see that? The other kings send him warriors when he asks, and furs and things.'

Ursel turned this over in her head. A king on top of other kings, like when the boys stand on each other's shoulders! Then they all fall down laughing. The story was starting, so she made a face at Winfrith, which Winfrith returned.

When everyone was looking the other way, Redwald's arm crept around Ursel's waist. Her body sang and she forgot about layers of kings that were nothing to do with her.

MEG

Hilda whispered in Meg's ear. 'See how he chose his spot in a shaft of light? He's got good lungs, we can hear him even here at the back.'

Does she think she's teaching me how to tell a story in the Great Hall? That's never going to happen.

Last night's dream of spear-sharp eyes bit her and she shrank her neck into her shoulders. But she noted where the light fell, and how the skinny man's belly moved out when he breathed in.

The Brother's first story was about a man being tortured to death by being nailed through his hands and feet onto a cross made of wooden planks. One of his friends had traded him to his enemies and they all turned against him. Meg felt sick.

But this man turned out to be one of the gods and he went to the Hall of the Heroes even though he had not died in battle. The story did not make much sense to Meg, but this Brother told it with dignity – it evidently meant a lot to him. He held up two pieces of wood joined together like the torture cross and told them that the man had died willingly and somehow it was our fault – Meg did not understand that part. We could make up for it, though, by calling the man-god 'lord' and obeying his wishes.

Bertold was sitting at the front, close to the important ones. He asked what the man-god wanted us to do. The thin man talked about being good, not hurting other people, being honest, being respectful – and obeying their Headman.

Bertold rubbed his bald patch, 'We know how to do that already.'

The Brother tried to teach them a spell for staying safe. 'Pitter patter' it sounded like, in a language they did not understand. People started drifting away.

URSEL

Ursel tugged at Redwald's hand. 'Can we go now? I don't want to hear about friends betraying each other; we don't do that. Or men torturing each other – ugh.'

'I think there's more …' Redwald looked to see what everyone else was doing. There was shuffling of feet.

Ursel turned to Winfrith. 'What's so wonderful about fine cups and jewellery?' she asked.

Winfrith furrowed her brows, thinking. 'Remember when Meg used to make up worlds and we played at being squirrels and living in trees, or flying with the swallows to the dark side of the moon? Well, there must be other places where everything is different! Wouldn't it be fun to ride over the skyline and see what's on the other side?'

Ursel snapped at her friend: 'It was Meg playing at being ravens learning to fly that made us ruin the roof by sliding down, last harvest time. "Flap and squawk, we'll soon take off". Dimwits we were. You came and warned us Mother was coming and nobody found out it was us; but we knew. Now Meg pretends the loose thatch that caused Father's death was nothing to do with her.' Anger stabbed as sharp as the adze blade that killed her father. Winfrith was muttering the usual platitudes but Ursel couldn't hear them through her guilt. Redwald's firm hold spread warmth from her hand up to her heart and loosened the grip of pain.

The Brother cleared his throat and looked around to get their attention.

MEG

'I'm going to see to the horses,' said Wulf. 'Got no time to listen to this drivel.'

'Wait, stop.' Thane Roger made it sound like an order. Wulf looked around, confused.

He's not used to being spoken to like that, thought Meg. *Except by Mother, of course.* She almost grinned to herself.

'Tell them about the beginning of middle-earth,' Thane Roger asked the Brother. Wulf sat down, looking around to check with Seren if he was doing the right thing.

The story had a talking adder in it and an elf with wings and a sword; Meg liked those parts. She liked how the god made a man out of clay too. May and she did that when they got some clay to play with. She remembered the little people they made last summer and how May kept hers until it fell to pieces. When he talked about the god making the man the boss over all the animals, Meg wondered about that. It would be fun to give them all names. But what did the animals think about it? The story didn't say. She did not like the part where everything seemed to be the woman's fault – she was even the cause of people dying, so he said!

'What rubbish,' Seren said under her breath. Hilda wrinkled her nose and said nothing.

When the story was finished, nobody knew what to say. *What did I call him, when we first saw him riding with Thane Roger yesterday? Wood Mouse!* Meg remembered. Hilda thanked Wood Mouse for his story and asked, 'What is your name?'

'Mi-chal. Mi-hael' Hilda tried the strange name over on her tongue, sounding it out. 'What kind of name is this?' she asked. 'What does it mean, where does it come from, what people are you from?'

Wood Mouse smiled. When his teeth showed, he looked more like a water vole. 'I come from Erin, the land across the water to the west. When I took the faith, I took a new name for myself, to show that I belong to Christ. Michael is the name of one of His warriors.'

'And is this Christ, the tortured god, from Erin too?'

'Oh no, Christ lived far away in a land of heat and shifting sands.'

Gaufrid, Nelda's husband, asked him, 'So, what time of the year do people make rituals for the tortured god? What does he help with – harvest or planting? Weeding or digging?'

The man's answer was firm. 'He is lord of every part of the year, and there are no other gods but him. He is the only one.'

There was noise throughout the hall. Everyone shocked, horrified. Some looked outside to make sure Thunor the thunder god had not heard him and was not about to strike them down with a bolt of lightning.

Elder Edith tapped her stick on the floor. 'What about the goddess who gave birth to him?' she asked. 'What is her name and how do the people serve her?'

'There is no goddess,' the man insisted, 'Christ and God the Father are the only ones, and the Holy Spirit too of course. Christ's mother was an ordinary woman.'

Meg slid closer to Seren on the bench. Seren began to weep quietly. Elder Edith was shocked. 'How can you say such a thing? Earth Mother has fed us and held us every day of our lives!'

'These gods and goddesses you talk about, they are demons, sent by the enemy to lead you astray!' Brother Michael went red in the face, almost shouting. 'But Christ came to save all people everywhere from the enemy!'

'Who is this enemy you fight, Warrior of the Cross God?' Hilda's eyebrow rose in a way that told Meg she was laughing inside, although her voice was level. Meg felt her breathing ease, since Hilda was calm.

'I fight against evil in all its shapes.' Brother Michael's eyes glowed as he spoke, looking inwards. 'Sometimes it takes the shape of a dragon or a huge worm. Sometimes it is the evil thoughts that people keep hidden. Sometimes people have to be killed because the devil has taken over their whole self!'

They all got up and sidled backwards, keeping one eye on him and another on a clear path to the door. Hilda cleared her throat. 'Thank you, Brother Mi-chal.' Her tone was firm and flat. 'Very interesting. We must talk again another day. Ah, look, the rain has stopped and it looks as if Thane Roger would like you to help load the wagon.' Most of the men went off to the shed and the stables, but Wulf stayed close to Seren. *I like it when he puts his arm around Mother. It gives me a solid feeling.*

URSEL

'The way he talked about Earth Mother! The story about the woman causing trouble – by wanting to find out for herself!' Ursel raged.

'Ah, hmm, I see what you mean. Very confusing, not very respectful.' Redwald stepped aside with her as people streamed by into the sunshine. 'I'm not sure, myself. I've heard King Ethelbert's interested in all this, down in Kent, and some of my uncles speak highly of it … I think I'd better go and help load the wagon.'

Ursel caught up with Winfrith, who'd got Elvie on her hip again and was jigging up and down to make the baby giggle.

> 'Ride on your horsey as fast as you can,
> Don't let your brothers make you marry a man,
> If you're covered in babies, you'll never be free,
> To sing and to dance and to bounce up high – Wheeee!'

Elvie squealed in delight and Nelda glared at Winfrith. 'Your brothers are only trying to help when they suggest good matches for you, Winfrith. Thornthicket's not such a bad place. I liked growing up there. You could do worse than marry the elder's grandson. Don't be too choosy or you could end up on your own!'

Winfrith shrugged, handed the baby back to Nelda and drifted closer to Ursel.

MEG

The smell of wet grass was sweet. Meg breathed deeper now they were away from the brother-man and his angry god. They hurried away from the Hall to the belt of coppiced hazels at the edge of the settlement. All the women gathered to sit on the mossy lowest branches of a big beech tree or on fallen branches around it.

May couldn't stop giggling. 'Fighting a dragon! Him!' she spluttered.

Meg had to join in and soon they were rocking with laughter.

Seren was not laughing. She stood very straight, her back against the beech tree trunk. 'How can a man-god be for all people?' There were tears in her voice. 'What about us women? How can a man-god help us when we birth our babies? What does he know about it?'

'And being everywhere …!' Ursel frowned. 'We all know Earth Mother is with us, she's the land under our feet and in all the animals.' She stroked the delicate fronds of moss and Meg ached to be close to her friend again.

Seren fingered the Breejsh sign she wore around her neck. She made a new one every year at lambing time.

What was it Mother said while she wove the threads around the rowan twigs? 'Breejsh draws out the first milk for the lambs, like a thread spun from a cloud of wool, and her compassion shines in the sun's warmth.' Meg bit her lip. *Will Mother get a knock round the ears for speaking out?* Oswynne's face was stone.

Hilda didn't catch Seren's eye. She made her voice loud enough for everyone to hear, without seeming to.

How does she do that? Never mind, Meg, she told herself. *You'll never have to try. Open your mouth and they'll attack you. They won't attack Hilda, or not yet.*

Gloom set into Meg as she listened to the light tone Hilda used, 'I've heard that there was a goddess of this place before Earth Mother came over the eastern sea with you Angles and Saxons, Ursel.' Her head dipped to one side like a robin. 'Does anyone know what she was called? Oh, Seren, you might be able to help us here. Was she the same as Earth Mother or was she different?'

She's putting herself in danger! Meg thought. She could see Oswynne's hands twitching as if considering smacking somebody for cheek.

Now everyone was looking at her mother. Seren went pink and her words tripped over each other, but she cleared her throat and spoke. 'She looks after us like Earth Mother, but she's more … Her name in our language is Breejsh. That's the way my people from the coast at Ousemouth say it. Our relatives who live round here – or used to live round here – we don't know what they called her, because they have … gone.'

'Not all of them.' Wulf stepped closer. 'My mother's folks on Eel Island are from round here way back. They tell a story about a willow wand that's planted in the earth, that sprouts and grows into a tree overnight – that's where she lives, our goddess, in growing things.' There was a murmur of agreement.

'What does Breejsh do, Seren?' Hilda's voice was gentle, but her eyes gave a signal to speak.

'She's in the red heart of the fire, where the peat crumbles when it's hot. When I lay white ashes over the embers last thing at night and make patterns, I ask her to keep the fire in, to warm us through the dark, and stop it from flaring up and catching the thatch when we're asleep. She's in the well too. When the water bubbles up from underground, that's her milk for us; we're all her children. Sometimes you can hear her voice in the wind, when the willows blow. And the little wriggly worms in the earth, they do her work, making rich soil to nourish herbs and crops. Plants grow, animals eat; we eat because she feeds us. We all go back to her when our bodies are done with. Her name doesn't matter. She is the one the earth belongs to, the one we all belong to.'

Oswynne looked at Seren as if she had never seen her before. Seren coughed and looked down. Meg saw Wulf squeeze her mother's hand amongst the folds of her dress, out of sight. Meg glanced at Hilda through a mist of tears. The storyteller looked pleased with what she had achieved, thoughtful.

I want to do that, cried a voice inside Meg. *Never, it's not for you,* stormed another. She turned away and stumbled to hide in the sleeping house, longing for a blanket to pull over her head.

Aikin passed her and asked, 'What's wrong, Meg?' but she covered her face. She heard him telling Oswynne, 'Headman Kedric says, please come and give our guests a cup of cheer to speed the journey. They're nearly ready to leave with the wagon. Wulf, can you come and help with the horses?'

CHAPTER 12

HOW MUCH HAVE THEY TAKEN?

OSWYNNE

Thane Roger strutted over to his carters, issuing directions: 'Careful with that bolt of cloth, lads, it's heavier than it looks. Don't want it to get muddy – I'll trade that for spears for our men defending the rampart.'

Oswynne stood in the doorway and watched them take the blue woollen fabric out of her house and pile it on the wagon. *I wove that! I arranged the warp threads carefully to create a herringbone pattern, passing the shuttle to and fro with Adela, my daughter, on the other side of the loom. We had to shake our hands to warm up our fingers.* Anger sat in a cold lump in her stomach. She clenched her fists under her apron. Her voice jerked in her throat, 'That belongs to me!' Kedric silenced her with a fierce look and stood in front of her, so Thane Roger could not hear her protest.

Kedric took a small knife from his belt, the new knife that Wulf had made for him, still shiny. He laid it, with its sheath, in Thane Roger's hands. 'I would like to give this seax, my Thane. It's the best work of our smith, sharp and strongly made. I hope you find it acceptable as an offering for you, to strengthen your war-band that protects us all.'

Oswynne felt her son Edgar's eyes on the knife. Edgar edged closer, lusting after the weapon. Thane Roger hefted the blade to feel its weight, tested the point on the doorpost, turned it over to examine the craft of its making. Sun glinted on its newness. 'Good,' he nodded briefly, sheathed it, and shoved it into his belt. Not even a thank you, she noticed.

Kedric smiled, satisfied that his offering was well received.

Edgar watched, taking it all in – his father making himself small to show the importance of the Thane.

My little boy, Oswynne thought, her fingers itching to push back a lock of blonde hair from his eyes. *What is he learning?*

Her husband lifted the trapdoor in the floor of their house, slid the ladder down into the cellar, and called out, 'Give me a hand with this barrel of smoked eels.' Edgar pushed past to haul it out and onto the wagon, eager to show his strength.

She bit back the words that sprang into her mouth: *Careful, son, your wrists are so thin … He's grown out of his tunic again, must add a strip round the hem.*

'What's in that crock in the rafters?' Thane Roger asked.

Kedric scrambled up the ladder from the cellar and took Oswynne's pot of cheese down.

Thane Roger sniffed it. 'We'll have that. My rampart-builders are hungry fellows; we need all the food we can get. When are you bringing your chaps to come and help, Kedric?'

Oswynne watched her husband squirm. *Good,* she thought. *He should feel rotten – he lets them take all our best gear and our food and now they want our work-hands too.* She opened her mouth to talk about planting and weeding, when Grimbold trotted up. *I mustn't speak before Grimbold. Even if his beard's just fluff and he looks like a rat, he is Thane Roger's own son.*

'Father, I found this bag of peas in the hall down there. Do we want it?' Grimbold peered at it as if it smelled bad and slung it into the cart as Thane Roger pointed.

She found herself thinking what a disappointment he must be to his father. She imagined Thane Roger holding his new-born son and announcing his name: *Grimbold – fierce warrior!*

The young man asked, 'What about the Elder's hall – do we search there too?'

Oswynne caught Thane Roger's nod. She hurried to get there first – they must not bother Elder Edith!

Edgar shoved the door open and ushered Grimbold and Redwald in, trying to impress his Thane's son and the important foster-son. Edith sat alone, serenely spinning. Oswynne wondered why Edith was sitting on her clothes-chest instead of her chair, and why the oak clothes-chest was covered with a blanket riddled with moth-holes. Grimbold didn't seem to notice.

He paced round the hall, poking his sharp nose into all the corners. 'Have you got any foodstuffs in here, Ma'am?' He sounded a little uncertain addressing the old lady.

Edith smiled, showing her black tooth. 'Eh, what's that dearie? Good of you to come and see me.'

'Food,' shouted the young man, looking around rather desperately.

'Have a bit of bread if you're hungry. I think I left some from my breakfast,' Edith pointed to crumbs on a table.

Oswynne put her tongue between her teeth to stop herself giggling. What was Edith up to?

Edgar stepped forward. 'She's not usually deaf,' he said. 'Great-Aunt Edith, what's in the chest you're sitting on?'

'My clothes, dear. Got to keep the mice out of my winter cloak; they will make nests if you let them get into a clothes-chest, you know. I'm not sure what's in that box over in the corner.'

With a small squeak of excitement, which he hurriedly changed to a cough, Grimbold flung open Kenelm's tool-box. 'Just what we need! This is a fine adze. We can use it to shape props to keep the earth-mound in place while we dig out the ditch; we never have enough tools.' He cradled it and looked around.

Redwald bowed his head in respect as he stepped forward. 'Elder Edith, we're collecting tribute for my foster-father, Roger. He needs food for the men up at Thaneshall making our defensive earthwork, and any other valuables you can spare, for trade, to get weapons. What can we have?'

Elder Edith looked at him squarely. 'And our children go hungry, to feed the fighters? Nobody has asked us if we agree with building this rampart, or if we think it might annoy our neighbours on the other side, so they harry us more than before.'

Redwald shifted from foot to foot and chewed his thumbnail. Oswynne almost wanted to help him.

Edith took pity on him. 'You can take this belt I made with my tablet-weaving. It's a rare bright red, we had some alum from a trader last year.' She took it off and handed it to Redwald. 'Give it to Thane Roger's wife Alice with my best wishes. She'll need to look like a lady if she's entertaining a horde of builders. Rather her than me! That's if Thane Roger doesn't want to trade it for weapons.'

Redwald blushed as he took the finely worked belt, muttering thanks. He pushed Grimbold out of the house.

Shouts of: 'Come on, we're ready to leave,' came from the wagon.

Oswynne hurried back to her house and poured everyday ale for Thane Roger and his son and foster-son, passing the cups to the men as custom required.

'We'll see you next month,' Thane Roger announced, mounting his stallion, 'at the Beltane full moon, when you can get the Thornthicket and Mereham folks to come to Wellstowe for your Moot. We should get to Thornthicket in daylight tonight, even if sunset catches us out. Tomorrow we'll be home. Hretha's nearly full moon will light the last bit. Don't worry about the Moot, Kedric my friend.' He clapped Oswynne's husband on the shoulder as Redwald and Grimbold swung onto their horses and cantered away up the track, the cart rumbling after. 'I'll bring some stout lads to make sure there's no nonsense. I'm sure the other settlements will see things your way.' Kedric looked relieved. Then Thane Roger went on, 'Here's an idea – why don't we marry your niece Ursel to my son, Grimbold? She'll soon settle down once she's got a child or two. He could do with perking up. He'd rather fiddle with arrowheads than get out there and shoot. He needs some red blood in his veins.'

'But Ursel –' Kedric spluttered. 'She's a trouble maker, do you really want her to be part of your family?'

Oswynne gulped at the thought of Ursel being married to a man not of her choosing. She remembered the fond looks between Redwald and Ursel after the feast. *But that's just youngsters' foolishness. Of course, a girl of good family would have her marriage arranged for her with a suitable local man – as I did. It shaped my life. It's my calling and I'm not going to say it was wrong. Have they asked her mother, Ragnild? She might think it's a good match – indeed it is – the Thane's son!* She shifted uncomfortably. The men weren't asking her opinion, she noticed, a fact as irritating as a horsefly. Not knowing what to complain about first, she said nothing. *Perhaps the idea will die out anyway; surely they'll see it won't work?*

Thane Roger went on, 'My wife will tame her. Alice is solid, doesn't take any silliness. She's brought up our five, and fostered young Redwald too. She'll soon get the girl sewing and suchlike. I'll arrange a good morning-gift and you let me know what bride-gift she can bring – you're her guardian now since the father died, aren't you. Let's keep it to ourselves for now and tell everybody at the Moot.'

HILDA

Meg jabbed her fork into the compost heap and stuck her bottom lip out.

Hilda turned her forkful over and stacked it on the new heap. 'Stick him again!' she invited. 'There he is, get him in the ribs,' and pointed to the pile.

Meg's eyebrows lifted. 'How did you know what I was thinking?'

'Looks a bit like Thane Roger, doesn't it?' Hilda peered at the rotted dung. 'Go on, stab him, just like you'd like to do in real life but know you won't. I'll help!'

They both bashed the heap, harder and faster, until their grunts of effort turned into chuckles and gales of laughter.

'We've made a mess,' Meg noticed, with more satisfaction than worry in her voice.

'Good thing everybody's up on the bean-strip.' Hilda mopped her face. 'We've turned up the good stuff. Look at all those wrigglers.' She piled a shovelful of rich compost onto the wheelbarrow and Meg dug and loaded too. They talked in the rhythm of the work.

'What was it he wanted to do to me?' Meg dumped some in the barrow.

Hilda paused, her tool mid-air, but Meg avoided her eye. *She must know,* Hilda thought. *Maybe she doesn't.* 'It's confusing, eh?'

Meg dug. 'When Mother and Wulf do it, they sound – happy. The noises from the bushes at Beltane sound like fun. Sometimes there's arguing or grumbling. But what he said ...'

'Rough? Harsh? Frightening?' Hilda suggested.

Meg nodded, biting her lip.

They heard the rumble of a wheelbarrow coming closer and worked in silence until Nelda left an empty barrow for them to fill. 'Don't be too long,' she called over her shoulder, 'We need you to help spread this lot so we can plant as soon as Headman's Wife Oswynne gets back.'

'We've got to turn this other heap first,' Hilda called back. *I need to talk more with Meg.* 'We'll join you as soon as we can.'

A wail that sounded like Elvie missing her mam came from the bean-strip as Nelda pushed the weight of the load up the slope, calf muscles straining.

Hilda turned back to Meg. 'We can put the dry leaves and scraps in the middle for the worms to work on. Those red ones are twisting about looking for more food.' They worked together while Hilda gathered her thoughts. *I'm not the one to be telling her all this. But right now she needs to understand more, because of last night. I have to try to explain.*

Hilda leaned on her fork. 'You know how love should be. You can ask your mother more about it, if you want to. Thane Roger wanted to show everybody he's the boss, and picked you to be his victim. Sometimes a man uses his body to show his power. They can join with a woman without joy – I don't understand that, but I know it's true. He threatens and hits her and forces himself inside her body. It scrapes and bruises her soft inside parts, hurting her body and her self. It's called rape. It's not allowed, but sometimes men do it anyway. I'm sorry you have to learn about it, Meg.'

'Other men do it too?' Meg shivered.

'I'm hearing about it more and more these days. They seem to use it as a way to push women down, to confuse us and make us weak, while they take away our freedoms and rights. Sometimes the woman believes it's her own fault; that's when you can tell that her mind has been hurt too. You understand it's not your fault he picked on you, don't you?'

'Why me?' They dripped with the heat of the afternoon as they loaded the next barrow.

'I expect he sniffed around for a woman who looked as if she was of no value to any man. When men get stuck in violence, they think about women as things. He thought you would be considered of low value because you're not married and haven't got a father or uncle to protect you and also because you're not free.'

Meg crumpled, but Hilda kept on.

Got to tell her this! 'Watch out for men who talk as if a woman belongs to a man, in the same way that a dog or a horse does, and can be traded or beaten.'

'Why are they like that?'

'I'm trying to work it out. I put it into stories when I get a glimmer and see part of the truth – like Varagan becoming hard-hearted. Will you help me?'

'Why should I?' Meg pouted. 'I don't want to understand Thane Roger. I just want him to leave me alone.'

'I'm not talking about forgiving him, or any turd-faced rapist. They need to be stopped. But I do want to understand how it happens, so we can keep ourselves safe. It's not just women either. It hurts men when they wrench out their tenderness like a weed. And when they make themselves into weapons, they wreak havoc on the earth – spoil and destroy and treat her like dirt, so Earth Mother is raped as well as her daughters.'

Meg listened, eyes wide.

'Trying to kill a breeding hind fits into this pattern too. I'm not sure how, but that hunt has the same smell of greed and grabbing.'

Meg narrowed her brows; her face closed.

I'm losing her, thought Hilda. *She thinks it's just about Ursel, not her.* 'You are part of the tribes who love Earth Mother, however they call her, and that man wants to stamp out the ancient wisdom, so he picks on you as a representative of your people and all they believe.'

Meg was alive behind her face again.

'What Thane Roger didn't know,' Hilda caught and held Meg's eye, 'is how much the women of your settlement value you, and what risks they would take to keep you safe from harm. Not just your mother – everyone else, too. Every time women work together to keep each other safe, we make a bright circle that holds Earth too. We do it for ourselves, for each other and for her.'

Meg choked on her words. 'You – they would have hit you and made you leave, if they knew you were covering up –'

'If that man ever lays a finger on you, I shall take a fire-stick and shove it somewhere he won't like.' Hilda was only partly joking, but she contorted her whole face and Meg burst into laughter so hard that it shook the fear out of her. Hilda grinned and stayed close to Meg while the river of laughter ran its course. They finished their work and took turns to push the next load of muck up to the bean-patch.

As she tipped the compost out at the field-edge, Hilda wondered how many times the women of Wellstowe had done this: feed the earth, plant. The handles of the wheelbarrow slid smooth against her palms.

A cry of outrage came from the gateway to the field strip. 'How much did Thane Roger and his men take? That's all our food! What are we going to live on, until the crops grow?' It was Ursel, bursting with fury.

CHAPTER 13

BLISTERS, BACKACHE AND BICKERING

HILDA

Hilda joined the group of women surrounding Headman's Wife Oswynne. Oswynne held her shoulders aloft like the sails of a boat, *keeping herself afloat*, thought Hilda. *If she lets go one inch, she'll capsize*. Hubert had to cling onto her to stay aboard her hip. Oswynne continued her list: '... and the beaver fur that Kedric caught in autumn and we all helped to cure. Half the cloth we wove last winter. Knives and nails that Wulf made ...'

'Couldn't anybody stop them?' Ursel gasped.

'My husband helped him. He offered food from our cellar.' Oswynne's voice was flat.

How does she keep talking with that stone in her throat?

Then Oswynne spat out, 'Get back to work, all of you! We've got a whole field strip to plant!'

Hubert wailed as Oswynne dumped him onto the ploughed soil. He reached his arms up to her. 'Go and shoo crows away with the other children. You're big enough now!' She stamped away up the sloping strip to the hedge at the top. The child sobbed.

Hilda made a funny face at him, but he cried harder, snot running down.

Seren sighed and scooped him up, wiped his nose and nursed him, and Hilda caught a vicious glance from her to the retreating back of Oswynne. Hubert continued to fret until Seren stroked the curve of his cheek and her milk flowed. The little one fell asleep and Seren wrapped him in her shawl and left him amongst the daisies.

'Idling again, Seren! Rake this section where the compost's spread. We need a fine tilth, not all these lumps,' Oswynne snapped.

Hilda watched the blank look blot out Seren's face like a cloud across the sun.

Seren turned to Meg. 'Don't stand there with your mouth open; half the strip still needs fertiliser. If you didn't stand around chatting all day, we'd have it done by now.'

Meg's face closed as she picked up a shovel.

Hilda's head buzzed like wasps in a pot. *They're all hurting each other – how many times have they done this? How much damage can they do before their community is too broken to be mended?*

Oswynne barked orders: 'Take the end of this twine, Nelda. Put your baby down; she's getting in the way. Put the marker in and tie the twine to it. Keenbur, you're trampling on the row I've planted already! You do nothing but get in the way.' Headman's Wife Oswynne spread her misery wider with every bean that she took from her belt-bag and jabbed into the earth.

I've got to change this. Hilda pulled out her swan-bone flute and played a few notes.

Oswynne looked up. 'Haven't you got anything better to do, Hilda? Give Keenbur a hand spreading compost; she can't do much harm there. Ursel, if you're going to keep checking on Otred over the hedge, you might as well mend that thin place with some hazel wands while you're there. He's doing fine with the pigs; they won't wander far; there's plenty of beech mast for them on the edge of the wood. And Ragnild, you can start some more bean-rows over there.'

Hilda was relieved to put a little distance between her ears and Oswynne. As she got into the swing of muck spreading, the midden song came back to her. She sang softly, then louder as she remembered the words.

Run, Many-legs, Run!

Run, Many-legs, run.
If I had a hundred legs like you,
We'd have a lot of fun.

Everyone joined in.

Eat, Many-legs, eat!
Eat, Many-legs, eat.
You need a lot of food you know,
For all your little feet.

Hilda divided them up with gestures so they sang it as a round as they worked.

Joy, Many-legs, joy!
Joy, Many-legs, joy.
My sister or brother, child of Earth Mother,
Many-legs brings me joy.

Even Oswynne was singing now, softly as she bent over to plant, her skirt tucked up into her belt and her sturdy calves moving her along the rows.

Hilda asked Keenbur to sing her the earth blessing song, and they all joined in.

Their shadows stretched across the earth once they shouldered their tools, the work done.

Hilda stretched. Her hip joints ached. She strode over to join the women, gathering in a knot at the gateway of the strip.

'Aunt Edith, you should have asked somebody to help you.' Ragnild fussed. 'If you have a fall, that'll be more work for me.'

'Well I'm here now, so make the most of me while you've got me. Is nobody going to sit with me?' There was a twinkle in Elder Edith's eye as she scolded them. Meg slid an arm under Edith's elbow with the deftness of long practice and lowered her onto a log. Edith continued, 'I saved a little something from those over-eager boys when they came searching.'

She brought out a leg of dried venison from under her cloak.

Ragnild gasped, 'How?'

'I didn't lie,' said Edith, 'I did have my clothes in the chest with the moth-eaten rug on top; I had the meat underneath. Not hidden, of course, just … laid aside.'

Hilda chuckled, but spit leaped into her mouth too.

Edith told them to sit down and brought out a knife with a blade worn slender from much sharpening. It reminded Hilda of a waning moon in daylight and a thought pierced her mind. *How long have we got Elder Edith for?* It was a relief to see the real moon rise, pale but still growing, over the tree line on the ridge.

Edith joked as she passed slivers of meat around. The women wiped their hands on their skirts and chewed it gratefully.

'The largest piece is for Keenbur. You need some strength when you're growing a baby. If the mother goes without, the baby won't grow well. We all need to feed a new life. Oswynne, make sure Keenbur gets the best bits. Here's a bit for Elvie – even if she hasn't got teeth yet she can suck it and get the juice. I see you watching her every move, Nelda – yes of course you finish it up if she doesn't want it. You carry her and nurse her; you're growing our settlement's people for us too; take what you need, dear. Seren, put the rest of this joint in the stew tonight. The children can pick nettles to go in, too – wrap your hands up – there's plenty of nourishment for everybody.'

'Did they really search our hall, Elder Edith?' Ursel asked. 'I would've stopped them if I'd known. What did they take?'

'I directed them to Kenelm's old tool bag. I thought it wouldn't be too bad if they took that one adze.'

Ragnild muttered, 'I'm glad that's gone – I kept it separate because it dealt death to my Kenelm when he fell. Wulf's got all the rest of his brother's gear. Now I'll never have to see it again – good.'

Hilda's admiration for Elder Edith swelled, filling her chest. The women continued chewing the tough morsels. Sunset flared over the fen, lighting the scudding clouds with the colours of fire.

Nelda said, 'Hilda, in the story you told last night, it bothers me the way the queen stayed with her husband when he knocked her about. She should have left him.'

Hilda nodded, listening. She didn't want to explain, she wanted them to talk.

'She hadn't even chosen him! Her marriage was arranged for her and she didn't get to say yes – *or* no!' Ursel was outraged.

'That's not always a bad thing,' Oswynne said.

Her voice sounded a little too firm, Hilda noticed. She put a question in her head for later.

'Where could she have gone?' Ragnild shrugged.

'She should kick him out!' It was Winfrith joining them, followed by a gaggle of geese. 'Why should she have to go anywhere? The place was hers as much as his!'

'Get them out of here! We've just planted,' Oswynne snapped.

They shooed the geese out of the cultivated land and shut the gate. Winfrith hung over the gate to join in the talk.

Oswynne continued, 'The Queen has her plan – to unite the two tribes. That's a fine idea. Will it work, I wonder?'

'Will somebody please tell me what you're talking about?' Elder Edith asked. 'What have I missed?'

Hilda opened her mouth to give her a quick outline of the story, when ten voices broke in, telling snatches of it. Hilda explained about the ale, and how they'd foiled Thane Roger's lust to dominate Meg and to show the 'troublesome women' who is in charge.

Edith's face boiled with anger. 'If I'd known that this morning, I would have told young Roger what I think of him. You thought quickly to protect Meg, all of you, well done. But have you noticed what we're doing? Hiding things, lying, giving poison even though it was just enough to stop them, not hurt them – these are the weapons of people who have been silenced – we fear we could get punished for speaking out. Why can't we confront them and say, "Stop"? What's happened to the authority of women?'

Hilda let that question hang in the air. A cloud of starlings whirled round and down into the reed beds to roost. Ragnild's eyes rolled – Hilda could almost hear her thinking 'ranting on about the old days again'. Hilda asked softly, 'They took all the food stores and half the winter's weaving. What have we got left?'

'We?' Oswynne shot her a look that told her clearly – this is our place, you are a stranger here.

Hilda decided not to challenge it. She forced a smile.

Nelda grimaced and held up her palms to show them: 'Blisters.'

Keenbur eased her shoulders. 'Backache.'

'There's no need to make such a fuss,' said Oswynne. 'We can get eggs from the fen as long as we leave enough nests of each kind untouched for the waterfowl to raise their young. Use your sling-shots to get ducks; they may be thin, but better than nothing. Our own chickens and geese will start to lay in a week or two, and we've got sheep in milk. There'll be silver eel coming upstream soon. We can tie our belts tighter, as we do every spring. It's a bit worse this year, that's all.'

Blisters, backache and bickering. Hilda kept that thought to herself.

Seren drew out a piece of fleece from her belt-bag. 'The first ground-work of the year always hurts.' She passed it round and they all rubbed their hands on it, working wool oil into their skin. Seren rubbed Keenbur's back.

'Seren, there's no need to make everybody feel sorry for themselves. You're only making it worse.' Oswynne's jawbone crunched so tight it hardly let the words sneak over her teeth.

Meg hugged her sharp knees as if she wanted to take root.

Seren turned to Meg, 'Why are you still sitting there! Those tools won't walk to the lean-to by themselves.'

May and Roslinda played making the shovels and forks walk. Meg growled at them, 'Stop it!' She loaded up the younger ones with tools and took an armful herself. They all stamped off to the shed.

Hilda's stomach plummeted. *Just when I thought we were getting somewhere. How can I get them to support each other instead of picking fights?* A waterfall poured into her mind, from the hills where she grew up. *What are you telling me?* She felt the weight of the cascade batter her shoulders. *Thane Roger's theft* (she could name it in her head) *bashes Oswynne, so she bounces the pain off onto Seren just like a rock in the torrent. It pours onto Meg and she makes a whirlpool of misery since she's got nobody to slide the anger off onto. What would happen if Oswynne stood up straight?* She saw the rock in the torrent heave itself huge, streaming with weed. *What if Oswynne told them, No? She would take the full force of Thane Roger's rage on her back. What if Seren opened wide her arms and said, Stop? She'd probably get a thrashing from one of them. How can I push back this river of hate?* She saw herself splashing in the shallows, trying to catch spray in her fingers. *We need a fen to soak it up and turn it into water lilies, dragonflies, swans.* She stood up and gazed away over the mere, gold with reflections of sunset. In the dark place of her head, a voice spoke. *'Trust our stories, Hilda.'* It echoed like the voice of the wise woman in the depths of the cave. Hilda, startled out of her despair, addressed everyone with her back to the gate.

'We've got the good earth, we've got each other – and our stories. They can't steal them.'

Meg came panting back to join them. Hilda smiled at her. 'Meg, please tell Elder Edith the parts of the story that she's missed, later.' Hilda opened the gate and stepped onto the path. Meg checked that Ragnild was helping Elder Edith and hurried to join Hilda. The girl wrinkled her forehead. 'But I can't remember all the words! What if I get it wrong?'

'Everyone who tells a tale gives it her own twist, Meg.' Hilda laid a hand on Meg's arm gently. 'My stories don't belong to me. There's somebody standing behind me when I tell a story, the one who told it to me, and behind her there's somebody else, and behind her another, going back and back, across rivers and oceans and forests. By the time it comes to me, voices have woven and plaited it a dozen ways already; and I turn it myself, too. You can knot in your own pieces and snip away frayed ends.'

'But you said – about Brother Michael – changing the apple tree story …?'

'That's different – to take a tale and tangle it and tear it so it hurts people when it should be making us strong … don't let that happen! Guard our stories, let them tell themselves through you, with your whole self.'

CHAPTER 14

SEARCHING FOR THE MERE-WIFE

MEG

Meg tucked rugs around Elder Edith's slight frame in the big bed in the corner. 'Put another pillow behind my back, Meg, so I can sit up,' Elder Edith requested. 'I've come to join you all tonight because I want to talk with Hilda the storyteller.' The women's sleeping house was dim and smelled of warm bodies.

Meg put Elder Edith's personal pee-bucket down by her bed. *Why couldn't Edith use the general pee-bucket with everyone else, why did she insist on having her own right beside her bed?*

Meg ground her teeth. She couldn't wait to hear what happened next in Peony Valley – but Elder Edith wanted to talk. 'Now then, Hilda. Meg told me your stories. They seem to be recreating a time when the old ways were strong – a time when women ruled in peace. Where do they come from?'

'Over seas and through forests, down rivers and over mountains, down the rolling road of many tongues through centuries …'

The buzz of chat died down. 'In other words, you don't know,' Edith chuckled. 'What are the stories for? Are you trying to change the way we think?'

Hilda played a soft run of chords on her harp, looking round at the listening faces. Meg never forgot that moment – Elder Edith's wrinkles lit by the glow of the peat fire, a mouse scampering in the corner, Hilda plucking notes from the harp-strings as she spoke. The storyteller's voice was light, but she carved the air with her words, 'I tell stories that show friendship. You can choose what to listen to: tales that keep your nose in the dirt, or those that lift you. When you know what's being laid on your shoulders, you can decide whether you're going to carry it or throw it off. I show people who've been squashed what they are really worth: as much as any prince! Then it's up to them: they can stand up for each other and themselves, or go on letting things happen.'

'You're a breath of fresh air here, Hilda the Bard.'

Meg slid onto the sleeping platform and pulled a corner of her mother's rug over her knees, shuffling close to her.

Edith fixed Hilda with a gaze. 'You've got us talking – should that young queen go back to her nasty husband, or stay with the wise woman in the mountains?'

'What do you think?' Hilda asked, head tilted to one side, spine straight, ear waiting to catch something unsaid moving towards the surface. 'Husbands do sometimes hurt their wives, so I've heard ...' She trailed her bait.

Edith bit. 'Mine certainly wasn't much good. Should never have gone off with him, silly girl that I was then. My sister Merewyn tried to warn me, but I had my own ideas, thought I knew it all.'

Meg saw Hilda watch Edith's face until their eyes met across the smoky hearth. *So that's how she does it,* Meg thought. *She's hooked her fish; now to pull it out of the water.*

'Did your family give you a free choice?' Hilda asked.

'My father tried to stop me – he had somebody lined up for me that he'd chosen. That made me even more determined of course! My mother and father quarrelled about it. Mother wanted me to have sovereignty over my own life, in accord with the customs from long ago. It was such a bitter row that Father left to join the king's army.'

'How did you meet your young man?' Hilda's voice was warm. She sat back to listen.

'Wonderful Beltane feasts we had in those days! They'd all come – from Thornthicket and Mereham, even as far as Meadowhall and Breckside! He came from Wild Horse Ridge.'

'What did you like about him?'

'His eyes twinkled when he talked about going off to make a new settlement. He looked so alive! I knew he was a good man. My family talked to his family, and off we went.' Edith sucked in her cheeks and sighed.

'When we got there, he knelt on the ground and ran a handful of earth through his fingers. "This is the place, men! The soil's good on this ridge. We'll start clearing scrub and timber tomorrow, to make strips for our crops and grazing for the flock. The oaks will make good planks for houses. Women, get a cooking fire lit." I couldn't stop looking at the way his hair flopped over one eye. How foolish I was!'

Edith shrugged.

Ragnild, sitting next to her in the family's bed, patted her hand. 'Nobody would blame you for falling for a good-looking man.' Her beaky crow face softened as she reassured her aunt Edith. Ursel snuggled a little closer to Ragnild, her mother, in their big bed. Ragnild asked, 'Did he go on giving orders?'

'Ugh, yes. Months of hard work later, I was kneeling near the stream one morning, throwing up. I had been vomiting for months and was exhausted. I hung onto the handle of my bucket for comfort – it was one of my mother's, which we brought with us. My husband's roar put a thrush to flight. "Do you expect me to slash brambles without even a hot drink inside me? Bring me that water now!"

'I felt as if I'd thrown up my voice too. All I could do was shiver. *I want my mother. Two days walk to get there, three now I'm slow. I'd have to camp under a tree. Can I remember the way?* I filled the bucket from a pool. *What's that paw-print in the mud? It's big – bear!*

'I rekindled the cooking fire outside our hut and set a pan to boiling. He came over and warmed his hands as the sticks blazed. *His poor scratched fingers, calloused palms. It's so long since he touched me gently! We used to dance. When did he stop smiling?* I straightened up. "I need to get back home for the birth. Not long now. Can I take the girl who's not pregnant yet? She helped her mother birthing her brothers and sisters. We'll need a man with a spear to protect us. It's not just wolves, bears are coming out of hibernation, and they'll be hungry."

"'I need everybody here! The brambles keep on pushing back. If we leave off hacking, or delay planting, we'll starve." My husband gulped his nettle tea down hot. "Stop snivelling! Batten down that weakness. If we give in to fear, we'll be swamped."

'I didn't dare to speak my thoughts. *We're not in a boat, crossing the sea now.* He flung himself off, axe in hand, cursing. I stayed put, frozen. Regretted it ever since.

'When my belly griped, I pretended to myself nothing was happening. *It's too soon, can't be the pains, just stomach ache.* Water and blood ran down my legs as the cramps got heavier. I could hardly breathe with worry. *Mother, you always promised to tell me about birth. I need you!*

'The girl came. I think she wanted to help but she stood looking blank while I groaned, "Help me find the Mere-Wife, the one who helps us bring our babies into the world. Mother said we have to walk with her hand in hand. She protects us with her tusks and blue scaly hide." The girl flinched. I went on moaning, "Mere-Wife, where are you? Are you angry with us? Because my man doesn't even gabble a prayer now when he fells your ash trees? Can't you hear me? Are you too far away in the river of home?" I screamed. The Mere-Wife didn't come.'

Edith went quiet. Meg leaned forward, anxious to catch every word, every gesture. Edith noticed and spoke to her. 'What do you want to know, Meg?'

Meg checked Seren's face quickly, wondering if it was alright to speak in front of everybody. Seren glanced at Oswynne. Oswynne looked at Edith. Edith nodded.

'Did you ever find the Mere-Wife, Elder Edith?' Meg asked.

'Later I did. First I must tell you about …' Edith's voice trailed off. Ragnild wrapped a shawl around Edith's shoulders. 'You're good to me, dear niece Ragnild.'

Hilda tugged gently at the story. 'This is hard for you. Do you want to go on, Elder Edith?'

Edith sighed. 'Yes, I need to tell it. I tried to distract myself from the cramps with mending, but it hurt to sit down. I thrashed about on my straw mattress. I scratched my face with my nails, I can feel a scar still, here.' She ran her thumb down her cheek. 'The girl had to leave me, muttering about work. All day I laboured. When the hut got darker, the girl came back and gave me a drink. "You must get up," she said. I swore at her. *I'm going to die!* She stayed, that good-hearted youngster. I clung to her. She lifted me up. Thunder roared through my body. The baby fell out and half my insides, it felt like. When I opened my eyes, the girl was blowing into the baby's mouth. He was blue. I quaked with fear and shock. My husband looked into the hut, growled in anger and went away. When a faint cry came from the baby's mouth, the girl passed him to me. She stuffed me together again as best she could. I heard her being sick and crying outside the hut.'

A whimper came from the far end of the sleeping platform. Keenbur folded in on herself, hugging her growing bump, her face twisted in terror. Nelda, her sister-in-law, put an arm round Keenbur's shoulders and tenderly tucked her loose hair back from her face.

Edith looked up with a start. 'Keenbur, dear, this won't happen to you. We'll all take care of you when you birth your baby.' There was a murmur of agreement from everyone.

'But I won't have my mother with me,' Keenbur wept. 'It's a long time since she passed away. There's only my little brother Aikin to look after me and he won't be much use!'

'I'm here,' Nelda assured her.

Oswynne spoke up, 'I'll let you have Seren to help you. She has skills in birth and healing.'

Meg felt Seren stifle a snort under her blanket. *As if Mother wouldn't be there for a birth! You don't have to give permission!*

Ragnild asked, 'What did you call your baby, Aunt Edith? I've never heard about him before.'

Edith replied, 'Osgar. He was never right, my little one. When he should have walked, he went limping and trembling. He never talked. My husband frowned at him and curled his lip in disgust. I clutched my boy and my husband spat on the ground, at both of us.

'One day little Osgar fell in the stream when I wasn't looking and my husband said –' Edith's mouth worked until at last she found voice to speak with. 'He said, "Good, one less mouth to feed." I went cold. We buried Osgar's small body curled up in a shallow grave under a silver birch. I got the shakes when we threw the first handful of earth. I grabbed lumps of earth in my hands and pelted them down into my little boy's grave. The others drew back, not knowing what to say. They looked at me sideways and fingered their charms to keep away bad luck. It wasn't grief. I was angry! Wave after wave of rage shuddered through me. It's bitter to lose a child. But for him not to care …'

As Meg watched, Hilda went still. Too still. Her face was a mask with holes for eyes. *She knows about this,* Meg thought. *Could she have lost a child too?* It was only a moment. Then Hilda turned back to Edith.

'So much pain. How did you cope with it?' Hilda asked.

'Cope? I didn't. Something happened in my head. I wandered in the woods day and night, searching for the Mere-Wife. I called out for my baby. I didn't know where I was or who I was. My husband turned away from me. I lost him as well.'

'You sound so sad,' Hilda offered.

'Hah! There was me, still remembering his curly moustache and laughing eyes.

'Traders from Eel Island came to our settlement, with iron tools to exchange for fleeces. Their eyes were kind and I thawed. "Wendreda," they said. "Healer. We take you." My husband's face was like stone as we left. My one friend came with me.

'We trudged for miles. When we skimmed upriver in the traders' boat, my friend's face opened out. "My cousins on Eel Island will take me in. They'll find the healer for you."

'When we moored at Eel Island, I was led to a small hall near the water. Wendreda the healer lived there, with her boys. She brought me back from that lost place, into my life again.'

Seren's words burst out as she leaned forward, intent, 'How did she do that? What skills did she use?'

Meg checked Oswynne's face. *Is she angry with Mother for intruding?* Oswynne's eye rested on Edith, who was looking long at Seren. *Elder Edith looks as if she's never seen Mother before! What is she noticing?*

Edith smiled. 'Good questions, Seren! First Wendreda was kind in an ordinary way. She gave me good food, like the wise woman with the young queen in Hilda's story. All I could utter were groans and cries. She listened. When I wandered down to the bank of the river where last year's seed heads rustled, Wendreda walked beside me, shaking her bright brown curls loose around her shoulders. With the smell of damp earth in my nostrils, I called for Osgar, beseeching the Mere-Wife to come and save me. Wendreda's grey eyes shone with care for me. The light in them reminded me of the mere on a calm day.

'One day at dusk she drew me away from the settlement and up to the barrows. She raised her clear voice in a song to the ancestors about me, asking for help. I sat and plucked at grass and muttered, when a movement caught my eye. Out of an alder thicket drifted a hind. Mist was rising from the ground as she moved silently downhill. She looked at me and I knew I had to follow.

'Among the rushes the hind stopped and bent her neck to drink. I heard her tongue lapping – and then I saw her eye reflected in the surface. The heart of that brown eye beat with warmth, for me. Breath moved through me and my body softened. Every creature in the world was looking at me with love. The Mere-Wife swam up from the depths and rooted her twin tails in mud among the willows. Tusks and scales glinted but I was not afraid. The Mere-Wife stroked the hind's neck with one hand. Dew trembled in the air all around her.

'I asked her, "Where's my baby?"

'Her gentle voice boomed inside me like a deep-toned drum, "Gone out of this life."

'"Where were you? Why didn't you come when I needed you?"

'"I have always been here. Your fear drove me fathoms deep and you could not see past the boiling surface of it. I stretched out my hand for you to take, but you were swept away by the surge of terror. Now that you know the wild can bring you back to this calm place, you will never lose me again." She shimmered away then, but I knew she was still there. The hind stepped down into the river and swam towards a nearby island, but she turned her head to look at me again as she went. I recognised her then. This hind was the one who had come to me when I stepped into adulthood, dancing the antler dance – long ago.

'Wendreda led me back to her hut. She gave me hot soup and I slept. The next day, I could talk again. She asked about my son – what made him laugh, what he liked to eat, what his hair felt like. I told her about the time he found a swallow's tail feather in the grass and brought it to me and we played with it, swishing it through the air. She took my hands and together we made swooping curves in the air like a bird. She told me he'd flown to the dark side of the moon with the swallows and was resting there, waiting for summer. I cried then, properly, for the first time.'

Meg understood – Edith's had been hot tears.

'After that, sometimes I could help Wendreda about the place. I remember sitting by her door stitching up a torn blanket, still weak, feeling the sun on my face. Wendreda's twin sons ran in and out with fishing nets.

'That evening she sent the boys off to sleep in the men's sleeping house with their friends. She and I sat wrapped in rugs by her fire and talked. I told her my whole life story, not so much what happened, but more like … how I felt about it. She had a knack for making me see things differently.'

'Ah, how did she do that?' Hilda asked.

'Things I blamed myself for – like falling for that man because of his twinkly eyes – she showed me how that was life and love welling up inside me. I stopped making myself feel bad. It was quiet inside my head then! Wendreda helped me understand how my husband was driven by mind-thorns that got stuck and twisted deep, though he started out singing. She talked about how my husband's pride had stopped me from getting help at the birthing. He was caught up in a net of men folk daring each other, taunting and jeering, cheering each other on to do brave things all alone. Like the time the first boats came over in the Crossing! My husband had the other men in mind, as well as his battle against the land. He wasn't thinking about me, or what he could do to help me. He drove himself and chucked away his own needs as feebleness. So he pushed me aside for being "weak" when I needed loving arms.

'Then she told me – there was a time when women came together around the time of birth, to sing the baby out, to stroke and smooth the mother's back, to wash her with sweet herbs and dance with her, and hold her firmly. Babies can slide out with wonder in their eyes, she said, not bawling. Mothers can give birth and feel their strength. Keenbur, this is how we will help you, when your time comes.'

Murmurs of warm agreement came from all around the women's sleeping house. Keenbur glowed.

'So yes, Meg, I did find the Mere-Wife. She is always near us. I call on her for every birth, and she always comes.' Edith yawned. 'Smoor the fire, Seren, we need to sleep. I'll need all of you dear women to help me plan this Moot. We'll have to work together, no quarrels, no scrapping amongst ourselves. I can't think about it tonight, I'm too tired.'

CHAPTER 15

FULL MOON SIZZLES

HILDA

Hilda joined Meg carrying water from the spring. 'Try this game – tripling words,' she said as they hefted their buckets out of the water. 'You say a word, I find two more words that mean nearly the same. Then we change over.'

'Like – bucket?' Meg asked.

'Pail, tub,' Hilda replied. 'Now my turn – walk.'

'Step, er …'

'Trudge? Stride? Stagger?' Hilda supplied as her foot slipped in mud and they giggled.

'I've got one! Flap.' Meg suggested.

Hilda scratched her head. 'Flutter, fly. I'm thinking about birds for my turn – sing.'

'Warble, whistle, call, croak, cry …' Meg grinned and sang the words.

'Now, I'll say a thing and you have to say what he does, starting with the same sound. It doesn't have to make sense! The cat …'

'Coughed?'

'Yes! Your turn.'

'The hound …'

'Hurried. The woman …'

'Wobbled!'

'Hurry up you two, we need the water,' Seren broke in. After that, whenever Meg and Hilda got together, words bounced between them, bringing joy to both. *Games are good training for word-lovers*, Hilda thought, *and they keep Meg close but not too close. How long can I keep it going, so I don't have to pick open the scab that protects my heart?*

SEREN

As she ladled out nettle soup for everyone, Seren felt a sizzle in her blood. It tried to tug her away from the cooking-fire, out of the settlement … where she could not go without permission. Her eyes were free. She scanned the sky. *Sun's dipping low behind the barrow on Eel Island where Wendreda lies, far across the fen. Nothing to see yet in the east, beech and elm in the way, need to get higher.* In her imagination, she joined her hand with Wendreda's and they walked up to the heath … Somebody was watching. Her eyelids snapped open. *Only Hilda.* She breathed out.

In the sleeping house, Hilda asked, 'What is the custom here to honour the full moon?' *She must be feeling it too – the call. Is it safe for the storyteller to talk about it? Wouldn't be for me, of course.* She glanced around fearfully.

Oswynne's voice contained a reproach. 'Those old moon ceremonies don't fit well with our gods. We don't want to anger Ing or Woden by making a big noise on the hillside. They like women to be quiet.' Seren's stomach clenched.

Edith sighed. 'I can't get up to the barrow by myself any more; I need an arm to lean on. That's the best place to watch the full moon rise; you get a clear view to the east. I love to rinse my body in silver light. And the ancestors like a chant at full moon. What's the harm in that? It keeps us women in tune with our moon rhythms and teaches us to run when we feel like running and rest when we need to. The menfolk can drum for the sun but we sing the moon up into the sky.'

'We could help you if you want to walk up to the barrow, Elder Edith,' Hilda ventured, looking round at Meg and Seren. Seren kept her head down.

Meg sucked in her cheeks nervously and whispered to her mother, 'I'm scared Oswynne might chuck Hilda out.'

'It wouldn't be good for you to go traipsing about in the cold and damp after sunset, Aunt Edith,' Oswynne said. 'Elves will be about; your knees could get shot with those sudden pains again. Hilda, we need to take care of Edith, help me please by keeping her in the warm! All of you, there'll be no sneaking out when you think I'm not looking. We'll stay here by the fire and get on with our spinning.'

Seren felt the glint of Oswynne's glare. *She means me, sneaking out. So what if I sometimes go alone to make a ceremony for the moon? Somebody should.*

'We'll sing the old songs then, while we work,' Edith announced. Her voice creaked but they picked up the tune and followed. They sang about the swing of the moon across the sky, the dance of dark and light, and the glory of moonlight on the breast of the hill.

'How lovely!' Hilda commented. 'Are these songs from Wellstowe?'

'Mostly from Eel Island,' Edith replied. 'Wendreda taught me the British words and tunes, and I remembered my mother striding off up the track to greet the rising moon, with something similar on her lips. When I got to be Meg's age, the arguments between my mother and father made it hard for her to get away. So I never learned the Anglish full-moon customs. I had to piece them together with the shreds I could recall in my mother's voice, and Wendreda's verses. Have you heard the moon greeted in different ways as you travel around, Hilda?'

'In some places she's a silver wheel. In others, a great white horse carved on the hillside. Weary-Moon Hill has a beautiful one; it's only a couple of long days' walk from here. Have you seen it?' Nobody had.

'That's the country where the cattle-raiders live.' Oswynne's voice was firm. 'I don't want to hear about those old giants. I don't trust them.'

'How do you feel about the new god that Brother Michael told us about?' Hilda asked.

'Hmm, I've got enough to think about without all that,' Oswynne remarked. 'My husband keeps talking about lordship though, so I expect we'll hear more about it later.'

'Which gods did you grow up with, Oswynne?' Hilda sounded respectful, interested.

'Ing and Woden and Earth Mother of course,' Oswynne replied, leaning back against her cushion. 'They were always in the background, solidly there, taken for granted. But every day we spoke with the Nine Daughters of the Sea. We trembled with awe on the shoreline as we raised our arms to them. We threw gifts into the ocean – golden grain, apples, a drink of mead. We gave something for each of those sea sisters: the wave that light shines through, the billow that roars, the foam-crested one who threatens to overwhelm us, the bloody-haired surge that grabs and drowns sailors, the icy wave, the storm wave that pitches boats about like twigs, the riser, the frothing one, the wave that wells from the deep. When a ship was setting out from the harbour, my father would throw gold for those Nine. At the time of the new moon in spring, the Nine Daughters would eat great chunks from the cliffs, soak our orchards, and invade our houses. My mother gave her necklace once to appease their anger. She hurled it far out into the flood.'

'They sound terrifying!' Hilda said.

'I loved their power!' Oswynne's voice held a memory of exultation. Seren recalled when they were children – *Oswynne whooped as she flung her loose hair and raced along the strand, neither of us caring who was mistress or slave, the joy of the wind, splashing in the water's edge ... So much has changed!*

Oswynne went on, 'You knew where you were with the Nine Daughters, what to ask for, how to please them, what they're likely to do. Not like these murky spirits that the slaves call up – they make me shiver. How do we know what those old gods think of us, if they're planning to stab us in the back or poison us?' She shuddered.

Seren tightened her wrap around her body. *Maybe they would want you gone, since you and your people have taken the land from us, who revere them.*

Edith shifted in her bed. 'I've heard of those Nine Waves before,' she said. 'I think they may be cousins of the Mere-Wife. Could they be angry because we lay heavy ships on their backs and steal their children, the fishes? It's our own fears and suffering that twist their faces into monster-shapes, the grimace of our own greed that gapes back at us when we grasp too much. Not so long ago, all of us loved and lived close to earth and water – perhaps we can again.'

A beam of moonlight slid through the thatch and lit up Hilda's lopsided smile. *This storyteller loves a dispute. What kind of trouble will she bring down on our heads?* Seren shivered, hugged Meg and May close and tucked a blanket round them.

HILDA

In the next days, Hilda made herself useful. Oswynne's sharp look prickled under her skin. *All I said was 'we' when I asked 'What have we got left?' She doesn't think of me as one of them, got to be careful.* Hilda looked around for children under peoples' feet – she told them stories, taught them songs, showed them how to look for beetles under stones. They showed her which leaves are tasty – they loved the toothed ones with flowers as bright as egg-yolk.

Nelda and Keenbur came every night to join them in the women's sleeping house. 'When I'm nursing Elvie and Leofric in the night, it's good to have warm bodies around me, even if you're asleep,' Nelda explained.

'Our husbands are happy in the men's sleeping house, so why not?' Keenbur added. 'It's hard to get comfy with my belly growing, so I'm often restless wherever I am. I'm not scared when I'm here with you all.'

They talked about growing up together in Thornthicket, their journey to live in Wellstowe, how they missed their mothers – Keenbur's long dead, Nelda's still alive.

Nelda talked readily in response to Hilda's questions. Keenbur was shy, so Hilda circled round – whose births did you help at when you were an older child? What do you love most about the moment of birth?

When they realised Keenbur had never been at a birth, since her limited sight made people think she couldn't help, they were shocked.

They sought out words to name the things that everybody knows: how to tell when labour starts; how to move and sway to dance the baby down; what noises you make; the plop of the afterbirth coming out as you lift your baby to your breast and she suckles. Keenbur soaked it up, her voice grew louder. She asked more every evening. The waning moon gave them longer stretches of darkness each night to talk in the firelight.

All because of Edith's story! Hilda secretly glowed. *Let's get her talking again!*

'What happened when you went back to see Wendreda, Elder Edith?' she asked.

Edith looked into the fire, remembering. 'When Ragnild was young, she had a rash and a fever. I took her to Eel Island and Wendreda cured her. Slip of a girl she was then, but old enough to make the chaps look twice. Remember that, Ragnild? Of course you would, that was when you met your fellow. Kenelm and Wulf, Wendreda's twin sons, came and went while Ragnild was laid up in the hut. She took a fancy to Kenelm and him to her – covered in blotches she was, but that didn't put him off. Wendreda made salves and herbal drinks and sang all the chants over Ragnild, and bit by bit she got better – what a relief! Kenelm ferried us home and never did go back. Turned out to be a good one. Poor chap – never thought I'd last longer than him.'

Hilda started singing softly – a lament for Kenelm. Voices joined hers, making the old words fill the shadows. Ragnild rocked herself, taking comfort from it, and put an arm round her daughter Ursel.

After a silence, Edith's memories flowed on. 'Years later, when my sister Merewyn was ill with that terrible cough, I took her to Wendreda. We'd seen Seren's talent for healing so I borrowed her, to help, and to learn the herbs and songs. Meg came too of course. She nearly toddled into the fire, but Wulf caught her just in time. He picked her up so gently, Seren blushed when he put the little one in her arms. Do you remember that, Seren?'

Seren spilled ashes on the floor. Oswynne snapped, 'Sprinkle those ashes on the fire neatly, Seren, watch what you're doing, they're going all over the place. Need a good thick even layer, don't let sparks get in the thatch in the night.' *Oswynne snaps at Seren every day. They need to get closer to each other! I could help by opening up myself … if only I could take a leap and trust them.*

SEREN

As if I didn't know how to sprinkle ashes on the fire! Oswynne's scorn scratched her. Her neck muscles tightened. Seren hid her face under a curtain of hair and warmth flushed up her neck as she swept.

Wulf's tenderness had touched her heart. *It's not safe to speak about it.* The feeling stayed trapped in her throat. *Not safe for Wulf – young Edgar insulted him when he saw us together in the weaving house: 'No decent girl will go with you!'* The tone of disgust echoed in her memory. *Not safe for me either: 'slave'!* The word tasted of bile and carried the crunch of breaking bone in the sound of it.

Edith continued, 'We said we'd go back to Wellstowe the next day – but a mist came up so thick we couldn't travel. I thought it was the usual breath of the fen – until I heard Wendreda calling it up. She got out her broom and started to sweep, with a strange high-pitched tone to her singing. The hairs on the back of my neck stood on end. Fog rolled in, thick and eerie.

'When I asked Wendreda why she wanted the mist, she said, "You brought me a gift – Seren – a talented woman who wants to learn from me. I am learning from her too. Can you let her stay?" I shook my head. Wendreda sounded pleased as she announced, "You will all have to stay until the fog clears! Please bring Seren back whenever you can."

'Wulf and Seren peeled parsnips to mash with honey in ale, to ease Merewyn's chest as she rested by the healer's fire. They chatted – until Wulf told his mother his news: his girl on the next island was expecting a baby. Wendreda cried and laughed and hugged him and told him to hurry back to her, of course. But he had to stay until the mist cleared. I always wondered, Seren, did you help with the fog spell?'

Seren sat back on her heels, ash on her hands. *Mustn't say anything that could make Oswynne angry. It hurts so much that she doesn't trust me!* She closed her face. 'I was busy fetching and carrying for the healer, Ma'am,' she said, weighing each word. 'That's mainly what I did, each time Elder Edith took me to Wendreda's house.'

Edith explained, 'We went twice a year when the weather was good, and stayed a few days if Seren could be spared from the work here.'

'When did Wulf come to live here?' Hilda asked.

Yes, talk about when things happened, that's safer to talk about than magic! Seren sighed with relief.

'Three years later,' Edith replied. 'He came to tell his brother Kenelm that Wendreda had passed away. I went with them to lay her in the barrow on Eel Island; Seren came too, with little Meg. How we mourned! By then Wulf's hand-fasted woman and their child had died of a terrible fever. We packed up Wendreda's things – some herbs, this rug – and Wulf came back with us to Wellstowe. He was glad to find Seren again, and May was born the next year.'

Meg whispered, 'Why are you not hand-fasted with Wulf, Mother?'

'A slave with a free man? It's not allowed – not the custom, cushla. Now sleep.' She kept her voice level while the old anger twisted her guts. *To walk openly with him by her side – for him to speak with pride and claim her in front of everyone – to see him acknowledge May, their daughter – to have a bed that was theirs.* These impossible dreams tormented her.

CHAPTER 16

ONE WAY TO BRING PEOPLE TOGETHER

HILDA

Beside the vegetable strip, the next morning, Ragnild settled Edith on a stool. 'That's splendid, I shall be very comfortable here, thank you,' Edith's smile was so wide they could see her ground-down teeth. 'Now May and Roslinda, show the little ones how to dig up stones and bring them to me. See if you can find more of these flints. What other kinds can you find?'

Hilda's eye was caught by a new tenderness in Ragnild's hands. 'I hope you're warm enough here, Aunt. I thought you might be lonely in the hall by yourself all day long.' *This must be how Ragnild mothered Ursel and Otred when they were little. Now it's her aunt who needs her.*

'I do find the days drag sometimes. I like to chat.'

Seren brought a rug and tucked it around Edith's knees. 'Is this the same rug you wove at Wendreda's house, Ma'am?' she asked, glancing around with her head down.

She's checking that Oswynne isn't nearby to overhear, Hilda thought.

'It certainly is,' Edith replied. 'I've patched it a few times over the years, but this is the one I made for her. She showed me how to weave the pattern of checks and stripes, mingled together like all lives. Is that what reminded you of Wendreda?'

'I can recall everything about my times with her, Ma'am.' Seren's voice sounded as if it was edging out of the soles of her feet. 'When you told us about your son, it felt as if you gave us a precious delicate thing to hold – an iris flower.'

Edith looked at Seren with a depth of thought in her eyes, as she thanked Seren for bringing the rug. Seren looked surprised to be thanked.

I must find out more about Seren's times at Wendreda's hall, Hilda thought.

'The children are clearing the carrot bed nicely,' Oswynne observed. 'That was a good idea to make it a game for them, Edith. You're full of surprises!' She turned to Seren and her face closed. 'Get to work at once, Seren!'

The pile of stones grew bigger.

Oswynne scattered tiny seeds with care, snapping at Seren from time to time. Seren was grimly silent. Hilda's head ached from listening to it.

Hilda asked Oswynne, 'May I take Meg to show me the best places to forage for greens?'

'Go and see if there's enough tall stalks of watercress to pick yet.' Oswynne straightened up, rubbing her back, and waved in the direction of the stream.

They grabbed baskets from the lean-to and slithered down the path to the spring. Once out of earshot, Meg giggled with delight. 'Can we play my favourite: "What animal or bird is everybody?"' she asked. 'I'll start – Roslinda?'

'Hmm, fox cub?' Hilda thought. 'What about Ragnild?'

'Something with a pointy nose – vole? Pine marten? You called her crow woman! What did you call me when you first came here?'

'Otter girl, because you'd been in the river! What am I?'

'Too hard! This is the best place, below the spring, where the stream runs shallow and fast over chalk. Sometimes you're like a squirrel, running up and down trees, sometimes you're wise like an owl … What about Wulf?'

'Easy – badger!' Hilda said.

They both laughed.

'What's Elder Edith?' Hilda asked.

'I used to think something like a dormouse,' Meg replied. She tucked the skirt of her tunic up into her belt, rolled up her sleeves and stepped into the water. She picked the longest stems of watercress from round her feet, washing the dark green leaves in the current, elbows wet, hem splashed.

Hilda followed her into the water. 'What's changed?'

'She seems more … real … now, bigger. Maybe a wolf with a grey muzzle that's loped a long way.'

'Ragnild seems to have more patience with her today.' Hilda retreated from the icy water and sat on the bank rubbing her toes back to life. 'And your mother was warmer with her too – seems to trust her more. Do you think giving Edith a chance to tell her story made a difference?'

Meg sat next to her. 'It did to me. I feel hot when I think I used to grumble under my breath about having to carry and empty Elder Edith's pee-bucket. When I heard about her problem with her insides, I remembered Mother calling for a bucket after May was born. It was really hard for her to move. Can that kind of birth make a body so many years later still need to go in a hurry?'

'You'd better ask your mother, Meg.' Hilda could hardly move her mouth. She looked away into the trees to avoid meeting Meg's enquiring look. *When would the pain leave her? When would she stop seeing the little cairn on the hillside?*

'Why did you ask Elder Edith to tell her story, Hilda? I saw you fishing for it. You were like a heron standing on one foot by the water's edge!'

A laugh came out instead of tears. This girl was a treasure! 'Is there more watercress further down?' Hilda asked. 'Let's fill the basket. I may have to stand on one leg to keep my ankles from going numb.'

They waded in again, mud squelching between their toes.

'It was like watching a fish under water,' Hilda agreed. 'I could see something needed to be said, so I went after it. I wasn't sure how it would go – I've tried before to get people to talk about why they came to be where they are, and often they seal up their lips as tight as a freshwater mussel. I had a hunch it might be a good way to spark some warmth between people. I didn't know it could shake things up as much as it has! I think I might have found one way to bring people together.'

Dripping, they panted their way back up towards the settlement. Meg looked uncertain. 'There was a woman who came to see Mother for healing last year – from Mereham. She gabbled on constantly! Mother couldn't get her to stop long enough to help her. In the end, she massaged salve into her shoulders and the woman quieted down, but then she started up again in the sleeping house and we had to wrap blankets round our ears to get some peace. She never asked anybody anything or even left a space for them to speak!'

'What did she talk about?' Hilda wondered.

'What she'd done, who she knew, things she'd seen – her, her, her.'

'Surface stuff? Like those pond-skaters that skim on top of the water, never noticing the deeps below?'

Meg grinned. 'Yes. Maybe that's it. She wasn't talking like Elder Edith did, about things that matter, or how she felt. How did you get her to do that?'

'I kept asking – that's the strike of flint on iron; and listening – that's the tinder that catches the spark and curls it into a flame. I didn't judge her – I didn't feel like that – I wanted to know what it was like for her. That's what helps friendships blaze.'

The clarity of the sky rippled with promise as Hilda realised what she had to do next. 'If I can just get your mother and Oswynne to talk like that, tell each other their stories, maybe they'll discover how much their friendship means.'

Meg shrugged. 'I don't know if that would work. Friendship? Is that what it is? Mostly they seem to just annoy each other … So when are you going to tell us about you – how you come to be here?'

Hilda felt her whole being clamp shut like the mussel shells she had spoken of earlier. She ignored the question and carried on playing. 'What's Headman Kedric? Jackdaw? Raven?' Anything to shift Meg's thoughts away from her. The hedge round her heart bristled with thorns so sharp that not even she could go near it.

URSEL

'Come on, Otred, don't let those piglets wander,' Ursel called to her brother. 'I want to meet up with Winfrith before the sun sets,' Otred's skinny legs carried him scrambling round to catch them all. They herded the swine down to the meeting place where three tracks cross. Slanting rays lit up snowy goose feathers – Winfrith was already there.

'Roslinda, get some more juicy charlock for the geese,' Winfrith instructed. Her young niece brought an armful of green leaves. She scattered them, made gobbling noises and giggled as the geese ate.

Winfrith put down her bow and quiver. Ursel sent Otred and Roslinda searching for beech mast, and she sat down with her friend on a mossy log with relief.

'How long until they can do it on their own?' Ursel mused.

'Ros can't keep up with the geese yet, if they run after frogs in the marsh. Her legs aren't long enough. How's Otred doing?'

'If he'd just concentrate!' Ursel flapped her hands in despair. 'He goes climbing and poking for bees' nests in every hollow tree, runs off after butter-coloured flies … He can cope with the pigs close to the settlement, but not out here on his own yet. It feels never-ending!'

'What's so bad about being out here? Do you want to get married off to some oaf from Thornthicket? That's what my brothers keep talking about for me! I don't want them choosing for me, I'd rather pick somebody myself – if I have to settle down. I don't want to get stuck in endless cooking anyway. I want more! Oh, are you still thinking about that boy?'

'Redwald's not like the other men,' Ursel fiddled with a hazel stick.

'He's got pretty hair, it's true.' Winfrith teased her, then spoke seriously, 'Remember what your Great-Aunt Edith said? She went after a man because he looked nice, and he seemed reliable, but he turned out to be a disaster. Poor Edith. I didn't know she'd been through all that. I don't want any disasters to happen to you!'

Winfrith put her arm round her shoulders. Ursel didn't want to shake it off, as it was warm and her friend meant to take care of her, but it reminded her of the yoke used for the oxen, keeping them in one accustomed path.

She straightened up and met Winfrith's eyes. 'It's not just that. He listens to me. He didn't mind that I looked ugly with my face all bruised – he wanted to know about it, why it happened, and how I felt. He talked about when we used to meet up and climb trees together. Remember that, Frith?' The arm gave her a squeeze and let her go.

'You're really taken with him, aren't you? Do you think he'd come and live here?'

'I don't think he can. He's got to leave his foster-family soon and go back to his own people, to Rendlesham, way over on the coast. He wouldn't talk about it much. He shifted and shuffled when I asked. His father's sick, and there's things to sort out, was all he said.'

'Would you go with him? You wouldn't leave, would you?' There was panic in Winfrith's voice.

A pair of dunnocks chased each other, flitting through elm branches. *Easy for them!* Ursel thought.

'He hasn't asked. I don't know.' The hugeness of the idea banged in Ursel's head. *Go without Winfrith, who knows where, with a man, any man, even Redwald? Unbearable!* But the excitement of it beckoned as well. She covered her face with her hands and shuddered as tears prickled. 'Watch out for the pigs!' she shouted, jumping up as Winfrith's arrow thudded into a target hawthorn.

'I am. They're heading down home with Otred. We'd better get going. The moon's up already and the sun's sinking behind Eel Island.' Winfrith's jaw jutted in the way that meant she was upset, so Ursel helped herd the geese and they hurried towards the savoury waft from the cooking-fire, in uneasy silence.

OSWYNNE

In the dim warmth of the sleeping house, the women and children settled in for the night. Oswynne was glad to be with them again.

Edith began the talk, 'Hilda, I have to apologise for taking up the whole evening with my own story last night.'

'How like a well-bred woman to be sorry for talking as long as she needs to, Elder Edith,' Hilda chuckled. 'There's no need to apologise; your trust warmed us through. When you told us about your wounding with such honesty, we lived it with you. We went down to the darkest places of our hearts, where we hide our own grief. We've all lost somebody dear. When that happens, part of our self can vanish and we yearn for that too. We think it's our own fault and nobody will understand. Listening to how Wendreda helped you, we all felt held along with you.'

Edith mused, 'Held. Yes, that's a good word for what Wendreda did for me. She talked with me until sparrows chattered in the thatch. You all held me last night, too, with your listening. You put your own needs aside and made a place for me. That's hard to do! It warmed me right into my bones. It felt strange to be letting all that pain out, after I'd buried it for so many years. I feel – light – today, wobbly, but clear.'

A well-bred woman can talk as much as she needs to … That's me, thought Oswynne. *I'm always watching that I don't make too much noise. What will happen if I ask when I want to know, say what I think, shout?*

'I knew you'd lost a son, Edith, but I didn't know how. I'm sorry,' Oswynne said, trying out a quite loud voice. *It feels good!*

Adela's plump cheeks flushed pink. *My little Puffin!* Oswynne thought. *One day I'll have to stop calling her that, now that her head comes up to my chin.* Her daughter pushed aside the blankets she shared with Oswynne, and spoke up too, 'Why was your husband so nasty to him? Poor little boy!'

Oswynne pulled the blanket back over her knees. Without thinking, she shot her daughter a look as if to say: Be quiet; this is grown-up talk. *Oh, but perhaps Adela needs to know she can speak out loud too!*

But Edith nodded and answered. 'You are right to be outraged, Adela. Children should be cherished. Whether they can run or not, all are precious. On Eel Island, there was an old custom of arranging games in the summer, after barley-harvest. Wendreda went to the elders and insisted on keeping the tradition. That was after a fisherman came to her hall to grumble about her sons getting in his way. They would keep diving into the river just where he wanted to position his nets.' She chuckled. 'So they made sure there were places to dive and swim, out of the way of the fishing. The girls and boys ran races in the stubble fields; they dug trenches and jumped them, piled up dry grass and leaped over it. They all joined in. The older people cheered when a young one finished their run, whether they were first or last.'

What if everybody cheered for Puffin when she ran, instead of telling her to keep up? If my father had watched me swim, instead of being busy all the time? Oswynne shook her head to get these silly ideas out of it.

SEREN

'How long did you stay at the healer's hall, Elder Edith?' Hilda asked.

'I was there for years. My one friend found another man, bundled up her things, and went to the next island. As she stepped onto the boat, I thanked her for saving my life and she smiled. Wendreda taught me so much. I hadn't got the talent for herb-learning ...'

As Edith spoke, Seren smelled again the clean tang of feverfew pinched between her fingers, in Wendreda's herb patch. *'I sniff too, to tell if I've got the right daisy,' Wendreda's voice echoed in her memory, serious but with a smile. 'My grandmother showed me how. She said chamomile's not so effective against a fever, and all those flowers look so alike.'*

'My grandmother too!' Seren had exclaimed. 'Nana, I called her. She didn't have her own herb patch, but we found all kinds of plants down by the beach. We harvested seaweed after a storm ...'

'What did you use seaweed for?' Wendreda had asked, and Seren explained how good it is to fertilise fields, and all the ways Nana used it in remedies. She felt again the tingle of joy she had known then, to be sharing herb learning with another healer!

Elder Edith talked on '... but I soaked up everything Wendreda told me about elder craft. I learned how to lead the antler dance, where young people step through the door into adulthood. She taught me how to listen for the voices of our ancestors when they speak from their barrows; rustling on the wind or whispering inside our hearts.'

Seren's words burst out without her usual caution, 'How did she teach that?' She clamped a hand over her mouth, too late. Oswynne's growl started, but Elder Edith spoke first.

'We went together to the barrows, Seren. There were chants and rituals, which I shall pass on to my successor, when I discern who that may be.' Elder Edith's eyes hooked hers and held them with a deep look. *What can she see inside me? Would she teach me? I yearn to hear all about elder craft! That can never happen, of course. I'm a slave.*

Hilda turned the talk with a question. 'Did the people of Eel Island appreciate what a wise woman Wendreda was?'

'Oh yes!' Elder Edith replied. 'Every day somebody was at her door with a basket of eggs or a jar of honey, to thank her for a healing. They mended her hall and made it comfortable. Wherever she walked, people would greet her with respect and wish her good health. I was honoured to be part of her household.'

'But you came back to Wellstowe at last, Elder Edith. How did that happen?' Hilda asked.

'After a few years, we heard there'd been a fire out at my husband's place and everyone had left, or died. That's when it came to me – I had to come back here, to Wellstowe. I found a boatman to bring me home. Luckily for me, my sister Merewyn welcomed me – she was the mother of Ragnild and Kedric. She said I could stay, and I did. I went back to see Wendreda often, as long as she lived.'

An old longing surged through Seren. *I want to use my skills with the same freedom that Wendreda had!* In her mind she escaped to live in a hut by herself, people came to consult her, and gave gifts in return – she could taste the honey they brought … but it was only a dream. She wrapped herself in the comfort of fantasy and slept.

CHAPTER 17

WHO WILL SIT ON THE CARVED CHAIR?

MEG

'Meg, I need you.' Elder Edith beckoned to her. *But I'm helping Mother!* Meg checked Seren's face. Instead of the blank look she expected to see, a smile twitched the corners of her mother's eyes. Seren took the spoon and stirred the broth herself.

'Heave open the lid of this chest, Meg. Ah, here's the speaking-staff.' Elder Edith laid the ancient whetstone on a table. She caressed the carved handle. 'Oh! It's come loose from the shaft. The stone part is sound, but the wooden handle is broken.' She turned it over, with a grimace.

'How old is, it, Elder Edith?' Meg asked. *I've seen it being used often in my life, never looked at it carefully before.*

'My mother's grandmother brought it with her on the Crossing, and all the way upriver to Wellstowe. We've taken care of it, but the wood has split with age. Lend me your arm, Meg, I'll take it to Kedric to mend. He'll be back from his field work by now, whistling and whittling in his shed.'

Elder Edith leaned on Meg's elbow over the rough grass, past the Great Hall, beyond the stable. *None of us would dare interrupt Headman Kedric! Should I warn her? But she's his aunt. He has to be polite to her, surely?*

'What have you brought me, Aunt Edith? Ah, the speaking-staff.' Headman Kedric unwrapped it from its linen cloth. 'Ah, I see, nasty split down this side.'

'Can you mend it?'

'Hmm. I'll have to make a whole new handle. I can copy the patterns.' Kedric ran his fingers over the pattern of intertwined hounds. 'It needs to be a bit bigger, more solid, to fit Thane Roger's hand.'

'Thane Roger? What's this got to do with him?' Elder Edith sounded surprised. 'At the Moot, we pass the speaking-staff round to make sure all the folk put forward what they know and think and feel. It brings them all in.'

'Ah, we're not going through all that endless talk and argy-bargy again, Aunt Edith! Thane Roger will command the Moot himself.'

'What? One man can't do that! He has not got the authority ...'

'Oh yes he has.' Headman Kedric frowned so darkly that Elder Edith lurched back, stumbling. Meg had to put an arm around her waist to steady her.

'Are you letting him take over?'

'I'm proud to help him! He will get the job done fast and thoroughly. What does it matter what some back country lass thinks? Or some oaf who's never been to court, never seen thanes making deals in their mead-halls? We don't want that sort meddling in important discussions!'

Meg felt ice grip her spine. *Thane Roger in charge? Headman Kedric helping him? Ugh!*

Elder Edith drew herself up. 'It took me years to learn the art of bringing people together. Making decisions in a group requires skills: listening, taking note of all the different views, helping them talk things through. That's where my authority comes from. Roger doesn't know anything about that! When Merewyn – your mother, my sister – thought I was ready, she chose me to succeed her as Elder of Wellstowe. It is my duty and privilege to preside, seated in my carved chair, as the elders have done through the generations.'

'We're not taking our orders from old women any more! We're not back in the old country now. This country was won by men's strength and courage. The pioneers forged their way upstream, deep into the backcountry where the natives fought with poisoned arrows. Nobody sat around talking then! They chopped back the forest to wrest it from the wild. Every day they beat back the natives and the weeds. We still do – thanes and farmers and headmen are the true heirs of those heroes.'

Elder Edith flung words back at him. 'The pioneers wouldn't have lasted long without their wives! Our foremothers led shiploads of women out of the old country, bringing cattle and pigs, spades and butter churns, looms and spindles. They brought their healing skills. They knew how to brew, make bread, and salt the fish and meat to keep them through the winter. They held the skills of weaving people together, hands and hearts and heads. Settlements would never have survived without the traditional wisdom of those women!'

Meg felt like cheering. *Elder Edith's words are like a wind blowing away fog – I can see women's work weaving the web of our lives. Why was I ever annoyed with her? She's special. Must look after her …*

'I'll mend this, my own way!' Headman Kedric grasped the speaking-staff and stamped away towards his house.

Elder Edith looked shaky. 'Come to the cooking fire,' Meg invited her. 'Mother will have a brew to put strength into you, Elder Edith.' Meg took the old woman's arm and helped her over rough tussocks. 'This makes me think of the invasion of Peony Valley! You are like one of those wise women who resisted, holding onto the ways of peace.'

Elder Edith stopped to smile at her. Then the pleasure faded from her face. 'As long as these "lords" don't take over. Those tales the Brother told, they make my blood run cold. This is not just about how we run one moot: they want to change everything and push our ancient wisdom into the mud. We've got to save what we can for the children, and their grandchildren, and the earth herself. Ah, Seren, hot sage tea please!'

That night, Elder Edith sat straight against the pillows Meg plumped up for her.

'I was full of brave words earlier, arguing with Kedric about how the Moot will be run, and who will be in charge. But now I'm not so sure! What have I let myself in for? It's years since I presided at a Moot, let alone an important one like this. This is not a simple dispute between niece and uncle, it's complicated. Thane Roger thinks he's the one to give out laws and tell everybody what to do, and my nephew Kedric wants to help him.'

'What would Wendreda say about that?' Hilda asked.

'I know exactly what she'd say!' Edith exclaimed. 'She had plenty of rude words. She'd tell us about a clan mother who rests in the barrows on Eel Island. This woman stood up, big and bold, in front of the warriors and brandished the talking stick, requiring their attention. "You're not listening to the women!" she yelled. "If you silence us, you lose the voice of Mother Earth. You could end up snatching food out of the mouths of children instead of sharing fairly. Women get a voice!" The warriors looked at their feet and shuffled, and women's thoughts were always heard at moots and meetings. Wendreda told me that story over and over.'

May jumped up and stood on the sleeping-platform, waving an imaginary stick round her head. Meg couldn't help grinning, even while glancing at Oswynne. *Are we going to get into trouble?* Seren shushed May and made her sit down.

Elder Edith didn't seem to have noticed. She twisted her thin plait between her fingers and went on, 'It's up to me to call the Moot, sit on the carved chair and run it; and make the judgment. I need you all to help me. My sister Merewyn had faith in me when she chose me to succeed her as Elder, I mustn't let her down. My knees are creaky, my teeth hurt, I get tired, and it's too difficult. I'm not sure I can do it.'

Meg glanced round. *Somebody say something. Well if you won't, I'll have to.* Her voice came out squeaky in front of everybody but she cleared her throat. 'I'll bring your stick and fetch things for you, Elder Edith.' It sounded like a sparrow's chirp in a storm. Nobody laughed, thankfully.

'Why is it important, who sits on the carved chair and leads the Moot?' Hilda asked. Meg had the feeling that Hilda knew some answers but wanted Edith to explain.

'It's not who, it's the way we do it! I lead a moot the old way: we talk until we have an agreement; I announce the judgment. Then we feast.'

'If Thane Roger and Kedric run the Moot, what will they do?' Hilda asked.

'Tell everybody what to do! If that doesn't work, there'll be arguments. If there's still disagreement, they'll use fists and knives. Or bribery.'

'If they try any of that, I'll get my dagger out!' Winfrith threw her hair back. Meg could almost see her hooves pounding the air as Winfrith sat bolt upright among the blankets. Meg's heart lifted – this was how her friend used to be, full of fire!

'We love your courage to defend what's right, dear! We certainly have to resist a takeover. Better still if we can prevent it. If the Moot turns into a fight, what happens next, do you think?' said Edith.

Winfrith wrinkled up her nose. *What she's thinking smells bad.*

Seren muttered, 'Bandages and poultices needed. More healing work!'

'I suppose people get hurt ...' Winfrith said. 'The winners make everybody do things their way.'

Edith nodded. 'Whether it's a fight or an argument – the side that loses will grumble. It'll be buried, not sorted out,' she explained. 'They'll have the feast anyway, and plenty to drink ... and it will all start up again.'

Hilda snorted. 'Hah! I saw something like this happen in a place down south last year. The women were tired out with looking after children and sick people, and their elder got confused and shouted. There were scuffles. The thane took over, said he owned the land and everyone had to work for him.'

'Instead of all of us working for the settlement? The land belongs to all of us, surely?' Oswynne sounded surprised.

'The people belong to the land,' Seren murmured. Only Meg heard her.

'What happened there?' Winfrith asked. *Elder Edith set her dagger idea aside so kindly, she's not crushed. Winfrith's trying to work things out now, instead of stamping.*

Hilda told them about that troubled place down south she'd seen. 'They got along all right until their food stores ran out. The thane gave most to his friends. Children starved. They trashed their woods to get fuel. They ate their seed corn. The women felt small and weak, didn't dare speak up. When I told them what I saw happening, whoosh, through that hedge I went, backwards.' Hilda twisted her mouth into a grin.

'So it's everywhere, not just here.' Elder Edith sighed. 'I'm just one old woman. I'm not sure I've got the gumption to guide them.'

Everywhere! Hilda's like an eagle, looking down at a flood rolling across the land.

'I'm sure you'll be fine, Aunt,' Ragnild said. Murmurs of agreement.

'Thank you for your reassurance, I know you mean it kindly,' Elder Edith replied, 'But please listen, there's more. My heart is with Ursel – when I saw the bruises Kedric gave her, I had to stop myself whacking him with my stick. But I have to make sure all sides get a fair hearing at the Moot.'

Winfrith broke in, 'Of course Ursel's right and her uncle's in the wrong! There's no doubt about that, surely?'

Elder Edith continued, calm but concerned. 'As Elder, it's my responsibility to think clearly, but also to go beyond thinking. I reach out in my spirit to seek the mind of the ancestors. I stand in line with them. Wendreda taught me how to listen to them and find their long view.'

Seren leaned forwards. Edith sent a searching look her way. *Is Elder Edith angry with Mother? No, her eye-wrinkles are smiling. What's that about?* Meg wondered.

Edith went on with what she was saying, 'This Moot will echo down the generations – so it's important for us to reach the best solution for everyone. Kedric may have valid points to make and some may agree with him. I have to be unbiased between Ursel and Kedric. I'm finding it hard to set my feelings aside. How can I do that?'

'Do you have to do it alone?' Hilda asked.

Edith rubbed her chin. 'Well, the elders from the other settlements will be coming along with everybody else. There's Mildreth from Thornthicket, she's a distant cousin of Kedric's. Elfric from Mereham will come too, he's a sensible chap who can see all sides of a problem. I can ask them to sit beside me and talk it through with me to come to a judgment.

'We'll need all of you to help as well. We can't have somebody thinking she's more important than somebody, or another one hissing envy. I know what we women can be like when we're trodden down! This is our chance to lift up our heads. If we rebuild the ways of our foremothers, our daughters will inherit our knowledge.'

'What are the ways of our foremothers, Elder Edith?' Winfrith sat forward, intent.

'We get everyone together first for a blessing, so they know it's important. Everyone gets heard. We listen to each other, root to root. We ask questions to burrow underneath the words and get to the hurt places, and down further to find the needs. Chew all that over, without shouting or name-calling. Then we start putting together ideas for a path out of the swamp – not a punishment, but a way we can all live together again. When we've all agreed, the elders announce a judgment. If the elders get it right, the folk feel we made it together and it lasts.'

Oswynne shifted, sitting in her big bed with her children. 'Why do you say foremothers, Aunt? What about our forefathers?'

Edith smiled. 'Our ancestors knew about the tenderness that floods through women when we birth and feed our babies. We heal children when they're hurt, soothe them when they're upset, hold them when they cry. We need to do this for each other when there's disagreement in our settlements. Compassion can draw out venom and heal pain not just for each one of us, but for our community – this is women's particular skill. Men share it when they stand back and learn from us, and care for little ones or animals – if they haven't had tenderness beaten out of them.'

'What about women's strength?' Winfrith lifted her chin. Meg imagined a whinny.

'We need all of that too!' Edith's eyes crinkled with warmth. 'The vivid courage of the young, the wide view of the old – all working together with love. All of our talents are vital for the making of a settlement – and a moot. Link arms with me!'

Oswynne fidgeted. 'How, Elder Edith? What do you want us to do?'

'Help me plan the Moot. I can sit on the carved chair, but you'll make it happen. That's good, because then you'll know how to do it, for next time. None of us is here forever,' Edith smiled. 'Soon I'll be choosing the next elder, when my time on middle-earth fades away.'

'Will you choose the next headman too?' Winfrith wanted to know.

'Headmen choose themselves nowadays, from the families who made the Crossing and tamed the land,' Elder Edith replied. 'Whoever's dedicated to the farm and willing to take on the burden. But for elder, we need someone who can see below the surface of the world. I'll seek the ancestors' guidance to find her, or him, or them.' Her gaze travelled round the sleeping house, taking in everybody.

Elder Edith turned to speak directly to Oswynne. 'I am so glad we have you in our settlement, Oswynne, you're such a talented manager. You'll know how to bring them all together, get them talking, make sure there's enough food, and everything runs smoothly. If you will help.'

Oswynne rubbed her neck and Meg could see how tense her shoulders were. *She needs some of Mother's ointment.* Oswynne looked up at the rafters, then levelled her look to Edith. 'I don't know if I can support you, Elder Edith. As Headman's Wife, my duty lies with my husband, and I think his way may be the best. All this talk and talk, it can go round and round and get nowhere. At least with one competent person in charge, the decision is made and carried through. I am not sure.' She shuffled down in her bed and pulled blankets over her head. All night she twitched, keeping Meg awake with her sighs.

CHAPTER 18

POT SHARDS

OSWYNNE

Oswynne stepped out of the dazzle from the east, into the gloom of the storage shed. When she could see again, she hefted her empty jar onto a shelf. *We'll need this again when the barley I planted this morning grows. Surely there was more seed corn? Couldn't find it in our cellar, is it here? My job to feed them all.* Dust choked her throat. *If I can't – who will we lose next? Nelda's little Leofric? His thighs are getting too thin. Not my Hubert.* Her chin set. *Edith? She's looking strained, what was it Ragnild said, her teeth? She needs soft food – is there any oatmeal left?* Her hands groped to check the pots. *A glazed one for cooking, this black bowl's got a chip in the rim, how did that happen? Another storage jar … stopper's gone, have to make another. What's in the bottom of this one? Only a spider.*

A shadow struck across the wedge of light from the open door. 'Where were you last night, wife? I waited in our house for you. What do you think I am, a slave to drag around after you?' Kedric hurled the words at her.

'I had to look after the children. It's all right for you men, drinking and laughing all night long – I heard you!'

'We worked hard and got the Moot planned out last night. Thane Roger needs a proper shelter; we're building him one up by the barrow. Our neighbours from Mereham and Thornthicket can camp on the flat ground on top of the ridge, near the barrow.' Kedric picked up an axe from the bench and tested the blade on his calloused thumb. 'We're cutting posts for the bothy this morning, better get on with it, I want to carve the end-posts to show respect. There's so much to finish before Beltane.'

'Why does Thane Roger need a shelter? They always bring tents for a moot, our kinsfolk.'

'Couldn't expect our Thane to bunk up with everybody else – he needs a private place to talk with the Headmen, peace and quiet to think and make his decision.'

Oswynne was glad he couldn't see her neck flush red, as she stood in the shadows. Her head thundered with thoughts but her jaw stuck firm, not letting them out. *'His decision – private talks!' Even if it's not Edith's way with all the talking back and forth, surely it has to be out in the open, everyone able to speak if they want to. I know what I'll have to do, if all the talk is between Headmen in the private bothy: refill the mugs with ale, look elegant, smile, keep quiet.* She glared and sucked in her lips but said nothing.

Kedric went on, 'I hope Roger gets Ursel sorted out. She's getting unruly – needs a husband. We'll get her married off, she can start breeding and forget about telling me what to do in my own settlement. How dare she defy me like that?'

There were scabs on his knuckles. *Do Ursel's bruises match those scabs?* She touched her own cheek, half expecting to feel Ursel's graze. Her fingers remembered Ursel's fat baby cheeks. Words slipped out through her teeth before she could stop them. 'Our settlement.'

'What's that you're saying, woman?'

'I said it's our settlement, not just yours, we all live here.'

'Are you standing up against me now?'

'You expect me to agree with everything you say, without even asking. What if I don't?'

'You're my wife; of course you support me. That's your job. What else is there for you to do?'

Her father's hall flashed through her mind, back at Ousemouth. *What colour were Father's eyes? They never lit on me. He always turned away, talking with merchants, overseeing loads on boats or carts. Mother's gone, only a burial mound. Father would tut-tut and sigh if I arrived back as a divorced woman, even if I brought my goods with me, my dowry and the morning-gift Kedric's family gave at the marriage. Father would get me hitched up with one of his friends right away. My children – would they come with me? Would Kedric keep them here?* She shivered.

'The wind's cold out there, Oswynne. There's miles of fen or forest between here and anywhere.'

'Are you threatening me?' She stepped back.

'I expect you to back me up.' Kedric shot her a frown under his eyebrows, ducked out of the shed and swung his axe so the blade glinted.

Coming nearer, women's voices. *They'll go quiet when they see me.* The warmth of last night's hearth in the sleeping house felt far away. *If I help Edith, I risk losing this life here, even my children. If I help Kedric, the women will turn away from me and I'll live alone at the mercy of my husband.* A pale curve of waning moon lowered over the fen, as narrow and frail as she felt. She pulled her shawl tight around her shoulders.

Seren stepped into the shed. 'Is everything alright Ma'am?'

'Of course it's alright, Ser–' The pots crashed to the ground and broke, knocked by Oswynne's elbow as she swung round. 'Oh now look what you've made me do!'

Seren's eyes turned grey as pebbles dividing a stream. She looked down, away from Oswynne, glancing towards Meg. Hilda came in behind her and scuffled around in the dark, among the shards. 'Can we mend them? No, too many pieces …'

'We'll have to make new ones,' Oswynne decided. 'Get the wheelbarrow, Meg, and spades, buckets, trowels and the rags we use for clay-work.' Oswynne's jaw was so tense it was hard to get the words out.

Hilda looked at her with such a warm smile that tears sprang to Oswynne's eyes. 'I'll help if I can, Oswynne,' the storyteller said softly. 'I'll pick up the pieces.'

Oswynne turned aside. Her father's voice echoed in her head, his parting words, as her lip wobbled. *Chin up, girl, don't let them see you weaken, can't trust any of them, there's work to be done.*

She stepped briskly over the broken pottery, out into the sun.

Meg and Seren set off for the clay-pit, past the Hall and the stables and down the droveway towards the water meadows. Hilda finished sweeping the shed and loped along to catch them up. Oswynne heard them chatting and felt a stab of envy.

She stopped to check that her little Hubert was still playing with May and Roslinda. The eight-year-old friends looked after him most days, along with her ten-year-old daughter Adela. May hauled Hubert back from the ashes of the cooking-fire and into Bertold's hall. He protested until she sat him on the place where her hip would widen when she grew up. May staggered along under his weight, and Oswynne followed them. *I remember being carried like that – who by? Seren, of course, hardly bigger than I was, so my toes bumped on the ground.*

Adela looked out from Bertold's hall. *My daughter!* A stab of love took Oswynne by surprise. She touched her cheek to Adela's sleek head. 'What's bothering you, Puffin?'

'Don't call me that!' Adela pulled away. 'May and Roslinda won't do what I tell them any more, and Ursel wouldn't take Elstan out to help with the pigs even though she takes her brother Otred because, she says, Elstan is Father's son as well as my younger brother, and she's got a feud going on with Father because he beat her, so Elstan hangs around and annoys me, and now he's gone to climb the beech tree and rob the blackbird's nest and I'm not supposed to climb trees any more, and Winfrith doesn't want me to help her with the geese and I know it's because she practices throwing a spear when she's away from the settlement and she's afraid I'll tell Father and she'll get into trouble, but I wouldn't. It's not fair!'

Oswynne heard about half her daughter's troubles. As she watched Seren walk through the shade of the alders in the lane, a thought hit her like a stone from a slingshot. *What if I had to leave the settlement – would Seren want to come with me? Of course she would, she's my slave ... But she's got Wulf here. Could I make her? Can I trust her? What about me?*

She sighed. 'Come with us, Puffin – er, Adela, you're good at making pots.' The pout vanished.

'What is a puffin anyway, Mother?'

'A little bird with dark feathers and a stripy beak. They nest in burrows in the sea cliffs, where I grew up.'

'Where you and Seren grew up?' Their feet slithered where the lane led them onto the layer of clay between the chalky soil of the ridge and the dark peat fen. Cuckoo pint flowers spiked pale among ferns, under the arch of bare branches. The smell of damp grass filled their nostrils.

'Yes. Hurry up.'

They caught up with Seren, Hilda and Meg at the corner of the field fenced off for clay digging. Oswynne shut the hurdle behind them. Frogs leaped away into long grass as they stamped and slipped.

'Mustn't let the heifers in here or they'll fall in the holes. Now, Seren, you dig. Meg, fill the wheelbarrow ...'

They were already hard at work and looked up briefly. *Why won't Seren meet my eye? All I did was tell her to pick out any flints she found in the clay, now she's muttering under her breath in her scary old language so I can't understand. Seren can be so annoying!*

Hilda took a trowel and moved a little way apart, among the buttercups. She stabbed down through the turf into a layer of sludge. 'That's too wet, Hilda. Find a drier place.' Oswynne called. Hilda moved towards the willows. She dug again, finding cleaner grey clay.

Meg edged over to Hilda. Oswynne watched her getting closer to the storyteller, as she ground her own spade in with her heel. Meg asked question after question – Oswynne couldn't hear what she said but she could see Hilda getting exasperated. At last Hilda snapped something and Meg turned away, bottom lip stuck out. They both jabbed at the clay, using up their precious strength for hardly any outcome.

Worry clawed at Oswynne. *How many meals left from stores in the cellars; how many mouths to feed; what can we pick from the wild; how many moons until crops ripen for food? What would happen to this round-faced little daughter of mine if I wasn't here?* She delved deeper, grabbed chunks of clay, tore plantain plants off them and stuffed them into a bucket.

Hilda slipped over with a squelch, then sat up giggling. She pushed her hair back, got mud on her face, laughed some more and smeared clay all over her face.

Meg grinned and smeared her face too. Hilda loomed up over Meg. 'I'm a grendel-bogle, yaah!' Meg pretended to be scared.

Seren spluttered, covering her mouth with her hand. Her deep-set eyes glanced towards Oswynne. *She wants to know if I will allow her to chuckle. Does she think I'm some kind of monster?*

'That's enough clay now. Bring the barrow.' She marched off towards the settlement, hardly caring if they followed or not.

Oswynne chose the grassy flat space outside the weaving house. *This spot is always peaceful.* It was quiet, facing away from the busy middle of the settlement, towards the water meadows and the stream. She shuffled her back against the south-facing wall of the weaving house; she craved comfort and the oak planks had soaked up sunshine. *Mustn't idle.* She continued her instructions: 'Spread the cloths in the sun so the clay dries.' She knelt and prodded some in its linen folds. 'This lot's dry enough; work it in the shade, Seren. Here's a piece for you Meg.' The tang of the clay mixed with the scent of violets from the slope by the stream.

She took a piece, too, and began to wedge it to smooth out air bubbles. As her knuckles drove into it, she imagined her husband's big nose in the ridges, his jaw under her fists. She slapped it flat and pounded it, kneaded, folded, punched. When it was workable, she rocked back on her heels, tore a piece and rubbed it between her palms.

'Wouldn't it be good if we could beat all the struggles out of our lives like this.' Hilda remarked with half a smile, 'Cruelty, unhappiness ...' She bashed her lump flat. Oswynne gave hers another pounding, grim faced. 'Hunger, illness, exhaustion …'

'And toothache!' It was Edith, navigating the turf to join them. 'Give that a beating for me, please, I can't reach.' She sat on a bench beside the wall. 'I can start shaping it, if you pass me a piece. Ragnild, fetch your pot-stamps, dear, we'll need them to mark patterns on the pots. If we make some good storage jars, perhaps we can trade them for food from our neighbours when they come to the Moot.'

'Did you make that, Puff … Adela?' Her daughter's storage jar was neat, evenly worked and smooth. Adela's cheeks went pink, reacting to Oswynne's delight.

'Please will you show me how to do the pot-stamps, Aunt Ragnild?' Adela asked, passing the jar she'd shaped to Ragnild.

Oswynne made room for Adela to sit beside her, melting gently against her daughter's warm body. Her sister-in-law bent over the damp clay pot with her crow-sharp eyes, pressed the end of her carved bone stamp-stick onto it to make a star, turned it and used the other end to stamp a flower shape, another star, flower … with rows of dots above and below, all round the jar's shoulder.

'It looks like a path! May I try?' Adela asked and Ragnild gave her a scrap of clay to practice on.

'Our storyteller is making new paths and patterns for us with her age-old stories,' Edith inclined her head towards Hilda. 'Let's hear some!'

Hilda was clearly pleased with the invitation to tell more of the story. She looked away over their heads at a thrush threading song into the wind from the top of an ash sapling, then brought her gaze back to them. Oswynne leant back against the sun-warmed planks and let a little tension slide out of her shoulders.

'I'll tell you more of the story of the wise woman and the young queen. This part is about …

Peonies Trampled in Dirt

Huldran, the healer, and the young queen, Marelda, were high up in the mountains. Their boots crunched over a crust of ice on top of snow. They chopped wood for the fire. They stacked logs under the eaves of Huldran's house. The bucket, the axe, the fire, round and round they went. Marelda got blisters on her soft hands for the first time in her life.

Hilda set her clay aside to show them the palms of her hands and her companions could almost see the blisters.

They ate well! Huldran unpacked boxes of smoked salmon and trout, barrels of pickled cabbage and beetroot. She had a root cellar full of carrots and turnips. She pulled down rings of dried apple, peach and apricot from strings looped round the rafters. Sometimes they caught a hare.

'Eat, have some more, suck the marrow out of this bone,' said the wise woman. 'You're growing muscles, see? Hard work is good for you.'

They sorted crocks full of beans and seeds – some so twisted they had to be thrown on the fire, some sprouting already, some good to keep. They talked as they worked – sorting Marelda's memories one by one. Some were bitter in her mouth – Marelda spat them out, cleaning herself of weakness and fear with talk and shuddering. Huldran listened, nodded and asked questions. Often she said, 'If I'd been there, I'd have helped you.' Some they talked through and through until they changed their shape. Some they laughed over. 'You have more strengths than you know,

Marelda. I'm glad you told me how you worked out how to use all the herbs in the garden of your home. You compared them and tried them out, one by one and together. That took determination. You've got a feel for that skill, and a powerful memory.'

They soaked beans and set them to sprout; Marelda's mouth watered as she crunched the tender shoots. Outside the blizzard howled. The fire flickered but they stayed warm while snow drifted over the roof. 'How did you come to live here, Huldran? How do you survive out here on your own?' Huldran took up the story:

'Varagan and his fighters poured over the ridge and splashed across the ford. The earth shook under their hoof beats. The first we knew about it was the blare of their horns. Out of a blue sky arrows rained down, thudded into people, screams rang out. My husband ran to Queen Velika's side – I saw him go down with a spear in his guts. I knew he was beyond healing. I shinned up the sacred tree in the courtyard – where the queen used to sit with her council to hear complaints and give judgement. I chanted and wept and called the spirits to save us, I made the gestures of protection – but the spirits couldn't hear me, with the din and stink of blood and shit. I slid down and grabbed Marn, my little son, from my friend Piroshka. "Tell them I'm dead, it's not safe for us to stay."

'I ran through the forest, carrying Marn, until I couldn't move. He could toddle by then, but he couldn't run as fast as we needed to go. I rested and ran some more, stopped to breathe, ran. Next day, when I knew they weren't following me, I sat down to feed him with my back against a rock – it held me. It was this crag where we are now. Sweet grasses blew all around. I looked out over waves of green and dark green and blue and purple forest as far as I could see. It felt like a shore, an edge. I thought – the spirits can find me here, I'll reach out to them. I had a picture in my mind of spirits scared and hiding, like me, curled up, trembling. I wanted to make a safe place for them, for me, for all of us.

'Jackdaws tumbled around the cliff and I looked up – there was a slit in the rock face – the cave. It looks different now with the door built on. I slipped inside and we sheltered there. I showed Marn how to gather nuts and berries. I made snares and fish-traps and dug with a stick to make a garden. We did all right through the summer.

'In the autumn, Marn got ill – he must've eaten something bad while I wasn't looking. His bowels ran; he threw up over and over again. He cried and then he stopped crying, and that was worse. He shivered and burned, his eyes glazed over. I fed him from my breast and that kept him alive – but then he couldn't even suckle any more. His breathing got very quiet. I tried not to panic. What could I do? I wanted my herb garden, back in Peony Valley. Had Piroshka kept it weeded? I strapped him on my back and set off. His legs dangled heavy where he usually bounced and chuckled.

'I stumbled through the woods, whispering to the spirits – help me find the way. There was Peony Valley, below us. I hid where I could watch a raiding-party ride out, with the king out ahead; then I slipped in among the houses and found Piroshka, with you, Marelda, playing in a corner. I gave my friend the fright of her life! She nearly fell into her cooking pot. Said I looked like a ghost, thought I was a ghost, poked me to make sure. Laughed and cried and hugged me. I couldn't laugh – I showed her my son's pinched little face. She held him while I found the herbs I needed and brewed them up and dripped warm liquid into Marn's mouth with a hollow reed. In the evening he began to suckle at my breast and I breathed again.

'He was sleeping soundly when women came to Piroshka – their arms around a mother in labour – the baby was stuck.

177

Piroshka had never dealt with that before. I stepped out of the shadows. We heated water over the fire and filled a half-barrel with it, I stirred lavender in and helped the labouring woman climb into it and soak. I called on the spirits to help while I rubbed her shoulders and back. They clustered round and sang through my hands to help the baby move down. At dawn, a guard banged on the door: "What's going on? Who's in there?"

'Piroshka called out through gritted teeth, "Go away, it's a birth, you're scaring everybody and slowing it down!" We helped the mother out of the tub when she asked. The baby slid out, we helped her lift him to her chest and wrapped them both in a blanket. I slung Marn on my back and turned to go.

'Piroshka hugged me. "You're not coming back, are you? You can't, it's not safe. If Marelda talked about you" – gesturing to where you slept – "they'd kill her like the rest of her family. There's always trouble, men muttering about getting rid of Varagan, they'd think it was a plot."

'I looked at you sleeping, Marelda, your pink cheek on your hand, your mouth open. I said, "They'd kill you too, Piroshka, and Marn, and me." I told her the way to my cave. "Send people to me, if they need me."

'Sometimes they come, in great need. The women don't tell. They give me things I can't make – a spade, seeds, a needle. They sent their husbands and brothers with logs and thatch, to help me build my house and make the entrance to the cave. The house is more convenient, but I need the cave for dreaming.

'I had no energy for making trouble. I began to love living alone. Marn was always making something or dreaming, watching otters in the stream, drawing patterns in the sand by the pool. He made a knife with a flint blade and carved curves on bark. Dragons, he said. He saw them in the shadows among the trees – I did sometimes too.'

'So he got better, your little Marn?' Marelda asked. 'Does he still live here?'

'He's a bronze smith now. He lives and works in the smiths' halls over on the next ridge. He soon bounced back. It's amazing how little ones do that, isn't it?' Huldran smiled.

'I wouldn't know.' Marelda's lip stuck out in a pout, her chin wobbled. 'Other women get babies, I don't. I can't.'

'I think I can help you bring a child into the world, from what you've told me about yourself and your body.' Huldran took Marelda's hand between both of hers. 'It'll take three moons at least. It's a big thing, to weave a new life. We need to find the lost threads of your body and spirit, and braid them together. You've drunk bitterness and tasted despair so deeply it'll take time to rinse those out of you. You need healing, tending – hah – and to do more hard work! I need to send a message to a friend to come and help us. May I have a thread from your dress, please?'

Marelda frowned. 'Why?' as she teased out a loose thread from her hem.

'You'll see.' Huldran took a thread from her own sleeve and wound the two together. 'The storm's died down. Good.' Huldran climbed the ladder in the middle of the house and stuck her head out of the smoke-hole. She opened her throat and uttered a noise that made Marelda jump – a loud croak. Again and again she called, until an answer came from far away. Huldran grinned as she stepped down the ladder and shoved open the door, heavy against drifted snow. 'Come,' she beckoned to Marelda and they went out into the bitter cold.

A raven hopped from the roof onto Huldran's outstretched wrist. Marelda blinked – was it the dazzle of snow-light or was there a shimmer of the spirit-world in the air?

Huldran introduced the bird to Marelda, 'This is my friend Star, you can recognise him by this white feather on his wing. Star, this is my friend Marelda.' She tied both threads around the bird's leg. 'Find Ziske!' Star bowed his head twice, looked at Huldran with his bright eye and leapt into the air. His strong wings whisked him over the crag and away into the mountains.

That night, Oswynne took refuge in the women's house again. The memory of her husband's sour tone turned her stomach. She ached, remembering the wind that keens outside settled lands, sharp as a pot shard. She held Puffin close, until she wiggled away. She cuddled Hubert. The women's talk soothed her.

CHAPTER 19

THE SHATTERED HEARTHSTONE

HILDA

Hilda laid a bundle of withies to soak in the shallows of the stream. She wiped her wet hands on the back of her neck, her brow, and her temples to ease the throb in her head. She lifted a handful of water to watch the drops catch fire from the sun, in no hurry to go back to the ranting and whining from the willow thicket.

Meg slithered down the bank on her haunches, slipping a look over her shoulder to make sure she wasn't missed.

Words fell out of Hilda's mouth before she could catch them. 'They've been arguing for days! Is it always like this?'

'Mother and Oswynne? Often. It's worst when food's short or something's worrying them. I try to keep out of the way.' Meg's nose wrinkled as if at a bad smell.

'I wish they would talk to each other, really talk,' Hilda said. 'They have to decide whether the Moot will be the way Elder Edith wants it, with groups talking and mixing, or if the Thane's word will settle the dispute. Either way, they have to plan it together – the food, where the tents go, the midden-pits, everything.'

'How does talking to each other help? Can't we just – get working on it?' Meg squatted among the marsh marigolds, eyes screwed up.

She's trying to understand. Hilda drew a bundle of well-soaked willow shoots out of the water, last week's crop. Their smell of growth cleared her head.

She passed them to Meg. 'Are these bendy enough? I don't often get a chance to make baskets.' Meg wound the young shoots with their thin brown skin and leaf-buds through her fingers, testing them. Hilda explained, 'A bunch of sticks is fine for poking or bashing.' She grinned as the words twined on her tongue. 'But if you want to hold something precious – eggs or seeds – you weave the rods together. When one stops, another one threads through without a break. Some stand tall to make a framework, others duck and dive between to build up the walls. Each one has to be tough, and flexible enough to wrap around the next one to make the whole basket strong.'

Meg's brow wrinkled. 'Do you mean – talking weaves people together?'

'Mmm, it can do; especially if we tell them what's happened to us before, how we got to be here, why we stayed. But only if it's the whole heart speaking, not just … a bark!'

Meg stifled a laugh behind her hand as snapped commands echoed over from the osier beds.

Hilda grew more serious, 'And only if the one listening leans towards the one talking and gives her a hug with words and looks.'

'That's what you did with Edith!' Meg's eyes lit up; then clouded.

You tried to do that with me at the clay-pit, to draw my story out, Hilda thought but did not say. *I dug in my toes and resisted. I can't even tell more of Marelda's story. I'm stuck!*

Day after day Meg had asked, 'What happened next? When can you tell us about Star – and who's Ziske?' Each time, Hilda suggested a game.

Hilda couldn't meet Meg's eye. 'It feels dangerous, to show the spots where we can be hurt. People have to pick their time. If you poke a snail with a stick, she goes back in her shell.' *As I've been doing for days.* 'She comes out when she's ready …'

A bee buzzed, visiting red clover. Huldran's voice sounded through it, trying to get her attention – again. Hilda had been trying to ignore this voice for days and nights. Every time she reached for the Peony Valley story to tell some more, Huldran tried to speak to her. Hilda yanked a curtain across her mind so she wouldn't have to hear the wise woman's nagging.

Hilda blinked and went on, 'When we see the shape of somebody's life, we stop saying – you're wrong, you shouldn't have done that – and start seeing through her eyes why she did it. That's one way to get closer, deeper, more in touch with our friends, so we can work well together.'

Meg nodded. 'I'd better get back.' She pulled her tunic over muddy knees and scrambled up the bank behind them.

I'm losing Meg! The bee was in the blackthorn now. At last Hilda harkened. *Is that you, Huldran or the bee? You're always in the back of my brain, waiting to give me good advice that I don't always want to hear.*

'Listening at last eh? Show them how to open your heart. Tell them what happened to you.''I never do that! I get the women to talk, and when they get uncomfortable they chuck me out.' Hilda spoke to the wise woman in the leafy shadows of her mind.

'That's handy. You can hide behind our tales and never throw off that cloak.'

Hilda wrapped her arms round the soft parts of her body. *'They don't want to know about me, I'm not special. They might blame me for what happened. What if they call me names? They won't listen to my little troubles, and I'll be left without a shred of dignity.'*

Huldran's buzz was deep and warm. *'There's the hurt you went through, and fear on top of that when you think about trusting them.'*

Oswynne's voice, scolding Seren, rose to a pitch that scraped Hilda's eyeballs. The bee flew away. Seren was silent.

Hilda shivered. *'I can't stand the way Seren swallows it. I want to pick up my pack, fill a water-skin, and get out of here.'*

Now Huldran's voice held a hint of sting, 'Like you always do, when things get tough.'

'I could say a few things to Headman Kedric first!' Hilda chewed over some juicy insults. *'He'd shove me backwards through the hedge.'* The imagined thorns felt familiar, almost comforting.

Huldran's voice resounded in Hilda's brain. *'This settlement is the place we need to be, you and I, to work changes with our tales about the peaceful queens of Peony Valley. Wellstowe is sliding fast into the rule of the fist. If you run, I'll be screaming inside you, dying to reach out to these women. They claw each other – because they can't see what's hurting them. You can give them tools to turn this around, before it's too late – if you stay.*

'Edith shelters ancient teachings in her frail heart. She knows how to make a Moot work, and a settlement, a whole clan, not by ordering people about but drawing out their urge to work together. She's aching to share her wisdom because she won't be here much longer – when she dies these skills will vanish from the land. The daughters of our daughters will think men have always ruled because women are weak and that's how it has to be. Is that what you want?'

Hilda screwed her knuckles into her eye sockets.

'How will Ursel get along without your coaching?' Huldran's voice was soft but her challenge prickled. Hilda imagined Ursel at the Moot, stumbling over words, saying her vital message backwards, sideways, losing the thread. Red hot and tearful, looking at her feet, clenching her fists, drying up. *'She wants to tell the truths that you and I clothe in story; we are all Earth Mother's children and our lives weave together, so all can flourish. Help her speak out!*

'Look at the shifting in Oswynne, the way her power jags and judders as her awareness grows. Which way will she settle? If she works for women, she could sweep away injustice. If she gets bogged down in obedience, her life will dribble into the mire.

'And Meg?' Huldran's voice again. Hilda thought how the life would bleed out of Meg if she couldn't be a storyteller. *'If Meg doesn't learn our tales, they'll die with you, Hilda. Oh, they'll still be told, but twisted and deformed so they drain women's strength and make us pale and limp. Meg can breathe life into them so they thunder down the years – will you walk away from that?'*

Hilda shuddered.

'And you. This is your chance to change what you always do. You'll only be doing what you want them to do – unwrap the bandages round your heart, sit with it raw, trust your friends to heal you. Show them how, even if it doesn't feel safe.'

'All right, I'll try.'

'If you didn't think you couldn't do it, it wouldn't be worth doing.' Huldran *chuckled gently. 'It may hurt more than you can bear. Maybe your pain will touch light to such a blaze that people will warm their hands at the embers years from now.'*

The dazzle of light from the stream leaked though Hilda's fingers. She washed her face, straightened up and went to join the others.

Oswynne was pointing at the edge of the stream. She snapped at Seren, 'I've told you before! You must not make pictures of your old gods. If our gods are offended – Ing and Thunor – we won't be safe. Rub it out, this – whatever it is.'

'It's mine.' Hilda stepped between Oswynne's glower and Seren's hunched shoulders. She met Oswynne's eye with a level gaze. 'This drawing of the Goddess was my prayer before your Feast, to ask her to help with my stories. It's washed away at the edges, but you can still see her face where the ripples lap around it.'

Hilda knelt on the chalky sand. 'These flints are her eyes, with the glisten of water on them – we call her Neath, Shining One, where I come from. These snaky patterns are her voice, twisting up from her tongue. I put white stones for bright words to sing out on, dark ones from the heart, leaves for airy notes – they've drifted away. Twigs join them all together. I asked for power, to make the stories come alive for you and your guests.' Hilda squinted up at Oswynne, where she stood against the bright sky.

'Where do you come from?' Oswynne asked.

Hilda stood up, brushed sand off her skirt and wrung out the wet hem. She picked her place to sit with her back to a willow trunk, among celandines. *All the community's women are here, even Edith with a blanket over her knees. Everyone has a task. Some are weaving baskets, and the older children looking after the younger ones. They'll be happy making mud-stew and we can all keep an eye on them. There's nothing to stop me. Now is the time! Oswynne's given me a way to start. Follow my journey last year … take myself into the past step by step …*

'I come from a place where the hills look over your shoulder and buzzards soar up above.' Hilda shut her eyes. 'There's a river named for Neath, near the place that was my home. It flows out of a cavern, gleams dark, and the earth swallows it in caves downhill. Streams stitch over and under through the turf, come out to shine in the sun then dive underground again. You hear the mutter of water even when you can't see it. That's the country I grew up in, where Neath is telling a tale all the time if we listen.'

Longing for home welled up in her with the words. Seren looked up with a smile. Meg took up eight willow rods, split four with a bodkin and threaded four through to start the base of a basket. Oswynne was listening – they all were.

Hilda breathed in; words came on her outbreath.

'I went back last year, hunting a story in the hills. I kept hearing shreds of it, in the west and the south, and I half-remembered my mother telling it to me.'

'Did you catch it?' Meg breathed.

'I headed north up the backbone of the land, when the swallows flew south. At nights I sang for my supper or told tales by the fire. I found wisps of that story snagged on bushes and drowned in streams and muddied in bogs, never the whole thing. I followed memories like cloud-shadows down into valleys and up over ridges.

'When the first snowflakes fell, I saw a curve of mountain like a breast, and the path dropped into a valley. The settlement was just where I knew it would be. I saw a woman pressing whey from a cheese and my mouth said her name without me knowing I knew it. She looked at me blankly. I told her, "I used to live here. An old woman took me in." Others gathered round but nobody recognised me. They gave me soup for supper and straw to sleep on, as you would for any traveller, but didn't talk. I had never really been one of them, and I'd been away so long. In the morning I couldn't wait to leave.

'It was a steep scramble up through scrubby holly and oak, over the ridge and into my home valley, with a weight in my chest as heavy as the bruise-coloured clouds. I walked over turf and stones, right past the settlement where I was born. Bracken and nettles covered all that was left, and I never saw it. Only when I found a single rowan tree by a pool

I knew where I was. I sat down and memories rushed back …' Hilda hesitated.

Edith asked, 'Painful memories?'

Hilda dared to go on. 'That pool was the best place for trout if you kept still. I was good at that, eight years old and freckled as a trout myself. My brothers said "Go away" when I followed them, so I hid. On the day I remembered, the others had run off down the hill home, laughing and shouting. I was glad to see them go, they disturbed the creatures. A fish came and hung under the rock where I lay on my stomach. Its fins moved gently up and down, light radiated through them; they looked like wings. I could see its mouth moving. I told myself I would catch it, when I was ready. My breath barely moved behind my lips.

'With a flick of its tail it was off. Noises came banging into my ears, like something caught in a trap, but not animals. I think I peed on my tunic. Smoke billowed up from my home settlement – burning thatch. Flames snapped. My throat hurt. I heard shouting, men's voices roaring. Women screamed, cows bellowed. There were feet running, arrows thudded. I slithered backwards into the gorse, and kept very still. I breathed like a fish with a tiny mouth. My heart dinned like a storm cloud.

'Then there was only the croak of ravens. I moved when my legs cramped. Nobody was there. I rubbed my legs. I needed to drink so I went to the stream but the water was a bad colour. There were legs sticking into it from the bank but the legs didn't move. Nothing moved. My feet found moss to walk on. No twigs broke as I crept. It wasn't a settlement any more. I choked and gagged on smoke from smouldering rafters. The great hearthstone of the hall lay broken, the spiral patterns my father carved on it scattered in the dirt. I found my mother but she was not my mother any more, she was a bundle of rags and her face was cold. She was not singing now. Her throat had a ragged red hole in it where the song had gone away. I understood she was not going to sing again. Other people were there too, on the ground, but I did not look at them. They were quiet and a red kite came to eat them. My stomach clenched and I threw up till it hurt.

'My little girl feet took me over the ridge, then down through scrubby holly and oak. I stopped to drink bitter cold water from the waterfall.

Shivering made me sick again. Cooking smells drew me down into the Saxon settlement, the one where nobody knew my name. People crowded round, asking questions. I didn't understand a word, but I expect they were, "You're from the next valley, aren't you? How did you escape? Did anybody else get away? Any cattle left?"

'My mouth still breathed like a fish, making no sound. An old woman put a scratchy blanket round me, brought me to the fire and gave me food. The shivers eased. I lay down in the old woman's bed with her arms around me. Although she smelled funny the warmth of her loosened something in me and I slept.

'As well as my life, the old woman gave me words. I didn't talk at all until the year turned and the snows melted. When the first elder tree leaves came out, she made a game for me – she showed me a leaf and gave me the word in her Saxon language, then looked at me, head on one side, asking for my word for it. I gave her two – Mam's Pictish language and Dad's British. She was delighted, tried another: "sparrow". I offered her a word: "barley-bread". She savoured it and smiled and gave me the Saxon word along with a bannock. After a while she gave me words for the things I'd seen: "cattle raid", "grief". When I got the hang of her Saxon language, she explained about the raid. The people who'd destroyed my home village were the same ones we used to trade with. My head hurt with trying to understand.'

Oswynne looked puzzled. 'Pictish people are from a place of heather hills, aren't they? We saw traders from all over, back in Ousemouth.'

Hilda nodded. 'My mother had kin from those mountains. The Picts were never enslaved, just driven further north. There were plenty of free Celtic Britons in my home hills too, my father's people. Sometimes they mixed with the Angles and Saxons, sometimes they fought.'

'Free Celtic Britons?' Oswynne mused. 'We don't have such people here. Our Celtic Britons are our slaves.'

'The shepherds on Weary-Moon Hill live only a couple of long days' walk from here,' Hilda reminded her. 'They shared what little food they had in exchange for stories, when I spent mud-month with them.' The memory made her smile.

'Eel Island has a mix of people,' Edith added.

Oswynne asked Hilda, 'How did you get on in the Saxon settlement with your kind old woman?'

'When she got my tears flowing I began to grow again,' Hilda replied. 'She made patterns with words – poems and stories – like the patterns Mam made with her songs, or Dad's carvings. I tried words over on my tongue and fitted them together. I strung them like beads and braided them together – they were strong enough to carry the weight of a heavy heart. I climbed up a rope of words, out of my dark silence, hand over hand, into daylight.

'I got so tall I could pick her up, my little old second-mother, and whirl her around and she giggled and pounded me with her fists on my back to put her down, but she didn't mean it so I hugged her – "too hard" she said. We danced and told stories until the embers glowed.

'When she died, there was nothing for me in that settlement. The others still treated me like a stranger, spitting "Pict" at me as if the name dirtied their tongues. They didn't see a person when they looked at me, only something not like them – because I came from Mother's settlement. It was the last one in those hills. I've never heard my mother tongue spoken since then. It's all Anglish and Saxons in my home hills, now.'

'How did you leave there, Hilda?' Ragnild glanced up from the basket taking shape between her hands, with a sideways crow-sharp look.

How can I talk about this? She can be so sharp with her daughter Ursel, dare I trust her? Hilda locked eyes with Ragnild and saw a woman just wanting to find out what happened next, no judgment. 'One day a peddler came through the village, a good-looking lad, and he did see me. He noticed I was a woman, so I did too. I was up and away with him. We came down the spine of the country, singing. Sometimes people liked my stories, sometimes they threw things and we had to run. We laughed about that, the two of us together. He sulked when my stories brought more goodwill than his needles and beads. We quarreled, more and more often.'

Edith tut-tutted. 'Jealous of your talent, eh? When will men learn to enjoy their women's strengths? It must have been difficult for you, Hilda,'

'Mmm. The next bit is hard to even talk about.' *It would be nice just to watch the ripples* ... A water vole plopped into the stream from its burrow in the opposite bank. Nearby, a bee buzzed on a clover flower. *You again, Huldran. I hear you.*

Hilda looked around. So many warm eyes met her that she found strength. She cleared her throat and took a run at it, speaking too fast. 'We stopped at a settlement where they made strong ale. Two men got into a fight over a badger-fur my peddler offered, the thane blamed him rather than his own friends, and threw him out in the cold. But they still wanted my stories. I played my harp and the thane gave me a brooch. As I stepped outside, my man was waiting, furious, swaying with drink. He lashed out, slapped and punched and pushed me – shouted that I'd lain with the thane. I still don't know – did he mean to kill our baby? When I fell, I bled and bled. I called for help and women came. They got me in the warm but the baby in my body died. She was big enough for me to hold and to recognise as my daughter, not big enough to live. Through the weeping and the pain, those women wrapped me and wiped my face and put broth to my lips even when I retched. When I came to myself, the peddler had scarpered and I was glad he was gone. We made a cairn to honour my baby who never took a breath. I carry my own pack now, filled with patterned words and songs.'

Seren's fierce hug took Hilda by surprise while she saw the world through a shimmer of sadness. Meg sat so close that her body warmed Hilda. May and Roslinda snuggled close to each other, each with a thumb in her own mouth. Edith keened under her breath, 'Poor baby.'

Oswynne growled, 'What a coward.'

Ragnild asked, 'Was nothing left of your settlement, your birthplace, when you went back?'

They were holding her with looks and words, listening to her. Although she felt raw, she risked it.

'I searched among the nettles that day last autumn. I found this.' Hilda pulled out a grey stone from her belt-bag. 'It's the last, broken bit of our settlement; all I've got left of my home, my people.' She caressed the stone and passed it to Meg.

Meg touched it tenderly and put it in Seren's hand. 'The patterns look like the curves you make in ash to smoor the fire at night,' she said.

Seren gasped as she held the stone to her ear. 'What gives this stone its power?'

'My father carved these spirals into the hearthstone of our hall, while my mother sang. He said he was pouring her voice into the stone.' Hilda held out her hand to take it back.

Seren whispered something under her breath as she laid it in Hilda's palm. 'I'm just giving it a blessing,' she explained. *She's trying not to look at Oswynne in case of trouble*, Hilda thought. Seren asked, 'I'm worried about that bruise-coloured cloud you told us about, Hilda. What happened next?'

'While I was ferreting around, snow started to pelt down so I looked around for shelter. I scrambled up scree to an overhanging cliff and half fell into darkness; a crack in the rock led into a cave. I crawled in, shivering. Snow blocked the entrance and daylight withered. I lit a fire – habit made me pick up sticks and tinder on the way up and my flint worked at last, as you can tell because I'm sitting here.'

Meg smiled. 'I'm glad you made it!'

Hilda nodded and went on. 'Water flows into earth and out again. Life coils into death and out again. I told myself this as I traced the patterns on my piece of broken hearthstone with my fingertip. All I knew was – loss. I don't know how long I was in the dark, days and nights, long enough for hunger to turn from sharp to dull. That gash in my mother's throat filled my eyes, even though it was thirty years ago. If I shut my eyes the wound went on gaping. I rubbed them to wipe it away – it still bled through my fingers. I shuddered and rocked myself and wailed until my throat was dry. Pictish words swirled round my brain like mist – Mother's voice.' Hilda hummed a fragment of tune. 'I woke clutching the hem of her song – something about a dress the colour of rowanberries. That was all I ever found of the story I went hunting.'

Seren's eyes opened wide; then narrowed over a shut mouth. Even from her far place, Hilda noticed it.

'Did you visit the cairn, for your daughter?' Meg's voice was small.

'On the way south, I looked. Nothing left.' Hilda stood up and climbed up the bank away from them. Her limbs shook as if she'd run up a mountain. She gazed out across the fen, filling her sight with plovers' wings and her ears with the fluting of lapwings. *This is now, and I am here.*

She didn't voice her thoughts. *I've been searching ever since for an apprentice to replace my lost daughter, and now I've found you it won't do me any good because you're a slave and you aren't free to come away with me if they make me leave. A thorn stuck in my heart when I left my baby's body under stones, but a dagger will stab me if I have to turn away from you.*

CHAPTER 20

A RUSH OF WINGBEATS

HILDA

Shouts from outside woke Hilda before dawn. She sat up on the platform in the women's sleeping house and yawned. *It's those two boys, Elstan who loves to climb trees and Otred, Ursel's brother with the grasshopper legs. Sounds like they go fishing together before anyone else is awake. They don't care if Ursel is arguing with Elstan's father Headman Kedric. They're enjoying being first with news* ... Otred's squeak added to Elstan's yell: 'There's a shoal of bream in the mere! They're jumping all round the willow roots, spawning in the shallows.' Men pounded past the sleeping house.

Oswynne shoved past Hilda as she looked out. 'Don't stand in the doorway, storyteller! There's work to be done. Hurry up, Seren.' Hilda jumped out of the way, pulling her blanket round her shoulders. Seren stomped out and the other women streamed after her. For the last couple of days they'd been tender with her and asked nothing of her. When they mentioned her journey back to her shattered home settlement, they spoke with delicacy.

This must be an emergency, Hilda thought. With no moon, the only light came from a faint gleam of grey in the sky through the beeches.

Only the occasional swear-word! The men know where to gather their gear – nets, buckets and barrels.

Hilda warmed her hands at the cooking-fire. Feeding it with sticks gave her a job she could understand while Seren stirred porridge and Oswynne shouted instructions. Once the trampling feet disappeared towards the jetty, she could hear blackbirds calling up the dawn.

When it was light, Ursel tapped her on the shoulder. 'Will you help me sort out my speech for the Moot? I've got to tell everybody why I saved the hind, and all about the antler dance. I've not got long to get it straight. Otred can look after the pigs; he's big enough, or thinks he is. Otred? Otred!'

'He's gone to the mere in the boats – he was so proud to tell the men about the fish. Give me a hand with this?' They hauled the oak top of a trestle table out of the store shed. Ursel on one end, Hilda on the other, they carried it to the edge of the cooking place and heaved it up onto its trestles.

'When I've let the pigs out of their pen, I'll have to lead them far away before the men get back with their catch, or the swine will knock over the salting vats and gobble half the fish.' Ursel sat down on the end of a bench and put her head in her hands.

'I'll help you practise your speech another day,' Hilda assured her. 'When will the Moot be – full moon? We've got fourteen days.'

Meg, dragging another bench, shot a look of hatred towards Ursel, now surrounded by snorting pigs. Hilda asked, 'Meg, if I get a chance to tell the next part of my story today, please will you tell it to Ursel later.'

'Meg, fetch Elder Edith, we need all hands,' Oswynne snapped. 'Ursel, get the swine out of here – take them upwind where they won't smell the fish-guts.' Ursel grumbled and the herd grunted as she led them away up the slope into the beech trees.

They'd only just got everything in place when Gaufrid came panting up the track from the jetty pulling the first handcart laden with barrels of fish.

The women worked fast, by feel and habit. They grabbed slithery bodies still alive out of pails, whacked them on the table, opened the bream and smacked them flat. Fish-guts plopped into buckets. When they started to stink, someone slopped the mess into the pigs' trough in their pen. In the vats the layers built up – fish head to tail, a thick layer of salt, more fish.

Oswynne looked round. 'Everybody got a knife? Hilda, stop mangling that fish please and tell us some more of your story about Peony Valley. The young queen and the wise woman were in deep snow, in the hut. Huldran sent off a raven messenger – what next?'

Hilda reached for the story in her memory. *It's not slithering away this time. There you are Huldran, waiting for me. Speaking my own pain must have freed something in me!*

Hilda felt a smile spread warm inside her. She wiped her slimy hands and stood where everyone could see her. 'Can you smell the fresh air of the mountain?

Marelda, with an armful of logs for the fire, sniffed the clean scent of pine needles. Her eye was caught by movement …

A WOMAN SKIED DOWN THE MOUNTAIN

The stranger skied down the steep slope, leaving a track as sharp as a scythe blade. Her blond hair streamed out behind her. Beadwork on her tunic sparkled in the sun. With a whoop and a leap, she slid to a halt by Marelda's feet, showering her with snow crystals. She pulled off a red felt cap patterned with green stars and hearts. 'The air tastes delicious but don't eat it all up!' the girl joked. Her skin was so clear that Marelda saw a vein pulse in her temple.

Marelda snapped her mouth shut and frowned. 'If you've come to see Huldran, she's out and won't be back until sunset. Would you care to wait inside?'

'I'd care for a large meal – whatever you can stew up.' The skier pushed the door open, flopped down and pulled off her boots. She grinned, showing even teeth.

Marelda felt a need to take control. 'I am Marelda, Queen of Peony Valley.' She placed a dish of nuts on the table with stiff formality.

The young woman grinned. 'I'm Ziske, I'll be queen of the Mountain People one day. They've chosen me to be next. I've picked out my husband already but I haven't married him yet. He's telling all his friends. What about you? Married? Children?' She talked with her mouth full and put her feet up on the bench.

Huldran got home and greeted Ziske with a hug. She asked for news of the Mountain People while she shook snow off her snowshoes. Ziske pulled gifts out of her leather backpack: a goats' milk cheese, cloth bags of walnuts and dried herbs, woollen mittens, a jar of small, sour black fruit. 'A trader brought them from the south, said they cure everything.' Ziske laughed and shrugged. Huldran tasted them.

'All for you, dear.' Huldran offered. Marelda sniffed them and drew herself back into her shawl.

'Tomorrow,' Huldran said, putting an arm round each of them, 'you'll be out all day. Ziske, you'll teach Marelda how to ski – I've got spare skis by the door.'

Marelda took Huldran aside to secretly tell her she preferred not to go. A bit later, Ziske whispered privately to Huldran that she'd rather go home than spend a day with this wooden woman, Marelda.

Huldran just smiled and told each of them: 'You will go.'

Seren skewered fish over a cooking-fire and handed them out to the women listening and gutting bream. They licked their fingers and worked on. Children crammed cooked fish into their mouths, spat out bones and dribbled savoury juice. Hilda sharpened knives on the whetstone and passed them back to their owners.

'What is "ski"?' Meg asked.

Hilda told her skis were planks bound to boots with leather thongs. She had seen people sliding upright using them on northern hills. She mimed wobbling and the women chuckled.

They told Hilda how they strapped bones to shoes to skate on the mere when it froze.

'What happened next?' Oswynne was netted in the story.

Hilda went on, 'We learn how to …

Stretch Our Wings Like Swans of Ice and Fly!

Over and over, Marelda got to her feet, gritted her teeth, checked her skis and tried again.

Hilda's hands slid and bumped to show the effort.

'I won't be beaten – not with Ziske watching,' Marelda muttered under her breath. 'I've got snow up my sleeves and down my neck. I've bruised my knees and jarred my elbows but I'm not giving in.'

It cramped Ziske's bones to watch Marelda's awkwardness. She skimmed a circle round the struggling figure. 'Slide your feet; don't try to walk. Keep your weight in the middle.'

Ziske's dancing turns shook Marelda. 'I want that smoothness,' she thought, knowing she would never attain it, and hated it instead.

At the end of the day, they returned to Huldran's house and she greeted them at the door. Her voice cut through the blur of Marelda's weariness. 'Come with me to the Cave of Dreams. The spirits are calling us there for our first night of work together.' It was not a request.

'I can't, I need to sit ...'

The wise woman's arm was warm around Marelda's shoulders as the old one helped her up the crunching snow slope to the cave. 'You've sorted your memories with me through many dark weeks. You spat out fears and found strengths you never suspected. I think you're ready to take a step into the spirit world. When you've worked hard and your body is tired, you may find you can open to meet ... your helper or ... whoever will come.' Huldran took her hands and drew her through the carved doorway.

Marelda and Ziske gasped. Lamplight blossomed on every ledge. Huldran put a log on the fire and pale flames ran along it. She drew white fox furs out of a box and wrapped them round their shoulders. She fastened bone beads round her own throat. Her eyes shone.

'Can you feel it?' she whispered.

The air shivered with spirit-light so clear that it tingled in Marelda's nostrils. She recoiled from it, hunching into the white fur.

Hilda played a ripple of music on her swan-bone flute.

Oswynne tilted her head, closing her eyes to listen. *She's deep inside the cave with Marelda,* Hilda thought.

She went on:

'Ziske, what does cold mean for you?' Huldran asked.

'When the snow drifts up to the eaves, we stay in our lodges and stoke the fire. It's quiet; everybody works – some carving horn, others spinning. I like to think things over by myself. We say

Mother Holly is shaking out her quilt and covering the mountains with feathers.'

Huldran smiled and turned to the young queen who shivered in the shadows. 'What about you, Marelda?' the wise woman asked and sat beside her.

Marelda bit her lip. Choking, she answered. 'When he grabs me and his breath smells of strong drink, I freeze. I ... can't. I pull away. He calls me barren. He curses, I cry.'

'What!' Ziske's voice rang with shock. 'You mean your husband? He can't do that! Why don't you have him thrown out?'

'It's not like that, where Marelda lives,' Huldran explained. 'Her husband would likely call the guards and she'd be the one thrown out.'

'Does he – force you?' Ziske shuddered.

'No ... not really. He has got tenderness in him. It's just buried so deep I only glimpse it when he thinks he's alone. It's never for me. He'll fondle the ears of a hound or a horse, but his hands are rough on my body. As soon as it's over, I roll out of our bed and go to Piroshka, my old nurse. She snores but she makes room for me. After a night like that, he doesn't speak to me for days and weeks.'

'Why do you stay with him?'

'I want to make a baby with him, to bring our peoples together,' Marelda's jaw tightened.

'But if your man is not good to you, why have a baby with him?'

'I have a plan – to bring the folk of Peony Valley and the Plains together, that's my people and his. They're still fighting after all these years and spitting on mixed-blood children. A royal child of mixed parents could unite them. That's what I dream of. Huldran has told me about how queens ruled with mercy and compassion, asking advice from their councillors, at peace with nature. It wasn't so long ago! I see now how my own child could bring back those ways. I want a daughter who can stand proud before all her people and claim both the strength of the Plains horse-people and the wisdom of the Valley as her birthright.' Her eyes filled with tears, her fists clenched. 'Huldran is the only one who can make me well so I can grow a baby.'

'This is an honourable plan, Marelda, though it will be hard for you.' Huldran said.

'You have to sacrifice yourself?' asked Ziske, outraged. 'Set your own joy aside to make this come true?'

'Not necessarily,' Huldran spoke firmly. 'Let's see what can be shaken up, who comes to meet us from the depths. Drum for us, Ziske.' The wise woman beat a rhythm with a seed-head rattle.

Marelda glowered and edged backwards from where she sat. Huldran drew her to her feet, holding both her hands. 'We're with you.' They shook their arms and legs. Marelda felt the tension in her muscles ease. The drumbeats quickened: Huldran stamped. Marelda tapped her toes. Nobody told her to stop being silly, to be quiet. She stamped her foot on the earth; it felt good. A shudder rolled through her body like rocks falling. She kept moving as Huldran encouraged her.

'Earth is my mother. This is my place. I plant my feet on this patch of ground and I belong right here.' Huldran chanted and Ziske joined in. Marelda whispered it then spoke it out loud. Earth spoke back to her through the soles of her feet. Her chest opened. She bent and stretched her knees, her thighs strong as mountains. She decided not to try to dam this surge of strangeness; stones slid off her shoulders, rivers rolled through her frame and burst out in leaps and turns. Ziske drummed and Huldran clapped while shadows on the walls danced with Marelda.

She shouted the words and wept. 'I never knew I had a place, they never told me that. I plant my feet on this patch of ground and I belong right here!' Taps on the drum skin dinned to the rhythm of the words. She leapt and whirled and yelled; her arms sliced out her space.

As if from a distance, Marelda heard Huldran call: 'Look at your hands.'

With a hiss like a fir cone catching fire, snowflakes crackled out of the tips of Marelda's fingers and whirled across the cave. Spirit-thin, they glittered, scattered, vanished. She raised her arms and carved an arc of icy sparks; another; again. She filled the cave with patterns of light. The air began to tremble.

Far off in the root of the mountain, something shifted.

Wingbeats surged out of the depths of dark, towards them. The brilliance of feathers filled the cave. A swan, transparent as ice, filled their vision. She stretched her neck and beat the air with her pinions. Breath fled from their mouths; awe overtook them. The eye that turned to look at each of them met Marelda's eyes, and knew her to the core. She was held by a look as deep as a mountain tarn, edged with gold. The swan's voice rang through Marelda's body, soft as faraway thunder, clear as lightning.

'Have you heard of swan-maidens who choose human husbands, mate with them, and leave when winter calls?' the swan asked. 'They are my children. Do you remember the river-mud figures of you and me merged, which women used to make? You are my daughters; listen to the thrum of the wild in your bones! Like me, you can dive under the surface of troubles to find calm; you can swim unruffled where waves and currents run; you can rise up when you desire the sky. I am glad to fly with you.'

Every nerve tingled in Marelda's skin.

'I'll show you how to ride the tides of trouble,' the swan fluted. 'When life crushes you, rest your cheek on the down of my chest. Breathe in love with each beat of my heart. Stretch your neck high, feel your strength lift you! Spread your wings.'

The three knelt on sheepskins and copied the swan's wings. Ziske moved gracefully, entranced. Huldran moved into the rhythmic stretches with delight. Marelda also watched and followed. Each touched her hands together at her heart, then opened her arms wide and low, breathing in deeply. They touched hands to chest again; spread their arms wide and level, breathed deep. They repeated the movements, arms lifted higher each time.

'Fly over the mountain,' the swan told them. They followed her steady wingbeats and slowed the rhythm of their breath. 'Leave the mud of trouble far below. Clean your lungs with draughts of air. Feel how this takes you out of the din of your mind.'

The women touched their fingertips above their heads, reaching high.

'My arms are wings', Marelda thought. 'Whenever I'm stuck, I can unfurl my swan feathers. I've never felt so strong! Oh, yes I have, when I mounted my mare and rode out of my home. Was I strong all along and never knew it? Now I can breathe myself up and out and over the mountain!'

'You are children of air; drink in the wind,' the swan told them. 'Now, slowly, evenly, glide down to the lake.'

The women lowered their arms as if flying downward, stroke by stroke, eyes closed.

'Water and fire are your home too. The shine on the lake greets you,' the swan chanted. 'Daughters of life, Earth sings because you are here!'

They opened their eyes. The swan had vanished.

Sorrow welled up in Marelda. She reached out her finger to touch one white down feather floating in the air.

'It's for you,' Huldran told her. 'When there's no softness in your life, remember this dance. When you need the swan, she will answer your call.'

Oswynne sighed and Hilda caught a watery gleam in her eye. *Marelda's tears*? she thought.

Geese gabbled in the water meadows as the handcart rumbled back again. More fish.

Oswynne rubbed her face with her sleeve and stood up as Kedric strode over, followed by Evrard and Bertold who were hauling the laden cart.

Headman Kedric clunked tubs down on the table, full of live fish slopping and churning. 'Lazing with stories again, I see. We've been wrestling with wet nets, shoving our boats through mud and mire, so you can sit on benches in the shade.'

Ragnild jumped up, her nose at the level of Headman Kedric's chest, and shouted, 'You think they gut themselves, do you, and lie down themselves in the vats? How do you think we get these raw chapped hands with salt rubbed in the cuts? Lolling about in a punt is the soft work!' *Ragnild shouted at him to defend her daughter, when he beat Ursel. Now she's standing up to him again! Is she getting braver? Are my stories helping?*

'Shut your mouth, sister!' Kedric roared. 'Wife, keep these women in order,' he ordered Oswynne and backed away.

What will Oswynne do? Hilda wondered, trying to catch her eye.

Hilda almost caught a rush of wingbeats as Headman Kedric's wife lifted her chin and stood tall, spreading her arms wide. 'These women work hard. We all do.' Oswynne placed her hands on her hips and said, 'Husband, we have work to do here. Shouting won't gut fish. Seren has cooked food for you men; take it and move out of our way.' Her hand pointed where they should skedaddle to.

Her fingertips sizzled with snowflakes. Hilda glanced at Meg. *She can see them too, judging by the grin she's smothering under her hand.*

Chapter 21

Salt in
a Wound

Oswynne

At last, all the fish were layered and the vats dragged into the cool of the cellar under her house. Oswynne got away by herself to the stream. She avoided the beady eye of Hilda's goddess and knelt among the tender points of rushes to dip her hands. The sticky fish-guts washed away, she laid cool wet hands on her temples and the back of her neck. As the thunder in her head eased, a faint kee-uu! caught her ear.

High above, two buzzards wheeled, calling to each other. They climbed the sky, riding on warm winds.

I want to soar like them! So much of my life I spend paddling muck in the shallows like a teal.

How did the swan movement go? She knelt on the grass and circled her shoulders. *Hands join at breastbone and then stretch wide and you're flying.* In and out, up and up, and her imagination took her over the tall hill and down again to the shine of the mere.

What would her husband say to that? As she slipped off to the weaving hut, she imagined the argument she'd have with Kedric if she ever tried to do anything out of the ordinary.

She took a half-made woven belt out of a basket and sat down to work on it, in delicious silence, alone. She tied one end of the warp threads to the doorpost, the other to her own belt, just taut enough. *So much easier than using a big loom, when you have to rely on somebody working on the other side to get it right!* She chose skeins of wool from her basket, woad blue and weld yellow. She crossed the threads in different ways to make the pattern. Lozenges and diamonds formed under her fingers. The rhythm comforted her as she passed her shuttle back and forth. *Shall I add a zig zag in the middle? Yes, that looks good.* She relished her own skill, the fit of the wooden tools to her hand, the way the threads did not argue or sulk.

Above the open door, last year's swallows' nest clung to the lintel. *They'll be back around Beltane to patch up the nest and fill it with eggs again. Why can't everything be so simple?*

The drift of her thoughts snagged on a memory – what Thane Roger said to Kedric, as he swung up into his saddle, about marrying Ursel to Roger's son Grimbold. *Has Thane Roger talked to Ursel's mother, Ragnild, about it? Has Kedric? Kedric and Ragnild are hardly speaking to each other. If they've discussed it, have they told Ursel? What does Ursel think?*

Ursel's face, still bruised, floated into her mind's eye – pink and shining as she looked at Roger's foster-son. *Isn't he from some important family from over by the coast, the one they choose kings from? What tangle is Ursel getting herself into?*

It's not up to a young girl to decide her own future. How can someone so young understand what's best for a settlement? She's just looking at the man's pretty hair. We know where that leads … Edith's husband with his floppy curls came to mind and she shuddered.

It's wise for older people to choose. That way, we can make sure she gets somebody reliable. It's not likely the royal boy will be interested in her for long; he'll be off to the court at Rendlesham and get caught up in feasting and fighting.

Now Grimbold might be the one. When they loaded up their cart with my well-made blue cloth, and all our food stores, I hated the callous way he thought he could take anything. But he was being helpful to his father, I suppose. He isn't beautiful, but his father makes sure there's always enough to eat and he's secure in his place at Thaneshall. And his teeth are sound, if a bit like a rat's. She could do worse.

Oswynne imagined packing a wagon with linen and pots for the wedding, with Ursel sitting at the front, her face wooden like the prow of a ship. Her mother Ragnild would be weeping.

She knew the wooden feeling of the face like the prow of a boat; it had been hers so often. She was proud to be part of a long line of women following a set path, going to live in a new clearing, setting up home in some wild place without their mothers nearby, bearing children without their sisters to help. The tight bind of this heritage stopped her feeling anything below the throat.

It's my job not to be swayed by feelings but to think clearly about what's best for the settlement!

It would be useful for Wellstowe to have a strong link with Thaneshall. Maybe Roger would go easy on the tribute next time. Kedric would calm down and be easier to manage.

But feelings were beginning to well up inside her.

Would I trade a girl for cheese? For bolts of woven cloth, for a quiet life? Send her off like a hostage? Will they ask my opinion? Kedric thinks I should always agree with him.

These stories Hilda and Edith are telling confuse me. What was Edith suggesting – a moot where everybody talks? The tongues of women pushing matters round and round ... That's what my father used to say!

Shadows fell across the doorway, breaking into her rumination. *Here's Hilda, popping up as she does to ruin the peace and behind her ... Ragnild – last person I want to see right now. Seren – nothing better to do.*

'Not now. I need to concentrate,' she growled.

'We've come to offer you ... friendship,' Hilda said.

Oswynne blinked. 'Don't sully that lovely word. You've come to try to get me to support Elder Edith and her tongue-wagging moot, against Thane Roger. You want me to back Ursel against my husband.' She tied off the threads of her weaving, folded the half-made belt and packed it away. 'Have you got any idea how dangerous this feud is? It could break our community and destroy everything we've worked to build. It's not just me who could get turned out – it could be all of us, children too.'

'I told you,' Ragnild whispered. 'It's best to leave her alone when she's in a mood.'

'I am not in a mood!' Oswynne turned on them. 'You're not listening! This is more important than women's ways or men's ways, old ways or new. If a thane sits in judgment, what's wrong with that, if he's fair and honest? Breaking up a settlement – what could be worse?'

'It wasn't us that started beating young ones – your husband …' Ragnild started.

Hilda turned to face Ragnild, 'Does it still hurt, seeing your daughter's lovely face all bruised?'

'Of course it does!' Ragnild snapped. 'I'd like to give him a smack – Ursel as well! I told her not to annoy him, and what does she do? The worst thing anybody could do when the hunt's on. The trouble is, we depend on him now. If he turns us out … where would we go?' She shivered.

Oswynne looked up from tidying her basket of weaving kit. 'That's what I said. We haven't got any choice; we've got to get along together. If that means putting up with the men-folk spouting rubbish sometimes, what does that matter? Keeping everybody safe – that's what's important.'

Hilda's face screwed up. 'Scary to think about, if you – if we – had to move away.'

Oswynne nodded. 'It would be such a waste, everything I've worked for, for so many years, could get chucked on the midden with yesterday's bones.'

'You've built up the settlement, helped everybody get along …'

'I came here to make peace. If it's thrown away, what's left of me? What's my life been for?'

'Were you a peace-weaver, to settle a quarrel?' Hilda asked.

'Yes, I married Kedric to make a friendship-link between my family and his, after the fight.' Oswynne passed Seren a blanket. 'This is full of moth holes, can you patch it?' She pulled another rug out of the mending pile, looked it over, took shears out of her belt-bag and cut it in half. She pinned the edges together so that the sides were now the middle and began to tack. A slant of sunlight through the doorway lit her work. 'My life is not just entertainment while we work.' Oswynne tucked pins between her lips.

'It can be hard to talk about what happened before,' Hilda offered, picking up a spindle and fleece from a basket. 'If it's painful, and you feel you're not allowed to talk about it, loneliness is like salt in a wound.'

'Salt! That was the start of it,' Oswynne hemmed with quick stitches.

Hilda lifted one eyebrow, asking a question.

Oswynne laid down her work and looked out towards the willows, seeing the bustle of a port settlement long ago, hearing the sea. 'My family lived in Ousemouth. The place was full of traders there for salt, some from Wellstowe, some from the north or across the sea. Father treated me like valuable goods, now that I was grown, so I was never allowed out. I wanted to see everything – the ships at the wharf, cargoes of spices, traders yelling in their foreign tongues. Father was busy making a bargain – salt from his salt pans for amber – Mother was ordering the feast to seal the deal. Not even Seren knew I'd sneaked out.

'The sailors tethered a dog in the middle of a yard. My brother, Torold, brought his favourite bitch, so I had to look, even though I wasn't supposed to. They set the other dogs on the one tied up and made wagers on which one would kill it. I watched from behind a pile of barrels. Teeth ripped its flanks and blood sprayed onto the sand. The snarls and stink made my throat catch. I was scared to push through the crowd in case somebody recognised me – my parents thought I was at home sewing tapestry.

'My brother laid his wager on the pile – a beaver-skin he'd traded last year. North-men passed round a bottle of some strong drink; it made the men roar and swear. My young brother swigged and staggered and retched, but he wanted to be a man among them, so he laughed. He loosed his hound and the sand flew. There was growling and a horrible gurgle. His dog was ripped to bits. My brother went crazy and started pushing people; when somebody told him to cool down, he stuck him with his knife. I struggled to get to him, shouting "Stop" but he couldn't hear me in the din. My heart battered at my ribs, I wanted to cry. The one my brother stabbed was Kedric's uncle. Somebody hit Torold so hard that he spun across the yard and crashed into the beer-table. Fists flailed, blades flashed. I ran for help but, by the time Father got there, only bodies were left. One was Torold, his head at a bad angle, in the dust. I cradled him and talked to him. I think I told him to wake up, everything would be all right, but it wasn't. They dragged me away in the end.

'Father called his war-band. They found the Wellstowe men and skirmished all round Ousemouth. Thatch caught fire, men shouted and slipped on cobbles slick with blood.

'Every night we worked, tending wounded men on the Hall floor. Mother and I ripped up linen and bound up cuts alongside the serving-women. Mother kept her face blank, trying not to feel the loss, busying her hands.

'In the end, the two sides had to talk. They always have to talk in the end … Why don't they start with talking and forget about fighting? We lost so many lovely boys because of that. The two sides walked out, came back, and talked more. They finished by exchanging gifts, including me.'

'You were traded like a bushel of salt?' Hilda frowned.

Oswynne turned her head away. 'Not at all! It's an honourable calling, to make peace between settlements.' She tasted salt on her lip where she'd bitten it. She wiped her face on her sleeve.

'You're like Marelda in my story,' Hilda's voice was gentle, 'using your life and love to bring two peoples together. It must have been hard to leave your home and the freedom to choose your own husband, as well as losing your brother.'

In the night it hurt so much I couldn't sleep. But when I stood before them all dressed in my best, Mother nodding and smiling, so proud of me … Aloud, Oswynne said: 'I thought I'd found my fate, to bring justice and friendship between Wellstowe and Ousemouth – a high calling.'

'What a brave young person you were!'

'I held my head high as we rowed upriver. I still do.'

'Was there any chance you could have said no, if you hadn't liked Kedric?'

Oswynne was silent.

Seren spoke quietly. 'We joked about that when I did your hair, the morning when Headman Kedric came for you. You said he'd have to bring a gold cup as a gift for you – as if a backcountry farmer would have that in his treasure-chest!'

'You two have been close for a long time.' Hilda noted.

Is she trying to make me and Seren talk to each other? Oswynne winced. *We're fine as we are, Storyteller!* 'The bronze cup Kedric brought me is fine workmanship – my brooches too. My father gave me my dowry: a box of salt, a wolf skin bedcover, a yellow cloak with a hood, as well as the large rowing boat we still use. Kedric gave me cows and sheep for my morning-gift after the wedding, and a mare. I was a wealthy woman when I left my father's hall.'

'You created a lasting peace between Wellstowe and Ousemouth.' Hilda took up her spindle again.

'I see what you're doing, Hilda,' Oswynne looked pointedly at her. 'You're trying to bring the women together with kind words, to help us understand each other, so that we stand side by side to fight the rule of thanes and kings and headmen. I can see that, though I don't know if I stand with you. Headmen, thanes and kings are not monsters. People doing what they're told to do is no bad thing. I wish they would! Women's chatter gives me a headache.' Oswynne heard those words in her father's voice and was at once three years old, playing in the rushes on the floor of her father's hall while he stamped past without seeing her.

She stretched and stepped outside the open door. The sun dipped low over the fen: 'Time to cook, Seren.' The blank stare she hated slid over Seren's face.

Hilda was at her elbow. 'Did you ever want something different?'

Her thoughts still in Ousemouth, Oswynne considered. 'I liked the trading. Otter furs coming downriver; chessmen made of walrus tusks from the north; turquoise beads from some hot land. I loved hearing about the places they came from, where rivers of ice fall into the sea, or seas made of sand blow into waves. I liked the patterns that formed when a deal was struck. Men shook hands. Alliances were forged that could last generations. Then if there was greed and men cheated, I noticed how quickly their friendships turned sour.'

'Did they ever let you think you could have done some trading yourself?'

'Me? Girls don't do that sort of thing. They do what they're told.'

Hilda's eyebrows moved up and down. 'Wouldn't it be good if we could do all the things we're capable of!' She grinned in her lopsided way. 'What about Adela?'

'Puffin – my daughter? What do you mean?'

'Is Kedric setting up a marriage for her? Whichever headman offers the most cattle? My stomach twists when I see young girls waving goodbye to their mothers and going to live far away, especially when they're too young for such a pairing. How will you feel about it?'

'Not yet –' Oswynne's heart sank into the ground. 'She's just a child!'

'You'll help her as much as you can, of course. I hope we can open things up for her and her friends – and their daughters and granddaughters. What wonderful things they will do, if we help them grow confident and strong! They won't be treated like merchandise – they'll choose where they live, who they marry, even whether to marry or not and use their talents to create settlements full of laughter.'

Oswynne was back in her father's hall, but standing on a table now, eye to eye with her father and the other merchants. She shook her head and the vision vanished. She ran her fingers through her hair, twisted a strand and pinned it back into place. 'You mean we have a choice. What we do here will echo down through the generations? I can back Edith and the endless hours of tongue-work we'll have to do to come to an agreement at the Moot, or let the headmen rule us and slide into despair alongside other women, all trodden upon and going further and further down. You make it sound easy, but there's danger both ways, as I see it. I'll have to think about it, Hilda.'

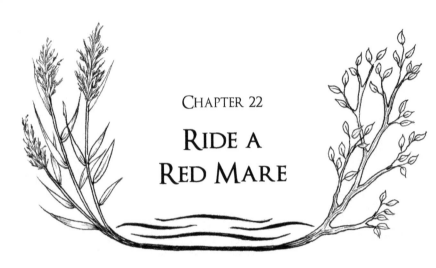

CHAPTER 22

RIDE A RED MARE

MEG

Wind gusted into the sleeping house, whirling smoke around the rafters. Winfrith and Ursel banged the door behind them, grumbling about draughts. They rolled themselves up in blankets and pushed their feet close to the fire.

Huh, thought Meg, *you should try the slaves' corner where the moss always falls out of the cracks, if you want to complain.*

They hadn't even thanked her for telling them the story of the White Swan, and she'd told it as well as she could while they penned up the pigs and geese. She jiggled her foot where she sat on the sleeping platform.

At last everyone was ready.

Hilda placed sticks on the fire, so the flare lit her face. 'Can you handle another deep story tonight?'

There were nods and murmurs of agreement.

Meg watched Hilda. *How does she call in the smell of pine, the glare of snow, with her throat or her hands? When will Hilda show me how to do it?*

Meg was drawn into the story as Hilda started to speak. 'Marelda and Ziske have work to do before they can hear:

Hoof Beats in the Cave of Dreams

One clear morning, they went out to ski. Marelda gritted her teeth, tried again and tumbled hard, winding herself. Her confidence crashed. 'I'm not getting stronger. I've never had to work this hard in my life! Doesn't help to have Ziske peering at me.' She wiped snow from her nose and eyes.

Ziske told her, 'You're thinking too much. Just slide one foot, then the other.'

'It's easy for you! You've been skiing since you could walk,' Marelda snapped.

'Don't they ski, where you come from?'

'The peasants ski, when they have to. We people of the royal household travel by sleigh. We have matched pairs of white horses with plaited manes. When the peasants hear us coming, they scatter into the ditches and bow as we go by.' Her sigh of longing was for the prettiness of the sleigh-ride.

But Ziske took it differently and snorted, 'Where I live, when the queen travels around, people wave and smile and tell her all their problems.'

Marelda would not let another word out of her tensed jaw. She got moving again. Sometimes she stayed upright. By sunset, she was bone-weary.

When Marelda opened her eyes the next morning, in Huldran's house, her shins ached. More rocks waited for her.

She laid her cheek on woven wool – and heard the beat of the spirit-swan's heart in the core of her. She breathed love in softly, remembering the swan saying: 'Daughters of life, Earth sings because you are here.' When she stretched her neck like a swan and opened her arms wide, strength lifted her.

She planted her feet firmly on the ground, lifted her chin and growled the words: 'I'm not going out today', in defiance.

Ziske's jaw dropped in amazement.

Huldran quickly got control of the surprise on her face and smiled. 'Please could you split this pile of logs then?'

Out of sight, Marelda stretched her fingers, hoping for snowflakes. She shook out her wrists and elbows – was that a shimmer? She wielded the axe carefully, as she'd learned to do over the winter months. Fix the blade in the rough-cut end; lift; bang it down and through. Catching a rhythm, her arms swung high over her head. The voice of the spirit-swan rang out in her memory: 'You are my daughters; listen to the thrum of the wild in your bones!' She whacked harder, breathed deeply and grinned as spirit ice-showers sparkled around her. Then, clunk! A cut branch bounced and grazed her knuckle.

'Leave me alone,' she snarled as Ziske came to see why the chopping had stopped. Marelda sucked blood from her hand. 'I don't want you coming to gloat. I can't do anything right, that's what you think! Get away from me!'

She swung a fist in Ziske's direction. Ziske dodged and Marelda went over. She pounded her fists against the rough bark of the house wall, yelling. She hardly noticed when Huldran helped her up.

Huldran brushed snow off Marelda's clothes. She checked Marelda's hand and smeared salve on the cut.

'We've got a nice blaze going now,' the wise woman remarked. 'Just what we need for more spirit work.' She led them into the Cave of Dreams.

The blaze of the fire in the hearth or my rage? Marelda wondered.

Huldran gave them warm sage tea. While they drank, she took a bowl of red earth and scattered it where the firelight lapped at the darkness, singing, 'Spirits of fire, turn your fierce eye on us! We dare to go deep into anger. Don't scorch us; burn away dross. Hold our hands when smoke blinds us.' She turned to the younger women. 'Now you.'

They took a bowl each, smeared ochre on the rock walls and sifted it through their fingers onto the floor.

'Now sit. Tell me what's been happening, one at a time, the other one listen. Marelda first.' Huldran's voice glowed warm as embers.

'She looks down her nose at me ...'

'I do not!'

'Wait! We'll start again. Ziske, you'll get your turn soon. Let Marelda speak now. Marelda, say how you feel – no accusations please. When Ziske looks at you, you feel ...?'

'Squashed. Tiny. I think she's thinking I'm no good, not worth bothering with.'

Ziske's mouth fell open.

Huldran turned to Ziske with a beckoning gesture.

Ziske jumped up. 'You don't know what I'm thinking! Listen to me.'

'We're listening,' Huldran assured her.

'I hate to see a girl fumbling about like that, almost on purpose, not giving herself a chance. I've taught lots of girls to ski; I can help you. I hear my auntie's voice, the one who taught us turns and jumps, shouting, "There's an avalanche coming, what are you going to do? Fall over? No – get out of the way. Could be enemies riding up the hillside, keep your balance, know where your arrows are, keep your wits sharp."'

'I thought you spent the day milking goats and playing with snowballs,' Marelda muttered.

Huldran's laughter took them both by surprise. They couldn't help giggling too. 'How are the ski lessons going?' Huldran asked.

'Trouble with the footwork, but Marelda doesn't give up. She's strong as knotted pine roots. She tenses up and that puts her balance out.'

'So, the squashed feeling – it's real but it doesn't have to stop you learning, Marelda. Where does it come from? Can you remember another time you felt that?'

Marelda looked away into the back of the cave. 'When my husband shouts...' She bit her lip.

'Nobody should shout at you. You deserve respect.' Marelda looked up, astonished to hear Ziske's voice supporting her.

'Does it sound like this?' Huldran pointed her finger and pulled a stern face. 'Blah! Blah-de-blah-rah.'

A small giggle crept out of Marelda's mouth. 'Blah!' she copied. 'Blah-de-blah-blah ...' She was laughing now.

'Stand up and do it!' Huldran drew her to her feet. 'Look, that's him on the floor.' She pointed to a woodlouse creeping past. 'Tell him what you think of him.'

'I'm bigger than you, creepy-crawly! I could stamp on you, and stamp ...' Marelda growled and shouted; wordless yells tore out of her chest. She jumped and roared, waving her fists.

Huldran drummed. 'Keep going! This is why you stretched yourself to the edge of exhaustion, to get here. Let the rage pour out!'

Ziske took up a seed-head rattle. They filled the cave with sound and Marelda danced. Huldran picked up the rhythm of her feet with her frame drum; speeded it up; syncopated ...

Meg watched Hilda's hands jump and twist and saw the shadows on the walls of the cave stamp and leap.

Noise like a whirlwind howled out of the shadows at the back of the cave.

'Here comes your helper, Marelda,' Huldran said quietly. She set down the drum. 'You called her with the din of your heels on the ground, the drum-beat of your heart, the wild light in your eye.' She fastened a cloak round Marelda's shoulders.

Wild neighing rang out. Ziske gasped as a clatter of hooves echoed round them.

The air was full of flying mane, snorts, and the smell of sweat from powerful muscles. A spirit-horse, red as ochre, raced into the cave, bucked and reared and pawed the air.

'Jump on my back, Queen Marelda!' the mare neighed.

Marelda left her body in a trance in the cave while her inner self put her foot in Huldran's cupped hands and clambered up. Ziske drummed and Huldran played her bone flute, as the spirit-horse leaped out of the cave mouth and onto the wind. Over the forest and high above crags they raced. Marelda clung to the horse's mane, her breath freezing in her throat. Clouds whirled by, rain dashed on her skin. Earth fell away below them as they galloped; her stomach dropped with it. She screwed her eyes shut. In a field of stars, they slowed to a trot. The mare's whinny rang out – was she laughing?

'Sit tall, young queen,' the horse told her.

Marelda had found her balance. She and the spirit-horse moved together.

'Listen inside yourself and you will hear my hoof beats. I am your rage; I belong to you! I'll whinny when your moon-time comes: throw open my stable door. You control what we do together. Nudge with your knee if we need to turn. Grip with both knees to slow down. I'll rear and snort when you want me to! Let me loose to destroy fear and greed!'

Marelda tried a trot, then a canter and a gallop. She laughed out loud and her hair streamed behind her. She whooped as they roared through the sky like a comet. Wind whipped clouds around them and she sang without words, revelling in her strength.

The drumbeats slowed, drawing them back into the cave. In spirit, Marelda slid off the mare's back. Huldran showed her how to rub her mount down with straw and give her water to drink.

The mare's warm nose nuzzled her as it faded into the dark. Marelda melted back into her body and rubbed her eyes.

'It won't be easy for anyone to squash you now, Marelda,' Huldran smiled.

As they munched dried peach rings, Marelda asked, 'Do you mean it was my fault? I should stand up for myself and then they can't hurt me?'

'It was never your fault, dear, ever. They should not push you down. '

'What do you mean?'

Huldran lifted a pot of soup into the glowing embers of the hearth fire. As she stirred it, the earthy smell of turnips and parsnips made Marelda's mouth water.

'Next time somebody speaks to you with disgust in their voice, you will know it's that person's pain coming out of their mouth, jagged and sharp.'

'So I should feel sorry for them?'

Huldran ladled out hot soup for them. 'You feel what you feel; it's not for me to tell you. Don't let harsh words hurt you. You know they are not true. Whistle for your spirit-horse! Sit tall. Ride on the power of your anger; use it to cleanse what's filthy, break up what needs to be destroyed, trample your fears. Insist people speak to you with respect. If they don't: gallop away, or yell for help. Do what you need to do, to keep yourself safe. You are precious.'

Her fingertips drew out deep notes from the centre of her frame drum. She began to sing.

Hilda's voice softened to intone Huldran's song as heads nodded in the sleeping house:

Earth Mother moulded red clay in her hands,
Mixed in her moon blood and blew!
Creatures sprang up from the pulse of her heart
Roared and wriggled and flew.

She swung her hips and danced like a snake,
Made woman so strong and so sleek,
She made woman bleed with the turn of the moon,
Our bodies have tides like the sea.

Girls grow to women, the bleeding can bring
Heartache, anger and pain.
In care for each other, we dream with Earth Mother,
Turn blood to a blessing again.

When a new baby rests on her mother's skin
And starts to suckle at breast
She stanches womb blood flow; her mother is safe,
To croon and kiss her and rest.

When death comes to loved ones,
We weep and we sigh. We give grave-goods for the journey.
We sprinkle red ochre to bring them new life
And smear their dear lips with honey.

Redwings are drawn to scarlet on thorn,
They chat and feast on ripe berries.
Embers glow warm in the dark of the night,
We sing and chat and tell stories.

Hilda's face wrinkled into a half-smile as her eyes met Meg's. 'They're all asleep.' The drone of her voice faded into smoke, she pulled her blanket round her and lay down. Meg gazed into the fire.

'Smoor the hearth for me, Meg, will you?' Her mother Seren's voice was quiet. 'I'm covered in children, as usual. Can't move.'

Meg scooped ash from the sides of the sand-box and sprinkled it over the top of the fire, saying the blessing she'd heard her mother repeat so often. She wasn't sure of the meaning of each word, but their weight rolled on her tongue like roasted apples.

'Come and snuggle here, cushla, breath of my heart.' Meg gently moved May's floppy body aside and slid under the rug next to their mother, so warm. 'It will be your turn soon, Meg. You're coming into womanhood. I sewed cloths for you; they're in my bundle. I'll get them for you tomorrow. You know how to tie them, you've seen that often enough.'

'Does moon-bleeding hurt?' Meg's words came in a rush. She didn't know she wanted to ask that, until now.

'It's not like a cut. Sometimes we have grumbling belly-pains, when we haven't had time to rest and take care of ourselves, mostly. Tell me if you do, and I'll get you something warm to hold on your tummy.'

'Do you bleed with the moon, Mam? Does everybody?'

'Sometimes I do, now that May hardly ever runs to me for my milk, and Oswynne's beginning to nurse her own little Hubert more often. Already I have to take care I don't have another baby. Oswynne has started again because she kept giving me Hubert to nurse. The moon doesn't help us so much as we get older and our nurslings come and go. Elder Edith keeps her wise blood inside now, since her hair turned moon-colour.'

'Will you keep your wise blood inside when you're old enough?' Meg wondered sleepily.

'If I'm lucky enough to live that long,' Seren murmured.

Meg rested her head on Seren's chest and fell asleep with her mother stroking her hair.

CHAPTER 23

PIG'S IN
THE HOUSE

MEG

Grunts and squeals came from the pigs in the settlement behind her, and peoples' shouts. Sweat trickled in Meg's armpits as she edged past the hurdle that closed the pathway into Wellstowe between the hedges. It was open now for daytime – but if anyone saw her …

Must keep off the track. If I get sent back, Oswynne will belt me for running off without permission.

She narrowed her mind to getting out quietly. *I could ask,* one part of her said. *Too slow! It's dangerous,* another part said, *I might get a smack for just thinking about going off alone.* Another voice in her mind said, *they're together, Hilda and Ursel, I don't want to see it.* Her legs took no notice of any part of her brain – they ran. Each breath stabbed her chest as she pounded uphill through the hazel coppices. The beeches thinned out further up the slope. *Keep going.* The sun was high in the sky and made her squint. Panic clutched her throat. *What if Ursel says no?*

Can I find the deer-scrape Ursel's always talking about? Haven't been up here for so long … The hinds shelter under the root-mat of the fallen beech, near the barrow, bit further east, not the edge of the forest. Young trees have grown up round it … there! Where are Ursel and Hilda? They'll be hiding, peering down through the lattice of roots into the pit torn out of chalky soil when the beech crashed. I can just about climb over the fallen trunk, if I grip these shoots growing up from it. Ugh, it's slippery with moss! It's hard to see, with the sun in my eyes. Oh, I see legs sticking out of last year's dry beech-leaves. It's them!

Heads together, whispering; Hilda's teaching Ursel – should be me! There's never time for me to ask Hilda all my questions, I always have to scurry and scrub. What I've got to say is nothing, straw in the wind, but Ursel – her voice matters …

In spite of the clamour in her mind, Meg's shins carried her forward. Her foot cracked twigs.

The hind leaped out of the sun-trap and away into a tangle of oak and hawthorn in the direction of Thornthicket, her calf at her heel. The scent of fear hung in the air after their flight.

'Meg, look what you've done. You're such a nuisance!' Ursel yelled, catching sight of Meg.

Meg worked her way round the root mat and scrambled down into the chalky hollow where the deer had sheltered. A few of their hairs floated on the wind. Meg looked up at Ursel and Hilda, still in their pile of leaves above her, half-hidden by roots. With the sun behind her, she did not have to squint now.

'Ursel, you've got to come back right away. Please,' Meg screwed up her face and spoke the thing she'd come to say. 'The pigs have got into Headman Kedric's house and they're wrecking it. Otred tried to get them out but he can't and he's crying. He wanted to do it and be a man like his father – your father, I mean – and Headman Kedric wants to beat him, and Edgar wants –'

Ursel jumped down into the chalky pit beside Meg. 'Don't you dare talk about my father, you little shit-wipe!' she hissed, right in Meg's face, 'Who sent you, anyway?'

Whoa now, said Meg to her spirit-horse, and took a step back, holding her stomach rigid. *This is serious. We have to go steadily, and fast.* 'This is what I came to say: Headman's wife Oswynne went to see Ragnild, your mother, because Headman Kedric and Ragnild aren't talking to each other. They all shouted, and then Oswynne said, "Let me make a bargain with her." So Oswynne talked to Ragnild and they made a deal.'

'What was the bargain, Meg?' Hilda asked, coming round the root tangle to join them.

Meg spoke clearly, making each word as firm as a horse's hoof print. 'Oswynne will support Elder Edith to be in charge of the Moot, and run it her way with all the talking, if Ragnild will ask her daughter Ursel to get the swine out of Oswynne's house. Ragnild said yes, but she doesn't know where you are, so I came to fetch you.'

'I'll stop Uncle Kedric hitting my little brother Otred! What were you saying about Edgar?' Ursel asked over her shoulder as she scrambled up out of the hollow and turned towards the track.

'Edgar's got his spear and he wants to kill the boar ...'

'He wants to kill Yorfor?' Ursel's face drained white as a full moon. She broke into a run towards the settlement.

All the way back to Wellstowe, Meg avoided Hilda's eye. Hilda was talking to her, saying something about Ursel, but Meg could not listen. 'If she makes a mess of her speech at the Moot, Thane Roger will be able to take whatever he wants, whoever he wants ...' Hilda's words fell like pebbles into a pool.

How could Hilda just stand by and let Ursel insult me? This morning's dew glittered in her mind's eye; Hilda and Ursel walking together up the track, heads close; Hilda's voice, helping Ursel; Hilda showing Ursel how to breathe deeply, how to send her voice far. *I want that! It's mine.* Meg's knees galloped as fast as a red horse and left Hilda behind. When she got to the corner of Elder Edith's hall, Meg hung back until Hilda caught up. *Don't want them to notice I've been off in the woods without permission!*

The door crashed open and Ragnild stamped out, shouting. 'My brother had better watch out if he thinks he's going to hurt a hair on the head of any of my children!'

Seren slipped out from behind her with May clinging to her skirt, while Hubert gripped May's skirt.

'I wouldn't mind hiding behind May's skirt myself,' Hilda whispered to Meg. 'If only it was big enough to hide behind.'

Meg could not giggle; her stone heart weighed her down. *You think you can go off with her without telling me,* she thought, *and it's still the same between us? You think I'm going to laugh at your jokes, when I know you're only passing the time with me, the slave, waiting to get back to Headman's niece? She's important; I'm not.*

'Mother, calm down, this is my job, I only came by to find Otred.' Ursel grabbed hold of Ragnild's arm. 'Otty, there you are.' Ursel bent over so her face was level with her little brother's. 'I know you did your best, Father would be proud of you. Wipe your nose and get a bag of acorns. We'll catch Yorfor together.'

'Meg! Where is that girl?' Ragnild's voice was shrill. 'Skiving as usual, daydreaming. Where's Aunt Edith's stick?'

'Didn't you send Meg to find me?' Ursel asked her mother.

Ragnild shook her head. 'Maybe Oswynne sent her.'

Meg ducked into Elder Edith's hall and fished the stick out from under the bed where it always fell. 'Here it is, Elder Edith.' Edith rested her bird-bone elbow on Meg's forearm and pushed herself up with the stick. As she stepped over the threshold, Edith paused and looked the group over.

'I want to see this: the capture of the great boar. It will be sung in stories years hence.'

May and Roslinda hopped like grasshoppers round them, shouting, 'Percession, percession!'

'Shush, May, this is serious.' Meg tried.

'You're right, children. It is a procession,' Edith smiled. 'Lead on, Niece Ragnild and Oswynne, Headman's Wife. Make it snappy!'

In the centre of the group, with all eyes on her as she supported Elder Edith, Meg felt hot.

May went right on skipping, behind Ursel, who led the little group with her hand on her brother's shoulder – Otred clutched a bag of acorns. Ragnild and Oswynne followed, with Edith and Meg. Seren carried Hubert. To add to Meg's embarrassment, Hilda played a merry tune on her pipe as they marched the ten steps to Headman's house.

'I want to watch from a safe distance.' Edith said. 'Meg, fetch me a stool from my hall. Oh, and a rug too.' Meg made her comfortable. 'Sit by me, Meg. Edgar's brandishing his spear and boasting. They've been arguing for a while now, but nothing's happened yet.'

'Yee-ar! I'm going in to spear him. Get ready, Father, he might charge.'

Edgar's trying to be a warrior, bare-chested like that, though he's a year younger than me, thought Meg. *Why's his father letting him try this? Maybe he's proud of him, even though Edgar's skinny as an ash sapling.*

Edgar rushed towards the house. Kedric crouched down, his boar-spear at the ready. Meg held her breath.

'Stop!' Oswynne yelled, running towards them, but Ursel was quicker.

She launched herself at Edgar, head down, and her shoulder rammed into his ribs. He sprawled, winded, and the spear rolled from his grasp.

Oswynne leaped on it and whacked the blunt end sideways against Kedric's spear-shaft, knocking his weapon from his grip.

Meg stood up to see better as Kedric's short, heavy spear rolled away. Hilda pounced on it, brought it to Edith and presented it to her with a playful bow.

Oswynne put her hands on her hips. Meg heard the echo of hoof beats as Headman's Wife pulled herself up to her full height. 'Have you got no sense, husband? That's a good breeding boar! Our Thornthicket neighbours want him at harvest festival, when we've got our new boar from Mereham. Yorfor will give us more fine piglets first, when our sows from last year come into season. His daughters won't be ready for months yet. You've already castrated the last male piglet. If you kill Yorfor, what can we swap to get a new boar?'

'It's breaking things – making a mess,' Kedric muttered, taken aback.

Meg peered through the doorway as crashing noises came from inside. Pots were hitting the floor. The stench made her gag – the boar must be frightened.

'What kind of mess are you planning to make with blood all over the house? Good blood – for making sausage!' Oswynne raged.

Oswynne gripped her fists and her knuckles turned white – *she's holding her anger in check with a red horse's reins!* Meg realised.

Oswynne's voice was taut, loud, controlled. 'How can you think about wasting the countryside's best boar – do you know how much work

225

it takes to make enough food for everybody through the winter? Have you got any idea?'

Edgar picked himself up, limping slightly. 'Let me finish the …' his voice squeaked. He stopped, coughed and started again in as deep a voice as he could muster: 'Let me stop the brute, before he tears the walls down.'

'No, son, your mother's right, we need Yorfor,' Kedric admitted. 'There's only one little male piglet now, since … and he can't breed. If we can't carry on the swapping arrangement, we'll have no herd. Come and take care of the horses. They're nervous with all this noise – hear them?'

Kedric's shoulders drooped as he went towards the stable, kicking turf, his arm around his son's shoulders. Meg had never seen him so deflated.

Otred spread the acorns in front of the door and made a trail leading towards the pigsty. Ursel gently pushed open the house door, crooning love-talk to the boar.

This is what I fetched her for, Meg thought. Pride, and tenderness, and resentment tugged at her throat.

The crashing stopped. A snout appeared.

Ursel scratched between the boar's ears with her gnarled swine-stick. The hackles lowered on his curved back and his black bristles lay flat against his hide. He snorted with pleasure.

Otred joined in, telling Yorfor what a fine fellow he was, stronger than all the others, father of many piglets, even the wild boar were afraid of him. The pig grubbed up Oswynne's mint by the door – found the acorns and snuffled them up. Talking calmly, Ursel and Otred walked with the pig down to the shed, one on either side, and shut him in. Nobody would ever know that it was Meg who brought Ursel back. Everyone gasped with admiration for Ursel. Meg hated Ursel harder.

'Meg, see if there's some hot water somewhere, we'll need a brew.' Seren ordered. 'May, search out Headman's Wife's needles, they're scattered in the muck. Oh, your favourite spindle's broken, Ma'am, what a shame, and your sewing basket's trampled.'

When Meg got back with the tea, Nelda was sweeping, Hilda wielding a shovel, Ragnild had kindled the fire, and outside the door Edith sat on the bench, winding tangled yarn into hanks.

Oswynne cradled her mug of balm tea, her hands shaky. 'My son looked so young – I couldn't help thinking about tusk-gashes on his pale skin.' She shuddered.

Edith nodded. 'On the cusp of manhood – it's a hard time for boys. Remember when Gaufrid and Evrard used to tussle like puppies? Are you alright, dear?'

Oswynne rubbed her elbow. 'The spear-shaft jarred up my arm. So slender, so brave, so – infuriating!'

Edith chuckled.

Meg, on her hands and knees picking shards out of dirt, heard the sound of laughter from a long way away. *This is my life now, picking rubbish out of dung. Not the golden work for me, making the old stories come alive. This is what I'm used to, this is what I'm for, nose in the muck.*

Ursel looked in. 'How bad is it? Oh … I should never have left Otred to look after the herd; he's not big enough yet. He wanted to do it so much! Hilda offered to help me sort out my talk at the Moot, so we went. It's a good thing you sent Meg to get me, Aunt Oswynne, or it would have been worse.'

'I didn't know she'd gone. I expect your mother Ragnild sent her. Now take the other end of this rug, help me shake it out. So much to do …'

Meg found she'd been holding her breath. When her mother called her to the cooking-fire, she went gladly, head down.

As she yanked Aikin's arrow out of a hare, skinned the meat and cut it up, Mother talked. Chopping and stirring, Meg fretted. When would they realise she'd been out without asking? She shivered as her skin remembered the last time Oswynne took a belt to her. *I had to, though; I knew where Ursel was. Nobody else notices. Only me.* That's what she could say – if they gave her a chance to speak – before the beating.

Mother was speaking: 'Give me a hand with these dishes, Meg. I can't carry them all to Elder Edith's hall. You weren't listening, were you? They've gone over there to plan – Ragnild and Edith and Oswynne – they haven't asked me what I think! All the moots I've seen in Ousemouth, all the ancient lore my grandmother gave me, and not a bit of it will they hear. They never think to ask …'

Meg's throat closed down more tightly than ever as she trudged to Elder Edith's hall, head down, trying not to spill hot stew.

Oswynne hardly looked up, even when savoury steam from Seren's ladle wafted to her nose.

Ragnild went right on talking as Seren filled her bowl. 'Do you remember the last Moot we had, about our bull that got into Thornthicket's herd? They spent days arguing about whose calves they were!'

Elder Edith mused. 'I think we can do it differently this time. I'll ask Ursel and Kedric to lay out their sides of the complaint, and then I thought of making a talk-group for the women, mix them up from the different places, another for men. What do you think?' She spoke to Ragnild and Oswynne, head on one side, spoon to her lips. 'Meg, cut the meat up for me, will you?'

'Why the talk-groups?' Oswynne asked.

'We need to hear what everybody has to say, because good thinking arises in unexpected places and people,' Elder Edith replied. A little sparkle in her eye told Meg there was more. Her mother plonked herself down on a stool in the shadows with her bowl. Nobody took any notice of Seren.

Meg avoided her mother's look. *No trouble now, Mother*, she pleaded silently, *I want to hear this.*

'I suppose that will make sure they're all involved and feel as if they've contributed,' Oswynne offered.

Edith snorted. 'Not just feel like that – that is exactly how it will be. We'll use the speaking-staff, as our ancestors did. Did Kedric finish mending it, Oswynne?' Oswynne nodded and Edith continued. 'If we don't respect every person, young and old, woman and man, we're not treating them like children of Earth Mother. We'll miss something vital, a contribution we might never hear if we don't pay attention to everyone's voices. When everybody joins together, what comes out is more than all the bits that go in. Like this stew – the flavour's good because the hare-meat and thyme, onions and carrots blend together. They're better

Marelda tore strips from her linen under-tunic, packed them with snow and bound them tightly round Ziske's swollen ankle. Holding her breath, her lip gripped between her teeth, she dabbed a damp cloth to the gash on Ziske's head.

Huldran drew a silver mirror out of her box and polished it. She saw a glimmer of firelight, a dark head and a blonde one close together. She wrapped the mirror in linen and put it away and smiled. Her plan was working. Marelda's strength had grown to meet the emergency. The storm had blown away the mistrust between the two young women. She pulled out the mirror and looked again – how serious was Ziske's injury? She hadn't planned that!

Ziske opened her eyes, murmuring, 'What … where?'

'Shh! Rest,' Marelda told her. 'You had a fall. We're in a cave. Snow has drifted across the entrance, so we'll stay here tonight.'

'How?'

'I carried you. Do you want to eat?'

Ziske shook her head and winced. 'You – carried me?'

Marelda grinned. 'Don't look so surprised! Phew, you're heavier than I thought. Water?'

Ziske sat up and took a sip. She felt her head and then both legs, exclaiming with pain, 'You did the bandaging?'

'I think it's a sprain, not broken, but there's so much bruising I can't be sure yet. Don't try to walk on it.'

The blizzard howled outside. Far away, Huldran put away her mirror and slept.

Marelda and Ziske shared the dried fruit and rested.

After a while, Ziske propped her head on her elbow and asked, 'You made a big effort for me. I thought you didn't like me.'

Marelda looked away from her, embarrassed. 'I thought about … your hand reaching to help me up. What you said, how I don't give up … how I'm getting stronger all the time. Nobody ever said that about me before. Or noticed.'

'What about when you were young and out playing with other children – didn't they help you?'

Marelda shook her head. 'I wasn't allowed.'

'So what did they teach you?'

'What to say. What not to say. Mostly what not to say and what not to do.'

'How's a kid supposed to learn like that!' Ziske was enraged. 'No wonder you can't do anything – sorry, I mean, er –'

'I watched Piroshka. When people came to her for a bandage or were feeling ill, she let me help. I remembered the herbs she used. I was allowed to sew as well, and weave and spin, of course.'

'But nobody ever said, look at you, so full of life, look at all the things you've learned to do?'

Marelda wrinkled her nose. 'Did they say that to you?'

'Of course!' Ziske propped herself up, groaning a little, 'We children all grew up together, climbing trees and rocks and shouting. If we got stuck, one of the older ones would help and make sure we learned how to work out the way down for next time. Me and my friends, we got into and out of trouble all the time, so we knew who was good at making dens and whose talent was finding excuses. I always had scabs on my knees and elbows.'

'You still do,' Marelda teased. 'When I watched you, so ... free, I hated my own cramped littleness and that made me think I hated you. Will you help me learn?'

'I was trying to. You wouldn't let me!' Ziske's exasperation flowed. 'But ... something changed. Just before I fell, I saw you, your blue cloak. You were speeding along. I was expecting you to go over, but you kept going. I was so surprised, I lost my balance.'

'You fell over because I didn't!' Marelda giggled.

Ziske chuckled. Soon their hoots of laughter echoed round the cave. Marelda's cheeks glowed as red as a peony.

'I don't need two cloaks. I'm warm now.' *Ziske offered the blue one back.*

'Let's share it,' *Marelda suggested, tucking it round their knees, 'You're still white as snow ...'*

Gaufrid stuck his head round the weaving-house door and nodded respectfully to Oswynne. 'We've finished ploughing the barley-strip, Headman Kedric says to tell you it's ready for muck and planting.'

Oswynne sighed. The women laid down their spindles and shuttles and went out to their next tasks, murmuring about the story they'd heard.

A warm breeze blustered as Oswynne stepped over the ploughed land, scattering just the right measure of barley for each stride. Too much and the plants would crowd each other; too little and weeds could bunch in bare patches. Wedged against her hip as close as a baby riding in her belly, the woven rushes cradled next year's life: their bread and beer. It wasn't a baby – her body was empty.

Laughter came from the strip behind her, where Nelda and Keenbur were showing the toddlers how to chase crows.

In the strip over towards the fen, Kedric led the two black oxen while Gaufrid guided the plough. They whistled to the beasts to tell them when to turn and called to each other, intent on the steady progress of the blade.

What will Kedric say when he discovers we've tricked him? She pulled her shawl close round her shoulders and ground her teeth.

Ragnild and Edith weren't around. *No doubt warm in their hall!*

Downhill from where she stood, Hilda, Meg and Seren had their heads together over a barrow of compost.

Would they mind if I joined them? Oswynne stood in the furrows, feeling very alone, then turned back to work, trudging up and down. *Have I ever had a friend? Could I?* She edged closer to them. Usually, she'd have a command to issue, but the words dried in her mouth. The wind threw their talk towards her.

Hilda was explaining: 'Wind-walker – that's the name they used in Peony Valley for people who see under the surface of everyday life. They can feel a person's thoughts moving under their skin like fish in a stream. They smell the wind and know what weather it's bringing. They sing along with the hum of the changing seasons. Sometimes they catch the tune so well they can make the clouds move with their footsteps, as Huldran did. I've heard them called seers, and chant-singers. What's the word in your language, Seren?'

Seren spoke a word softly in her native language, the tongue of the slaves. 'My grandmother told me it means "ones who go through the door".'

Oswynne shivered. She hated doors flapping in the wind. *What might get in?* She hesitated. She wanted to hear more – would they think she was eavesdropping?

Hilda had seen her, but Seren hadn't – she had been bent over the barrow with her back to Oswynne.

Hilda asked Seren, 'Do you – go through the door?'

Meg looked up from scooping and scattering compost and, catching sight of Oswynne, coughed in warning.

Seren whipped round, swift as a snake, dark eyes glaring.

Oswynne took a step back from that look and stumbled on the furrows, spilling the seeds she carried in a puddle. For some reason water got in her eyes as she scrabbled around, picking up handfuls of seeds mixed with mud. *What's wrong with me? I should be angry.*

Hilda squatted down to help her.

Seren seemed frozen. Meg reached for Seren's hand, a sulky scowl on her face.

Hilda looked round. 'I think we got most of the seeds,' she said, straightening up – then, to nobody in particular: 'It's a fine profession, chant-singing, making weather-magic, whatever it's called. Never know when we might need a sudden fog or rainstorm.'

Oswynne looked skyward. Clouds glowered as wind massed them over the fen.

Hilda laughed. 'That's ordinary rain coming! Nobody's called it.' She turned to Seren. 'Can you go through the door and make weather-magic, Seren? Did your grandmother teach you – or Wendreda?'

Words seethed out of Seren, roiling with bitterness. They scorched Oswynne's ears. 'I push on the door and I can feel it opening … Sometimes I see through it, just a crack. I hear voices deep and far as if they're under water, or high and sweet like birdsong. But then somebody always shouts – do this, do that – and I lose it. Then I never find it again.'

That's me: do this, do that, thought Oswynne. *Is that what she thinks of me? Is that all I am to her?* Rage lifted Oswynne up off the ground. She brushed down her tunic and drew herself up. 'I forbid you to ever use this magic. You may not dabble in it – who knows what fearful bogles you could stir up!'

Meg whipped in front of Seren. 'Mother never does any harm. She only heals people! How could you think she would hurt anybody?'

Oswynne's hand rose to slap her. 'Don't you give me that cheek!'

Seren pulled her daughter aside and stepped close to Oswynne. 'It's me you're angry with. Don't take it out on her.' All the birdsong fell silent. There was a bustle of wings into the hedge.

Never had they spoken to her like this before. Oswynne's mouth fell open.

'Look, she's protecting her young,' Hilda spoke softly, urgently, and pointed to the rough turf bordering the field, 'pretending to be injured.' A female lapwing fluttered away from her nest, dragging one wing. Bright baby eyes peered out through fluff in a nest inside a scraped hollow.

A sparrowhawk sliced through the air, talons spread to catch the wing-dragging bird. Meg leapt, Oswynne shouted, Seren waved her arm in the sliver of time before its claws would strike. The hawk swerved aside and was gone.

The mother lapwing scurried back and spread shimmering black wings over her nest.

They looked at each other.

'Am I the hawk?' Oswynne croaked. Before they could reply, she turned and stamped down the hill towards her own house, wiping her nose on her sleeve when they couldn't see her face.

At the edge of the stream, Oswynne's overdress was getting wet to the knee, but she didn't care. A pile of pots waited there for scouring. She grabbed a handful of chalky gravel and scrubbed the inside of one, hard, then rinsed it in the flowing water and set it on the bank. *Don't want any mouldy last-year's grain to spoil the new season's harvest. Hope we get a good one.* She took another pot from the pile. *The way they looked at me!* She scrubbed fast, arm-muscles straining. *I spend my life keeping everybody safe, and this is the thanks I get! I could have been a slug in the cabbage, how they curled up their lips at me.*

Hilda slid down the bank, empty bucket on her shoulder.

And now the storyteller's coming to scold me, no doubt!

Hilda sat down beside her. 'Did I ever tell you about the time when a squirrel bit my thumb?'

'What?'

'I was sleeping in a hollow under some dead leaves and I woke up to find it running over my head. Its feet got stuck in my hair. I reached up to get it off and it bit me. Really hurt! You can still see the scar.' She waved her thumb towards Oswynne.

'Why are you telling me this?'

'No reason. What's that poor pot done to upset you?'

'The way she looked at me! I'm not a sparrowhawk. I'm not going to … steal her babies. I give them all bread and a warm place to sleep at night! Why won't she be my friend?'

Hilda spluttered.

'What's the matter? Have you got a cough?'

The storyteller leaned back and gazed at Oswynne with a smile. Hilda's eyes wrinkled with kindness, but they pierced right through Oswynne.

Oswynne turned away and stacked her pots neatly.

'Headman's Wife, your hands are raw.' Hilda took Oswynne's hands and held them as if they were baby chicks.

'I'll be fine.'

'Tell me about Seren. Why is it hard for you to be her friend?'

'We grew up together but there's always a part of her I can't reach. She keeps her feelings hidden from me, won't let me near. When she blanks her eyes, anything could be going on behind them. I don't know what she's thinking.'

'That must be scary. When you were little, what did they tell you about slaves?'

'My grandfather said, you can't trust any of them. Always plotting behind our backs in that singsong language of theirs. They aren't quite human, not like the rest of us. That's what he said.'

'Did you believe him?'

'Ousemouth was always full of slaves trying to get away, if they got hold of a dagger, there'd be murders, and thieving too, of course.'

'I see. Tell me about your grandfather.'

'He was the only one who had time for me, with my parents so busy. He told me tales by the fireside.'

'He sounds lovely! It's possible he may have been wrong about some things. Has Seren ever stolen anything?'

'No.'

'Or tried to get away?'

'Not that I know of.'

'Do you think she's human, like us? If not, why do you let her look after your children? Perhaps we need to check some of the things you were told when you were growing up. Rigid old ideas can block the light, like stiff shutters. It's good to give them a rattle from time to time.'

'My grandfather was wise! How could he be wrong?'

'I think you know Seren well.'

'Yes, but –'

'There's more? Tell me.'

'You want me to go against my own people! I can't stand … naked, out in the cold, alone.'

'I want you to know what you think, your inner self that you've been since you were a child, the real part.'

The stream gurgled as it flowed. They sat so still that a wren came down to drink.

'When Seren mutters to her goddess, I don't know what it means.'

'It's frightening for you, because you can't understand her.'

'There's smoke in her voice when she talks in that other language. She's far away from me,' Oswynne shivered, 'and it sounds dark.'

'Ah, dark.' Hilda sucked her lips in. After a while, she said, 'I've got more to tell about Ziske and Marelda. Please come to the women's sleeping house tonight.'

'I don't know if I want to.'

Hilda looked up. 'You sounded like Marelda just then, in her falling down stages. I think of you being more like Ziske.'

'Me, like Ziske? How?'

'When you decide to do something, you make it happen as brisk as a skier on a mountainside. In fact, I take some of Ziske's strength from you.'

'What do you mean?'

'I have the outline of the story, but it changes every time I tell it depending on the people I meet. When you took charge of planning the Moot, I saw Ziske's courage in you.'

When I plunged into sending the messages, I felt alive like Ziske, Oswynne thought. To Hilda, she said, 'I'd like to have Ziske as a friend. She's not afraid of anything!'

'Oh she is frightened sometimes. She gets on and does it anyway – just as you do. Come and hear more about her tonight. Perhaps you may get to know Seren better, too.'

Meg appeared at the top of the bank.

How long has she been listening? Oswynne wondered.

Meg spoke to her directly, 'Mother says the chickens are laying again at last and she's making griddlecakes so everyone can have a share of the eggs. She asks please will you come and share them out?'

CHAPTER 25

PATTERNS
IN THE DARK

HILDA

A bat swooped down to sip a drop of water from the spring, the fur of its round body lit golden by a ray of setting sun. Hilda straightened her aching back, set down a bucket on the grass and scanned the sky. Seren looked up from scraping the griddle – her gaze led Hilda's high and south of sunset, where blue faded into violet. There it was – the first thin sliver of moon. Hilda lifted her arms and began a chant in her old language.

'Shush!' Seren grabbed her arm. 'Not so loud, they'll hear.'

Meg twisted her face. 'Headman's Wife Oswynne clouts us if she hears us greet the moon. You've heard her scold Mother about old gods – she calls them dark spirits. I think she's afraid.'

Hilda continued the song quietly and Seren joined in, under her breath. Meg watched and mouthed a chorus, the only part she knew. Hilda put a hand on Meg's shoulder and told her the words, repeating them until she got them all. Seren gripped her hand briefly.

'My tongue's tingling with story. Get everyone settled in the sleeping house, I need them all to hear this part.' Hilda shivered. *The myth I'm giving them tonight is deep like the sky beyond the sharpening moon. Dear goddess Neath, please help me tell it well!*

In the sleeping house, peat smoke wreathed the rafters. Hilda looked round to gather the women. They shuffled, settled, turned to listen.

'Can you walk, Ziske? Lean on Marelda.'

Huldran led them to the Cave of Dreams. 'Tonight our work will be ...

Painting Beads: Red, White and Black

In the quiet place inside the mountain, Ziske was glad to put her foot up – Marelda's poultice had drawn out the swelling, but her ankle hurt and her whole body ached from the bumpy sled-ride home from the mountain. She felt shamed to be dragged like a log by Huldran and Marelda, but their teasing was kind.

Huldran lit lamps and stirred the fire. From a box she brought out wooden beads, squirrel-hair brushes and pots of colour. 'Paint some of these beads red, some white and some black.'

'Oh, moon-necklaces,' Ziske took a handful of beads. 'I've got mine in my pouch. I added the beads we made when I came here before, Huldran, into the necklace my mother gave me when I had my first bleed. What's yours like, Marelda?'

'I ... I've got lots of necklaces, but what's this about the moon?'

'Did nobody give you red beads when your first moon-blood came? Or help you string beads to remember the pattern of your days through the month?' Ziske's mouth opened in shock.

'That's what we're doing now,' Huldran put in.

'So what did they do, to celebrate your growth out of girlhood?' Ziske persisted.

Marelda looked down at her feet. 'We shouldn't talk about it; it's shameful. Piroshka told me to make sure nobody sees. That's all.'

'You shouldn't be ashamed! They should be proud and welcome you as a woman and tell you how beautiful you are and make a feast and ...'

'It's not my fault. Why are you shouting at me?'

'Sorry, I didn't mean to yell.'

'Let's paint them now. Before we start a baby, there's often a pattern that follows the moon,' Huldran smiled. 'The beads will help you get to know your own rhythm, Marelda, as you string one each day. We all know the red days – one red bead for each day of bleeding. Have you noticed the fine rage that can come with it?'

They nodded. Ziske painted quickly, coating beads and setting them to dry. Marelda held her tongue between her teeth and used the tip of the brush to make delicate swirls.

'Harness that red mare – her strength can rid the world of wrongs.'

Marelda outlined a rearing horse on one bead, hooves pounding the air. Ziske looked in amazement. 'Oh, will you do one for me?'

'When the bleeding stops, have you noticed a thick, white goo?' Huldran asked.

Ziske nodded. Marelda looked confused. 'When our bodies make this barrier in the neck of the womb, nothing can get through – so even if the man-seed is there, it can't make a baby. Thick white is there for a few days each month. Then, we have a time of outward flowing, when you can sail out on your journey through this world and makes links with friends. That's the time to carve a space for your own work.'

Marelda drew a swan wing on a white bead and fringed it with feathers.

'When we're ripe inside, our bodies make clear, stretchy stuff to draw the man-seed in.' Huldran rolled rock-crystal beads into the palm of her hand from a drawstring bag. 'Here, take some.'

Marelda reached out and took a bead. 'Is there only one day in the month when I can start a baby?' She held it up with her fingertips, turning it to catch the light.

'No – more than that! Man-seed can live for days if it finds the welcoming slippery wetness. But the white will stop it when you take your own space.'

'Do you mean …' Marelda wrestled with the idea, 'Women can choose to make a baby – or not? What if the man doesn't agree?'

'They have to work that out, the two of them. But if the woman knows her body, she has power.'

'What about the black beads?'

'Those are for the days before the bleeding starts when we turn inwards. Darkness calls and our whole self longs to rest in its warmth. If we make a place in our lives to honour ourselves as women, we can grow dreams that nourish us then. If we're beset with busyness, we get headaches and snap. It's a fine thing to help each other take time when we need it.'

Marelda asked, 'Can we start babies then?'

'We often find we don't want to be touched during those times – the inner life is so rich, we need to look deep inside. But if a woman does choose to enfold a man, she may find love ripples through her like a snake swimming in a river. There will be no baby – unless there's some of that slippery stretchy stuff that she hasn't noticed.'

'Is it the same every month?'

'It changes after a baby's born. Once the breasts start their work, thick white in the mother's body keeps them both safe from another baby for a while. When the little one needs the mother less intensely, the rhythm starts again. When we're feeding more babies, patterns come and go. We may get to a time of no mothering, before we change. Use that time to throw off your bridle, snort and kick over what you want gone! Flex your wings and fly! At last we keep our wise blood inside and hope for rest. You'll learn to run your beads through your fingers and notice what's happening day by day,' Huldran replied.

'It's like the steps of a dance. Does everybody go through this pattern?'

'Everybody's slightly different – so you have to learn your own body's ways. It's good if you've got a knowledgeable woman to answer your questions. Ziske will help you. Now, my dears,' she took a deep breath and stretched, 'put out the lights. Let's sit in darkness. Listen to your breath, your heart, your thoughts.'

Outside the oak door, the wind wailed.

'It sounds like fierce creatures coming to destroy us.' Marelda hugged her knees.

'It's good to feel afraid of a hungry animal! You may meet a human animal who is so hungry for love that they're trapped and can't find it,' Huldran said. 'Fear makes us take care of ourselves. If we're scared by the wild feelings inside us – we can listen to their roar and learn their language.'

Ziske shivered. 'I don't like it. It reminds me of the blackness I saw when I fell and hit my head. I thought I was dead.'

'Our lives whirl away like thistledown.' Huldran's words drifted deep into the cavern. 'We shout with joy and shriek with pain – and then we're gone. When we step through the door of death, who knows what we shall find? Will it be gentle Hel to welcome us, with a horn of mead in her hands? She's queen of the misty lands of the dead; and she is old Mother Holly, who shakes out her feather bed to make snow fly in winter, so the earth can sleep. Or will it be ... the dark?'

Hilda breathed out a slow sigh and sat for a long moment in silence.

The women in the hut began to stir and Ursel asked, 'Hilda, did you get moon-beads when you became a woman?'

'No, my second mother was too ill by the time I came of age. We just barely kept alive. It was a sad time for me. I missed my real mother.' A bleak feeling swept over her. She set her grief aside for another time and asked, 'Oswynne, did you have a celebration when you first came on?'

Oswynne's voice was smaller than usual. 'When I told my mother, she looked up from her sewing and said, "I see," then turned away with a look of disgust on her face. So I went to find Seren and she showed me how to tie the cloths. She's a couple of years older than me, so she knew.'

'Seren, what about you?' Hilda asked.

'I looked after her, of course,' Seren replied, surprised.

'No, I mean, did you have a ritual or a party for starting your moon-cycle?'

Hilda could almost hear Seren thinking what to say, to avoid getting herself into trouble. 'Nana took me down to the beach and told me to listen to the tides as they rolled in. She said if ever I had pains with my bleeding, to put my hands on my belly and remember the sound of the waves. She hadn't got anything else to give me; we had nothing.'

Ursel said, 'I've never heard of a special necklace before. I like the idea. Have you got one, Mother?'

Ragnild pushed the blanket down and sat up. 'Wendreda gave me something when I was at her place, when I was so sick – a little carving of a moon. I don't know if I've still got it, maybe at the bottom of my clothes chest. She didn't really explain it to me, or maybe I didn't listen.'

'There's a lot of that about: not listening,' Edith observed.

Ragnild looked worried. 'Do you mean me, Aunt Edith?'

'I mean everybody. I tried to get the antler dance back, with all the preparation for adulthood that goes with it, but nobody listened. Part of the learning for it was a moon story, and making a token. I'm too old for that now … too tired.'

'Some of us are listening,' Hilda said.

There was only muttering in reply as Edith and the others settled into sleep.

Hilda lay awake, thinking.

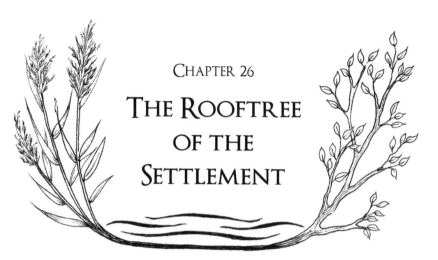

CHAPTER 26

THE ROOFTREE OF THE SETTLEMENT

HILDA

At first light, Oswynne and Seren began arguing. Even planting vegetables up on the end-strip, still they niggled and nagged.

Hilda straightened up from her work and watched cloud-shadows chase the wind across the fen. *Oswynne's worried: is Edgar safe? Have the messengers said the right thing? She bickers with Seren when she's tense. So many times I've tried to get them to open up to each other, but they resist or edge away.* Hilda stuck close to them. *If I can't get them to stop, they'll wreck the Moot with their snarling. We need calm; we're trying to create peace. Think, Hilda, think!*

Meg buzzed at her. 'Hilda, can we play the three words game? I've got one: fly!'

'Wasp, bug.' Hilda responded, looking from Seren to Oswynne.

Meg tried again. 'Now you do one!'

'Go away,' Hilda said, without thinking.

'Escape, run off … Oh.' Meg's mouth dropped. 'Did you mean it?'

'Your turn,' Hilda said brightly, wishing she could suck back the words she just said. They went on playing, but she could feel Meg watching her with a crease between her dark eyebrows.

'Meg, bring that bundle of hazel wands over. Fix this broken bit of fence between the apple tree and the plum,' Oswynne ordered. 'Did you hear me? Stop chatting to Hilda. She's trying to make a support for the peas; she doesn't need you bothering her. Seren, wheel the barrow over here. We need more manure in this corner.'

May and Roslinda brought bread and weak ale for them, then played leap-frog and giggled so loudly that Oswynne shouted at them.

Hilda grasped at the chance to get Seren and Oswynne alone together. 'Could Meg find Ursel and take over her job herding the swine this afternoon? I need to work more with Ursel, to help her sort out what to say at the Moot,' Hilda said.

'Meg – off you go,' Oswynne commanded. Meg trudged off, her face tight.

Hilda only had a short time to work with the two of them on their own. She pushed the sight of Meg's hurt glance aside; she could talk to her later. 'Let's shelter in the hedge-corner. I feel rain.'

It was only a few drops, but they were glad to take a break. They sat on the ground, thick hawthorn studded with plum blossom keeping the shower off their heads.

'How did you do Oswynne's hair that day when Kedric came to fetch her as his bride?' Hilda asked Seren with a smile.

'I used her new ivory pins, traded all the way from some icy place where the seals have tusks. Walrus – that's what they're called. Why do you ask?'

'I'd like to know what it was like for you when you first travelled here,' Hilda said, thinking: *I want Oswynne to understand how much you give her, day after day.* 'What did you say when they asked you to go with Oswynne to this new place, Wellstowe?'

'They never asked me what I wanted to do! I was told to go. Me and my man Drem and baby Meg. We were sent here, like the bags.'

'That wasn't my fault!' Oswynne protested, cheeks flushing. 'Did you want to stay in Ousemouth?' she asked, surprise in her voice.

Seren thought a while. 'Nana died before Meg was born, and my brothers went off to sea, so there was nobody close to say goodbye to. No, I wouldn't have left you to go alone. You needed me.'

Hilda turned to Oswynne, 'What would it have been like here without Seren?' She was not expecting an answer, just planting seeds. 'Tell me about the journey, Seren.'

'We'd never been so far upriver.' Seren looked across the fen, remembering. 'We were in the front boat, with Kedric and some rowers, then came a boat of Wellstowe men. Oswynne's father's reeve came in another small boat. What was his name?'

Oswynne drew it out of her memory. 'Edbald. He used to give me treats when he came to see Father, when I was little – sometimes samphire from the saltmarsh, or a bunch of lavender. He came with us upriver to make sure the wedding feast was fitting and the morning-gift cows were healthy and to check the sheep's feet and count the mare's teeth.'

'I was glad he was there,' Seren added. 'It was scary when the creeks we knew rippled away in our wake and the roar of the sea fell behind us. I wasn't used to sitting still for so long. I had Meg on my chest in a shawl. When she fidgeted I took a turn at the oars with Drem and the rhythm soothed her. There was a place where trees crowded right down to the bank of the river on both sides, so we couldn't see past. Noises came out of the shadows – horrible laughter, a screech. I looked around for otherworld beings, but there was only a bird that looked like a dragon, green with a fire-red head. Another one disappeared into the woods – with a flash of blue. I learned their names – woodpecker, jay. I've got used to them now. Then the booming started in the sedge. We shivered on the damp riverbank all night, terrified. In the morning, the Wellstowe men laughed. "Bittern," they said, and showed us a speckled bird as it whirred past. Whenever I roast one now, I think about that night.'

'How long did the journey take?' Hilda asked Seren.

'A few days, but it felt like forever. We pushed through miles of reeds and it felt like the sky weighed us down. I got used to the squawk and quack from the flocks of fowl, but every time a fish splashed, I jumped. The last morning of our river-journey, everything was still. Clouds covered the sky, so we couldn't see the sunrise. It was hard to say what was pool and what was river. Water stretched as far as we could see – clear dark brown. Mist wreathed up from the surface. I hardly dared speak, the air was so thick with spirits. All the dead of the place came down to peer at us newcomers. That's how it felt. We whispered, everything was so hushed.'

Hilda looked out of the corner of her eye at Oswynne's face, full of memories.

Seren went on, 'I asked where we were. "The mere," they said, shrugging. Somebody passed me a shawl, even though it was warm, and I wondered why. Then the gnats came down, buzzing. We wrapped every part of ourselves, just leaving a slit for our eyes. But they bit us anyway – on our eyelids, fingertips, even under our clothes. The itch, ooh ...' Seren shivered.

'I felt sorry for Edbald, the reeve,' Oswynne put in. 'He got the worst of it. He was stout and getting on a bit. His face swelled up all red and puffy from the midges. He finished his job and scooted off as fast as he could, after.'

'What was it like, coming to this place as strangers?' Hilda asked.

Seren replied, 'We did our best to fit in. Then Drem fell sick with the four-day fever. At first, he seemed to get better, and I thought my remedies were working. I tried everything Nana told me, and everything I could find out from the women here – mint boiled up to bathe him with, sweet gale with willow bark brew to drink ... but even mugwort couldn't save him. That was the first time I used poppy – it helped a little. But the fever the elves sent was too strong for me; it took him.'

'He died?'

She choked with tears. 'I couldn't save him – my hand-fasted husband: Meg's father.'

'Such a lot you lost, Seren, to help Oswynne with her peace-weaving.' Hilda's tone was gentle.

Oswynne bit her lip.

'Ah, but she lost so much, too,' Seren said, looking kindly at her old friend, 'Your mother died the year after and we never knew, not until months later. It was so hard for you. I heard you crying in the night.'

Oswynne looked away, her eyes welling.

'You missed the chance to marry whoever you fancied. I think you had your eye on that walrus-ivory trader.' A note of mischief in Seren's voice jerked Oswynne into laughter.

'I did not! He stank of blubber!'

They both giggled.

In Hilda's mind, two snakes twined together. They hissed and spat at each other, then lay down in the sun. She rubbed her forehead. *What next?*

'I didn't know it was so hard for you, Seren, coming here,' Oswynne muttered, fiddling with a twig. 'When Edgar was born, I didn't know what to do. You rubbed my back and when I thought I was going to die, you told me, "Not long now." I always remember that.'

'He wasn't so bad coming. Elstan was the worst,' Seren spoke softly. 'Your life nearly flooded away with blood. I gave you a mix of rye with dream-mould on it; I thought I'd given you too much, as it made you wild all day, but it stanched the bleeding. I had to feed Elstan until you stopped shaking. We nearly forgot about him, poor little one. He had to cry to make us remember him!'

'You saved him as well as me.'

'I wouldn't let the dark goddess take you, then or now! We've got more days together first.'

Hilda's breath moved softly over her tongue. She dared make no sound to disturb them.

Over on the far side of the settlement – movement caught her eye. Bright brown hair was waving like a flag in the wind. It was Ursel jogging down the track between beech trees.

They hadn't got long, so Hilda pushed a little: 'Oswynne, you stopped Thane Roger from touching Seren – why did you do that?'

'Of course I did!'

Seren ventured a question. 'Was it because I'm something that belongs to you?'

'What, like damaging my goods? No! I would never let him hurt you. I care about you!'

Hilda nudged a little more. 'Seren, when you feed Oswynne's children, is it because you might get a slap if you don't?'

'No. I feed them because they need it. Sometimes it's a chore when I'm busy cooking and sometimes I wish you would hold them more yourself, Oswynne. But then they latch on to me, I get that sleepy feeling and I can't help loving them. When you were little and I was not much bigger, I used to cuddle you to sleep.'

'My own mother didn't look after me as much as you did, Seren. She was always busy. You were always there.'

'You were all chubby. Even though I was only a little bit taller myself, I used to carry you around – drag you, more like!'

'I've always been a burden for you.'

'No. Well, yes, sometimes. Sometimes I help you because I have to and sometimes I want to help you because I see what you're doing and it's good, and sometimes – because there's a warm place in my heart for you.'

Hilda spread her hands wide and spoke to them both, 'Your friendship is the rooftree of this settlement, as strong as the giant oak trunk that holds up the roof of the Hall.' Her voice was quiet, but she made the words ring like pebbles dropped on stone. 'We don't see how women's friendship holds a settlement together, just like we never think about the rafter, even while we rig the cauldron-chain around it to make stew for everyone.'

Ursel waved to her as she went inside Elder Edith's hall. 'I've got work to do with Ursel,' Hilda said. She smiled at them both, wiped her eyes, and turned towards the next thing.

CHAPTER 27

FIERCE AND DELICATE, DEEP AND WARM

HILDA

After a long afternoon trying to help Ursel with her talk for the Moot, Hilda stopped feeling clever. They stood either side of the loom in Elder Edith's hall and passed the shuttle back and forth. *Can we weave Ursel's tangle of words into some kind of pattern like the threads of this cloth?* Hilda wondered. *If we can't get the argument clear, nobody at the Moot will understand what she's talking about. I don't myself. She goes round and round in circles …* Hilda pushed down the wooden baton, to firm the rows of weaving. She tried to hide her face from Ursel, and from the group of women spinning by the fire. Hilda felt wide open after witnessing Seren and Oswynne's new gentleness. *If I cry with disappointment, that's not going to help Ursel,* she thought.

Ursel noticed anyway and wrinkled her neat nose. 'I'm not doing very well, am I? It's hard thinking about speaking in front of everybody, with them all looking at me.'

'There are so many threads and I can't see how they fit together.' Hilda scratched her scalp. 'You'll have to explain it to people who understand even less than I do. I can see that it's not just you and your uncle Kedric – it's about how he treats women, and how thanes and headmen, everywhere, treat women. I see their rule of the fist growing stronger as I travel around. I'm glad you're bringing it out. Then there's the forest and the hind, and that's important, too, and the hind is a female so that part hangs together. If you get angry and start raging at Kedric, nobody's going to listen to you. It's off-putting. They'll start worrying about whether he's going to punish you again or punish them for listening. Then there's the antler dance – how does that fit in? We need to know why all of this is so vital, and not be put off by your frustration.'

Ursel rubbed her face in misery. 'I'm doing my best!'

'I know you are. We're both tired. Let's take a break and come back to it tomorrow. My fingers are too cold for weaving, anyway.'

'Come and sit by the fire,' Edith called. 'Ursel, you can sit with your mother, if you move up a bit Ragnild dear. Hilda, there's room for you on the mask-box next to Seren. There are spindles and wool in the basket. Help yourselves when your fingers can work again.'

'Mask-box?' Hilda asked.

Ursel poked the fire and it flickered into life.

Elder Edith wrinkled her brows into furrows brown as ploughed earth. 'They're for the antler dance, that we haven't done for so long. I hid the horned mask in the box when Roger's men came sniffing round for valuables. Our animal ancestors are there, waiting for us to wake them.'

Hilda gazed into the fire, seeing feathers in the flames. *Something Seren said – what was it? About the place where she grew up, where the great river flows into the sea* ... 'Seren, you said something once about a moot your tribe held, long ago. Your Nana remembered it. Where they used masks. Tell us about it!'

Seren looked over to Oswynne, who nodded permission.

'It was when our tribe held the saltpans and traded with sailors from across the North Sea. Ousemouth prospered so they needed to build another jetty to cope with more boats coming in. They couldn't decide where to dig into the mud for the struts. The best place to catch the current was right where the little terns nested. They called a moot to talk it through. The sailors got together to tell their side of the debate; the saltpan workers, too; and the builders and the traders. Then in swooped a flock of terns, with their high-pitched piping and white plumage. They were people in masks and feather-cloaks, but they called and moved just like real birds – fast and fierce and delicate.' Seren raised herself onto tiptoes and spread her arms. Breathing hard, she went on. 'They told how there's only one place where they can make their nests – they need open beach with small sand dunes, nothing to disturb their chicks, and plenty of sand eels. Those people wore the tern masks and cloaks from our ceremonies.'

Hilda caught a look passing between Seren and Oswynne – and Oswynne nodded encouragement. *Did I do that?* She allowed herself to feel a glow.

Seren continued, 'The spirit of the terns moved them to speak out for the wild creatures.'

'Remarkable. Did it work?' Elder Edith asked.

'The moot discussed some more and agreed to find a different site for the new jetty, far away from the nesting beach. The little terns are still there – I used to love watching them shoot along like arrows, then dive into the waves and catch a fish in one swoop. After that, every time our folk held a moot, they cast around to find who would speak for the wild. One time a group of seals came bobbing in to make sure their sandbank didn't get dug out. I would've loved to see that!'

Edith nodded to Seren and smiled. 'You have a lot of wisdom; will you take part in our Moot, Seren?'

Seren went pink. Hilda could almost hear her thoughts: *About time! Of course!* But Seren said only, 'Yes.'

Oswynne gasped. Her fists clenched and unclenched, as if unsure whether to slap her slave. She rubbed her temples, closed her eyes, then opened them and gazed up at the rafters. 'Hilda pointed out to us both – our friendship is the rooftree of this settlement. Seren and I have travelled a long way together. Yes. Seren shall be included in the Moot.'

Seren stood up straight and folded her hands in front of her apron. 'Elder Edith, Ma'am, everyone, thank you. My Meg should speak too, she's growing up,' she dared.

Edith nodded again. 'Yes, the young should take part, not just the creaky-kneed ones like me.'

Seren was still on her feet. She cleared her throat. 'The wisdom I can share is not mine. It belongs to my people, the native British who were here first. I think we should also invite the other slaves to speak and take part, all of us.'

Elder Edith stared down Ragnild, to quell any objections. 'We need all the wisdom we can get, from whatever source. The slaves shall have a voice.'

The chat brightened as they planned details of food preparation, tents, bedding ...

'I still haven't found the story I need for the Moot,' Hilda fretted to Seren, 'the one that ties it all together, with the woman in a rowanberry-red gown.'

Seren stood straight as an ash sapling after her talk with Edith. 'Come down to the spring with me.' Seren smiled a little and handed Hilda a bucket.

At dusk, the weary, mud-stained messengers arrived back from Mereham and Thornthicket. Yes, they'd got there and spoken the message, they grunted between mouthfuls of broth. Yes, everyone was coming. They rolled into their blankets in the men's house and sleep felled them. Hilda saw Oswynne and Ragnild exchange a look of satisfaction, swiftly hidden.

'I have a deep story for you all tonight, come to the women's sleeping house,' Hilda invited everyone she could find. They were all there at last, with peat smoke drifting into the thatch. 'They are still in the Cave of Dreams. This is where they meet ...

Dark Goddess Bear

Scratch, scratch at the door – the noise woke them. Ziske and Marelda sat up, breathless, and looked at each other.

Huldran, still lying down, called quietly, 'Open the door and let her in. It is our Dark Mother, who can help us.'

A huge bear shuffled into the cave. The air shimmered with spirit as she snuffed them in turn. Her claws rasped on the stone floor and Ziske shuddered.

Marelda pressed herself into the shadows, shielding her soft body from those teeth, as long as knives.

'No need for fear, little ones,' the bear growled, 'I love you with the heart of all the mothers who ever lived or ever will. You came out of me – all things come out of my body.'

'Brush the snow off her back, dears.' Huldran sat up on one elbow. 'This is our great mother, mother of all things, who holds our darkness and our weakness. We are honoured to welcome her tonight.'

Marelda crept closer and put a hand on the bear's back. Her fingers glowed; a feeling of safety flooded through her. She rubbed her cheek against the soft fur.

Ziske swept the bear's pelt. Ice crystals chinked onto the floor, flared and melted. Some circled high to the roof of the cave and chimed.

The bear's body filled the cave, glittering with constellations. 'I am the space between the stars.' Her voice came from the root of the mountain. 'I am silence – I am darkness – I am emptiness. Every creature is my child. I rock you inside your mother before you are born; I rot you into rest at the end of life; I breathe you out into life again. There is nowhere to fall but back into my womb.' The huge body drew itself down into bear-shape again and she swung her head towards Ziske. Ziske reached for Marelda's hand and gripped it.

'She touched me with her tongue!' Ziske was overwhelmed with tears. 'I thought she was going to bite me.'

'It's not death I'm afraid of.' Ziske shuddered. 'It's the suffering that comes before it. I can't stand to see sickness that gnaws at the gut or flays the skin.'

The bear growled. 'You are right to stay alert. I like to watch my children gathering together when sickness threatens. I gave you wits to avoid it and kindness to overwhelm it.'

'I'm scared of cruelty,' Marelda murmured.

The bear rumbled, 'Humans can hunt each other worse than any plague. I lollop panting alongside you when you run to safety. I rear up tall and roar with you to stop danger. When you've found a nest, you can sink into my fur to rest. I'll sniff your wounds and breathe on your sore places to help you heal. My tongue will wash away your tears.'

Huldran shivered and pulled her shawl tighter round her shoulders. 'I am afraid of dark places in myself. Sometimes I hang on the edge of a precipice and can't look down.'

'What is in that chasm, wise woman?' The bear looked at her with eyes as deep as river pools.

'A dream unfolds. I watch myself creep to the King's hall and set fire to the thatch. I am skilful with my bow and arrows – I could catch him in the throat as he flees. I would sit on his throne and give orders. I allow myself to think – wouldn't it be simpler that way? I taste his rage, no different to my own. My fist crashes down, as cruel as his. I become the same as him,' Huldran shuddered, 'and then I am lost ...'

The bear sat back on her haunches, listening. 'Tell us about this rage you feel.'

'I hate to see those men of war beating men and women, destroying homes, leaving orphans to starve!'

'Let's dig below this hate. Perhaps we can unearth the roots of your pain. You love the people. You're delighted when they build houses and take care of their families. How does it feel to rest in that love, at the root of your rage?'

Huldran wept.

'Once you feel the fullness of your love, new shoots will grow. You work with hope already. You know those fighters can be lovers, fathers, friends, when their hearts turn. These cubs of yours,' the bear's snout pointed to Marelda and Ziske, 'will take your love to the valley and the mountain. The season of growing is here!'

The bear turned, nuzzled each of them with her wet black nose and lay down by the fire. She seemed smaller now, more like the brown bears in the forest.

The animal turned round and round, whimpering, and strange lights radiated around her belly.

'Let's help her get comfortable,' Huldran invited. Ziske brought a dish of water and the bear lapped it up and groaned. Marelda brought her own sleeping-straw and tucked it round the bear.

They stroked her, crooning. Lightning sizzled through the bear's body. They jumped back, startled.

She stretched up on her hind legs, crouched down and roared as she birthed a tiny cub. Pink and naked, it wriggled up to its mother's chest and fastened its mouth there, as the mother bear sat back. All the light in the cave gathered round the newborn cub. The mother bear licked and licked her baby, growling tenderly.

When Marelda cleaned up near them, the mother bear licked her too. As Ziske refilled the water-dish, she nosed the girl's fingers.

Mother and baby settled down together.

Weariness rolled over Marelda and Ziske. They wound their arms around each other and slept. Huldran kept watch in the dark.

In the middle of the night, Marelda woke. She couldn't stop shaking, even when Ziske held her firmly. 'She's gone!' Tears dribbled from her eyes as she looked wildly around.

'The bear? Yes, she's left us now,' Huldran's voice was calming. 'We'll see her again.'

'No, no! In my dream – she stroked my head, I thought it was the bear licking me, but it was her hand. There was sticky on my cheek – it was the honey on her dress. I was close in to her side, riding on her hip. I snuggled into the black cloth; it was warm, and it smelled of her. I rested my head on her shoulder and her black hair blew all around me in the wind. She was crowned with peonies, red and white. We were stepping in a circle, everyone together, arms round each other's shoulders, pipes and drums playing, flowers everywhere. And then … then …'

'What happened?' Ziske asked. Her arm was still round Marelda's shoulders. Huldran sat close, following Marelda's face with her eyes.

'A terrible noise – hoof beats, shouts, screeching. Smell of burning thatch, bits of ash sting my eye so I can't see. I'm falling on cobblestones, peonies smashed, hands grab my arms, bruises …' Marelda crunched her arms round her body, head down.

Huldran took both her hands. 'What next, Marelda, my dear? Take a breath.'

Marelda bit her lip. Words crashed out. 'Riding round and round, big man, can't see his eyes under his leather helmet. Lips pulled back in a snarl. Waves a blade in the air, sleek and dripping. Swinging from his saddle, he's knotted her hair – her face is bone-white and bleeding. It's her head – my mother's head!' Marelda screamed. 'She can't see me! Her eyes are staring. She can't hear when I call – Mother!' Sobs swept through Marelda from the pit of her stomach. Ziske and Huldran held onto her.

'Let the weeping flow.' Huldran stayed calm.

Ziske had tears running through her nose.

When Marelda could hear again, Huldran told her, 'It's not a dream. That was old King Varagan, your husband's father. He killed your mother the Queen. All your family were murdered – they kept you to marry to Bors, to make the people obey them. You didn't speak for a year. Piroshka nursed you back to health. Your memory must have closed over this, to stop you feeling the pain.'

Marelda's voice shook. 'I needed her, every day of my life. She could have soothed me to sleep, taught me how to be just and kind like her, how to climb and swim. She could have given me moon-beads! Now, girls don't learn those things. They drag around with their burdens. Boys don't know how to dance, they only learn fighting and shooting. How could I forget?'

'Your wounds must have scabbed over. If nobody talked about it, how could you remember? Piroshka had to keep you quiet to save your life. King Varagan's version was that they saved you from an uprising of your own people.'

'Yes ... that's what they said. But they always looked away when they said it. They lied to me!' Marelda seethed. 'Took my Mother, then they took my memory – and the peonies, and the circle dance. They never told me about being a woman, the power of it. When they burned down the queen's roundhouse, they destroyed everything – the way Mother listened to people, her wisdom, getting them all to talk together ...'

'That's right, Marelda. Now you've found it, you can make it again. That's why you're here. That's why I want your daughter to come here when she's nearly grown: to learn how to make new ways rooted in ancient strength.'

'I don't think I can. It's too big. I'm tired.'

'You're not alone, Marelda. We're here to help.' Ziske still had a hand on her shoulder.

'Yes, you'll need your friends.' Huldran smiled.

'It's because of you I remembered this. You put your arms round me while I slept, Ziske. Nobody ever held me like that before, not wanting anything from me, simply being there. And because you listened to me, Huldran. That's new for me.'

'What we've done in this cave together, these past moons, is not only for us. We've melted ice and freed fire. When we go out, we'll bring passion to our work, because we held each other in the dark.'

'The bear thawed my fear,' Ziske murmured. 'Before that, I liked you, but I didn't know if you'd mind if I hugged you. With the touch of the bear's tongue, I stopped thinking about myself and saw you, looking like you needed warmth.'

'When you put your arms round me, it felt solid, as real as the bear's fur. How can that be, Huldran? She's a spirit-bear isn't she?'

'She's the only thing that is real, in all our changing world,' said Huldran. 'We are puffs of her breath, the print of her paws in the snow.' She threw open the cave door. Light ringed her head and cloaked her arms. Her face was in shadow as she turned to speak to them. 'Goddess Bear will show herself whenever we open our eyes to her. In all the heart-wrenching pain our lives bring us, her compassion shines clear. Look.'

Mist shifted and coiled in the valleys, rolled up the hillsides, thinned and blew away across ridge after ridge of snow. Icicles dripped. 'The spring thaw has begun.'

At the end of Hilda's story, there were sighs as they all settled down to sleep. Arms were flung round each other, bodies shuffled closer.

Hilda noticed Oswynne slide out of bed, careful not to wake Adela, unwind Hubert from Seren's blanket, take him back to her own bed and hug him close under her rug.

Fear paced chill steps across Hilda's shoulders. *What will happen when Kedric finds out how he's been tricked?* She repeated Huldran's words to herself: *'We are the print of her paws in the snow …' I can worry about Kedric tomorrow.* She imagined bear-fur and lurched into sleep.

CHAPTER 28

IS THAT A
PACKED LUNCH?

SEREN

At first light, Kedric's roar set everyone running.

'You said what? They're coming when?' The two black oxen shifted in their harness and snorted.

Wulf stroked their necks and talked to them. *His voice would calm a wolf,* Seren thought with a rush of pride. *Didn't work on Headman Kedric, though.*

'So we thought we'd take the tables and benches from the Hall up there today.' Evrard faltered, his arm on the wagon full of wooden trestles. 'We'll dig latrine pits as well, and we'll have to fish …'

'I know what we've got to do!' yelled Kedric. 'We should have half a moon to do all that, with time for a game of knucklebones as well. Whose idea was this?'

Seren eased herself silently backwards, one foot behind the other, wanting to hear, but keen to stay away from trouble. The other women seemed to be doing likewise.

Edgar looked at Bertold. Bertold looked at Evrard. Evrard looked at Edgar.

Edgar cleared his throat, 'Great-Aunt Edith gave us the words. She made us say them over until we got them right.'

'Old Edith? Her wits must be stewed.' Kedric looked round, rubbing his chin. 'We always hold the Moot at the full moon. Oswynne, what's going on?'

Seren didn't want to run now. Her breath came shallow, as Oswynne stepped forward out of the crowd. A memory flashed in Seren's mind: *Oswynne as a small girl chasing a puppy, a crash as an ale-jug hit the floor, her father's frown as he looked round – a young Seren swooping down on the child not much smaller than herself with, 'Bedtime, young lady.'* She longed to whisk Oswynne away now – but Oswynne was standing her ground. Seren caught her eye and held it, stretching her mouth into what she hoped was an encouraging smile.

Oswynne straightened her shoulders and spoke loudly enough for them all to hear: 'It is important for Elder Edith to give judgment at the Moot, along with the other Elders. She will hear speakers for women and men, young and old, and give them equal weight. She'll make sure we all listen to each other with respect, ask questions, and understand each other's concerns. The Elders will talk through the matters laid before them, ask everyone for their thoughts, and make an agreement that helps us move forward together. We don't know yet what they'll say. If Thane Roger sits in the carved chair, he will shout what he thinks, which may be quicker, but it will leave us still at odds with each other.'

'You mean – you've done this on purpose, you and Edith, to cheat Roger? To trick me?' Kedric was hoarse, his fists clenching and opening.

Oswynne lifted her head to look him in the eye.

Seren saw the tension in her jaw and went over the ingredients for headache tea in her mind: feverfew already springing green in the herb patch; willow-bark powder in the jar; better put water on to boil soon …

'This is the old-style Moot as the folk have held it for hundreds of years. We used our mother wit to cook up peace in the cauldron. It's not for anyone or against anyone – we're making it for all of us and our children, and their children after them, and our mother, the Earth.' Oswynne stayed steady.

'I don't want to hear that claptrap. It's bad enough you're going against me, going behind my back!' Kedric glared at everyone. Nobody moved. 'Are they coming from our neighbour settlements – on their way already?'

'We left the Mereham folk packing up their gear, getting ready.' Bertold spread his hands wide.

Evrard nodded. 'Thornthicket, too.'

Kedric stamped off, swearing and muttering. 'Half a day to Thornthicket with a good horse, a full day from there to Thaneshall. Another full day for Roger to get back to Thornthicket. Stay the night there, then it'll take him half a day to get here.' He counted on his fingers. 'Wulf, come here, I want to talk to you.'

Seren found Wulf poking the eye of his fire in the forge, making nails, even though Headman Kedric's stallion was tied to the fence nearby. 'What's eating you, cushla? Here's your pack-up: a piece of hare-meat from last night, a flatbread, some dried apple-rings. Where are you going on Dragon?'

'Headman Kedric wants me to go to Thornthicket and then over to Thaneshall. He wants me to fetch Thane Roger and bring him back in time for the Moot, or part of it at least.'

'Oh, no, you can't do that! We don't want him here – he'll take over!'

Wulf put down the poker. 'That's what I thought. Why do you mind so much? I didn't really understand what Oswynne was saying.'

Seren felt colour rush to her face. She picked words to give him, like tender pieces out of the stew. 'If Thane Roger is in charge, he'll do it the Saxon way. He'll tell us what he thinks and make us agree, with knifers standing round to make sure we do what he says. If Elder Edith sits on the carved chair, she will help them sort it out, like a loving mother.'

Wulf scratched his head. 'So, it's not just about Ursel's quarrel with Headman Kedric?'

'No, it's about how we decide.' Seren stroked his badger-striped hair as he sat fiddling with the bellows.

'Why's that important, again?'

'We all need to be heard, for justice and fairness. If women have a voice, they'll talk about what children need, what hurts them, what helps them grow. We can all make sure no harm comes to the Earth, because Earth Mother feeds us.'

'Oh, honey-sweet, you make it so simple! Sounds like I shouldn't fetch Thane Roger. What can I tell Headman Kedric, if I don't go? He'll yell at me.'

She loved the way his face wrinkled up, then brightened, like cloud-shadows blowing across the fen.

A new thought struck him, 'I can get on with mending the four-seater punt. Except I've run out of resin to caulk the joints. I thought Thane Roger would bring some over when he came but he must've forgotten. There's some good pine trees up on the ridge beyond Thaneshall, the best for tapping for resin anywhere round here, it makes good waterproof joints if you mix it up with reeds and rags.'

'Thane Roger wasn't thinking about what we might need, only about what he could take,' Seren said. 'That's what I mean!'

Aikin sauntered up. 'I'll finish off making nails, Wulf, if you've got to fetch Thane Roger. Oh, you're not …? So what's Dragon doing tied up here? If I go, can I ride Dragon?' He stroked the stallion's nose. The big animal whickered and nuzzled his hand.

Wulf rubbed his ear, as he did when he was trying to get his thoughts straight. 'You mustn't, Aikin. The women have got a plan and it's about taking care of the Earth, I'm not quite sure how, but Headman Kedric doesn't like it. He wants Thane Roger here but …'

'Mmmm. Is that a packed lunch?' Aikin stuffed the leather pouch into the saddlebag, tightened the girth and swung astride Dragon. 'I love going to Thaneshall. This is a great chance! Grimbold, he's my friend now, wants to show me his new pattern for arrow-heads …'

'No, Aikin, wait …'

'Hey boy, steady – he's ready to gallop, what a horse, he's so strong … See you soon!' Divots flew as Dragon's hooves tore into the trackway, Aikin whooping in the saddle.

Seren sat down with a bump. 'Why didn't you stop him?'

'I tried, but …'

'Can you go after him?'

'There's no horse can catch Headman's stallion. It's too late in the day for anybody else to go, could get caught in the dark. He doesn't mean any harm. He doesn't understand what's going on. He's trying to be helpful.'

'What are we going to do?' Seren wailed. 'I'll have to tell Oswynne.'

KEDRIC

The clomp of Bertold's hand, as broad as an oar on Kedric's shoulder, almost winded him. 'We need to check the eel-traps, Kedric. Elstan says the silver eels are running well. Roll this barrel down to the jetty, will you? I need some help.'

Out on the mere, Kedric jabbed the punt-pole down and pulled it up with a twist, drops wetting his tunic-sleeves. 'Steady on, there's a trap down under that willow-snag. What's the mud done to upset you today?' Bertold teased.

A muscle jumped in Kedric's jaw. 'Oswynne's pushing me too far! Fixing the Moot so Roger can't get there in time – or trying to.'

'Ah, the wife.' Bertold pulled up the wicker eel-trap and tipped the wriggling contents into one of the barrels, filled with water to keep them fresh. 'What difference does it make, if Elder Edith sits in the carved chair, or if Thane Roger does?'

'Roger could get everything sorted out quickly, no fuss. Her way, we'll be there for days wittering on.'

'Would Roger leave more time for feasting? I like the sound of that,' Bertold grinned.

'It's not so simple, Bert. Thane Roger knows what's going on all over the countryside. He rides to Rendlesham, to feast with the king every year. He hears about wars overseas, and all the news from Kent and York and Durham. Everywhere, he says, thanes are getting to grips with local places like ours, getting organised, putting up defences against raiders, making sure the settlements pay their dues to keep the fighters on guard. These old women with their endless chatter, their time is over!'

'It's not that you think Roger would favour you in the argument with your niece, then? Watch out, you'll have the boat over, we're shipping water already.'

'Don't care if you do fall in. Don't push me! You always used to wangle me up when we were lads, but this is serious.'

'Sorry. I can see it's scratching in your innards. What's the worst thing about it, for you?' Bertold bailed with a pot.

'I keep thinking I should send Oswynne back to her father's house in Ousemouth.' Kedric put his head in his hands, shame burning his throat.

'What! Your brain-pan's addled, Kedric. Why would you do that?'

'She's making everybody laugh at me. I can't stand that.'

'Nobody's laughing at you. Why would they? We're all feeling like a bowstring tied too tight, but I can understand what you're trying to do. The women too – they're doing what they think is best for the settlement. They see the bairns with their skinny legs and worry about them getting enough to eat. I watch Nelda and my grandchildren. She saves them bits from her own bowl. It's a disagreement, that's all. Surely you'd miss Oswynne, wouldn't you?'

Kedric rubbed his beard. 'Sometimes I can't bear the looks she gives me.'

'Oh, well, we've all been there. I used to fight with my wife, Emma, often enough, but I miss her every day and every night. There's nobody to match her in all the settlements round here. And, believe me, I've looked! You could find some pretty young thing, but you need a manager like Oswynne to run a place like this. She's got the strips planted up as soon as the ploughing's finished. Nobody's starved this year, though we've come pretty close. That's down to her storing food carefully, keeping the pots and vats clean, getting the women working hard every day. Nice looking too – not that I'd notice, of course.'

Kedric felt a pulse in his groin, remembering the softness of her arms. He took up the pole and expertly sent the four-seater punt out from under the willow fronds into open water. 'Where's the next trap?'

'Where the current flows round the corner of that little island. You could let them do the Moot their way and see what happens. You'll be able to lay out what happened with Ursel and the deer, why you were so annoyed, why it matters so much to have a fine feast when Thane comes.'

'Do you think they'll listen to me? Won't they all be on Ursel's side, women together?'

'Edith isn't all cosy with Ursel. She often scolds her, my Winfrith says. Edith can't abide Ursel trying to do her hair or look after her – too clumsy, always calls for Meg.'

'Oh, so do you think there'd be a chance I could get a fair hearing?'

The pointed end of the trap was stuck under an alder root. When they'd worked it loose and tipped the eels into a barrel, Bertold said, 'From what I've heard, they're planning to have you and her put your cases, then everybody talks, and the Elders give judgment at the end. Not so different from what we usually do, bit more talking maybe. It's your chance to tell everybody from the three settlements how you reckon things should be done, how the world's changing and we've got to keep up.'

'Hmm. But Thane Roger is coming! I sent Wulf to fetch him.' They both counted days of travel on their fingers. 'He should get here about noon, in the middle of the Moot. Sooner if he's got a fresh horse.'

'Well then, he can have his say too, and everybody's happy.' Bertold seemed satisfied.

Kedric wasn't so sure. Bert always avoided conflict if he could. *But sometimes you have to take a stand.* He shoved with the pole to move the punt away from the bank, sucking thoughtfully on his moustache.

With both barrels full, the punt wallowed along between flat muddy islands and winding reaches of river, upstream from the mere. Bertold bailed faster. They stopped to rest by the shore of Great Clay Fen, with the afternoon sun warm on their faces. 'What do you like about Roger?' Bertold asked.

'When he talks about the rule of kings and thanes, it makes a pattern like a tapestry studded with gold. Swords flash, spears line up and march together. They'll tell tales about our kingdom, years in the future. All this is going on, and I could be part of it.' Kedric turned to squint at his friend as the low sun dazzled him.

'Oh,' Bertold nodded, 'like with your brothers.'

271

'What do you mean?' The light that bounced off the surface of the water outlined wrinkles on Bertold's face, which was red and shiny where it wasn't smeared with mud.

'Those two were always up to something, weren't they? And you trailing along behind, wanting to join in. When they went off to trade down the coast, you kept saying they'd be back to fetch you. All that summer you bleated about it. You only stopped when the storms blew in, and you knew your brothers wouldn't come. Proper miserable you were then. I had to teach you how to shoot a goose, to get you out of that mud-mood.'

'We'll both be in the mud if we don't look out.' Kedric was glad to shift out of that memory, even if the punt was sinking. They bailed, but as quick as they sloshed water out, more seeped in between the planks.

'I thought Wulf mended this one?' Bertold grumbled as they scrambled out onto the bank and hauled the eel-barrels with them.

'He did. Well, he was working on it. Oh. I sent him off without checking if he'd finished. Do you think we can walk back?'

They tried to move away from the water's edge and sank up to their ankles in squelch. 'It's too far to walk home, too dangerous with sinking mud and no paths. We'd never make it before dark.' Bertold shook his big head.

'What are we going to do?' Kedric coughed the panic out of his voice. He could always rely on Bert.

'Shout!'

So they did.

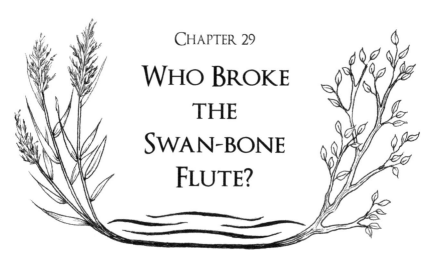

CHAPTER 29

WHO BROKE THE SWAN-BONE FLUTE?

OSWYNNE

Oswynne's back niggled this morning – wet weather always made it ache. She stood on one side of the loom, propped against the wall of the weaving-house. Seren passed the shuttle back to her, smooth as water flowing, moved the heddles to form the pattern, talking softly as she wove.

I wish she'd stop wittering on about it, Oswynne thought. *It's bad enough she let Aikin go off to fetch the Thane. Now she's on about stopping Roger with magic or some such nonsense. I've got enough to worry about without that.*

The loom-weights clinked softly to the rhythm of the work. She passed the shuttle back to Seren, feeling her mouth draw tight like the warp thread. *Nowhere to escape to with this rain drenching down, too many people cramped together in the weaving-house, the smell of damp wool and armpits.*

Returning the shuttle, Seren tried again. 'The spirit I need to speak with is the same one Elder Edith told us about – the Mere-Wife …'

Pictures from Edith's tale flashed through Oswynne's memory: tusks, blue scaly skin, a voice that sent shivers down her spine. 'How many times do I have to say no!' she snapped. She pressed their weaving down with the baton, to firm the cloth. She avoided Seren's eyes. When she glanced back expecting river-pebble blankness, Seren met her gaze, alive behind her eyes. Oswynne felt naked.

She turned away. *Stop bucking and rearing, anger horse! There's no room for me to ride you now, as I'm longing to. I've got to haul on the reins; you've got to slow right down. You can stamp and snort as much as you want, I can't let you free!*

Aloud she said, 'Ragnild, please take a turn at the loom with Seren here. I need to get on with my tablet-weaving.'

Oswynne had to ask Elder Edith if she minded if her chair was moved so she could use the back strut to set up her warp threads. Edith grumbled, 'I need to stay close to the fire. It's smoky but it keeps out the chill.' She had to have the table just in the right place too, for her needle and thread.

At last Oswynne got old Edith comfortable. She smoothed her woad blue and weld yellow yarn, and comforted herself with the rhythm of the small shuttle. She could wind herself into her own little world of the emerging pattern … until something else bothered her. *Will I never get any peace!*

On the loom against the opposite wall, Hilda and Ursel's weaving was progressing slowly. They talked more than they worked. Ursel's hands flew about in gestures; Hilda tried to slow her down.

From the slope of Hilda's shoulders, Oswynne saw it wasn't going well. Anxiety poked her. *If Ursel can't make a sound argument, the whole Moot will be wasted, Kedric and Thane Roger will triumph, women's voices won't be heard ever again. Hilda's getting exasperated! What if she gives up? She must take a break. It's my job to take charge.*

Oswynne ordered, 'Hilda, stop what you're doing please. Tell us some more of the Peony Valley story.'

The storyteller looked confused. 'I can't just now, Oswynne. Meg's not here.'

'Never mind that. We're all getting across each other, crammed in together because of the downpour. We need some entertainment.'

Hilda frowned. Oswynne realised – *the bard doesn't like me calling it entertainment. She thinks it's bigger than that! Well maybe it is but how am I supposed to find the right word when everything's annoying me!*

Elder Edith came to her rescue. 'You can tell it to Meg another time, Hilda. Or one of us can. We've all missed bits and had to catch up. Meg's a good girl, she won't mind. Come along now, what happened after the bear's visit?'

Hilda played a trill on her flute and set it down on the table. Her face was not as lively as usual, but she told them the next piece. She continued weaving as she spoke. Oswynne lost herself in the story gladly.

MEG

'"Help! Help!"' Otred squeaked. 'It was so funny when Gaufrid told us about saving his dad and Uncle Kedric from the leaky punt.' He doubled over with giggles. 'I had to stick my fist in my mouth to stop laughing, Evrard was doing the same. Bertold snorted like a sow,' he stopped to imitate the noise, 'and Kedric gave him such a look! Then Bertold dug him in the ribs and …'

Meg was not listening. She strode ahead, eyes narrowed to squint through the rain. 'Stop blethering, Otred.'

'I'll tell Ursel you're mean to me!'

'You do that. Maybe she'll look after the rootling pigs herself, instead of sitting in the warm getting a storytelling lesson all to herself.' She waved her stick as one of the small pigs ran off. 'Get back to your mother, you dumb piglet!'

'Don't do it like that, Meg! You've got to talk to them like your friends, then they'll obey you. Like I did when we got Yorfor out of Headman's house.'

Meg pulled her soaked shawl tighter round her head. At least she could cover her ears to keep that little oaf's chatter out all the way down the slope. They got the pigs into the sty – off he went to his mother, *to grumble about me, no doubt.* She dashed drips from her face and looked for the smoke that showed where the women were.

Chat buzzed from the weaving-house. *Cosy – if you're on the inside.* Meg elbowed the door open, heading for the fire.

Hilda and Ursel passed the shuttle to and fro across the wall-loom, all peaceful. *Ursel is in my place, getting all the jokes and word-games and deep teaching from Hilda, while her little brother shows me how to poke pigs with a stick, in the rain. How can Ursel pout like that when she's spent a whole day with Hilda?*

Hilda looked around to gather their attention again and spoke, her tone showing she was coming to the end of a story.

Towards dawn, when the morning stars came out, a new sound woke the court – a baby crying. Marelda's baby daughter took her first breath, and the young queen cradled her little one in her arms.

Meg rocked backwards as if she'd been punched in the gut. All the life drained from her. *Hilda told the last piece of the story – without me. To Ursel. To everybody – not to me.* Things went blurry around her. *Something of Hilda's is on the table – nothing to do with me. Hilda's nothing to do with me, not any more. She's siding with Ursel, who hates me and hits me.* A mudslide of misery dragged Meg down as she shivered in her soaked clothes. She staggered a little and knocked over the table.

A crunch, crack, and Meg slipped on something that rolled under her foot, among the rushes on the floor. She banged her shoulder and it hurt as she went over, but nobody took any notice of her.

'What have you done?' Hilda's face was skull-white. She scooped up the pieces from the floor. 'My swan-bone flute. You broke it, Meg.' It was a whisper; she cradled the sharp ends in her palm.

'It wasn't my fault. I didn't know it was there. I didn't mean …'

Pain, as her hair was yanked from behind. She twisted to see – Oswynne, eyes narrow as lightning. 'Ursel, get the strap. This clumsy, careless girl needs a whipping.'

Hilda's eyes opened wide and her eyebrows twisted together, then up. *She'll never speak to me again,* jagged through Meg's mind. *It's my fault. I'll never tell stories now.* Snot ran out of her nose.

'I demand the right to punish Meg myself.' Hilda spoke slowly. 'She must make restitution. She must get me a suitable swan-bone and learn how to make it into a flute herself. I need her for the whole day tomorrow, and I'll make sure she does all her normal work as well.' Her face loomed close to Meg's, her eye sockets skull-sharp. 'We'll go out into the fen and I'll sort you out there.'

Meg stared at the floor. She didn't care about the beating she was going to get from Hilda. Nothing could hurt more than this.

CHAPTER 30

MIST MAGIC

SEREN

Seren's heart jumped in her chest like a stranded fish. Last chance, today, to use her skills. 'Mist would delay Thane Roger.'

They heaved one hearthstone into the cart, rubbed their backs and reached for the next.

'He's galloping from Thaneshall to Thornthicket today,' Oswynne snapped, 'hoping to get here by noon tomorrow, when we're in the middle of the Moot. Why would a mist rise over on the heath and into the forest?'

This feels like one foot on the jetty, the other reaching for a boat that slides away.

'If it wasn't forbidden,' Seren faltered, trying not to look at Oswynne, 'I could raise a mist and make sure it finds him, wherever he is. He'd get lost, go round in circles, maybe turn back.' A wave of heat swept through her. 'Wendreda showed me how, but it was a long time ago …'

'I told you, we can't trust dark spirits!' Oswynne snapped. She nearly dropped her end of the stone. They steadied it on the edge of the cart then piled it on top of the last.

May and Roslinda threw in logs and ran to get more.

While Oswynne eased her back, Seren tried again. 'Sometimes dark places hold the wisdom we need. Edith told us about the Mere-Wife: she's the one I need to help with weather-magic, the ancient one who belongs to this place. Or maybe the place belongs to her …'

Oswynne shuddered. 'The one with tusks and scales? I don't want her around here!'

'She's certainly fearsome,' Seren replied. 'She sucks unwary travellers into the bog if they disrespect her, underestimate her power over winds and weather, or if they're rude to people who live here. We have met her already, you and I: when your births went hard I called for help to all the spirits of the land, the ancient mothers who've helped women give birth for years. The Mere-Wife sent you strength, sent me courage, and your beautiful children slid into your arms. We can nourish her by offering up our feelings of weakness to her. That's what her tusks are for, to crunch up terror and chew it into useful food. She lives far away from our settlements because people mistrust her now. We'll need to bring her gifts.'

Oswynne asked, 'What sort of gifts?'

'Bread and salt on the flat stone beside the hythe track.'

Oswynne commented, 'Merewyn used to leave that offering, long ago, on moonlit nights.'

Seren moved closer to her. 'Is it this bit?' She rubbed Oswynne's back just where she knew the ache was sharpest.

Oswynne's ribs expanded. 'But this uncouth spell-making – isn't it dangerous? Can you really control this otherworld being?'

'It won't be me controlling her, more like we work together. She does what I ask because she sees the need and she understands that we honour her, and we ask politely for her aid. We could bring to mind Hilda's dark bear goddess, to give us confidence and show we have powerful friends.'

'We have to feed her our fears?'

'It will help us to be rid of them, and they will give her great strength.'

Seren worked with the warmth of her palm to undo the knots in Oswynne's lower back. *When I rub into the tension with my thumbs, something inside Oswynne seems to loosen as well.*

'This is not a curse?' Oswynne checked.

'No, there's no ill will behind it. I'd start with making a shield around our settlement to keep anything bad out, and one for Thane Roger, too. I can't say he won't meet a hungry wolf or trip and break his leg, but he might do that anyway, it wouldn't be because of me, because of us.'

'If I say yes – what would you need?'

'A quiet place to work with nobody coming to break my mind-work; in the wood at the edge of the vegetable strip, above the water meadows. I need Wulf to help me, and my herbs and my drum. And time to do it, without having to stop and cook.'

Oswynne scratched her head and pushed back her hair. 'You could have just gone off and done it, Seren, without telling me. Why did you ask?'

Seren spoke slowly, daring to speak from her heart. 'That would have been – not right. There is friendship between us, Hilda said it holds up the settlement. I don't know about that, but I feel it deeply, and honour it.'

Oswynne put a hand on her arm, smiling. Seren breathed out. *My friend was not offended! Even though I'm her slave, I can talk to her.* She smiled back.

Elder Edith shuffled over to join them. 'Weather magic, eh? I say we should try it. If he has a fall, that's his lookout. Can't mollycoddle these chaps, they can fend for themselves. Besides, he won't be coming alone.' She made sure they were both listening. 'He'll bring a troop, well-armed, to the Moot. He'll hold us at spear-point until we make the decision he wants – or else take over as judge himself. The Elders from the other settlements, my friends Elfric and Mildreth, are no heroes. Life tastes sweet when there aren't many months left to us. They'll do what Thane Roger says. And Roger can do exactly as he pleases with us women.'

Oswynne went pale. 'Do it, then, Seren,' she said.

'Here are some heavy fears,' Seren acknowledged Edith's words. 'May I take your hand, Elder, as we offer them to feed the Mere-Wife?' She offered her other hand to Oswynne, and felt it firmly grasped.

Oswynne spoke, 'I offer up these fears: will Thane Roger and my husband take away our power and leave us speechless? What kind of man will my Edgar grow into? What will happen to my little Puffin?'

Seren added: 'Will Meg's womanhood be full of groping hands and men who force themselves on her? Will good men stand and watch and say nothing?'

They all shuddered.

Seren reached for the Mere-Wife in her mind and spoke words she didn't know she knew. 'Please accept these fears, dear Mere-Wife, spirit of this land, loving grandmother who waits for us in the dark and the wild. We offer them without shame, without cringing, without hate, sure that you can transform them as you do dead bodies and dung, into rich life.' *Nana must have taught me this! I'd forgotten until now. Oswynne's trust has loosened something knotted up inside me, too.*

They squeezed each other's hands, then lifted them palms upwards. They turned them downwards so the feelings could roll down into the earth.

'Take what you need, Seren,' Oswynne said. 'I'll get the men to help me take these cooking things up to the campsite. We have to stop Thane Roger.'

HILDA

Greylag geese flew up grumbling, as Meg poled a punt out into the stream. 'Where are we going?' she asked. Her eyes slunk sideways, avoiding Hilda's.

Hilda tensed as Meg's misery gripped her own gut, then breathed out deeply to push it away. 'I asked Nelda to milk instead of you, and your mother said she can manage without you today. She even gave me this pot of weak ale for us to share. We can take as much time as we need, to find a swan-bone and … everything.' She looked around. Ahead the mere opened out, dotted with flat islands no bigger than a barley-strip, held together by alder roots. Far to their right, the river meandered towards Mereham. Boats were expected sometime today. Upstream to their left would be quieter. There the current eased past water meadows, drifting silt into the mere. 'Let's go to those big willows,' Hilda said, pointing.

Pollen puffed into their faces as they brushed through swinging willow catkins. After the sun-dazzle on water, Hilda blinked. The riven heart of one great trunk stood bare and pale, with new leaves flaming from withies along each branch, even those branches that lay half-broken along the ground.

Hilda ran her hand over the mother-of-pearl wood. 'How can something be so shattered and still live?' She turned to find Meg sitting, her face shielded by her hair. She drooped over her folded knees like a creature curled inside a seashell. *Can't pull this worm up, I'll have to coax her out or lose her in the depth of her despair.* There was nothing outside the hanging leaves, nothing inside but the thump of tenderness in her heart. Hilda sat close and leaned to trace the silver line of a scar on Meg's cheek with her fingertip.

'What's this from?'

'I spilled a whole pail of milk, the first one last year. Headman's Wife had her ring on.'

'They should not do that to you.'

Meg's shoulder twitched, a small shrug. 'That's how it is.' But she didn't pull away.

Hilda closed her eyes and said, 'I don't want that for you. You deserve respect.'

A sound like a snort came from under the hanging hair.

'What did you say?' Hilda asked.

The strangled noise came again. 'Don't pretend to care!'

'Oh, I see.'

Meg pushed her hair out of her face and rounded on Hilda. 'No, you don't. You said you'd train me. You said I could tell stories in the mead-hall. Then you sent me away.'

'You felt I was pushing you away?'

'You made me go and mind pigs while *she – she* got all the teaching, all the wisdom. It should have been mine!'

'You think I'm giving Ursel something I'm not giving you?'

'Of course! She gets everything. She's Headman's niece, the pretty one, and I'm just a slave!'

Hilda could hear how often those words had burnt through Meg's head, even if this was the first time they singed her tongue.

'I wanted to be a storyteller. I wanted to be like you. You said I could – then you took it away. Just don't pretend! I can't stand it.' Meg hugged her legs and rocked to and fro, her teeth sinking into her knee.

'You thought I wasn't going to get back to you. You don't trust me. Why should you? Everybody else treats you badly. That's what you expect. I didn't ask you to wait. I didn't explain I had to attend to Ursel first because, with the Moot coming up tomorrow, it's urgent. Oh Meg, I'm sorry.'

Sobs broke out from Meg's throat, without breath between them. She wailed. As Hilda put an arm round Meg's shoulders and drew her close to her side, a tear slid down her own cheek.

At last Meg gasped, 'Just get on with beating me.'

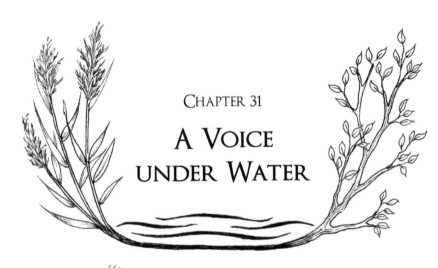

CHAPTER 31

A VOICE
UNDER WATER

SEREN

Seren smelled damp grass as her breath sank through her feet, down her roots, into the earth. She drew up green through her soles; it snaked over her skin. The sizzle of growth filled her ears. She reached up. Her gaze fixed on a walnut sapling; her fingers uncurled as crisp as its leaves. Her palms drank sun; warmth glowed through her. Light seeped down into soil; moisture rose like a blessing. She sent a chant out in a wave to curl around the settlement: people, animals, crops, buildings. She wrapped safety round Meg, wherever she was. She drew Thane Roger's face into the shine and saw him frown. She breathed love and asked it to hold them all.

She settled cross-legged on the ground. Wulf's drumbeat kept her company. She could trust him to take care of the fire and bring her back from … wherever she needed to go. She sank deeper inside. Fear trembled in and she watched as it passed by like a cloud-shadow. She sent her awareness out over the fen, searching. *Where are you? How can I find you?* Her fingers strewed vervaine on the flames and offered the smoke as a gift.

Wingbeats overhead! Seren jumped up and ran, following the line of the swan's flight towards the mere. She slithered down the slope to the water meadows and leapt across tussocks and mud, past dreaming heifers, through rushes, to the bank. The pulse of Wulf's drum kept pace with her heart, not so far away, by the fire. She trailed her hand in the margin between reed stalks, and poured water over her head and arms; she squatted by the edge. Sun-sparkles washed her sight. A voice singing under water circled her ears. She held her breath and leaned closer to listen.

Bits of light swam together into a pattern – fish-scales. Fear darted through her again, swift as a kingfisher. The scales formed a tail – two tails. Laughter like running water. 'Who are you? Are you the Mere-Wife, the spirit of this place?' Seren breathed. Something flashed and was gone. A tear fell from her eye. 'Please, we need help. Thane Roger is travelling here, to take power over our Moot and silence us women! He plans to plunder forest and fen to feed his fighting men. He doesn't care about your beautiful creatures. Please keep Meg safe, wherever she is; he sees her as his prey. He wants to plough and plant the bodies of our daughters like fields. Goddess of the fen, Mere-Wife, I'm sorry I don't know your ancient name. Sister of Breejsh – if we can stop him, we women will make sure we keep your waterways clear and clean, care for the wild and take only what we need. Can you help us? Send mist to wrap round Thane Roger and slow him down!' The fish-scale light pattern swam back into her sight

'Who are you?' The voice resounded through the water, through her body. Her question was being sent back to her.

Seren spoke her name, the names of her mother and grandmother and tribe. She brought to mind images of herself cooking, nursing babies, helping a mother lift a newborn to her breast, preparing remedies, singing for the dead, killing chickens. In her far memory, she played in sand dunes, paddled, watched waves, dived, swam, floated, felt herself part of the ocean. Then her visions slowed.

She stirred her feet in the river water, cool on her skin, and came back to the present. 'I am your child, Great Mother.' she whispered. 'We all are – even if some of us don't know it.'

She saw the breasts of the water-goddess now. Fountains flowed from them over the earth.

Joy cascaded through Seren and washed away her worries. A stream of notes burst from her, echoing the song that poured from the Mere-Wife's mouth.

Green water-weed hair billowed and myriad creatures glistened in its fronds. Seren reached out to them in wonder. The Mere-Wife's radiant face shimmered with love. Seren rubbed her eyes.

When she looked again, she saw only the flat surface of the mere. *What's that swirl? Coils of mist are rising from it!*

HILDA

'I'm not going to hit you, Meg.' Hilda used the hem of her overdress to wipe Meg's face.

'Why not? I broke your flute.'

'Yes. Why did you do that?'

'I didn't mean to. It was an accident.'

'Hmm. The kind of accident that tells us something, perhaps?'

'What do you mean?' Meg looked surprised.

'Sometimes feelings boil up inside us and jump out and knock things over. You were angry with Ursel and with me. It forked out of you like lightning.'

'Oh.' Meg's head hung down again. She picked petals off a buttercup. Her hair muffled her voice, 'You told the end of the story to them. Not to me. You waited until I wasn't there.'

'I didn't do that on purpose,' Hilda screwed up her face. 'I'd tried all day to help Ursel get her story straight. She's got the part about saving the hind and taking care of the wild deer so that they can increase, but then there's something about the antler dance that she rushed through, and I don't understand it. Her father comes into it, but she can't explain how he fits in. He died recently, didn't he? Perhaps she's too upset to talk about him. She kept zigzagging from him to the deer and back to hunting, and I got lost. And exasperated! I'm afraid she'll make a mess of her speech at the Moot, and if she does –'

'– Thane Roger will be able to take whatever he wants,' Meg finished the unspoken part of Hilda's sentence, '*Who*ever he wants.' She wrinkled her nose.

So you were listening, Hilda thought, nodding. 'Could you help Ursel, do you think? You know her better than me.'

'She won't listen to me.' Meg went back to destroying buttercups.

'Maybe there's some talking you and Ursel need to do together.'

'She'll never talk to me. She only shouts and hits.'

'You were friends not so long ago. What happened? She might tell you, if you sound as if you want to know. You'd need to listen well, even if it's hard for you.'

Meg shifted uncomfortably.

'I am asking you to do this, Meg.'

'Is that my punishment?'

'It's not a punishment. Something needs to be cleared up between you, not just for the two of you but for all of us, and for the forest and fen.'

A whirr of feathers passed overhead; ducks were on the wing. Behind the willow veil where they sat, Hilda and Meg couldn't see what kind.

'Is that what I have to do, instead of being beaten?'

'I want you to listen to me while I tell you why my swan-bone flute was dear to me.'

Hilda propped her back against the gnarled trunk, one hand laced amongst willow leaves. She looked out between branches across the shining mere. 'When I blew into it, my breath came up ... from the ground under my feet, from the growing part of my bones, from the heart of my heart. What is it your mother calls you? Beat of my heart. That's how it felt. The tunes came by themselves; I never had to work them out. Sometimes I practiced, of course, to get a trill right – but the melody came' – she paused – 'not from inside me ... more like through me.'

She glanced at Meg to see how she was taking the weight of this sadness. Meg's face was white as a high full moon, but resolute.

'Where did you get your flute?'

Hilda watched water move behind willow leaves. 'My teacher gave it to me, in the marshes of the far west. I learned songs and stories from my mother and my second mother, and everywhere I went, I picked up more. My teacher was the one who showed me how to take the songs and stories deeper. She showed me how to dance with pain, not push it down out of sight, not to let it blind me to what's happening here and now. On the morning when I told her everything – about my child who died, the man who left me – we were walking beside the mere. She brought her loving gaze to my heart's wounds. I saw that I didn't have to squirm away from those injuries in terror. I could simply feel how much they hurt, and I would not break apart. The warmth of my teacher's voice calmed me. What she was saying sank in at last. In that moment, a swan flew up from the mere right beside our feet. Water droplets fell and sparkled from its feathers as it carved the air with its wings.'

Meg breathed, 'Was that the swan in your story? Did she speak to you?'

Tears welled in Hilda's eyes. No one had ever understood the way her stories and her life meshed with each other. She had never let anybody as close as this. The glitter of sun on the river merged with the glory of her memory of that long-ago swan's flight. She blinked. She couldn't believe what she was seeing. Again there was a swan, in this place, on this day, taking to the sky from the water. She pointed – 'Look!'

They listened while the wingbeats grew fainter.

Hilda sat down and her eyes met Meg's. 'Something spoke,' she picked up her thread, 'It was me speaking through the swan-bone flute. I felt like my real self. My ordinary self went shimmery like a heat-haze. The self who spoke through me was bigger and wiser and lovelier than the usual me.'

Meg sat silently for a while, cross-legged. She looked up and asked, 'The swan in the story – was she real? Or was it Huldran speaking, or the swan talking through Huldran?'

Hilda breathed gently, savouring the taste of this new thing, a seeker. 'It's all the same. The notes I played made a pattern with wing-feathers and webbed footprints, air and water, cloud and sun, and me. In the story, Huldran and the others, and the swan and the cave are all shine and shadow, stone and song, boulder and dream. We all are. When I took this in, I stopped mithering about my own small being. I made space to work and found new tunes. My teacher gave me her flute and said, "Now is the time to walk your path."

'When that flute broke, I thought, I'll never feel what I felt then ever again. A new flute might be as good, but again it might not.'

Meg spoke softly. 'Hilda, I am so sorry I broke it.'

They sat quiet for a while.

Then Hilda broke the silence with, 'Soon you will have a swan-bone flute, Meg. You need to know how to make it sing.'

Meg's head jerked upright as she said, 'What do you mean?'

'You'll make a fine bard. You have a feel for words. They ripple out of you. You understand the tales in the marrow of your bones, not just in your head. I've walked from hills to plains, from cliffs to marshland, searching for the one who will be my apprentice. And here you are. The first night I was here, when I heard you telling Marelda's story in the dark, I knew. I thought you knew too?'

Meg was silent.

'What's the matter, Meg?'

'Something's happening. I don't know if I should show you. Is this what Mother told me about?' There was blood on her skirt. Her cheeks reddened as she rose onto her knees.

'Ah, my dear, is this the first time your moon-blood has come? Congratulations! Welcome to womanhood.'

Meg looked up, shy. 'What am I supposed to do? Mother told me to carry this cloth with me all the time.' She fished a strip of linen out of her bag.

'Let's get you comfy. Here's a bed of sphagnum moss, you can just sit here and let the flow take its course. When we move on, you can tie a pad of moss inside your cloth, and take some for later too. Here, I'll damp some moss so you can wipe off your thighs. Although this blood is a blessing, it can chafe a little when it dries. I should give you beads, like in the story. What ceremony is done in Wellstowe when a girl becomes a woman?'

Meg settled on the soft moss, cross-legged. 'When Ursel started her moon-time a couple of years ago, we were setting up a small feast in the Great Hall to honour it, just the women and children, but Headman Kedric burst in and stopped us. He was furious! "Get on with your work!" he shouted. So we met later for it, in the women's sleeping house. We shared out blaeberries – not many, but they were a treat, and Elder Edith taught us a special song … I don't think they'll do that for me.'

'They should celebrate. A new woman is a gift for any community. For you, Meg, this is a time of great power. Take a while to feel the sun on your face and the changes in your body. Whenever your flow starts, and a few days before, it's a time for rest and turning inwards to listen to our inner wisdom. If we don't, or can't, take time for that, we can suffer pain and tension.'

'Mother told me we can get cramps if we can't rest enough.'

'Remember that red mare? I think you've been feeling her hooves trampling you these last few days. The rage that dragged you down into misery is part of the pattern. Each month we women have the chance to deepen our awareness of the things that are hurting us, to sit with them, not push them underground. Sometimes we simply live with things and work our way through them – like turning a compost heap – and find they change. Maybe we can ride on our rage to put things right. We haven't helped you yet learn how to harness your wild mare. Your anger towards Ursel tells us how much your friendship means to you.'

'Meant.' Meg growled.

'You miss her deeply, and Winfrith too, I think. What did you like to do together?'

'It was me that made up the games we played. They followed when I said let's be rooks and build nests in trees.'

'You liked leading and being creative. That's a good way to be in the world. Let's find ways to set you back on that track. It's not that your moon-cycle makes you feel bad – more that it makes all our feelings more intense and gives us the chance to work through them. You were angry with me too – maybe you still are. Let's look at that.'

'I wanted to be a storyteller. You said I could. Then I realised I'll never be safe. I can't stand up in front of people. Thanes and headmen don't like it; they want to shove me down. So you lied to me! Then you went off with Ursel and left me alone.'

'Thanes and headmen will always be a danger. But we can't let them stop us being who we are, singing our songs, telling our stories, standing up tall. That's a time to jump on a strong mare of anger and lift up our heads and neigh!'

Meg smiled.

Hilda went on, 'Did you notice how all the women worked together to put a stop to Thane Roger's vileness? Even Oswynne. All of them made a circle of protection round you. That's what we have to do. It's not fair we have to, but it's our skill. When your moon-time comes round again, remember how that ring of women held you. Let their warmth sing to you, like a voice under water.'

Meg looked down, shy again, 'Do you have to work with Ursel all the time?'

Meg's whine irritated Hilda like a swarm of biting flies. She took a moment to breathe before she answered. Huldran's voice spoke inside her: *I know you're doing your best! Meg's stuck in thinking about herself. This is hard because Meg is so important to you. Listen to her, Hilda.*

Aloud Hilda said, 'That hurt is still stinging where you said I lied to you and went off. I am sorry I hurt you, Meg; I didn't mean to. I can't wait to get back to helping you learn more storytelling skills. When the Moot's over, if Ursel speaks well, we'll all be given more respect for our crafts and more time for them. And I will have more time for you. That's why I'm asking you to help Ursel get her mind clear and her story straight. She will speak for all of us.' They were quiet together in the warmth.

'How long does the bleeding last?'

'A few days usually. After the bleeding many women feel a rush of energy. You'll get to know your own pattern, if you give yourself some inner-listening time every day. I wish you every blessing, dear Meg, for the flowering of your moon wisdom.'

They rested until the sun moved past noon.

Meg stretched, tied the cloth with moss inside and stowed some in her bag. 'See that hawthorn thicket across the water? There's a fox-earth under its roots. The day you came, May and I saw the vixen drag a swan-carcass up there out of the rushes. There might be bones left from it.'

Hilda noticed Meg stood taller than before. Her arms moved with fluid grace where there had been angular elbows before.

'I'd love to show you the dancing cranes near here,' Meg smiled.

'Bones first, cranes second,' Hilda declared.

As they pushed off from the shore, a tendril of mist drifted over the water, then another and another, translucent in the sunlight.

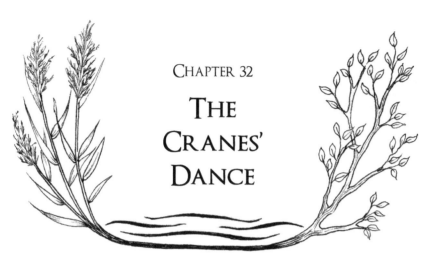

CHAPTER 32

THE CRANES' DANCE

HILDA

Meg's strokes with the punt-pole settled into a rhythm as they searched the margin of the mere for the fox-earth. Hilda leaned forwards as she told her story, to make sure Meg heard every word clearly.

'This is the part I told when you weren't there …

RETURN OF THE QUEEN

Marelda and Ziske roamed the woods together. Marelda knelt to pinch and sniff leaves and count the petals of gentian and orchid; Ziske showed her how to climb trees and swim in fast-rushing mountain streams. They splashed and gasped in icy melt-water. They found a pool in the woods loud with frogs; lily flowers nearby made them giggle with their man-shaped stamens in pale cloaks.

'Are you really going back to your husband?' Ziske asked, suddenly grave.

'Yes. I know I can change him.'

Ziske grimaced. 'I've heard that before – usually from women with hidden bruises. What if he goes on hitting and shaming you?'

'I've seen how he is truly. He hides behind roughness but he's tender inside.'

Ziske shook her head. 'When it all goes wrong, I'll help.' They walked back to Huldran's house in silence.

That evening, Huldran served delicate slices of smoked trout after their usual turnip pottage. As they licked their fingers, she announced, 'Tomorrow morning it will be time for you both to go back to your homes. I'll miss you so much, dear cubs! I'm pleased to see how strong you've grown. I know you can take up your work as queens.'

Marelda and Ziske smiled and wept a little and gave each other small gifts.

They stood outside the door of the Cave of Dreams in the first rays of sunshine. Marelda ran her hand over the sinuous carvings, to remember them. Huldran blessed them, 'You've travelled so far on your inner and outer journeys! As you go your separate ways, the sureness of our friendship will travel with you. Come back when you can!'

Marelda made her way down through pine and oak, singing to keep her courage high. The earth answered the beat of her feet. At the edge of the forest she stopped and looked down at Peony Valley. Smoke rose from cooking fires; children's voices blew on the wind. She imagined her own child's voice mingling with the others. She took a deep breath and murmured, 'Now I have to be the Queen, like my mother and all the queens before her. Come with me, Swan, Mare, Bear! I'm not sure I can do this – but I'm doing it.' She strode down to claim her future.

Hilda paused as Meg steered towards the shore. 'There it is! The hawthorn above the fox-earth.' They poked amongst reeds and bramble – 'Look! The swan wing is still here. I hoped it would be.'

The wing was decaying and muddy but still tough. They pulled it apart, dug feathers out of muscle, and stripped away flesh with their knives.

Hilda grinned with relief. 'It's strong and whole with no cracks. It's hollow already, apart from some fine struts inside. All I need to do is clean it, file it clear, shape the mouthpiece and cut holes in the right place.'

Meg scratched around and pulled the other wing-bone out of scraped-out soil near the entrance to the foxhole. It was scored with tooth-marks but usable. With a mutter of thanks to the swan that lost its life and the fox that spared the wings, they sat down at the water's edge to clean their finds.

'We'll borrow Wulf's tools. We'll have two fine flutes to sing the songs of our bones – one for me, one for you.' Hilda watched delight wrestle with disbelief in Meg's face – a mix of feelings that she shared.

Meg caught tiddlers in her net while Hilda built a small fire, well away from the fox's den. They strung the fish on a stick, toasted and ate them, sucked their singed fingers and laughed. They drank the weak ale that Seren had given them. When the ale pot was empty, they searched the margin of the mere for mallard nests and filled the pot with eggs. They left plenty of nests untouched so the ducks could thrive.

Gnats whined up from the reeds. 'Have some of Mother's sweet-gale salve,' Meg offered a small jar to Hilda. 'It helps to keep them off.' They rubbed it onto their faces, arms and legs.

'Are you ready to see the cranes?' Meg asked.

Hilda looked at the swirls of mist rising from the surface. The sky was blotted out by a layer of it, pale as the inside of fresh-water oyster shells. 'Can you find the way, in this mist?'

Meg shrugged. 'What happened when Marelda got home?'

Hilda took up the tale:

In the Great Hall, King Bors lounged by the fire, picking his teeth with a little bronze dagger. He turned to his friend Olgor, 'I like to see the men edgy. Keep them at each other's throats, then they'll be ready to fight any time.' Olgor nodded and poured him more strong peach liquor. Bors drank it down in one gulp and wiped his coppery bristles with the back of his hand.

A scuffle broke out amongst the men playing dice and Bors cheered them on. 'Go for him, Sweyn, nip in under his guard and throw him. Oh, Argulf's got him down. This dagger for the winner!' It rattled across the floorboards. As they elbowed each other to grab it, a shadow fell across the doorway.

In she stepped. Silence fell and they all looked up. Bors blinked. This tall woman looked like his wife. Could it be? Her dark hair was bound back and there were swan-feathers in it like a crown. She stooped to pick up the dagger and he recognized a bracelet shaped like a serpent that he'd given her. The wrist that had been pale and thin was brown now and sleek with muscle, but it was her.

'Better keep this safe, husband,' she said. 'Somebody could get hurt.' Her voice was musical, deeper than he remembered, with a hint of laughter in it that needled him. She placed the knife on the table. 'A dispute, Sweyn and Argulf? We'll help you sort it out. Bors, is it still your custom to hear requests in the mornings? I'll sit in counsel with you. Come to our Hall tomorrow, Sweyn and Argulf. Don't squander your strength squabbling. We'll need your muscles to plant trees – replacements for the groves cut down when this Hall was built.'

'Where in the name of all the gods have you been?' Bors yelled.

'I stayed with the wise woman and learned what we need from her.' Marelda half-smiled. Her ears were full of swan wingbeats and she felt the air lift her.

'Thought you were dead – been choosing my next wife!'

'I'm alive.' Her eye was merry. Some kind of noise was building up from the back of the hall: laughter, stamping feet, crude suggestions.

'Fun and games tonight then!' somebody called out. Bors whirled round, fury rising, but Olgor laid a hand the size of a ham on his arm.

'Keep them edgy, that's what you said,' Olgor whispered. 'That's all it is. Laugh it off.'

Bors frowned, spat and called for more drink.

Piroshka brought mint tea and honeyed nuts for Marelda and fussed over her, scolding and patting her by turns, as the men drank steadily. 'Such pretty embroidery, the stars and flowers on your hairband, dear, such neat stitching – who made it for you?'

'A friend.' Marelda missed Ziske and the clean air of the mountain. 'I gave her a pouch of dried rosemary ... I think I'll go to bed now,' Marelda said. 'Please leave me a bowl of warm water to wash with.'

'Bed, bed!' shouted a rabble of voices. They cheered as the royal couple retired to their quarters, one straight as a spear, one lumbering and belching.

Bors pushed Marelda onto the bed and grabbed at her clothes.

She rolled aside and stood up. 'Not like that.'

He roared and lunged at her.

Her ears rang with a wild neigh as anger surged through her. In her head she sprang on the back of a red mare, reined it in and rode. 'You're upset because I'm not whining and cowering like I used to do?' She stood tall.

He growled again and went for her. He was heavy-set, bigger than her. He dragged her by the hair to the bed and pinned her down with a knee while he fumbled with his garments.

'I said – no. Not like this.' Her eyes unnerved him. He looked away, at her breasts, at his hound bitch whimpering a little beside the bed. Marelda got a knee between him and her own body. 'I will make love with you, but not this way.'

He pushed her down, his hand on her throat.

She reached out in her mind for help and heard a rush of feathers. She grasped his arm with both hands and forced it away from her neck. 'No!'

Bors was so surprised that he fell off the bed. The hound licked his face. He felt tears well up – the final humiliation.

He flung himself back on top of her and thrust – or tried to. It was limp. He cursed and tried again, but his body would not do what he wanted. He covered his face in his hands so she couldn't see him cry. The fight leaked out of him through his traitor eyes.

Marelda wrung out a cloth in the bowl of warm water and washed his neck and hands, then his face, when he let her. She spoke soothing words about his dogs and horses, the birds she'd seen in the forest, and asked how the planting was going this year. She combed his hair with her fingers and massaged his scalp. He sat on the edge of the bed, with his head drooping. She rubbed his shoulders with herb-scented oil, then his back. A great sigh left his chest. He rubbed the ears of the brindled bitch and watched as Marelda slid off her clothes.

She turned to him and asked, 'Shall we make a child together?'

He nodded.

She drew him back to bed, settled over his body and folded herself around the gentle man that only she knew.

Many months later, on a night of storms, a new sound woke the court: a baby crying. Marelda's daughter took her first breath, and the Queen cradled her little one in her arms.

Meg sighed a deep sigh. Hilda watched the story settle into Meg. *At least I gave you this. The first part of this story is complete. But you need the next bit!*

SEREN

'Mam, Mam, can I go and join the percession, can I, please?' May hopped from one foot to the other.

Pipes and whistles started up from the crowd gathering around the barrow. Far away they could hear a deep-toned drum and the whinny of a pony.

'They're coming from Thornthicket. I can see them! There's a dapple grey pulling a cart and it's covered in mayflowers! It's wading through the cow parsley up to its knees. I think it's got the old lady in it. Has she really got hair like a pile of snow, Mam? Their headman's riding in front and all the settlement has come, people my age and grown-ups. They've brought chickens in cages and a lamb on a rope and I want to go and see. Please, Mam!'

Seren shaded her eyes and looked down the slope. She felt light-headed, hardly there.

Wulf laid a broad hand on her shoulder. 'Alright, my star?'

She looked up. *What does 'alright' mean? Am I?*

'I'll take you, chicken,' Wulf said as he swung May up on his shoulders. She giggled and whooped as he strode down to join the rest of the Wellstowe people going to meet their neighbours from the next settlement. *He's acknowledging her as his daughter!*

Seren checked around. *Smoke is rising from the cooking-fire down beside the Hall; up here at the meeting place the posts stand ready for tents; there's plenty of firewood stacked by hearth-pits.* A skylark sang high overhead. She scanned the forest. *No trace of mist in there, but over the fen it hangs thick as gathered wool. Meg is out there with Hilda.* A familiar tunnel of worry opened up but Seren did not scurry down it. She heard again the Mere-Wife gurgle with laughter and swish her two tails. Ripples washed her mind. She sighed, and then Seren did something she hadn't done for a long time. She rested.

HILDA

Cree-enk-cree-unk! The call of the cranes echoed through the mist. With no splash, Meg dipped the pole into the water and steered the punt towards an unseen island. *This is eerie! But Meg is confident.* Meg leaned forward and grasped a clump of reed to pull the boat in gently, tied the painter to an alder trunk, and showed Hilda where to step on the slippery bank. A nudge in her ribs told Hilda 'shush.' They squirmed their way behind clumps of sedge, trying not to rustle. They crept through the dark bare twigs and shimmering trunks of a birch grove, then dropped to the ground to watch a patch of turf in the centre of the island.

Meg lay on her front and peered between rushes. She quivered with the intensity of her gaze. Feathers edged through the mist, scaly toes pointed and trod. Meg turned to share an open-mouthed smile with Hilda as a pair of cranes stepped onto the grass in front of them.

The birds called and nodded to each other; the red patches on their heads glowed in stray beams of sunlight. They spread their wings, hopped and bounced from one foot to the other.

Hilda's breath stilled on her lips. Holding their wings up like feathered arms, the huge birds turned and bowed, then leaped and twirled. Sunset light gleamed through the mist, turning their white wings to gold. Beak and long leg, tail and curved neck, their shadows fell across the grass and danced with them.

Another pair stepped out of the trees, lifted their wings and greeted each other. They wafted trails of cloud between their snake-like necks and their pinions.

A dozen birds gathered, their strange eyes intent on their partners. They moved with slow grace, each foot-thump lofted by their wing-feathers, as they uttered their eerie calls.

Cold crept into Hilda's toes in the mud but she didn't flinch. Meg lay entranced and Hilda tasted Meg's joy, drank it in, savoured it with her.

The birds vanished into clammy whiteness as the sun slid below the horizon. Light lingered in the sky but chill struck. Hilda shivered.

They moved silently towards the punt where they wrapped shawls round their shoulders. Meg poled the boat out from the shore through reed beds into open water.

Hilda cleared her throat. After so long without speaking, the words came out rusty. 'They're wonderful.'

'I watch them every year.' Meg wiped a drip from her nose.

'Who have you shown them to?'

'No one.' Meg looked up and met Hilda's eye. 'Not Mother, not even May. What if she said something by mistake, and men came with arrows …?'

'You trust me with this secret.' The gravity of it weighted Hilda's stomach. 'That's the best gift you could give me. Thank you.' *You let me come closer than your mother or your sister,* she thought.

Tomorrow – her mind ran ahead to the Moot – *it's likely Thane and headman will blame me for the row between Ursel and Kedric, and kick me out. Without me putting ideas in women's heads, they can take control. This night could be my last here. I may never hear Meg telling the stories I've taught her. When I'm old, I'll have no apprentice to care for me, I'll die alone in a ditch and everything I've learned will die with me. So far I've walked, so many nights I've lain awake with bones aching to find her, or somebody like her. Nobody drinks the stories into their sinews like Meg does.* She buried her head in her hands.

'What is it, Hilda?' Meg's cheeks still shone with the glory of the crane-dance.

I should warn her. If I go, where does that leave Meg? She won't ever stand in her strength, telling a myth in the Great Hall. Her life will dribble away while she scrubs floors, mucks out pigsties, carries water. Hilda imagined the light in Meg's eyes going out like a tallow dip, her voice falling away into silence.

'Meg, they may make me leave, tomorrow.'

'Because of the stories? Because you make people think?'

'Mmmhmm.'

'Hilda – do you ever change the endings? Make the women more … tame, the men a bit … nicer? Would you, if it meant you could stay on?'

Hilda shook her head slowly. Her chest was empty – no breath came to carry words. 'I can't. Even if they kill me, I've got to tell the truth of the stories. My bones speak through me.'

Meg's eyes filled and she bit her lip. 'I don't want you to mess the stories up, Hilda, I just can't stand thinking about – if you have to go. When I talk about looking at clouds underwater or what mice think, you listen. Everybody else says don't be daft. When you say I can tell stories, I feel like it might be true. I'm still scared of standing up in front of them all, and Thane Roger might get me if I stand out. But if you think I could learn to do it … I want that. You've only been here since Hretha-feast, and already I feel different.'

'This mist seems to be wrapping round us, Meg. The Mere-Wife may be stirring. The moon seems to be clear over the forest, but we're wallowing in fog here. I think something's protecting you.'

'You see, nobody else would say things like that to me.'

Meg needs more learning with me. The fen needs us to tell the old stories, through all the generations. I've got a few more years in me until my body gives out, but after that, what? Without the stories that guide our care for Earth Mother, people could lurch into ravaging her. I can't let that happen! Only Meg can carry them into the years to come …

Hilda blurted out, 'Would it ever be possible … has a slave ever run away from a settlement? From Wellstowe, I mean?' Hilda heard a frog croaking more musically than she did.

'They'd set the dogs on anyone who tried that! Bring them back piece by piece.' Hilda could hear Seren's grandmother's voice, harsh with hate, echoing through Meg's. 'Do you mean me, leave Mother and May?'

'I … I'm sorry.' Hilda winced. The shock in Meg's voice told her: Meg couldn't do it. 'I only meant … I thought maybe, if I do get thrown out, you might want to come too and be my apprentice. I didn't mean to upset you … it was just an idea.' The silence was broken only by the slip of water past their hull.

'What did Marelda call her baby?' Meg's voice shook. 'If you have to leave, I might not hear the rest of the story.'

'Snow Storm. But they all loved her so much they called her Snow for short.'

'Did she go to the wise woman's house when she was ... my age?'

From far across the fen, voices carried through the murk. 'Help! Help!'

CHAPTER 33

MIST LICKING HIS HEELS

MEG

'Who's that in our four-seater punt? That's a Wellstowe boat! What are you doing out here, in the middle of Clay Fen?' The words jumped out of Meg's mouth before she could think.

'What do you think we're doing? Trying to get to Wellstowe, of course!' Thane Roger grabbed for their boat, making it rock. His grasping hairy hand made her wince and brought back his words at the Feast: 'I'll show her what a man is …'

She shrank back.

Hilda took the punt-pole and pushed against the gunwale of the Thane's boat, making theirs edge back out of reach.

'Don't leave us! Please help. We're alone, the two of us, out here,' Redwald begged. He clung onto a willow branch and pulled himself out of the half-sunk boat onto the bank of an island.

Thane Roger hunched in the punt, jaw set, boots in water.

Out of reach, Meg breathed easier.

'Where are all your Wellstowe men?' Thane Roger bellowed.

'Far away by their hearthside. There's just us. We're your last hope.' Hilda called lightly.

She's enjoying this, Meg thought with astonishment.

Redwald was teetering on the slippery mud. 'We were out on the chalk ridge, measuring up for the ditch, when the messenger from Thaneshall found us. He said to come back, but we knew if we went back overland with him, we'd take another day to get to Thornthicket, then another half a day at least, so we'd miss most of the Moot, and then we saw this boat and thought we could get downstream to Wellstowe quicker in it.'

'Do you lot leave a leaky boat there as a trap for unwary travellers? Is this some horrible fenland custom? A sacrifice for your dark elves?' Thane Roger muttered.

'Of course not,' Meg began. 'Ow!' Hilda's kick was small but sharp.

The storyteller's voice was sharp and carried clearly through the wreaths of mist. 'It's true the spirits of these parts are fierce, especially if any man harasses a local woman. They rear up out of the river in the form of twisted roots, seeking revenge.'

Meg had to pretend to reach down under her seat for something as she put her hand over her mouth to stop the giggles coming out. *How can Hilda be so bold! She's playing them like a fish on a line.*

'That's what happened to us!' Redwald gasped. 'I thought it was a dragon. It rose up out of the mist and bit into our hull.'

'Nonsense,' growled Thane Roger, 'it was just one of those ... what-do-you-call-em –'

'Bog oak!' Meg sat up to join the game. She pulled her jaw down to look solemn. 'That's the shape they take when they're rigid with hate for some human, such as a man who harasses women. They grab people with their iron-hard claws and drag them underwater to drown them.' *He filled me with fear,* Meg thought. *Now it's my turn!* She remembered the tales Edith used to tell, to keep them close to their mams when they were little. 'Have you seen will-o-the-wykes – the wavering flames – on the water's surface? Those are spirits from all the rotting corpses in the bog.'

'Yes! We followed one. We thought it was a lamp but it led us astray!' Redwald was pink under his coating of mud.

'That was you, trying to punt,' sneered Thane Roger.

'You weren't any better, Foster-father. We hit the bank when you snatched the pole.'

'Are you going to sit there talking all night? Take us back to Wellstowe!' A vein stood out on Roger's neck. He fingered his dagger.

Meg edged back against Hilda's warmth.

'I don't think we can travel anywhere, this mist is so thick,' Hilda replied loudly so they could hear, then whispered to Meg: 'How big is this island?'

'Tiny,' Meg whispered back. 'I come here often to get duck-eggs. It's a long way out from the river bank.'

'We'll all have to stay here tonight,' Hilda murmured. 'But don't worry, he won't hurt you. Do you know any more scary stories? Let's keep him bound here by terror.' She called over to the island: 'Thane Roger, your life is in the hands of this young priestess. I don't know my way back; only she does. None of us can punt – only her. She may consent to take us back to Wellstowe in the morning, if we do not anger the spirits of this place. Do you hear me?'

Grunt.

'If you try to lay a hand on her, or threaten her with rape as you did at the Feast, your body will be found suffocated in the swamp, many days dead and stinking.'

Redwald looked at Thane Roger in surprise and disgust.

'It's not me who will do this, but the goddess of this place, who looks after her own,' Hilda continued. 'Do you see the crown Meg wears? You might think it's only water-droplets caught in her hair – but why does the moon spear through the cloud to touch her – her alone? Why does the mist part for her?'

Meg gulped. *Me, a priestess? Hilda must be trying to impress them, to keep me safe. Can I look like one? I've got to. Mother's stories have priestesses in them sometimes – they're powerful.* She thought of Huldran calling up a blizzard. *What would it feel like to be in touch with the land, the light, the water, the wind?* She felt swan-wings lift her, like Queen Marelda when she returned home. Meg shut her eyes, breathed deep, and raised her arms to greet the waxing near-half moon. As she stepped out of their punt onto the islet, she felt nearly as tall as a priestess. 'Spirits of this place, we ask permission to stay here tonight.' She turned, bowing to willow, alder, birch and river. 'Gather sticks,' she commanded the men, and Redwald hurried to obey.

Hilda lit dry leaves with her strike-a-light and fed twigs and sticks into the flames. The two men huddled by the fire.

'If it was in your mind to steal the boat, Thane Roger, or hold me at knife-point,' Hilda spoke in conversational tone, breaking duck-eggs into the pot, 'you will get lost.'

Meg's heart stood still. *Will they believe it?*

Hilda carried on: 'The mist could last for days and I see it clinging to you in particular, but I think it will let Meg through. If you upset her, or hurt her, you could slither into the ooze and never be seen again.'

She bowed her head respectfully and passed the pot of scrambled eggs to Meg first.

Meg took a morsel of egg and laid the food reverently on the earth by their fire, her mouth watering as she spoke a blessing. 'Dark Mother Earth, thank you for your gift of life. Accept our first mouthful. Take our bodies for your meat and our whole selves to mingle with your being, whenever you choose.' She thought that sounded a bit tame, so she added some words in her mother's language, rolling them on her tongue, even though she was not entirely sure what they meant.

'Here, young Redwald, you can take the first spoonful,' Hilda offered the bowl to him. 'You're somebody important aren't you?'

'Not today, I'm not. I'm a simple lost traveller.' He dipped the one spoon into the pot, blew on it, slurped down some of the delicious mess, getting bits in his soft beard, and passed it on.

Each of them ate some of the eggs.

'How is Ursel? Has she recovered?' Redwald asked Meg.

'She's much better.'

Thane Roger wrapped his mud-slimed cloak round him and lay down. 'Wake me in the morning,' he growled.

'You and Redwald will need to take turns to keep watch with us,' Hilda ordered.

Meg narrowed her eyes. She had Thane Roger skewered now and she was not letting him go. 'The dragon may still be about, and who knows what elves and spirits. Have you heard about the dead hands that pull down anyone who tries to cross the marsh on tussocks? That bogle called Grendel used to live around here; they say his mother's lair is somewhere nearby and the hero in the story didn't really finish her off. How could he when she's got the fen on her side?'

'Foster-son, you sleep, I'll take first watch.'

Thane Roger wants to look tough, Meg thought. She recalled the horror that thrilled through the old tales. *They kept me and the other children from wandering off. Let's keep these two from trying to leave.*

Hilda nodded to her and Meg launched into a story that still gave her nightmares.

THE BURIED MOON

The moon, Queen of the skies, turned her ear towards the earth (just as she is tonight) and heard cries of agony, so she wrapped herself in a dark cloak and stepped down onto the land. She followed the crying to a marsh, and stepped across from tussock to tussock all the way to a dark mere. She clung to a willow branch and leaned over to listen – the screams came from under the water. Crack! The branch was rotten; it broke. Down and down she fell – her cloak floated away – her feet touched mud.

The moon knocked at a huge bog oak door.

The voice of the sludge greeted her: 'Ah, you've come to see me at last, have you, sister? Who d'you think you are, swanning around in a pale embroidered linen gown, all high and mighty? You can't come in here like that! You've got to be a bare little sliver, just your own naked self, to come in here. Drag it off her, boggarts!'

A hundred spiky hands tore at the moon and voices screeched. She crept into a corner and shivered.

Sludge-sister's belly heaved and shuddered. She writhed in agony and screamed. Out burst a dark jagged shape. She snarled and cast it from her – it joined the other bogles, searching for someone to torture. They found the moon. Nights and days went by and still they held her down in the cold.

In the settlements, people looked at the sky, expecting the moon. 'We can't see to feed the cattle, nor get the peat in for the fire. We need the moon. Where is she?'

They gathered in the wise woman's hut. She swirled water in her scrying bowl, and looked deep into the mysteries.

'I see the moon – far below the surface. She can't escape. The bogles and the boggarts have captured her. We must go where the water is in turmoil, beside the great willow.'

Out into the fen the people went, treading carefully, arms linked, clutching their charms in their hands.

In a narrow channel between islands, the river swirled and boiled. Was that a shimmer in the deep?

They threw a rope into the foam, weighted with iron. Down it sank to the muddy bottom.

The moon saw the rope, threw on her gown and climbed up it, hand over hand, towards the water surface. Bogles in the shape of beetles bit her toes and clung on. Boggarts got tangled in her hair and flapped like bats. Horrors hung on to her hem. Terrors sank their fangs into her ankles. Then they all burst through into the air together, scattering glittering drops.

The moon shook off her assailants and sailed up into the sky again, filling it with light. But the bogles and the boggarts, the horrors and the terrors, jumped down onto land and went searching for people to poke and gnaw and relish, to torture and to tear. They're out in the world still, seeking prey: such as any human foolish enough to roam the fen at night.

Thane Roger shifted uneasily and looked round.

Meg pulled her mouth into a serious frown and peered into the darkness.

Hilda started singing a song that Meg had never heard before:

Bogles and Boggarts

Bully boys and braggarts, watch out for the boggarts!
They'll poke you and bash you
And pull you down.

There's a bogle out to get you
Called Kill-Yourself,
And a horror lurking close to you
Called Hurt-the-Ones-Who-Care-for-You.
They'll stick you and scratch you and
In the slime you'll drown.

Shame and Blame, the twins,
Are working together;
They'll poke you in the eye; you'll be blinded forever.
Can't-Share will tear you, Can't-Cry will fry you,
I'm-No-Good makes you his food,
He'll grab your toes and chew you.

If you put yourself outside of
The love of Mother Earth
You'll feel a bogle shoving
Your proud nose in the dirt.

If you glimpse a bogle gurning over your shoulder;
Your stomach churns, you quiver!
But – don't run, don't fight, scream if you like –
Hold your ground – be bolder!

Listen to the blighter – what's he got to say?
He might tell you what you need,
What you needed yesterday,
Or a year ago or longer,
And still you lack today.

Thane Roger got up to pee. Meg noticed he didn't go further than the edge of the firelight. He slapped at tendrils of mist that curled round his heels as he moved. It dragged round him like a damp cloak. Back by the fire, he nudged Redwald with his toe and wrapped himself up in his cloak, pulling it tight around his ears.

Redwald sat up.

Hilda played the tune on her elder pipe and sang some more:

> Sit down with your bogle
> As he dines on your raw heart.
> Pass him salt tears and feed him
> With your wounds – how they smart!
>
> You fear him but he's part of you.
> As he mangles you and chews,
> This is the start of new
> Life for you and those you care for too.
>
> Hear him out. Ask nicely what he knows.
> When he's told you, you may find he wants to doze.
> Let him slide down into mud where the slimy creatures go
> To sleep in the magic of the ooze.
>
> His claws soften, his teeth fall out.
> At the bottom of the pond, you pupate together.
> You rest until you're ready, then you wriggle and you rise
> Up into the sky as – dragonflies!
> Now the earth is not just dirt to you.
>
> You spread your wings and learn
> How to love, not hurt.
> You know you're Earth Mother's child,
> Like all creatures of the wild,
> You can care for her now that you're free!

Redwald rubbed his head. 'It's too chilly for sleep, so I heard your story, but I'm not sure I caught all of it. Sounded pretty nasty. I think I've heard something like it – at my cousin Ola's court perhaps.'

'There are many versions.' Hilda nodded. 'We can work on this one, Meg, but how you told it tonight was perfect.'

'Are you really a priestess?' Redwald asked. 'I thought you were a – er, British.'

Meg noticed he didn't spit 'slave' as people usually did about her, but called her British – and with some respect. She felt a little warmth for him, then looked at Hilda, not knowing what to say in response.

'What she is tonight is a blessing for us all,' Hilda said firmly. 'And she's also tired. You should get some rest, Meg.'

Meg was glad enough to lay her head down, but she didn't sleep. She was too keen to listen.

'Are you really going to be a king?' Hilda asked.

'I'm waiting for my uncles to decide.' Redwald shrugged. 'There's six of us, brothers and half-brothers and cousins. Any of us could be chosen.'

'I see. And who is Ola?'

'My mother's cousin. I went to see her with my mother the summer before Mother died. Ola is Queen over the valleys and hills to the south, near the source of this river,' Redwald explained. 'There's a mix of tribes over there, all inter-married and mingled. I like the way she rules her lands. It's a bit like your stories, Hilda. I went to a moot there, with elders. It lasted ages but everybody had their say and got listened to.'

Meg wondered about him. *He sounds different from Thane Roger but is he really?*

'Ursel has a mixed heritage,' Hilda said. 'Her father, who sadly died, had a British mother ...'

'I know, I've been visiting Wellstowe with Foster-father since I came to his household when I was eight, whenever I could. I haven't been able to come for a couple of years because of illness and coming and going to Rendlesham. Ursel has changed! Do you know if she's promised to anyone?'

'I'm not involved in the families' discussions,' Hilda replied. 'I'm a visitor myself. You'd better ask her!'

Redwald smiled, 'As soon as I can.'

'Have you any influence with your foster-father? Can you make sure he treats women better – like people, not chattels?'

Meg squinted through one eye to see his reaction. His mouth twisted as he shrugged hopelessly.

'I have another verse of my song for you!' Hilda said.

> *If your brother's got a boggart that is chewing up his liver,*
> *Sit with him, stay close to him, listen while he shivers.*
> *Tell him I won't judge you, friend, look what this bogle's doing!*
>
> *It's really messing up your life! That's your family it's stewing.*
> *Where has it come from? What is its name?*
> *Let's dig a bit deeper*
> *And send it to sleep.*
> *Together we stand up for the weak and the small,*
> *Your bogles made you strong, kind, gentle and tall!*

Redwald's eyes were round.

Meg sat up and yawned.

The moon was setting into the fen, far to the west.

Hilda checked Thane Roger's breathing – 'Even and slow. I'll get some sleep now. There's still a stretch of night before dawn. You two, sleep. We need our wits about us for the Moot tomorrow. We'll start back as soon as there's enough light to find our way.'

Redwald whispered, 'Can you see antlers? Are there stags on this island?'

Shapes swirled between the night sky and the miasma. They were blindfolded by wraith-rags, with squeaks and flutters at their elbows – a gap opened to show dripping branches as sharp as teeth leaning over them.

'The creatures of the fen are with us,' Meg observed. 'They're all watching.'

'Do we really need to be scared of them?' Redwald spoke softly. 'Ursel talks about our lives all being twined together, animals and people.'

Meg assured him, 'I think we can sleep now. The dragons go back to their lairs, and the bogles and boggarts calm down once the men who treat women badly are out of action. They won't hurt us.'

She curled up beside Hilda. She remembered the old feeling of warmth in her friendship with Ursel. Sadness for its loss sighed out from the depths of her lungs. Would she ever get that friendship back?

CHAPTER 34

CLEANSING? I'M CLEAN ENOUGH!

MEG

Meg bit her lip to stop it wobbling when her mother ran to greet them, arms outstretched. 'There you are! I'm so glad you're safe!'

Meg pulled back, straightened her spine to make herself 'priestess' while Thane Roger was watching, although her sodden cloth chafed and her arms ached from poling the punt, and she longed for her Mam's hug.

Hilda gave her a little shove towards her mother, and spoke to Seren, 'Please dress Meg fittingly and take her swiftly to join the elders. I'll get this fire going, to warm our guests.' Hilda turned away from her to poke the cooking-fire behind the Hall, then shouted: 'Otred, Elstan! Come quickly! The pigs can wait for their feed. Please run and tell Headman Kedric and Oswynne we've got honoured guests – it's Thane Roger and his foster-son under all that mud. They need to borrow clean clothes.' The boys' mouths fell open.

Seren called as they scampered off, 'Ask Nelda to come down, to cook porridge and tea for them.'

In the dark of the women's sleeping house, Meg slumped into Seren's embrace and allowed herself a tear as she told her mother about her new womanhood. Seren hugged her, helped her change, and gave her a piece of new bread she'd saved from the morning's baking. Meg swallowed in haste, and explained as she washed herself.

'I took them all round the islands, through reed beds, past lilypads, round meanders and back again. I talked about treacherous currents and mud that can suck down a boat, how only a few know the ways of the river and how difficult it is to navigate. But as the sun rose above the chalk ridge, we saw cooking-smoke from around the barrow. I was hungry, so although I was trying to delay Thane Roger, to give everyone time to get going with the Moot, I poled fast.'

Seren rubbed her daughter's tired arms with a lavender salve. Meg slid into Seren's spare shift and undyed wool overdress.

'I'm supposed to be a priestess,' Meg told her. 'Hilda pretended so as to scare Thane Roger.'

'Better wash your face then.' Seren mopped her with a cloth and they both laughed. 'Stand still while I braid your hair. What happened with the mist?'

'Got to get up there! I'll plait and tell you while we walk.'

They met Edgar striding down the slope. 'Mother and Father have already been cleansed by the elders and they're in the moot-circle, so they sent me. Are the mud-covered men really Thane Roger and Redwald? I'm allowed to open the chest in Father's house.' His chin lifted, chest puffed out.

Nelda hurried down past him, without her baby.

'Hilda the storyteller's looking after the guests. Take over from her, please,' Seren called after her. 'And don't rush them. They're tired and chilled.'

Be as slow as you can, Nelda, thought Meg. 'Let's wait for Hilda to catch up.'

When Hilda came panting up the slope, Meg bunched the borrowed dress up with her belt and they hurried.

They stopped to draw breath at the place where three tracks meet. 'Let's make you look like a priestess,' Seren said and pinned Meg's braids around her head. 'You did well to slow Thane Roger down. If he'd got here last night, he'd be bossing everybody around today.'

'Have they started yet?' Hilda asked.

'Preparations. Elder Edith's insisting on the full ritual, with the elders blessing everybody first; Thane Roger would've skipped all that. Edith will be glad to see you, cushla. She's been fretting without your arm to steady her.'

They hurried along the churned-up track to the brow of the hill. A dozen tents clustered in two groups: Mereham's camp on the sunset side and Thornthicket's by the beeches.

Next to the barrow on the eastern side stood a new bothy made of branches and planks, roughly thatched. Lower down, the cauldron from the Great Hall swung from a tripod. More cooking-fires covered a flat grassy area.

The smell of stew wafted towards Meg. She asked, 'However did you get everything up here?'

'The oxen hauled cartloads of gear up all day yesterday,' her mother replied. 'It was just about ready by the time they all arrived. We'd better see where we're needed. They don't seem bothered about cleansing slaves.'

Seren had her blank face on as she gestured to the log-circle where all the folk were gathering.

OSWYNNE

Oswynne's heart thudded in her chest. 'He'll take over! Has he got weapons with him? How many of them are there?'

Edith laid a hand on her arm. 'The little lads said just Thane Roger and Redwald. I see smoke, so somebody's cooking for them. We've got a short space to get the Moot started our way. We've cleansed everyone who's here already. Let's make sure we do the cleansing thoroughly for those two.'

'You're trying to soothe me, but this is serious! What can we do if he comes barging in and tries to take over?' Oswynne pulled her chair closer to the elders and whispered loud. 'I'm not sure what Kedric would do.' She felt hot with embarrassment.

'We'll awe Thane Roger with the weight of the ancient words and the power of the ritual. Can you remember the opening chant? Sometimes we skimp it to get on with business, but this time we need to do it in full splendour.'

Elder Mildreth from Thornthicket drew herself up to her full height, taller even than Kedric, though slender. Her white hair blossomed around her head. She reassured Edith, 'I remember it, Edith dear. But I'll need my granddaughter to give me a hand if we walk three times round the barrow to bring in the ancestors and then three times round the circle. Let's have women from each settlement attending us, with frame drums and pipes or whatever they have with them. That's Wulf with the deep-toned drum, isn't it? He can play for us. Have we got any other music? Not the horn yet, Elfric; that's for summoning everyone.'

'Where's Hilda?' Oswynne saw her chatting with the youngsters. 'Ask her to come over, Adela.' Oswynne chewed her lip. She could not see how a few chords would pacify Thane Roger in full rant, but maybe it would help. 'What else can we think of, to take the wind out of his sails?'

URSEL

'Where've you been, Hilda?' Ursel's hand trembled as she grabbed Hilda's wrist. 'I can't get it straight, what I want to say. I know you've tried, but I keep getting sidetracked. Everything's tangled up in my head. What shall I start with? How do I end? You've got to help me!' she yelped.

She wanted the steadiness of Winfrith's arm around her, but Winfrith was busy holding Nelda's baby.

Adela arrived with a message for Hilda. *How annoying!*

Hilda turned from one to the other, confused.

Ursel blinked as somebody stepped forward from behind Hilda. She didn't recognise Meg at first. This new Meg stood tall as an ash tree. *Are those red beads at her throat? Is that a snake bangle on her arm?*

Meg's voice rang out like Queen Marelda's in the story when she broke up the fight. 'Ursel, I think I can help you, if you'll let me.'

Ursel's face crunched into her accustomed scowl.

Hilda sent Adela away: 'Tell your mother I'll be there as soon as I've tuned my harp,' and she fiddled with the strings. 'Ursel and Meg, I think you've got some sorting out to do, before you can work together.'

Meg spoke with authority, without shame: 'Something has come between us, Ursel, since – well, ever since your father died. I know you're grieving for him. I miss him too. Kenelm was a good man.'

Ursel flushed with fury. 'How dare you! It was you and me who killed him. He'd be here now if we hadn't been so dimwitted.'

'What do you mean?' Meg's voice cracked.

Hilda looked up from the tuning pegs in surprise.

'Don't pretend! You know what we did. You just don't care.'

Meg stared wide-eyed, 'I don't understand.'

'You and me, sliding down the roof of our hall. You saw how the thatch came off. We picked bits of it out of our hair – and laughed. That's where the sleet came in before Yule, from that corner of the roof. So Dad went up on his ladder to mend it. The rungs of the ladder were slippery. The thatch was greasy with frost.' She stopped and cleared her throat. 'He came hurtling down. I heard him cry out and came running. His tools were on the ground next to the ladder, right where he fell. He always kept them sharp.' She bit her lip. 'When I got there, he was … making a noise. Blood was pouring from a head wound. Then the sounds stopped. He died that night.'

'Oh! So you mean – if we hadn't played on the roof that day, the sleet wouldn't have come through and he wouldn't have had to mend it. Then he wouldn't have fallen off! Ursel, I am so sorry.' Meg's eyes were dark with sorrow.

'You … really … didn't know?' Ursel said slowly.

'No. I didn't think – I thought it was just an accident.'

Winfrith's mouth was opening and shutting in surprise as she patted the baby.

'It's hard to know what the Fates are doing, sometimes,' Hilda said, 'why they make us suffer so much. Do they weave all the threads of our destiny, or do we add some? That was hard for you to lose your father, Ursel. If the tools hadn't been right under him, he might have just been shaken and bruised – not killed. If the winter storms had blown from a different corner of the world, the thatch might have stayed put. Did you mean to hurt anyone? Of course not! You were simply children having fun. If, if, if ... Sometimes people fall off roofs and it's nobody's fault.'

A sigh from the pit of her lungs shook Ursel. She rubbed her face, then turned to Meg. 'When you came to find me, that time when we were at the deer-scrape and the boar got into Headman's house ... who sent you?'

Meg frowned with worry. 'Nobody sent me. I came by myself.'

'Why?'

'They needed you. The others were making things worse. You're the only one who understands the pigs; they listen to you.'

'They would beat you if they knew you'd run off like that. You risked that to fetch me!'

'You have skill with animals,' Meg levelled her gaze with Ursel's.

'And you have skill with stories,' Ursel noted. 'You told me Hilda's tales when I missed some, herding the swine. Maybe you can help me with my word-gift for the Moot.'

Winfrith gaped.

'Ah, my harp's tuned up.' Hilda swept her fingers across the strings. 'I'll play every melody I know, to give you time. Go to the deer-scrape – fast!'

MEG

Memories rushed through Meg's mind as they ran: Ursel climbing – wading in a stream – racing with a hound puppy – always moving. Even when she sat listening to a story, Ursel would be drawing with a twig in the ashes, or chewing grass, or swinging her legs. She was never still.

The two of them leapt down into the chalk scrape under the roots of the fallen beech. Nobody could see them there. It wasn't quite a cave, but the roots had torn out a hollow in the earth, which shielded them from the din of the gathering.

'Stand here.' Meg led Ursel to the middle of the small arena. 'Tell the first part.'

Ursel began.

When she started to get mixed up, Meg said, 'Is the first part finished? Good. Stand up on this lump of chalk.' She listened carefully. 'Ah, now it's the twisting-together part. Stand down again and show how things are intertwined with your hands.'

Ursel smiled as she brought in the strands of her argument from top and bottom, east and west. She did not stumble now when she talked about her father.

'Talk about your father as loud as you like, Ursel,' Meg instructed. 'His spirit is listening; he'll be proud of you.'

Winfrith galloped over to them, without the baby now. 'They need you! Come quick!'

On the way to the Moot place, Meg could see Ursel going through her speech in her head, gesturing with her arms and nodding as each part of her story fell into place.

'Earth Mother hold you,' Meg murmured to her as they reached the crowd.

Ursel smiled briefly and said, 'Thank you.'

A hot tear welled in Meg's eye.

OSWYNNE

'Here they come!' Oswynne caught sight of Edgar and Nelda leading Thane Roger and his foster-son up the slope from the settlement. Her son had given them tunics and breeches. *Those checked leggings that Thane Roger's wearing; I made those for Kedric last month.* Thane Roger moved as if still mired in mud.

'He doesn't look like a man who thinks he's in control of our Moot,' Mildreth remarked as she peered over Oswynne's shoulder.

'He seems quieter, thoughtful. Smaller somehow, not so cocky. What did you do to him down the fen, Hilda?' Edith asked.

Hilda chuckled. 'We told him stories.'

'Is that enough for a person to change?' Mildreth enquired.

'It's one good way to re-shape the way somebody thinks: to change the stories they tell themselves about who they are.' Hilda was not joking now. 'If important people see how human they really are, they may grow kinder.'

'So, is that all we need to do – keep talking to him?' Oswynne asked. *Ridiculous idea!*

'Also, we'd better make sure he hasn't got any weapons on him!' Hilda said with a small smile.

Oswynne hustled off to find Evrard and Gaufrid. They seemed to have forgotten the pile of spears propped against the barrow that they were meant to be guarding.

MEG

Hilda's fingers leapt into life, making a tune that started feet and fingers tapping. It grew into grand sweeping music as the elders linked arms and started the procession.

They walked round the barrow, then round the moot-circle to the beat of the drums, strewing willow branches and chanting as they went.

Edith's elbow was heavy on Meg's forearm as she steadied the elder. Meg didn't understand all the ancient words, but she filled her lungs with the peace they called into the meeting. Sixty voices joined the chorus, children singing along with their parents. The noise sent rooks flapping out of the tops of oak and elm.

Headman Kedric, straight as a spear in his best tunic, guided Thane Roger and Redwald to the moot-circle entrance.

'What fine workmanship!' Gaufrid balanced Thane Roger's blade on the palm of his hand. Respectfully, he added it to the stack of weapons beside the barrow. 'Thank you, sir. Please step this way for the cleansing ceremony.'

'Cleansing! I'm clean enough.' Thane Roger grunted.

'It's the custom.' Gaufrid grinned, leading him to the willow arch where the elders waited.

Meg kept her arm firm under Elder Edith's elbow. When Edith was steady in her place, Meg handed her a bowl of spring water.

Mildreth dipped a spray of hawthorn flowers and sprinkled it over Thane Roger's head.

The elders chanted a prayer – part blessing, part thanks – that ended with the questions: 'Has all anger fled from you? Are you calm and clear as the Wellstowe pool?'

Thane Roger's 'Hmph' did not satisfy the elders. He looked around angrily and scratched. Kedric's second-best tunic was made of rougher cloth than he was used to. 'Who is this girl? I thought she was a slave, but they're calling her priestess now!'

Meg saw Thane Roger jab his thumb her way. *I should be afraid – but fear seems to slide off me like drops from a mallard's feathers. There's a new stillness inside me!*

'People are often more than they seem,' remarked Elder Edith gently.

The elders began the cleansing again. *They're working so seriously to rid Thane Roger of the burden of his wrath! They seem almost tender.*

At last he sighed 'Alright' and shrugged.

They cleansed Redwald then, and he bowed his head and thanked them.

'Since you are one of the Wuffings, young man, we'd like you to sit with us in the council chairs,' Edith told him, and the other elders nodded in agreement.

'What're Wuffings?' May whispered, close on Meg's heels, eager to see everything.

'It's the family of our kings and queens,' Meg replied. 'Shush now, they're starting.'

Wulf placed a fourth chair next to Elder Mildreth's, for the young prince.

Thane Roger has to take notice of this important boy Redwald. They must have planned this, to stop Thane Roger interfering! How will he take it?

Thane Roger shrank down into himself. Headman Kedric led him to a bench where he took off his boots and emptied dribbles of sludge out of them. He sniffed the scent of rotting rushes and shuddered. *He's remembering bogles!*

The elders took their places. Their chairs were set to the south, so the sun could warm their backs but not dazzle their eyes, and they could see the crowd. Meg and her mother brought their stools close, to be on hand for the elders.

Elder Edith looks like a queen, Meg thought as the old woman settled into her carved chair and swept everyone with her warm gaze.

People from Mereham sat on logs and benches on the western side of the circle, those from Thornthicket on the east and Wellstowe folk on the northern curve of the ring. Children sat on their parents' laps or made daisy chains at their feet. Nelda suckled Elvie. Hounds dozed. Mildreth's pony cropped the grass.

Elder Elfric blew his horn. Lapwings rose from the turf and tumbled, fluting, high above.

Elder Edith asked for a blessing from the Hare Goddess of the Heath, who gives clear sight into past and future, and people's hearts. She called on Deer Mother, who makes tracks through wild places for us to follow. She rolled her tongue around the names of the people's ancestors, praising their wisdom and courage, and pointed out their descendants in the circle.

She sounds as if she's met each one for a chat, thought Meg. *How long is the list going on for?* She nudged her mother.

Seren passed Edith a drink and she took a sip of weak everyday ale, then moved on to thanking everyone for coming and outlined the dispute. 'I am honoured to serve you today with Elders Mildreth of Thornthicket and Elfric of Mereham. They will ensure no bias arises from my kinship to both participants.'

Elder Mildreth's bronze sleeve-clasps glinted in the sun as she opened her arms wide. 'Our aim is not to punish but to find ways for Wellstowe folk to live and work together. When we elders watched at the barrow by moonlight, the ancestors reminded us to follow customs from before the Crossing. Each of the complainants will lay their gift of words before us. While one is speaking, no one will interrupt. We shall all listen with

324

respect and open hearts. After both have spoken, we may ask questions to make matters clear. This is not a simple argument about cattle. Matters of deep principle will rise out of it. The way we talk is as important as what we decide. To draw wisdom from everybody here, we'll create groups to talk about what comes up in the word-gifts. A speaker for each group will keep track of what is said. As elders, our job is to hear everything and to make a judgment together that draws on the best of what everyone says. If all goes smoothly, we'll be finished by noon and can spend the afternoon catching up with news, trading and preparing for the feast.'

Meg glanced sideways at Thane Roger. *How is he taking this?* He was slumped on the bench so she could not see his face.

Elder Elfric stood up, leaning on his staff. Care tugged round his mouth, making his wispy beard wag as he talked. 'We decided the first to speak should be the one with the most injuries from the dispute. We call on Ursel, daughter of Ragnild of the family of Herewald and Beorngyth, Founders of Wellstowe. Ursel, lay out your word-gift.'

Meg smiled encouragingly as Ursel stepped up to speak. *Will she do it? Can she do it?* Meg willed Ursel on, gripping her hands together so tightly that her fingers turned red.

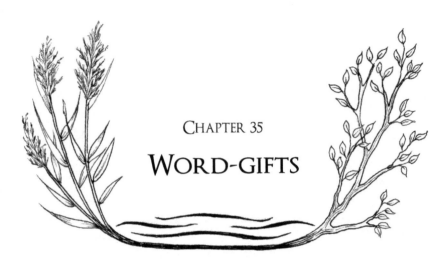

CHAPTER 35

WORD-GIFTS

URSEL

This is the moment I've lived all my life for, and dreaded. Ursel lifted her eyes above the heads of the crowd, seeking green leaves in the edge of the wood. She breathed them in, pushing fear out through the soles of her feet; that much she remembered of Hilda's teaching. *Tell them what happened:* Meg's prompting came back to her.

'I take the settlement's pigs out to find their food in the forest every day; I'm teaching my brother to look after them too. That day, he kept an eye on the herd while I tracked a hind I've been following since the rut. I was high in an oak, she and last year's calf below, when I noticed the hunters targeting her. I could not believe my eyes. It is against all sense and decency to kill breeding females; it was my duty to prevent it. I dropped down and scared the hind to flight. Headman Kedric, my uncle, leading the hunt, shouted and threatened me, so I ran, too.

'When he caught me, he beat me – a free woman – with the butt of his spear. I had bruising on my face, arms and back; they had to soak my tunic off because of cuts. I can show my scars if you wish – but the insults hurt most.

'The next day, Uncle Kedric took the young pig that was my perk for swineherd duties. He insisted it had to be killed to punish me and to serve to Thane Roger at our Hretha-feast. I planned to make myself a pair of boots from the hide and cook the liver for my mother at the autumn slaughter. He deprived me of my right to share out the meat and give it as I chose, earning respect from my family and friends for my year's work. He wasn't just taking something that belonged to me; he was undermining my standing in the community. He called me "witless" but I don't think he was using his wits …'

'She deserved it!' Kedric jumped to his feet, shaking his fist with rage.

Ursel stared at him and stood her ground, but her voice crept down her throat and congealed into a lump.

Elder Mildreth stood up and looked down at Kedric from half a head taller than him. She held her bony shoulders high and angular. 'Ah, Cousin Kedric, I see you're eager to speak. Your turn will come. For now, Ursel is laying out her view and we shall hear all she wishes to tell us. If you speak again, you may not remain in this Moot. If you wish to leave, of course you may at any time, but you may not then come back into the circle: we shall give judgment without hearing your side.' The Elder followed up her grim tone with a fierce look from her ice-blue eyes.

'Sit down, old chap, let the girl have her go,' Bertold growled, tugging at Kedric's tunic.

Ursel could almost see smoke pouring out of her uncle's nostrils as he muttered and sat down. Her mouth was dry, and she was glad of the ale Meg handed her, and for Meg's wink. She noticed that Thane Roger was blinking as if he had just woken up.

'Please continue, Ursel,' Elder Mildreth commanded. Many voices made encouraging noises.

There's so much more to say! How do I get to the most important part? Ah yes: step sideways, take a deep breath.

She told the crowd about the red deer herd; how many adults there were, where they drink, where they rest, how many of last year's calves survived the winter.

'Did you know that hinds carry their babies inside them all winter, but they don't start to grow until there's spring grass for the mother and her newborn? One morning a month ago, I saw this hind's hoof-print cut deeper into frozen leaf mould. Under branches frosted with mist, I realised: new life had sparked in the mother hind in the autumn rut; cold kept it hidden and sleeping until nourishment breathed on the tiny flame inside her. The calf had uncurled and the hind was growing her baby inside her womb. Can any of us do that? It's one of the mysteries. The hunters notched their arrows on the string. They just saw her as joints of meat.'

Before her she saw eyes were round and mouths open. *What came next?* She sought faces in the crowd – Meg returned her look steadily. *Now I take a step forward.*

'I had to stop them.' Ursel spread her hands. 'The calves are the future of the herd, and the wood needs red deer as much as we do. They gnaw bark and crop small saplings, so they create spaces between trees, glades where sunlight gets through and speckled butterflies and bees come for the flowers.' She heard shuffling around her – panic twitched in her gut. *Where was I?* Her eye steadied on Winfrith, who was smiling. *I'm doing all right.*

She took up her thread, 'Wolves thin out the deer by taking the old slow ones. That's what we should do, too. When hunters take care of the herds, they flourish and so does the whole forest. When men and women take care of each other, our settlements grow strong. If we take just what we need, we can work with Earth Mother. If we don't care, or take too much, everything starts to unravel.'

Heads nodded.

'What holds it all together?' Ursel went on. 'It's what my father, Kenelm, told me. He lies in the round barrow over there. Every year at Yule, he and my great-aunt, Elder Edith, used to lead the rite we call the antler dance. Back then the young people who came of age went out to the water's edge and waited for their night of vision. The deer, all the animals, came and spoke to them with spirit voices.'

I can almost feel them, here now! Hairs on the back of her neck prickled.

'At dawn, my father and Elder Edith led back the new adults. They raced through the settlement, whooping and yelling with the wind. Mothers left cakes out for them and hid indoors, afraid, or pretending to be. At dawn, the new adults brought back the sun and everyone gathered in the hall. They danced the messages the deer had entrusted to them: how we all rely on each other – every creature as well as humans on Earth – and how we can live together in peace. We need that ceremony every year, to keep the balance. That's what my father said. Now I see why.

'It was stopped years ago because Elder Edith's knees gave out and my uncle, Headman Kedric, wanted the feasting and drinking without the ritual. My father got tired of arguing with him. There was deep wisdom in it that my father said he couldn't share with me until it was my turn to become adult. My turn never came. There are lots of us who have never done this coming of age rite, and adults who have forgotten that the red deer are guardians for our spirits as well as for the forest. I want the antler dance for myself, for my friends, for all our people, and for the land.'

'Thank you, Ursel.' Elder Edith said with a smile.

KEDRIC

Elder Edith stood up to introduce him. 'Now, Headman Kedric, you may speak. You are Headman of our community, a descendant of Beorngyth and Herewald, and the uncle of Ursel. Tell us what happened that day and why.'

She's tottering, my old aunt! Unlike me. She's given me this chance though. Kedric stood straight as a pine tree. The matter to lay before them was weighty, like the bronze torc round his neck. All eyes were on him. A strange flutter in his stomach distracted him; he squeezed his innards together. *Nervous? Don't be a weakling. Make sure they all hear.*

'I'm not sure this meeting has the authority to make judgments in this type of case. We are subject to Thane Roger, and he should be the one to decide right and wrong.' He noticed the Thane start slightly as his name was spoken. In the warm sun after an uncomfortable night, his head was drooping.

The throng looked on expectantly.

Kedric continued, 'Times are changing and Thane Roger's rule will take over soon. With him at the helm, the small paddle of our settlement will join with all the others to move the great ship of the Eastern Angles towards a bright dawn.' *That came out well, great image I made up! Just like when I practiced it. Hang on, Thane Roger is glowering! Maybe boats are not a welcome thought for him today ...* Kedric cleared his throat. Edith's frown reminded him of his mother. He sighed. 'Out of respect for the elders, and you who have travelled so far, I lay my word-gift before you.

'The day of this event was the day before Thane Roger's visit at Hretha-feast. We'd hunted for days and caught nothing – it can go like that sometimes.'

Men in the audience murmured agreement. *They're all friends, neighbours and cousins.*

'So we had to catch a good size beast before sunset, to provide an honourable feast of venison for Thane Roger and his men.

'We coursed after red deer all day and it was getting late. At last, the hounds picked up a trail and the animal turned at bay. Our arrows were notched on the string when my niece, Ursel, dropped down out of a tree, yelling. Her noise startled the horses and set the deer off. It got clean away. She did it deliberately, to scare our prey.

'Such disrespect! Not just for me, but for all the hunters – and for Thane Roger. I shouted, of course, but she did not stay and apologise or offer to make reparation. She ran off! When I caught up with her, I gave her the blows that she complains about, to remind her of her duty of obedience to her headman. She continued to talk back, and we had only a hare for the pot, so I requisitioned the pig as recompense. It seemed only fair to me.'

The attention of the crowd buzzed in his veins. He rested a hand on his leather belt and straddled his legs wider apart.

'If a girl – or anyone – takes it into their head to defy the headman of their settlement, all kinds of chaos could creep in. We need children to take notice of what older people say, and do as they are told. Our safety depends on people following orders smartly, without question. The forest is not some dainty place with butterflies flitting about. There are bears and wolves out there, ready to attack the unwary. Outcasts and savages hide out there, on the look-out for settlements without strong leaders.'

Thane Roger was rapt, following his every word. Kedric threw his head back, looking far away. No one ever looked beyond the bean-plot hedge, except for Thane Roger and himself.

'This is not about me, or my pride. As Headman, I hold the land here from Thane Roger, who holds it from the King. Our kings received their lands long ago from our heroes. Shield, our legendary ancestor and great warrior, was the son of Sheaf, the farmer of mythical stature. Their royal line descends from the gods themselves.' Under his arm, which was raised in a grand gesture, he caught a sharp glance from his wife's slave. When he looked directly at her, Seren's sullen face was blank. *Why does Oswynne keep that stupid woman? She has some herb-knowledge of course, but sometimes I wonder about her.*

He pulled himself back to his argument. 'Let me explain. To this day, our shields – the armed men of our community – rely on the sheaf for sustenance. The sheaf is us farmers – who depend on the shield for our protection. It's our duty to sustain Thane Roger and his fighters, and it's theirs to keep us safe from our enemies. In the battle against the untamed – in the woods, in our communities, in ourselves – we stand together. He is my shoulder-to-shoulder man and I am his.' As Kedric sat down, Thane Roger clapped him on the back with a broad hand.

HILDA

Hilda's head buzzed as she kept track of everything they needed to talk over. Elder Edith invited questions. A woman from Thornthicket checked that this was not a long-standing feud and that it was the only time Ursel and Kedric had clashed. The Headman from Mereham wanted to know how the pig was taken. (He had a fine snout himself, Hilda noted.)

Redwald asked if she had decided beforehand to disrupt the hunt.

'No, I followed the deer as usual that day, to watch them, and couldn't believe what I was seeing,' Ursel replied. 'If they'd asked me, I could have taken them to the old stag's hideout. He's not so useful to the herd. But they never ask me what I know.'

Hilda looked from Ursel to Redwald, noticing that they took care their eyes didn't meet as they spoke. When they did for a brief moment, pink crept into Ursel's cheek and Redwald hastily covered his face with his hand. *She's chosen well,* thought Hilda. *This boy listened to us all night in the mud and now his ears are still open. One of the powerful family, eh? He's unusual.*

'I have questions for both of you.' Elder Edith turned first to Kedric. 'You spoke about protection, and keeping us safe – from wild animals, from enemies. We appreciate your care. Yet, you planned to kill a breeding hind – why did you, that day?'

'Of course I wouldn't normally go after a breeding female. I didn't like seeing her along my arrow-shaft. But it was our duty to get meat for the feast.' He beat one fist into the other hand.

'So there was a more pressing need – even more important to you than stewardship of the deer-herd?'

Kedric pulled himself tall and threw back his shoulders. He directed his words towards Thane Roger. 'We owe respect to our overlord when he comes to our settlement. He's our link with the world out there, beyond our kale-patch.'

Thane Roger nodded in agreement, the corners of his mouth drawn tight. Redwald was following the talk closely.

Kedric's not just saying this to please them, Hilda realised. *This is what all the headmen and thanes think, and it's getting bigger fast and hurtling like a kestrel down upon us.*

'Explain why we should bother about anything outside our own neighbourhood?' Elder Edith asked.

She's drawing his ideas out, even though she doesn't agree, thought Hilda. *That's even-handed – and skilful.*

'Things are changing!' Kedric leaned forward, to make sure everyone heard. 'We're thriving – settlements are getting bigger. We're taming the wildwood and bringing order, one strip at a time, making the land tidy inside hedges. All the settlements are being forged together, like links in a chain. Kings and thanes are creating this – and we can be part of it, even though we're only farmers. If we all pull together, we'll be part of a strong country. Anglia will be glorious with gold. Harp-songs will be made about us who fight for it, and they'll be sung for years to come.' He stopped, out of breath. Thane Roger sat upright.

Proud as a pigeon, thought Hilda.

'Where will your place be in this new order?' Elder Edith asked Kedric.

'I'll carry my spear and lead my men with my Thane's troop. Every man will have his place.'

He can't wait to get in line for a battle, Hilda thought. Her nostrils flared with the remembered smell of blood on trampled grass, but Kedric's eyes were on the horizon. *He's feasting after a skirmish, raising a silver-lipped horn to drink a toast and turning a new arm-ring to catch the light – 'My Thane gave me this!' Mead would never taste as sweet as words of thanks from his lord for his courage, for his service in the brotherhood of heroes.*

'What about the women?' Edith tilted her head to one side. Hilda loved the way she shifted the talk without squashing his dreams, as cool as the breeze that loosened her grey hair from its plaits.

'They'll help the men, of course.' Kedric sounded as if he had never thought about this. 'Cooking, farming, weaving, bringing up the children, that sort of thing.' He waved his hand vaguely.

'Will there be harp-songs made about women birthing babies, feeding them, keeping them safe?' Edith asked.

'Er …'

She couldn't resist, thought Hilda. *She's right to bring it out. He hasn't thought this through. I make stories and songs about women and their heroic mothering – I wonder if he will ever listen to me.*

Edith carried on smoothly, in spite of an outbreak of whispering among the women. 'Back to the day when Ursel broke into the hunt: I can see that she was putting to flight your vision of the world. No wonder you were upset.'

'No, not upset. Just a bit annoyed.' Kedric eyed the crowd. The men nodded, backing him up.

Hilda hid her face with her hand. She couldn't help rolling her eyes. *They can't allow themselves to know what they're feeling. What was that like for Kedric as a boy? Having to pull himself out of hurt without acknowledging it; strangling tears; stomaching insults or risking mockery and loneliness. He's leading us into a world where swallowing pain is normal, so we can hurt each other carelessly. When tongues are doused in bitterness day after day, people seek sweetness wherever their hands can grab it. When skin's scoured and scarred, it hides away shivering. Greed and fear will rule without mercy.* She folded her arms to protect her body.

As she looked down, Leofric toddled past.

That's why we're here, to make a place where little ones are safe to grow into brave, loving men and women. She lifted her head and looked around.

Redwald shifted uneasily. *He's one of those kings and thanes Kedric is so keen on,* Hilda thought – *but what is he thinking? He's wrestling with thoughts. Worry is ploughing furrows on his brow.*

'Thank you, Kedric, please sit down. Ursel, I have questions for you.' Elder Edith announced. Ursel stood and moved forward. 'There seem to be several aspects to your quarrel with your uncle: outrage at the hunting of the hind; the punishments, both beating and taking your pig; and our neglect of the antler dance. Which is most important for you?'

Ursel screwed up her nose, squinting behind it. 'It's all braided together! I can't take out one thread or I lose the pattern.'

Hilda hoped that only she heard the little sigh that sneaked out of the corner of Edith's mouth with those words of Ursel's. *We're both thinking – here we go, into Ursel's tangle again.*

Ursel moved her hands. *She's showing herself the strands that help her think. Good, she's taking it slowly.*

'They hunt a doe; they hit a woman; we're both females. That's part of the pattern. I know I'm not pregnant and not likely to be and I'm not so important –' She stopped and looked at a bumblebee on red clover, at a rook with a twig in its beak – anywhere except at Redwald while the blush flooded up her neck. A worry line tightened between Redwald's eyebrows as Ursel got stuck.

Hilda looked round for a way to help. Meg caught her eye and made plaiting movements with her hands, her face screwed up. Hilda picked up a basket at her feet, where the women had laid the skeins of wool they had spun and twisted together while they listened.

Hilda picked up three skeins of yarn, teased out the ends, and knotted them firmly together. She leaned over to Oswynne, 'May I borrow your sewing-scissors?' She cut the three strands and passed the bundle to Ursel.

'Show us,' Hilda invited.

Ursel took the threads, and tried again. 'I'm just one woman,' Ursel held up one thread, 'but if he can beat me, he can beat any woman.' She put that thread between the other two.

'The hind is just one animal – but if hunters don't take care of wild herds, they'll die out. The forest depends on all the living things working together. If we take too much, Earth Mother can't make it work.' She wound the second thread into the middle.

'The antler dance makes sure that all our men and women listen to the animals and understand how important it is to work with Earth Mother, not against her.' She wound the third thread into the middle.

'So the women, and the forest, and the winter nights of listening inside – they all come together.' She braided the threads and handed the plait to Edith, who held it up for all to see, then laid it in the centre of the circle.

I was wrong, Hilda smiled inwardly, *she's laid it out clearly. No wonder she had trouble before – she had a lot of ends to join up.*

She looked around. Oswynne's mouth was open; Elder Mildreth was bobbing her head like a robin; and the women from Thornthicket were commenting on Ursel's words.

Elder Edith turned to the edges of the gathering, asking, 'Do you see what she means?' Some nodded vigorously, eyes wide, some looked doubtful. 'We can talk more about this,' Edith promised. 'Now, Hilda the bard with a brain-pan like a grain-store, what have you hoarded from our talk? What questions shall we mull over in smaller groups?'

CHAPTER 36

ARE WE PEOPLE WITHOUT SHADOWS?

HILDA

Hilda rocked backward and forward on her feet – it helped her to think.

'Questions have come up regarding headmen and free people. How do we work together and what does each owe to the other?' She made a gesture of giving, her hands palm upwards, as she laid each bundle of questions before them.

Her heart beat fast. *Edith's relying on me to make this work.* She took a slow breath.

'Is the wild ours to take what we need, or are we simply one of the creatures who live here?'

She closed her eyes to think.

'Do we gather together in old-style moots with elders leading or should thanes and kings decide what we do?

'There's plenty to talk about inside each of those. Also we'll need to decide whether to re-start the antler dance.'

The word 'we' bounced around in her head. *Did anyone notice? It does feel as if this place is my place in the world. Don't worry; the prickly hedge will come soon enough. Maybe today, if the headmen don't like what we're doing.*

Elder Edith conferred briefly with Mildreth and Elfric. 'We elders will take the question about the antler dance. We need to touch hands with the ancestors' spirits later, in deep meditation, and ask for guidance.

'These talk-groups are to share our experiences. We may change our views, or find out something new. Pass the speaking-staff round so everyone who wants to speak gets a turn. No interrupting. Whoever holds the speaking-staff is the one who is talking. Hear them out. Good ideas can come from anyone when we listen to each other well. When we all have our say and our neighbours know what we think, we feel linked together. Even if the decision is not what we want, we know we had a hand in it; it's ours.

'If you want to join the group to talk about the rights and duties of headmen and free people, gather near the barrow. Friends from Mereham, did you bring your speaking-staff?'

Elder Elfric held it up. It had a little boat on top.

'Use that one,' Edith said.

Edith gestured towards the edge of the forest. 'To work on the ways people treat the land, meet under the big beech tree. May they use the Thornthicket speaking-staff?'

Elder Mildreth lent theirs. It was made from a sapling marked with spiral tracks of honeysuckle.

'Let's have a group beside that juniper bush to thrash out everything about moots and meetings, and leading and being led. Here is our Wellstowe speaking-staff.' Elder Edith passed the whetstone with a carved handle to Redwald.

He looked at it intently. 'Fine work! These are intertwined hounds, aren't they? Who made it?'

'Kedric put on the new handle, after the old one broke,' Oswynne said.

Redwald moved his thumbs along the sculpted details. 'I keep wanting to touch this, it's so delicately chiselled. Why is the whetstone so smooth?'

'We don't use it to sharpen our tools; we have a rough one for that,' Kedric explained. 'This one's to keep my wits sharp to protect the settlement.'

Redwald grinned. 'I like that! The figures are so intricate. What kind of wood did you use, Headman Kedric?'

'It's oak; I wanted it to last. The ancestral one served many generations before it broke. I added the hounds' lolling tongues, engraved the faces, drew out their tails.'

'The eyes have a shine to them! Those tails – one's wagging, one's whisking – they look alive.' Redwald clapped Kedric on the back. 'I'll take this fine whetstone speaking-staff over to the moots and meetings group. I see my foster-father's there already; I want to show it to him, and hear what they talk about.'

Hilda hoped Redwald might control his foster-father Thane Roger's temper.

Kedric stamped over to the barrow to join the group discussing the rights and duties of headmen and free people.

People milled around, muttering and shuffling their feet. Winfrith hurried round, questioning. 'They don't know which group to join,' she reported to Elder Edith. 'Do they have to stay in the same one?'

'Ah, I nearly forgot,' Edith announced, 'the blackbird rule! When you want to hop over to another group, go. We do need one person to stay in each group the whole time. Choose a thought-keeper; they will remember all that is discussed and tell everyone later.'

There was much chatter as people moved around and chose thought-keepers. The groups settled into serious conversation.

Hilda flashed a grin towards Winfrith – delighted to see her learning fast and helping. Winfrith went off with Ursel to the juniper bush group about moots and meetings, leading and being led. *Is Ursel following Redwald or wanting to challenge Roger?*

Elder Edith sat down, suddenly pale. 'Meg, bring me a drink please.' Meg was setting off towards the beech tree, but turned back when Edith called her.

What's happening here? Hilda wondered.

Sipping weak ale, Edith gestured to all the groups. 'We'll go round to each one and listen in, dear.' She leaned on Meg's arm to stand up. 'Bring my stool, will you? Hilda, come with us to remember things.'

Hilda's thoughts churned as they walked slowly uphill towards the barrow. *Is Edith thinking to teach Meg this way? Or has she simply forgotten her promise to bring the British slaves into the discussion?* She saw Meg look once towards the beech tree, lips parted with longing, and then back down to Elder Edith's feet pushing through the tussocks. Disappointment pulled Meg's mouth taut.

'I can assist you, Elder Edith,' Hilda offered, and slid her arm under Edith's elbow, 'then Meg can take part in the talk.'

'No, no, Meg will come, she's my kind helper, always by my side, such a good girl.'

Meg wavered. Hilda sucked in her breath as if she'd been punched. This was more danger than all the thanes in the land: this easy sense that everything would be given, coupled with the habit of doing what we're told. Edith didn't even know she was taking away Meg's rights; Meg noticed something slide out of her hands but felt powerless to grasp it back. Of course – a lifetime habit of taking what you want can't melt away with one good thought. A lifetime of following orders makes it hard to dig in your heels. *Stop standing there with your mouth flapping like a fish,* Hilda scolded herself. *You know words; say some!* She began to speak, but Edith shushed her.

'Help this group remember what they're saying, Hilda,' Meg placed the stool and Edith sat. Hilda felt torn.

A fiery Thornthicket woman was talking, hands on hips. 'What about if we're pregnant? Nobody should beat us then. It can hurt the baby! Even if we're not, it makes us hate each other.'

A man jeered, saying something about being tough.

'Have you ever patched up wounds from a beating? No, I thought not!' she went on.

Other women joined in about the time it takes to heal a skull and how it's nothing compared to mending the way people get along together. 'Even a single clout stirs up anger. How can we work together then?'

'Who's Thought-keeper for this group?' Hilda asked.

Nelda spoke up, 'I am. This is Tola; she's my Mam.' She put her arm round the woman who had spoken so passionately. 'We're discussing what beating really teaches people.'

Elder Edith asked, 'Have the children spoken yet?'

So she remembers them, thought Hilda, *even if she's forgotten the un-free.*

Otred stood up very straight. 'When I left Father's tools out in the rain, he shouted a bit and then he showed me how to use the whetstone to sharpen the blades and rub the handles with sheep-grease. It took all day and I couldn't go and play with Elstan like I wanted to. I felt bad; I didn't mean any harm; I just forgot. I never did it again.'

Ragnild, bursting with pride, laid a hand on his shoulder. 'You lived in a warm place in his heart, son, and you followed him from the first time you learned to crawl.' She wiped a tear away with her sleeve.

'Young ones learn when they're with someone who cares for them.' Hilda had to say it. 'If they are smacked or hit or beaten, or even shouted at all the time, it stops them taking anything in. They build a wall between themselves and everybody else, to hide behind.'

Where was Kedric? Already moving away to a different group. I hope he heard my words!

Hilda glanced at Meg, hovering at Edith's side. Young May was tugging at Meg's wrist, whispering something, and Meg followed her away to the cooking-fires.

MEG

Seren banged a basket of flatbread down on the trestle table. 'Here's some more.'

Meg winced to see the rage steaming off her mother's arms. She looked around. *Nobody else has noticed.* Seren turned back to the fire to rake the embers round the baking-stones. She muttered to Tegwen, the elderly slave-woman from Thornthicket, who was shaping pieces of dough in her hands. Seren took one, flattened it and slapped it on the stone. *She's seeing somebody's face on it.*

'What's wrong, Mother?'

'Carry this, do that. Don't speak unless you're spoken to. First they call you "priestess" and then they expect you to wait on them. Didn't last long, did it, Meg?' Seren spat in the British tongue, not even bothering to look round to see who could hear her.

'Oh. You're angry because of me? What have I done?'

'It's not you, cushla. It's the way they're treating you. Back to being just a slave again, fetching and carrying. All this talk – the rights of free people! What about the rights of slaves; don't we have any? Of course not! I might as well shut up before I get a cuff round the earhole from Headman and his fine friends.'

Meg spoke slowly, 'When I'm helping Elder Edith, it's clear what to do: keep her upright. If she falls, the whole Moot will scatter and break and Thane Roger will grab his chance. Grab anything, anyone he wants.' She and Seren both shuddered. 'But, we should be there, not just me – all of us.' She looked around the people spread over the hillside. 'Are there more slaves from Thornthicket here?' She asked Tegwen. No reply.

She said it again louder, and the older woman leant towards her with her hand behind her ear. 'Eh?'

Meg repeated her question clearly and Tegwen watched her lips. 'My man stayed at home to tend the animals. Just me and my son, Madoc, over there.' He was grooming the pony. Meg remembered his blank moon face.

'What about his brother?' she asked.

'He got traded. Thane Roger took him to work on his ditch, part of our tribute last time.'

'Is he alright?'

The old woman shrugged. 'Don't get any news. My son's lost to me now.' Seren put a hand on her shoulder and they both shook their heads.

Meg asked Madoc about Mereham slaves and he called over two young brothers. In the Saxon tongue, they told how grateful they were to the Mereham headman for taking them in when everyone else in their settlement, downriver, died from a terrible pox.

'Rights?' they laughed. 'What does that mean? You want to speak to Cafell; that's her kind of talk!' One jerked his thumb towards the biggest tent, as they lolloped off.

Like puppies, Meg thought. *I remember Cafell. She's the slave from Mereham who looks like a cat with those high cheekbones and her pointed chin. About my age, scrawny. After the last Moot, we sneaked away together for a dip in the river. She told me how she got there – her owners traded her mother away, but nobody wanted a sick grandmother and a sulky child. Her Nana died while they travelled, so she asked for shelter at Mereham in exchange for work. The headman's family took her in as a bondmaid.*

Cafell gave her a wary look with her green eyes. She was re-balancing the ridgepole across two crossed hazel branches. Her baby, tied onto her chest, grizzled as she heaved the heavy cover into place over the pole. Meg steadied the poles so Cafell could tighten the guy-ropes.

The elderly Tegwen's son Madoc came over with a mallet for the pegs, an awkward grin on his round face. 'Nice baby,' he said, 'Whose is it?'

'Mine,' spat Cafell. She gave him such a look that he shambled off.

Her glare reminded Meg of a cat that gave birth to kittens in the grain-store. When a hound came snuffling round, the cat lunged and dug claws into its nose.

'Last time, we swam in the river – you hauled yourself out of deep water with a willow root and gave me a hand,' Meg gulped. 'Can you help me now?'

'What do you think?' Cafell hissed.

'I don't mean work. It's the groups. We slaves should be in the groups talking, and they should be talking about rights for us too, not just free people.'

'It's them that have all the rights; that's what Pigface thinks.'

'Pigface?' Meg asked. The girl jerked a thumb and Meg looked over and saw she meant the Mereham headman.

Meg giggled. 'Good name!'

'He thinks he's got the right to take me, just because I belong to his family. I can put up with that. But he's not touching my baby!'

Laughter drained down through the soles of Meg's feet. The sky bore down on her. Thane Roger's words at the Feast rushed into her head and she shivered. 'Couldn't you stop him?'

Cafell shrugged. 'I bit and scratched him the first time, but he's stronger than me. He said he'd throw me out of the settlement if I struggled, and I've got nobody to protect me. He told me I was ungrateful; he took me in when I was all alone, gave me food and shelter. It's true.'

'The first time … you mean it's still happening?'

'When I started to feel sick, I couldn't fight. When I realised Cariad was inside me, I was afraid to upset him, in case he punched me and I lost her. I thought, I just have to live through this. I go away in my head. I don't let him touch her.' She wrapped her arms round her baby and tucked her tighter into the shawl.

'You shouldn't have to put up with that! Nobody should!' *I've got to do something, for this cat-girl, for her baby, for all of us!* 'Come with me, we've got to speak out.' Meg touched Cafell's arm.

'How can I? If they kill me, there will be nobody to look after Cariad.'

'Hello – is that Meg?' a musical voice called. Elder Mildreth's granddaughter came into the loose-flapping tent. 'Your grandmother needs you; she sent me to find you.'

'My grandmother? Oh, you mean Elder Edith!'

'Yes, of course! If you're not her granddaughter, who are you?'

Is she looking down her pointed nose at me? 'I belong to Headman's wife Oswynne, along with my mother and sister.' Meg summoned up *priestess crowned by the moon* and stood tall. 'This is Cafell from Mereham. We want to speak in the groups, but we've got to fix this tent because we are un-free; we have no rights.'

'Oh. That's not fair. Can I help? My name's Lynna. I could speak for you. They might listen to me because my grandmother is Elder, and my uncle is Headman in Thornthicket.' She tucked a stray curl behind her ear.

Meg was distracted by the girl's round brooches. *Could those be garnets?*

'If you want to help, take that mallet round and secure the tent pegs,' snarled Cafell. 'I need to feed Cariad.' She sat on the rug and loosened her shawl so the baby could nuzzle her breast. Her sleek black hair fell over her face as she purred a rhyme to help her milk flow.

'I don't know how,' Lynna almost whimpered. 'Madoc always does ours.'

Meg showed her. 'I'll pull the guy-ropes tight; you give the pegs a good thump.'

'There's an awful lot of sheep droppings here,' Lynna complained as she knelt.

'Yes, there is,' said Meg, trying not to laugh. She passed the girl a rag to wipe her dress.

Lynna went round all the pegs, taking care. 'Is that alright? Anything else I can help with?' She wiped her hands. 'Where's your drink, Cafell?' She brought a cup for the mother as she nursed. Meg warmed to her. Lynna continued, 'Your baby's only a few weeks old, isn't she? Have you had the healing bath yet?'

'I don't know what you mean.' Cafell spoke quietly, so as not to disturb Cariad as she dozed off.

'Every mother has it, to heal and soothe her and smooth her way into caring for her little one. I'll ask Grandmother if we can do it for you while we're here.'

'For me?'

'Why not? We're all women, aren't we?'

'Maybe you can help in the group,' Meg suggested to Lynna. 'Could you announce us, then we could say what we want? Would you do that?'

SEREN

'Thane's calling for drink,' Madoc panted. Seren pushed the pitcher into his hand.

'Tell us what they say?' she asked.

'Thane says Headman did well. Headman tells Thane he's a good chap. They have a drink. Thane grumbles about how slow this all is.

Headman tells him it's always like this. Thane gobs on the grass.' Madoc reported.

Seren couldn't help chuckling. 'Thanks for going. None of us want to be near that creepy Thane with his wandering hands.'

Oswynne bustled over. 'Seren, take the jug to the group under the beech tree. Elder Edith needs a drink. She's pale as a candle. We don't want her keeling over.'

As if she's the only one who cares about her, Seren thought.

Light filtered through the new, soft beech-leaves, dappling the people who sat in a circle underneath. Two were on their feet, arguing. 'The wildwood is our enemy, full of hostile spirits and ferocious animals,' the man insisted.

Hostile spirits? Seren wondered. *Maybe there are ancestor spirits stalking the forest, furious with these Angles who stole the land from our folk.*

He was still talking. 'We've got to fight the wild back. Our families are growing; we need to hack down forest to make our settlement bigger. Every year we have to get more strips under plough to feed everybody. I wish I had Thunor's hammer to blast the weeds; Mereham would disappear under them if we didn't keep clearing.' He chopped with the edge of his hands to make his point.

The big-boned woman wagged her finger at him. 'There's no need to be so angry about it. Let's think about how much land we need to cultivate, and how much we should leave for wild plants and birds and animals. Nobody's saying we have to let the weeds take over; of course we need to keep our strips clear so we can grow our crops. We say to them – out you come, you can't grow here; you can grow over there at the edge of the strip. We've left that for the birds to nest. And don't leave your roots behind; we know your game; you'll be springing up again as soon as our backs are turned.'

People chuckled, until the man cut in: 'It's not funny! We've got to stay in charge. If the pests flood back in, you won't be laughing then. We'll starve. It's all in our hands.' He spread his wide, calloused palms upward.

Elder Edith cut in, refreshed. 'Friends, you are addressing the points we need to talk about. But we can't have you shouting at each other like this. One at a time – that's the rule. And listen to each other! Who's the Thought-keeper here?'

Evrard raised his hand.

'Remind them if they get carried away, and pass the speaking-staff when they do.'

Weeds? Seren thought. *Are they talking about herbs and medicine plants?* A fountain of words rose up in her throat. *I want to help these people notice the healing all around them.* She tried to catch somebody's eye, but nobody could see her, it seemed. As she trudged back to the baking-stones, a tune rattled in her head. Words fitted themselves round it, from long ago – her Nana's voice.

'We are people without shadows, in the shadow of the trees …' Seren sang the lines that jumped into her head. 'We are people who have nothing, and we sing.' She clapped her hands twice to fill the beats.

Tegwen joined in, then said, 'My auntie used to sing something like that.'

Meg and the Mereham girl with the baby came to join them. One of the Angles from Thornthicket, a young woman in a fine blue wool dress, hovered around them.

'Can I help you, Ma'am?' Seren meant to ask but it came out in a growl.

The girl took a step back, twisted her belt with nervous fingers, and enquired, 'Are you Seren, the Healer? I hoped I'd see you here.'

What's she up to? *Assume they're the enemy, Nana always said; don't trust any of them.* Seren grunted assent, looking round for safety.

'Lynna wants to help,' Meg said.

Seren was still not sure. She looked the girl over, from the pretty bone pins in her neat braids to her muddy skirt.

The girl stepped closer and pulled her skirt up to show a scar on her knee. 'That's where I skinned it climbing a tree. The wound festered. You saved my life, Mother says, with your herbs and the chanting that kept me calm while you cleaned it up. Thank you.'

Seren warmed, remembering the anxious walk to Thornthicket with Meg on her back, little Lynna burning hot and shivering cold, the power that poured through her that long night as she worked. *An Angle saying thank you? That's new!* She didn't know how to respond.

'I'll talk to Grandmother,' Lynna said to Meg, who nodded.

Seren gathered her daughter in and taught her the song as they kneaded dough. Meg drummed on her thigh, catching the rhythm. Cafell rocked the baby, moving in time to it. Meg made a mistake as she sang. Seren did not correct her, liking Meg's words:

> 'We are people without voices,
> In the shadow of the trees,
> We are people who have nothing,
> And we sing.'

Soon they were all gripped by it, moving and singing under their breath.

Meg held up a hand. 'What if – we sing instead of talking?'

'What do you mean?' Cafell asked.

'Because we were supposed to be joining in the talk, be part of the groups. That's what they said, isn't it Mother?'

Seren nodded, tight-lipped. 'I reminded Headman's Wife Oswynne about what Hilda said and she said it, too: about our friendship being the rooftree of the settlement and needing our wisdom in the Moot.' Her mouth pulled tight, so the words had to crawl out. 'Oswynne said, "Don't bother me when we're in the middle of looking after all these guests."'

'When they ask for something, when we bring them food, or anything, if we just keep singing, all of us, in time, with the clapping as well, they'll have to ask why. That's when we say, "If we're not allowed to speak, at least we can sing!"' Meg sounded cheerful.

'And they say, "Get on with your work, girl," and clout us round the head.' Seren snorted.

'That's what we're doing, then.' Tegwen nodded. The old one had not heard Seren's words.

MEG

'Yes, that's what we're doing.' Cafell replied firmly. She settled Cariad on her hip, took a jug of ale and walked towards the group beside the barrow. Meg grasped another pitcher and hastened after her.

'We could ask Hilda to play a tune,' she panted.

'Who's Hilda?'

'The bard who's staying with us. She tells stories and plays a harp and a … er … elder wood flute. Hmm … she might get into trouble and get chucked out, and then we wouldn't hear the next part of her story. It's got a queen and her friend in it, and she learns to stand up for herself, and the next part is about the queen's daughter, Snow Storm, and I want to hear it!'

Elder Edith waved and called. 'Meg dear, take my stool, we'll go back to the rights and duties group by the barrow now.'

Meg's heart beat fast. She turned back, straightened her shoulders, smiled and started singing.

> 'We are people without voices,
> In the shadow of the trees …'

'What's that? Eh?'

> 'We are people who have nothing,
> And we sing.'

Meg's hands were full – jug in one, stool in the other, and the frail old woman hanging onto her arm. She could not clap. She looked round with panic choking her.

Seren came alongside carrying a trestle table with Madoc. She stamped twice where the claps had been, and Meg did too.

All over the hillside, the song rang out with stamps, or clacks with a ladle, where the claps had been. *When life crushes you, spread your wings.* Meg's voice lifted her. *If they beat us, I don't care – just to have this, now.*

CHAPTER 37

PIGFACE
AND THE
CAT GIRL

HILDA

'Nelda, what's been agreed about rights and duties?' Edith asked, as Meg settled her on her stool. Meg was singing for some reason.

'Beating rarely works. Nobody should beat a free person without consulting the whole settlement to say why, first, and without everyone giving consent. Also, free people should obey their headman, but they can ask questions or disagree; except if there's a fire or a raid.'

Movement caught Hilda's eye; people were coming over. Thane Roger's slouch looked aggressive and the jut of Kedric's chin meant danger. Winfrith and Ursel hurried after, worried.

'Enough of this drivel!' shouted the Thane. 'If I was in charge, this whole matter would be slaughtered and skinned by now and we could get on with trading. I say –'

Edith stood to her full height. Her frame looked frail against his bull-like shoulders; but she spoke with such power that he took a step back. 'That's not necessary, thank you, Roger. I understand you want to help by moving things along – but we need to listen to each other, even when it's uncomfortable. Especially when it hurts.' She winced as Thane Roger began another rant.

'All this chat gets us nowhere. We need firm decisions. That's what makes people feel safe. I know more about this than any of you. What can you know, with your noses stuck in pig-dung while I'm talking with the King's companions at court? We're the ones who defend our land against invaders …' His voice grated as he harangued the gathering.

Hilda looked round. *Open mouths, everybody frozen in fear at the raised voices.* Edith shrank, looking hunched. *If she collapses now,* Hilda thought, *it'll be the rule of fists forever.* She moved to Edith's side and tried an encouraging smile.

Edith grasped her arm and implored, 'The elders!'

Hilda covered ground fast to fetch Elfric, Redwald and Mildreth from the other groups. People streamed after them, following the noise.

Nelda's mother, fiery Tola, shouted, 'While you're off feasting, we're digging and sweating to fill your ever-so-important bellies. We know what helps us work together better than you do!'

Uproar rang out.

Hilda hurried the elders into the group just as Headman Kedric snapped, 'Our Thane is right. You've travelled a long way, neighbours; you deserve more than endless talk.'

Arguments broke out. People shouted to be heard.

Kedric roared: 'Where's the ale? Slaves!'

Two young women stepped into the circle, Meg and her slender friend Cafell with the baby, their arms linked. *Clinging to each other for support?* They sang:

> 'We are people without voices,
> In the shadows of the trees,
> We are people who have nothing
> And we sing!'

Seren's deeper tones joined them, alongside the reedy voice of the old slave Tegwen. Her son beat time with a spoon on a pot. Two young lads joined in.

People looked at them, puzzled, as the music threaded through the arguments. Thane Roger frowned at them. Kedric scratched his head. Hilda found her elder wood pipe and accompanied the singers.

> 'As we step out of the shadows,
> We are finding voice at last.
> As we hold our heads up high
> We – sing!'

OSWYNNE

Now what's going on? Just when the food is coming along and the talk flowing, they're up to something. Why can't they just get on with their duties!

'It's nice to hear you singing, but this is not the time for it,' Edith frowned.

Oswynne glowered at the slaves. *All this clapping and stamping, what does it mean?* The girl from Mereham filled a row of cups on the trestle table, grinning like a cat. Oswynne's hand twitched with an urge to slap her. *I'm not the only one about to lose my temper,* she realised, and her neck hairs rose. Thane Roger's fists were clenching and unclenching. *It's up to me to stop this nonsense, fast, or there'll be trouble.* She used her pay-attention voice. 'That's enough singing.' She took Seren's arm and spoke clearly, 'Stop it now!'

Her old friend looked her in the eye and continued to sing.

Thane Roger stormed to her side and grabbed Seren by the hair. Seren cried out in pain, her face white.

Oswynne turned on the Thane. Anger seared her. She felt a red horse buck and rear under her. She laid her hand on Thane Roger's shoulder and let flame flare in her eyes. If she pushed him, Seren would get hurt worse. 'You will let go now.' Her face was so close to his she could smell his breath. 'The peace of the Moot must be respected. Open your fist.' Thunder of hooves spoke in her voice.

The man dropped his hand and took a step back; his big shoulders slumped. He straightened at once – but everyone had seen it.

Grip with your knees to slow down. Nudge which way you want to go.
'Please tell me the words of the song, Seren.' Oswynne felt strength glow in her chest, knowing she'd faced down Thane Roger.

Seren rubbed her head, stood up straight and sang the words clearly, in Anglish. *'We are people without voices – we sing.'*

'What does it mean? You've got voices. I don't understand.'

Seren's dark eyes glowed. 'Thank you for asking. When you invited me to help plan this Moot, you said it was important for the wisdom of my people to be heard. You said we have much of value to contribute. Yet today,' she spoke slowly, making sure the people crowding round could hear every word, 'today we have been asked to prepare and serve food, to support you in your talk. We have not been allowed to join in with the groups. That's why we have no voices.'

Oswynne's headache was back, thumping in her temples. Thane Roger's glare stabbed at the edge of her vision. 'I must confer with the elders,' she said.

HILDA

Into the centre of the group stepped Lynna, Elder Mildreth's granddaughter. She carried herself with natural dignity, as graceful as a silver birch.

Hilda noticed the white knuckles of the hand that gripped her woven belt. Lynna raised her other arm in a grand gesture. *This is someone used to being obeyed.*

The hubbub died down. Roger and Kedric, caught off guard, didn't know how to react.

'Our sisters who are un-free have a word-gift to lay before us,' announced Lynna. 'There was an agreement before the Moot, as Elder Edith can confirm. Meg of Wellstowe, please speak.' She handed the speaking-staff to Meg.

Meg held it high. She looked just over the heads of the crowd.

That's the trick I taught her to avoid panic, Hilda thought. She breathed courage in Meg's direction.

'We slaves have rights too. Some of us are British and some Saxons or Angles, but we are all people.' Meg glared fast round the silent faces. 'We serve you, but we belong to ourselves. We should be in the groups, talking with all of you. Our voices need to be heard. We do not want to be beaten – or raped.' She gasped for breath.

Beside her Cafell narrowed her green eyes.

The old slave Tegwen grunted, 'What did she say, the youngster?'

Seren put an arm round Meg's shoulders as the crowd boiled with conversation and noisy shouts.

Hilda asked Meg for the speaking-staff. She sucked in breath to hurl her voice above the din. 'It was agreed that we need the wisdom of the native people. Isn't that right, Elder Edith?'

The crowd quieted as Elder Edith responded, 'I remember some talk about that. But I don't think we meant *all* the time, did we? Oswynne, what do you think?' Edith's unsure tone was not like her.

Thane Roger's challenge has rattled her, Hilda thought.

'It's very inconvenient to have this coming up now, when our guests are hungry,' Oswynne's familiar snarl was back. 'If you don't cook and serve, how are we going to feed everyone?'

'We could all help,' Hilda started, but a red-faced woman pushed in front.

'What's this about rape? Who's been raped, and who did it?' she demanded, hands on hips.

'That's Pigface's wife,' Hilda caught the thin girl's whisper to Meg. 'I think she really doesn't know. Everybody else does. If they kill me, look after my baby.' Hilda passed the speaking-staff to her. Stepping forward, the girl spoke in a high, tight voice: 'You have always been good to me, Ma'am Sunnifa, but your husband hasn't. This is his baby. I was not willing, but he did it anyway. Does it anyway.'

Sunnifa rounded on her husband. 'You told me it was the trader who came through last year!'

A ripple of laughter spread from the Mereham people to everyone else.

Her face went purple. 'Am I the last to find out? How dare you!' She lashed out at her husband.

He raised an arm to protect his face. 'It's only a slave – it doesn't count!'

'No, you're not the last to find out, Sunnifa. I am.' Elder Elfric shook as he clung to his walking stick. 'Did you think I wouldn't bat an eyelid, Osric? That I would be on your side because I'm a man? What sort of man do you think I am? This slave girl Cafell was sent to us by the gods while she was a child for us to keep safe. Osric, Headman of Mereham, you have violated the trust of the gods as well as this girl!

'If this is the way headmen behave, I will not support any of you. Any powerful person needs others to keep him in check, to hold him responsible for his actions. This behaviour could make headmen think they can get away with anything – and make good men and women feel powerless, just little mice all on their own. If headmen and thanes rule with violence and do anything they want, ordinary people will think they can't do anything.

'I vote for retribution for this man and help for this girl and for the old ways of running moots – even if we talk all day and half the night, and all the next day and night, to reach agreement.' Elfric sat down, less shaky now that he had spoken.

The Mereham headman Osric and his wife Sunnifa retreated to their tent, shouting at each other.

Meg and the girl with the baby looked at each other, wide-eyed.

Talk flared through the group. A man's voice cut through. 'Slaves won't work if they're not beaten. And the women, that's what they're for, to breed us more slaves, and have a bit of fun while we're at it.'

Winfrith found the speaking-staff and passed it to Elder Edith. 'Use the speaking-staff!' Edith instructed, holding it up.

Tola, Nelda's mother, reached for it and spoke with heat. 'Having fun together, men and women, that's one thing. We're talking about rape, when the person does not want it. That's different.'

Thane Roger shouted, without the speaking-staff, 'This talk is about rights and duties. Why are we veering off the topic, just because somebody's got a problem?'

Elder Mildreth held the speaking-staff high. 'Everybody has a right to feel safe in her own body. This is the most important thing we could talk about. Feeling secure is the source of every other right. Rape is the root of many wrongs.'

Seren held out her hand for the boat-topped staff. 'Rape hurts the soft inside places of the soul, as well as body. It's like crushing a flower; instead of the way a bee visits, gently. And when it happens, we stay smashed: afraid, angry, unsteady, our place to stand in the world is snatched away. A woman may have to give birth with resentment. I've seen those twisted feelings trap a baby so that it could not be born, and the mother and baby die. What about a woman who brings up a child who looks like her attacker? There's more courage there than on any battle-field.'

Tola took the speaking-staff. 'What does it do to you men when you spit on the children you make? If you despise your own issue, does that mean you hate your own bodies, too? Can you split off your head from your warm breathing body? Maybe that is what you have to do, to be able to split each other's skulls with war-axes.'

Winfrith spoke up: 'It's the headman's job to protect everyone in his settlement, not to go hurting us himself.'

Women nodded.

Nelda joined in, taking the speaking-staff from Winfrith: 'Seren said it right. Rape harms us all. If men see women's bodies as things to be used, they make their own bodies into weapons. Once they've hurt themselves like that, when they gaze at us women that way, they will look at Earth's creatures and see only things to be taken, and taken, and taken again.'

Lynna's finely woven blue sleeve stretched out for the speaking-staff. She looked at Seren and then spoke, 'The slave tribes keep Earth Mother as the centre of their lives. They say we're all her children and that makes us brothers and sisters with the deer and the trees. Raping a slave woman cuts a man off from Earth Mother. He is no longer in harmony with her.

Doing such a thing affects the way he thinks. It changes his attitude to everything. He begins to see his own body as something disgusting that he can poison and spit on. It turns his brother stag and sister willow into just dead meat and firewood. If he's so lost, he can gorge on the earth and guzzle it all up without care and still never be satisfied, because he lost his Earth Mother and she lost him.'

Seren's eyes stayed alive as she followed Lynna's words, nodding.

Thane Roger, apparently not having listened to anything Lynna said, grabbed the speaking-staff from her the moment her words stopped, seemingly impatient to say, 'How do we know the girl wasn't leading him on, our respected friend Osric, Headman of Mereham?'

'Leading him on?' Bertold spoke slowly, puzzled. 'Of course the woman can lead.' He scratched his bald head. 'If she says "No", you sit and have a chat and hope for better luck next time.'

'What if they say "No" when they mean "Yes"?' Thane Roger cut in, 'Girls often do that.'

Stern-faced, Cafell boldly snatched the speaking-staff away from him. 'When we say "No", we mean "No",' she growled. Her glare was sharp enough to scratch the Thane. 'What are we supposed to say instead of "No" when we mean "No", if you think we mean "Yes"?'

Thane Roger shrugged.

Snowy-haired Mildreth looked to Hilda to get the speaking-staff for her and to help her stand. The elder levelled her gaze at Thane Roger. 'Greed that grabs an unwilling woman hurts all of us, not just her. We have to stop this grasping now, before it ravages everything. I vote against the unbridled power of Headman and Thane, even if they are good men. We need all of us to link together, think together, and maybe have a drink together afterwards. So link, think and drink together and we'll make a better community!' She snorted at her rhyme and smiled to calm the situation.

Elder Edith politely took the staff from her elder friend and stood up, strong again. *She was wilting, but now she's uncurled like a plant that's been watered. It's all these voices speaking up that's nourished Edith's resolve,* Hilda thought.

Edith took control, 'We will eat now. We said we would be finished by noon, but now we see we've got far more to discuss than we thought, so we'll have to keep talking. We said unexpected wisdom could arise – and it has, so we must deal with it. We elders must confer about who may speak and what to do next. We have a clear decision from all the elders to continue discussions in the traditional way.'

MEG

Someone came whistling down the track from Thornthicket. It was Aikin.

'Where's the food?' he called as he tethered Headman Kedric's stallion, Dragon, near some juicy grass. He strolled over to the cooking area, where people thronged, talking. 'Hey, the baking-stones have gone cold. Give me a hand Wulf, get this fire going a bit better. Here's the dough, I'll put some more on to cook, shall I? Here's some bread that's done already. Help yourselves from the table, everybody.' He lifted onto the table the basket that Tegwen and Seren had filled. He noticed Thane Roger hulking over a drink of warm ale.

'Oh, Thane Roger Sir, how did you get here so quick? Have some flatbread. I've been having a good talk with your son Grimbold; he showed me all his arrowheads. He's really inventive. He told me how to make a special one for splitting chain-mail; it was grand!' Aikin struggled with a lid. 'Wulf, could you knock the pin out of this lid so we can open this barrel? There! Smoked eels! One each, leave plenty for your neighbours!' Aikin announced to the assembled crowd. He turned again to Thane Roger. 'When I got to Thaneshall, they said you were out, sir, and it was already dark, so I stayed over. They sent somebody out to fetch you yesterday morning. I thought you'd have to follow me back and get here later. But I hear you came by boat! Good idea!'

He's arriving without a care into the middle of this huge change that's happening. My life will never be the same again, but he hasn't even noticed how tense everybody is. It had taken all Meg's strength to speak out and now she felt so weak with hunger that she couldn't deal with the noise and the people streaming around the table.

Cafell noticed and, grinning, gave her a flatbread wrapped round a chunk of eel. She sank her teeth into it. *No one killed Cafell,* Meg thought with satisfaction and returned her smile, no words needed between them.

HILDA

As she waited, Hilda noticed Redwald heave a crock of cheese onto the food table and slice it up, putting some on wooden trenchers for people to help themselves. He licked his fingers as the moist ewe's cheese crumbled in his hands. He shovelled some onto a piece of flatbread and lifted it to his mouth – and stopped.

Hilda followed his line of sight to Ursel, waiting her turn in a queue.

Redwald pushed through the crowd to offer his food to Ursel. Their fingers touched around the bread. They smiled, but no words passed between them.

Ah, he's not supposed to talk to her because he's sitting in judgment with the elders, and she's a complainant. Hilda remembered seeing a marsh harrier, as quick and tender as this, pass food to his mate on the wing.

People were looking at them, so Redwald hastily made a basket of bread and cheese for Edith, Mildreth and Elfric, and passed it to Oswynne. Looking to see who else was waiting, he served Seren and Tegwen.

Then he handed Hilda a flatbread. She thanked him softly and added a blessing, 'Sun's warmth shine on you, cool of night enfold you.' She wasn't sure that he heard her; the talk around them was so noisy.

OSWYNNE

Oswynne set the basket of bread and cheese on the elders' table in their bothy, keen to hear their talk. Elder Edith offered Oswynne a seat on the bench and beckoned Redwald to join them.

'It's working rather well, this new way of everybody helping,' Edith said, as she pulled crumbs from her bread and chewed painfully.

Elder Elfric grimaced. 'I've got no appetite. Osric made a fool of me! What do they call him: Pigface? Good name. It's my duty to protect the settlement and everybody in it – or rather it's his duty to keep us safe; it's mine to guide us. I've failed.' He put his head in his hands.

'How could you guide him if he doesn't tell you what he's up to? You did your best, I'm sure,' Elder Mildreth reassured him.

'Women are better at noticing what's going on between people. I was too busy worrying whether we had enough fish to see us through winter, if there's blackfly on the bean-rows … I couldn't see what was under my nose.'

'That's a headman-farmer's job, surely, and his wife's. They put everybody in danger, leaving all that planning to you.' Elder Edith sighed.

Oswynne chimed in. 'Shall we let our slaves join the groups?'

Elder Mildreth searched her long memory for precedents. 'There was a slave woman who always spoke at moots and was deeply respected for her wise sayings. Can't recall her name, but she was wet-nurse to young Roger. She was sent away before he was three – much too young,' she tutted. 'Typical of Roger's mother to make such a decision.' She began to list other occasions when Thane Roger's mother had shown bad judgment.

Oswynne hid a yawn with her hand.

Elder Elfric quoted fragments from a long-forgotten agreement between the incoming Anglish and the indigenous Britons at the time of the Crossing. 'It spoke of hunting rights and parcels of land. There was protection for some British families in exchange for losing their freedom and something about speaking rights. But the agreement wasn't completely clear on everything and was broken many times by both sides. And even more bones were broken!' He embarked upon a list of occasions when fighting had occurred, with details of who hit whom, with what, and how hard; who had made the weapon and how well he'd made it; what had been said about the workmanship; and the relative musculature of the combatants. 'However, the agreement, though interesting in principle, is no longer valid. The bards who knew it by heart have died or forgotten the details.'

Oswynne had heard her mother talk about 'tearing her hair' but never knew what it felt like until now. She turned to Edith for help.

Elder Edith outlined the benefits of hearing Seren's views – her innate good sense, her calm demeanour. 'She told us something about feather-masks that saved a seabird colony. We talked then about the slaves perhaps having a say at our Moot. Do you remember, Oswynne?'

Oswynne recalled the warmth she had felt that day, sheltering from the rain with Seren, and how the talk shone in Edith's hall. *What words were said?* 'The bard was there.' She looked at Hilda.

'As I remember, Elder Edith,' Hilda said, 'you decided that Seren should take part in the Moot, because of her wisdom. Seren pointed out that her wisdom comes from her people, the native British tribes. You mentioned that we need all the good sense we can get, from the young as well as the creaky-kneed, from slaves as well as free people.'

'Did we promise that all the slaves would have speaking rights at the Moot?' Oswynne asked. She felt her eyebrows almost touch her hair.

'That's how it sounded,' Hilda spoke evenly.

The elders turned to each other, shrugged and nodded.

'If we invite them today, will they want to speak at every moot, on every topic? Where will it end?' Elder Elfric stroked the wisps of his beard.

'Did you see how Thane Roger pulled Seren's hair?' Oswynne put in.

'Outrageous!' Elder Mildreth spluttered.

'It's one thing for a headman to punish his own slave, if it's necessary and in proportion to the offence, and he stays calm as he does it.' Elder Elfric spoke with the voice of authority. 'That's his property. He needs to keep order and make sure he's obeyed. But you can't lift your hand against another man's slave without his permission, especially not in anger. Would anyone respect a man who is blown about by the storms of passion?'

'Seren is mine, and her children too.' Oswynne was firm. 'I will not allow them to be hurt. They are under my protection as well as my property. I stopped him, this time.'

'She's your respected house slave, isn't she?' Elder Mildreth asked.

'She nursed my children and took care of me when I had them, and she looks after all of us with her healing skills. She's more like a friend than a slave,' Oswynne said. Out of the corner of her eye, she thought she saw Hilda's eyebrows twitch and her mouth tug up and down, but when she turned to look, Hilda was simply smiling warmly.

'All the slaves shall have speaking rights in this Moot, for the rest of this day.' Elder Edith announced. 'Next time, the Elders will discuss beforehand who will speak. We need further talk, to settle the important principles that came up in the word-gifts. I think some women aren't speaking up because they're afraid of men shouting them down. We haven't heard enough from young people. How can we make sure all of these views are brought forward?'

Elder Mildreth, thoughtful now, asked, 'What did you mean about feather-masks, Edith dear?' Edith wrinkled her brow. 'Can "the bard with a brain-pan like a grain-store" help?'

Hilda grinned briefly. 'Seren told us about a moot that was held long ago at her home settlement, Ousemouth. They wanted to build a new jetty, and the chosen place was where the little terns nested. Some people worried about the birds; some cared more about increasing trade. They held a moot to talk the matter over. A group came dressed in feather-masks. Seren showed us how they whirled and called like terns, to bring the spirit of the seashore into the meeting. They found a different site for the jetty.'

'That's what we need: the voice of the wild, brought into our gathering! How can we do that?' Elder Mildreth asked. 'Edith dear, have you still got the masks for your antler dance?'

'Of course.' Edith sighed. 'They're precious. I've got them in a chest in my hall.'

'May we use those masks?' Elder Elfric asked.

Elder Edith scratched her head, thinking, then said: 'It wouldn't be right to use the masks without giving their spirits proper honour. It wouldn't be fair to those who wear them either. If they haven't been initiated and don't have a close kinship with the animal shown by the mask, they could be damaged, both inside and outside. No, we should not use the masks so lightly.'

Edith thought again, and announced, 'But we can bring in the voice of the wild, as you say, Mildreth. For this afternoon's talk groups, let's ask everyone to divide differently from this morning. We can have a group of people to speak for the forest and fen; one to bring the views of men; another for women; and a group to speak for generations to come. When they have put their heads together in their groups, a speaker for each group will bring their thoughts to the full Moot.'

The elders agreed.

'We must get back to work! Sound your horn, Elfric.'

Oswynne's heart hammered as a plan she had formed in her mind jumped into life. 'I'll rejoin you soon. There's something I need to do first.'

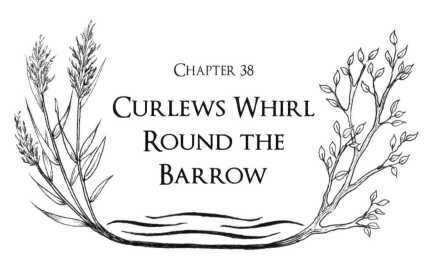

CHAPTER 38

CURLEWS WHIRL ROUND THE BARROW

HILDA

Hilda escaped to the south side of the barrow, away from the throng. She tried to follow the curlew's long liquid trill with notes on her elder pipe, but it sounded nothing like a curlew. *If it did, I'd have them whirling round my head, in love with a hollow stick.* She grinned and leaned her back against the barrow's curve. The sun warmed her face. Through half-closed eyes, she watched a lovelorn bird slide along the wind, his call spinning out to his little dun-coloured mate crouched in the grass. From the far side of the barrow, she could hear talk and movement; she drank in the quiet.

Ancestors of this place, you who rest in the long sleep in this barrow, thank you for cradling my bones; I mean no disrespect as I lean on you. Whose ancestors are you? You must have lived here before Angles and Saxons made the Crossing. Now they lay their lost ones in with you. Do you fight in the land of the dead?

Something rumbled in the earth-cave – laughter?

Of course, you are in the country of peace.

The wind wafted the smell of the fen to her nose – water, with a whiff of rotting leaves. *The first time I smelled that was right here. I'd stopped to sniff and look, as I strode down towards the blue thread of smoke from Wellstowe. It was an unknown settlement then but now it feels almost like home. I wondered:*

will they listen? Will they let me stay? I laid a hand on the grassy mound of the barrow and asked the ancestors lying inside: Let the truth on my tongue run clear and the notes of my flute find their hearts.

Now she asked it again. *I am so tired – can I do it?*

MEG

'Here comes Oswynne, look at the set of her jaw, cushla! You know what that means. She's made a decision and she's afraid her husband's going to scold her, but she's doing it anyway,' Seren whispered.

'There's something different about her, Mother. What is it?' They stopped whispering as Oswynne strode towards them.

'Cafell, you belong to me now,' Oswynne announced. 'I want you to start work at once. You'll do whatever Seren directs you to do. There'll be no idling.'

Cafell's mouth opened and shut. In Oswynne's wake, Sunnifa came back to the group.

May said what Meg was thinking but had thought better than to say: 'Aren't those Oswynne's amber beads hanging from Sunnifa's brooches, Mam?'

'She traded me – for beads?' Cafell breathed, outrage jostling with joy in her voice.

Seren spoke loudly enough for people to hear. 'That amber is not just a trinket. It was handed down to Headman's wife from her grandmother, and her grandmother before her. The amber holds warmth like the sand dunes where we grew up. When she drew the beads through her fingers, she heard her ancestors speaking in the voice of the waters on the shore. This is a great price to pay.' She narrowed her eyes. 'You will be worth it, I think, you and your daughter.'

Cafell buried her face in Cariad's hair.

'They could have asked me,' she mumbled.

Seren's face softened. 'Yes, they could,' she said quietly. 'I will take care of you and your child.'

Meg felt a stab of jealousy mixed with relief. What would it be like to have Cafell sharing their sleeping space? Sharing her mother? She cuddled May beside her until her little sister wriggled away.

'Can I hold the baby? Can I?' May reached up to stroke Cariad's head.

I'm even sharing my sister? thought Meg. Annoyed with herself for feeling bereft when she should have felt happy for her friend, she bit her lip. She didn't want Cafell to see the tear that welled in her eye. *Where's Hilda? I need her.*

The elders' voices called out, dividing people into groups – differently this time.

Meg couldn't take it in. She fled, moving slowly so as not to draw attention to herself.

At last she found Hilda behind the barrow. 'There you are! I looked everywhere!'

'What's happened, Meg?'

Meg poured it out – the amber, her mother's welcome, her sister. Hilda's face held her with a long, level look. Wrinkles rippled with kindness round Hilda's eyes; her mouth twitched and her eyebrows drew together.

She knows everything. She understands it all. She's right here with me.

'Must feel like you're being pushed out. Sit with me.' Hilda patted the grass and Meg flopped down, sighed and let some tears roll. 'There are most likely some of your ancestors behind our backs here. That's Eel Island way across the fen, isn't it? Do you remember Wendreda? She's taking care of us too. She'd be proud of what you did today, winning the right to speak in the groups. When are they starting?'

Meg had forgotten till now. She jumped up. 'Come on, they are gathering already!'

Hilda breathed deeply. 'I need to practise words and gestures for my story. It's the one I went hunting for all over the country. I found it here at last. Your mother gave it in trust to me. They need this story from me more than any I've told them yet.'

Meg was astounded. 'Are you nervous?'

Hilda made a face. 'I need to ask blessings from the Hare Goddess of the Heath, Deer Mother, the Mere-Wife and from Neath of my homeland. Yes, I am on edge. I must tell it with my whole self. Which group will you join, in the meeting?'

She's not pushing me away, just taking her space, like the swan said. Meg rubbed her nose in the familiar smell of Hilda's cloak, remembering when they first met. 'Hilda, your bony hug is hard enough to crack ribs!' She squeezed back and announced her choice: 'Forest and fen!' and ran back to the Moot.

HILDA

Later Cafell summoned her to return. 'Hilda the Bard? Elder Edith wants music to bring the groups together, please.'

'Which group did you go to, Cafell?' she asked as they went back.

'Oh, I listened in at nearly all of them. Not the men's group, though! I was in the women's group first, and then the young people's. It was mostly mothers in the group speaking for unborn generations – though not all. Some men came to that one too, and they said useful things.'

Hilda patted her shoulder and strode over to join the elders. Many urgent voices fell silent as her fingers swept across the strings of her harp.

'Let's hear what you talked about,' Elder Edith's voice was firm, though she looked frail without Meg at her elbow.

Hilda played another ripple of music.

Edith called to the crowd, 'Who speaks for unborn generations?'

Keenbur looked around, unsure. Aikin, her brother, linked his arm through hers and they stepped forward together. She rested one hand on the baby inside her. 'We, the children of the future, will need food and water, clothing and shelter, but most of all we want to know we will be loved. We call on you – put mothering first! Honour our mothers and all parents, so they can care for us. All of Earth's children: calves and fawns, lambs, pups and babies, we rely on you, the people who are here now. Plan for our safety, and all the generations to come.'

Hilda let her fingers roll across the strings, so the words sank in.

Bertold spoke for the men's group. 'The lads want me to say –' he coughed and continued, 'We should be good husbandmen to the Earth.' He shivered, talking about death creeping close in winter's cold and how hard it is to stay strong when we're scared.

Hilda noticed Elder Edith assessing Bertold keenly and nodding to herself.

For the women, the big-boned woman from Mereham talked about sticking together to stop women's rights from dribbling away.

'Who speaks for forest and fen?' Elder Edith looked around.

Hilda played again. *Are they here? What are they doing?* She gasped with everyone else as the forest moved towards them. *Oh, the leafy branches have legs – human legs.*

Little May just couldn't stay with the others. She ran ahead, waving her fern and shouting, until Seren called her back to walk solemnly with the group.

An oak branch spoke in Wulf's deep voice: 'Our tribe is close kin to your human tribe. We were flourishing on these slopes before you came, and will take back our land when you have drifted away like a dream. We help you with our bodies – use us wisely!'

The ferns danced and the faces of May and Roslinda popped out from behind them to giggle as they hopped.

Willow branches and bulrushes stepped forward. *Whose were those feet?* The fen spoke with Meg's voice, clear and strong, in a

Paean to the Fen

'We are feathered or scaly, some of us slimy.
We slither, we ooze, we waddle and dive.
We soar and swoop, we boom and drum,
We croak and gabble and honk.
We wheel and murmur, flock and flutter,
We swarm and buzz and shoal.
When you keep our water clean and clear,
We fill your nets, your baskets and pots,
And thrive in river and mere.'

Hilda found her mouth was open and closed it. It wobbled a little. Her hands worked on her harp, following the notes of Meg's praise-song to the fen.

She was lost in the words and music – until suddenly she realised that Elder Edith was calling her! Everyone was looking expectantly at her.

Now I tell the story. If I tell it badly, Ursel will be married off to some fool and women will be beaten by headmen any time. If I tell it well, I will get blamed for the trouble and get pitched out of the village on my ear.

Her mouth was dry as she strode up to the place where they could all hear her. She opened her heart to the ancient ones, opened her lungs to breathe and gave herself to the story.

THE ROWANBERRY DRESS

Goddess Breejsh walked through her woodland, weeping. Blackened stumps smoked where ancient oaks had stood. A rash of sawdust mottled the ground. No blackbirds sang. Trees crashed as they were felled. Woodcutters shouted as they burned branches, hauled trunks, sawed living beings into planks.

Like mist, the goddess drifted through the waste, writhing in pain.

At the edge of the mere, one giant oak still stood. 'Brother, what can we do?' Breejsh asked the tree.

The oak's voice rolled up from his roots and rumbled through his lichen beard. 'Bring him here, the one who did this. Let ash sting his eyes and the reek of destruction fill his nose. If that's not enough to stop him, give him to me!'

Breejsh replied, 'We must give him a chance to change. I made him too. He's a wondrous creature, like all my children, and we need his hands to set things right.'

'That's you with your kind heart. Look what they did to me!' The oak brushed one branch-arm across his trunk. 'They stuck this axe in my side.' Sap oozed from the wound. 'They came for me today, but I dropped a rotten branch on them. They went, but they'll be back.'

Breejsh cooled the gash in the tree with a spray of dew. 'I'll bring him here. We will make him find the answer to … the question.' She twisted into the shape of a white hind and bounded off.

Mathan, the king, inspected his ships being built on the river dock. So much trading and raiding he could do, with this new fleet. Bursting with pride, he wheeled his horse around and called his men. 'We'll hunt – boar or deer – up the slope where the forest's thick. Look out for good timber – we need more!' It was a long pull uphill; when he sighted the white hind, the rest of the men had fallen far behind. He set spurs to his mare's flank and tore after the glimmer in the gloom.

The hind swerved through the clear-cut land, down towards the mere.

The King's mare had to pick her way over half-burned branches, among cart tracks, through wrecked bushes. She stumbled and threw him. Winded, King Mathan lay with his face in the stench of burnt bark. His scalp was seared with pain – something had got him by the hair! It lifted him high up. Nothing but air was under his feet.

Breejsh watched, and changed her body into water drops on a spider's web. The oak-giant dangled the King, who shouted and kicked.

'Afraid, little man? What are you squeaking about?' The giant oak held him up to an ear with tufts of twig growing out of it. 'You want to keep your little life? Look at what you've done. Every one of my tribe who grew here was home to a settlement of living things: finches nested in our branches, squirrels scampered, mistletoe made the sign of the sun in our tops, jays feasted on our acorns. The swathe of forest you hacked down was home to badgers and owls, foxes and moles, moths and ants and bees and bears. No more!

'I could take off your head; that would stop you.' The giant held a glinting blade so close to the man's throat that his eyes stretched wide and tight as a drum-skin. A trickle of raindrops ran into the giant's eye. He blinked and sighed. 'Alright. Wondrous creature, eh? Kinglet, is there another way you can change?'

The man nodded, carefully, the axe blade at his neck. 'What do I have to do?'

'Find the answer to this question: what do women want? Come back and tell me, in a year and a day.' He was dropped. As he hit the ground, the giant told him what would happen if he failed. He rubbed his head, gasped with relief, found his mare and hurried to join his companions, who were hallooing for him in the wood.

Mother Breejsh stood with her hand on a birch trunk, her dress as red as rowanberries. She frowned as the men went home to the king's hall with their heads together. 'Are you sure he'll come back? Did you scare him enough?'

The giant chuckled deep as summer thunder. 'I told him, if he does not return, roots will trip him when he rides, ivy will bind him when he stands still, toadstools will grow out of his toes, flame will spit in his eye when he sits by the fire, beams will break over his head when he sleeps. Did you see how he looked about him as he rode away?'

'But will he find the answer? Will he understand it if he does? What will we do if he fails? I can't go on like this; I am so tired. I weave cresses in the brook, each leaf a gift – and they dam it. I pull out pollen from the sun's sleeve to feed my flocks of butterflies, I grow a million leaves out of my skin to wave on the hillside – and they smash stems, crush flowers, spill juice. I dribble moist desire between male and female, birth sleek herds of deer from my body, croon milk from the breast of spring – and they shoot, break bones, butcher. I hatch waves of starlings, constellations of starfish – and they burst the patterns, trample my creatures. When they stick my side with stakes, I bleed. When they chop and burn, I choke. I give them food, and all they do is snatch it and hurt each other or me – it's all the same. When I shake and boil with rage, they scramble and scream, but do they hear my voice? I'm not sure how long I can keep on giving.'

In the king's hall, Mathan sat, head in hands, utterly ashamed. Dangled by the hair! Bested by a lump of wood!

His nephew Gawane spoke. 'I'll help. We all will, Uncle. We'll ask every woman we meet: what do women want. We'll soon find out.'

Nearly a year later, they met again at Mathan's hall. 'What answers did you find?' The King set down his horn of mead, impatient.

One said 'gold' and another 'jewels'.

Some said, 'handsome husbands', 'faithful lovers', 'a skilful lover'.

'What did they mean?' the men asked.

'I had some fun finding out!' They all guffawed, except Mathan.

His pale brow beaded with sweat. 'None of these answers have the ring of truth,' he faltered.

A sparrow perched on a beam above them, head on one side, then flew out through a gap in the thatch. None of them noticed her.

'We'll ride out with you tomorrow, Uncle,' offered Gawane. 'If we see the giant, maybe we can think of a way to save you.'

They stopped in the glade by the silver birch and looked down to the mere. The huge oak still stood, hoary with lichen; a strange light shimmered round the giant. A voice from the roots shook them: 'One night left, little king. Come to me tomorrow. Have you changed?'

Mathan shivered. Gawane put an arm round his shoulders and drew him back. Someone else was in the clearing – a woman with her back to them, her gown the colour of rowanberries. Some of the young men pointed and jeered at her. 'Look at this old hag! Squinty eyes, warts on her chin. No teeth, just blackened stumps. Ugh, the stink!' They threw twigs at her, laughing.

'Enough!' Gawane stopped them. 'Grandmother, how can we help you?'

'It's me that can help you, dear,' she croaked. 'A sparrow told me you need the answer to a question, or the giant will slice your king's head off.' She cackled.

'Do you know the answer? Tell me!' Mathan thundered. She regarded him with a level eye. The gaze from her other eye wandered over the young warriors.

'I do, and I will – for a price.'

'Anything! Just tell us!' Mathan was pleading now.

'So, it is agreed. Did you all hear?' They nodded. 'I will tell the answer, in good time. My price is this: give me one of these young men for my husband.'

'Lady, I can't! That's not in my power.'

'No head for you tomorrow, then, dearie,' the old woman said, and chuckled.

Mathan gulped. He looked at each of his men in turn.

One said, 'Er, my horse needs grooming, I must go.'

Another said, 'I've just remembered I have to meet a man about a dog.'

One by one, they slunk away ... except for Gawane. Pale but resolute, he stepped forward and knelt before her. 'Lady, please do me the honour of being my wife.' With her knobbly hand she took his and raised it to her lips to kiss; he did not shudder as she slobbered.

Slowly they returned to the king's hall with the hag riding on Gawane's horse in front of him. Children pointed and laughed, and Gawane felt the old woman tremble. People stared and whispered behind their hands; he saw her head droop. After they passed, the sneering started. A tear slid from the old woman's eye and fell wet on Gawane's hand. When they got to the hall, he was white with fury. 'Bring an embroidered gown for my lady! Set the tables for a feast! She will have a wedding day as good as any.' If he regretted his bravery, he did not let it show.

He made the merrymaking last as long as he could, ignoring the pitying looks. But at last he took her by the hand and she hobbled beside him to their bedchamber.

'Sit by me. Poke up the fire,' she asked, and he was glad for the delay. The bed, fine though it was with soft covers, loomed at him in the shadows. 'Where did you play as a child?' she asked. 'I want to know you, my husband.'

He shut his eyes, not simply to avoid seeing the spit that drooled from her lips as she said 'husband'. The forest came alive for him again: 'I swam in the mere and hauled myself up on the roots of that old oak. From the highest branches I could see into the tops of all the trees – that used to be there.'

'Just stumps left now, as black as my teeth,' she mused, and his eyes snapped open. 'What did you see, my duck?'

'Early spring, a woodpecker with a red head drummed on a dead branch. I thought it was eating something, but it turned its head sideways and listened. Another one drummed far away. They were signaling to each other. They were marking out a stretch of land for one of them and another territory for the other one, so they'd have enough food for all the chicks in their nests.'

'If people made agreements like that, it would save a lot of broken heads and fatherless children,' she said, nodding.

'But the creatures eat each other! I saw a bracket fungus that drained life out of bark. Grubs ate the fungus and got caught in a spider's web. The spider sucked their juices. A blue tit gobbled the spider up. A harrier swiped the blue tit. So much death!' He shuddered.

'Yes, the flesh of one feeds another. Try seeing it as so much life! The fungus takes food out of the tree; it fattens the grubs that make the spider's dinner; they become blue tit song, until the harrier eats them – so it's life from the heart of the tree that soars up into the sky and flies far over the fen. What else did you see?'

'In amongst the roots, I watched a magpie snap up a black beetle with horns like a stag. I saw a dead hedgehog, its bristles melting back into the soil; a fern grew up through it and unfurled. I heard hedgehogs grunting as they got ready to mate. I watched a mother one suckling her babies.'

'You saw how life and death weave pain together with joy. Your own life is flourishing, and one day you will be old like me and die.' Her voice darkened. 'There's not much joy at the mere-side now. The balance is broken.'

Gawane shifted in his seat. 'We've taken too much. The forest will take years to grow again. Those trees were older than my grandfather's grandfather.'

'And I'm grown old before my time.'

'Who are you?' he breathed. Her eyes glowed with a smile while her mouth stayed set in sorrow. 'What can I do?' he asked.

'Kiss me, dear husband,' she invited, her voice like mead.

He couldn't help shutting his eyes as his lips touched her gnarled cheek.

The warmth of his touch melted frost. Her strength flowed again – her back uncurled from its hunch like green bracken opening; her clawed hands unfroze and grew soft; her lips kissed him back with the warmth of spring sun. Life pounded back into her body and blossomed into beauty.

He opened his eyes and gasped. He stroked her hair as dark as a raven's wing and gazed into her eyes, clear and brown like a peaty pool. When he kissed her cheeks, she gathered him to her.

'It's me, your wife,' she giggled. 'Your kindness turned the wheel of the year towards spring. Welcome to my arms, dear husband. Shall we go to bed?'

She enfolded him with her body, juicy and sweet as a ripe plum. He worked like a bee to please her, and her raptures sang in them both with the glory of all the birds together. Not much sleeping was done that night.

In the grey first light, he gazed at her body as she rested. The rise and fall of her breath was like mist rising from earth when sun warms it after frost. The curve of her shoulder reminded him of the chalk ridge as he caressed her. She opened her eyes and smiled.

'Will you stay like this?' The question burst out of his mouth. She sat up and gave him a level look.

'I'm not sure I can. When they cut and burn my forests, my flesh, it drains my life. When my children are wasted and killed, my cry wrenches strength out of my guts. I can't keep working the magic of transformation, not without help.' The tear that ran down her cheek furrowed her skin into wrinkles again. He hurried to put an arm round her shoulder.

'I'll help if I can.' Her skin smoothed. 'Are you Earth herself?' he breathed. 'I want to be a good husband to you, whoever you are.'

'I can stay young and beautiful at night, and change back into my winter self at daybreak. Or, I can be beautiful during the day and change to old and loathsome at night. I have just enough power left for that. What will you choose?'

Gawane sat on the edge of the bed, and rubbed his feet. He thought of the jeers of his friends. Even worse, their pity, if he walked about the court with a hag dragging on his arm. He remembered how she drooped as she endured their name-calling: to live through that every day would be torture for her. How envious they would be if he walked through the hall with her young and radiant at his side! She could be friends with the ladies and sit at the high table, but he couldn't bear to think about the night-times! He buried his face in his hands and wept.

'You're the wise one!' he choked. 'You choose. I'll follow whatever you say.'

Rosy light filtered between his fingers and he rubbed his eyes. She shone brighter than the risen sun as she threw open the shutters. Larks burst into song. 'You found the answer, dear husband!'

'Oh! Did I?'

'What women want is for everyone to follow the wisdom of the earth. When I was an old and ugly woman, you respected me. You listened and learned from me. When I was young, you adored me; your body worshipped mine with tenderness. We had fun, sweetheart! Respect for women and the old; listening and learning from the ways of the wild, tenderness and joy – this is the wisdom of Mother Earth. Tell them all.'

He looked at his knuckles and chewed his lip. 'What about … night and day? Which will you choose? If you are the Great Goddess, can you still be my wife?' He looked at her with longing.

She took his face in her hands. 'I am dragonfly and willow, badger and crane. I dance in rushes, sprout through shoots. I'm everywhere, in everything, and I'm the love everything springs from. I can be your human wife for as long as our bodies live. I have a special tenderness for you, Gawane. My name is Breejsh. If you and your friends work with me to help the forest grow again, I can be my young self both day and night.'

He started to kiss her again, but she laughed and said, 'Hadn't you best tell Mathan what you've learned? He may be worrying about his neck this bright day.'

Naked, he ran out into the hall, shouting, 'Uncle, I've got the answer! Everybody, listen! What women want is for us to follow their wisdom, that they get by listening to Mother Earth.'

They gathered round, scratching their heads. 'How do you know?'

'She told me – I found out! She said she could be ugly by night and lovely by day, or the other way around and I had to choose. I couldn't, I said – you're the wise one, it's your choice, tell me what to do, I gave her the power and then everything was alright, and the sun shone and now she can be –'

'You're babbling, Nephew,' King Mathan said, 'but I think you may have got something.'

She swung back the leather curtain of their chamber and passed Gawane his tunic. She was bright as lightning, strong and slender, and she swayed to the music of a robin's song. When she smiled, they gasped and their hearts melted.

Mathan's men crowded round the couple, cheering and clapping Gawane on the back, until the old King said, 'Now I must go and face the giant.'

'We'll come with you, Uncle,' Gawane said, and a merry throng flocked round them as they went.

The strop of a blade being sharpened on a whetstone stopped them. The blood drained out of King Mathan's face.

'You have the answer now, Uncle,' Gawane reassured him.

Mathan stepped forward and looked up at the oak giant. He put on a brave face, put his hands on his hips and swaggered.

'What do women want? They want lots of things, so they say: garnets set in gold; fine horses; gowns made of cloth they haven't woven themselves …'

At each wrong answer, the giant snorted.

'… handsome lovers; kind husbands; handsome, kind husbands who are also good lovers …'

The giant roared and swung the axe over his head.

'Wait!' Mathan shouted. 'What women want – is to lead the way for us all, with their wisdom, which they learn from Mother Earth.'

The giant set down the axe. 'Do you know what that means, little man?' he growled.

'I think the youngsters are going to teach me,' said the King, still shaking.

The giant laughed, a great, deep fruity noise that sounded as if it came up out of the belly of the Earth. The ground shook under their feet. 'What are you going to do with this?' He threw the axe down at their feet. Mathan looked around for help.

Gawane picked up the axe and looked to Breejsh for guidance. 'The mere will take care of it,' she said.

So he strode through the sedges and hurled the blade far out into the dazzling lake. He blinked; the axe was gone, ripples moved over the water's surface and the giant was just a huge oak tree.

Breesh stirred the ash with her toe and coughed as it blew into her throat. Rage surged through her and she threw her arms wide to hold it. She hovered over the grey ground and roared: 'This ash offends me! What shall we do with it?'

Hilda looked round – were the listeners tired? Some had round eyes and mouths as they followed every word; spindles grew fat with thread as spinners worked; one or two snored gently; some fidgeted.

'What should they do with the ashes?' Hilda asked.

'Stuff them down his throat!' called out a woman.

Hilda mimed choking and spluttering and they laughed.

'That'd be a waste,' somebody said. 'Use them in the privy-pits. A good sprinkle after each use and you'll have good compost in a couple of years.'

Hilda nodded and worked this into the story.

'Let's sweep it up to fertilise our crops,' Gawane said. They scooped up armfuls and carted it to their middens.

'Let me see the poor earth.' Breejsh tore up trails of ivy and dug with her hands. With soil under her nails, she patted and stroked, laid her cheek on the moist earth and blew gently onto it. 'It's ready!'

The giant oak dropped acorns into their hands. They planted seeds everywhere amongst the blackened stumps.

Breejsh danced over the soil. Anger drummed from the soles of her feet into the ground. At the next beat, love leapt up and into her muscles, warmed her womb, raced up her spine, shouted out of her mouth. Seedlings shot up at every touch of her toes. Aconites flowered, bees buzzed. She jumped and swooped, caressed the land with a fingertip. Shoots rose tender; stems fattened into trunks, branched into a tracery of twigs; leaves uncurled, blossom filled the air with fragrance; apples swelled with juice.

'Come!' called Breejsh and the canopy rang with whistles and cheeps. Cranes joined her dance, curlews and lapwings, starlings, grass snakes and moths. Each creature chose a human partner, as Breejsh beckoned the people to join in. Young men lolloped and laughed, girls linked arms and swung each other, hair flying in the wind. Her rowanberry dress swirled around her. At the kiss of its hem, butterflies burst out of their cocoons, stretched their wings and followed her.

'May and Roslinda, all your friends, show us how they danced!' Hilda invited, and played a tune on her elder pipe. Children whirled each other round, jumped and skipped amongst the seated adults, roared with laughter. Aunties grinned and clapped the rhythm. Hilda held up a hand to ask them to stop and dived back into the story.

A kingfisher flashed in the setting sunlight. Gawane chuckled at the snorting and cavorting of hedgehogs in love as dusk fell.

King Mathan sat hunched over, alone on the grass.

Breejsh saw his eyes fill with tears as she sat beside him.

'I was not chosen,' he said. 'None of them trusted me.'

She took his hand. 'You set yourself outside and above the dance of life; and now you wish you were part of it.'

As each of his tears fell to the ground, Breejsh made a clover flower spring up, white as the moon. After a while, she asked, 'What will you do?'

'I'm tired,' he sighed. 'I'll ask Gawane to be king, now that he has you. You'll look after the land. I'd like to get to know the oak giant, if he'll wake up again. He looks like the kind of chap I could share a horn of mead with, of an evening.'

Breejsh laid a cool hand on his forehead and he felt a blessing shiver down his spine. In the wood, owls hooted.

Every year on the longest night, the people gather by the edge of the mere. They dance with the creatures, whatever

comes to meet them: snail or frog, bat or eagle, stag or dragonfly.
Each person vows to protect the Earth and keep it safe for the
creatures and their children, and their own children, and their
children's children.

Her words dropped into silence. Gold from the sun lit a tear in more than one eye.

Hilda had seen people moved by her stories before, but never had she seen the effect run so deep. Now in silence people turned to each other, touched hands. Some murmured quietly.

Fierce gladness filled her. *If I have to go, at least I know something happened here and I gave voice to the words that made it so.*

Then Kedric stamped his foot. 'This is not fair. The storyteller is clearly on the side of my niece, against me.'

Elder Mildreth glared at him. 'You've had your say, Headman Kedric.'

Elder Elfric sounded his horn.

'We, the Elders, will now consider our judgment and decide what to do,' Edith announced. 'You, in each group, have spun good threads. We will twine them together, and make them strong enough to weave into justice and peace.'

Elfric sounded his horn again. 'The Elders withdraw to deem our Doom,' he announced. The three of them, taking Redwald along, made their way to their bothy and ducked inside.

'If the old ones lay shame on my back, I know who to blame.' Kedric snarled, looking at Hilda.

CHAPTER 39

THE HEDGE BECKONS

SEREN

'Wulf,' Seren called, 'help me with this tripod. One leg's shaky. If the cauldron tips, we'll lose the stew!'

'There's a big lump of clunch in the way,' Wulf poked at it. 'Madoc, lend me your hammer and a tent peg. There, the spike's split the stone; it's gone deeper, won't wobble now.

'That was good what you said, honey-sweet, about mothers having to love babies when the fathering was violent. My mother – Wendreda – told Kenelm and me how the Thornthicket headman of that time forced her. Finding she was pregnant with us twins was the wound that broke her in pieces. During the months of her sickness, she was in a land of spirits. When she came back to herself, she had healing powers. She said the water of the well made her whole. She was keeper of the Thornthicket well, along with her grandmothers. She could not stay there, having to see that headman every day. When she ran to stay with kinsfolk on Eel Island, all she took was a jar of water from the well. Nobody went after her; the headman knew he'd done wrong. She made sure he didn't get us; we would have belonged to him. We were born on Eel Island, free.'

'You never told me all that!'

'Elder Mildreth is the cousin of that headman. I'm not going to claim kinship with – the man who begot me and my brother.'

May ran over. 'Oswynne wants the tooth-worm tea for Elder Edith, Mam.'

'I'll stir the pot if you need to fetch your remedy, honey-sweet.'

'You help your Dada, May. Make sure he scrapes right to the bottom of the cauldron!'

Seren's heart was full. She heard Wulf's deep tones tell May she could go and play, and smiled. It was strange to hear Hilda telling the rowanberry dress story. Her grandmother's voice echoed in her memory, rooting the story into her.

Hilda changed details to make it come alive for the people here; Nana's version had the sea in the background. Sun-glitter was the same – when they plunged the axe into water to get rid of all violence. How can a woman half-drowned in agony, as Wendreda was, reach up and out of herself to help others?

Seren measured powder from a jar and mixed it with water. She spoke a blessing over it, in her grandmother's words. *I taught those words to Wendreda and we used the chant together, so many times. Whose voice is this in my throat; mine or Wendreda's? Nana's or her grandmother's? I'm a channel for all the wise women through the ages singing together!*

HILDA

Kedric's harsh voice jolted Hilda into old fear.

Every man who's threatened me – their spit, their venom, their knuckles – it all comes back again round a man like that. I joke about thorns in my backside, but last time I got chucked out of a settlement, I limped for a month. The thwack of a club left me bruised and shaky – and worrying I'd got a broken bone. That would finish me, on my own in the wildwood.

Aloud she said, 'It's not my fault! You were sliding into this long before I came. If you hit your women, if you don't listen to them, if you try to squash them – you're bound to get trouble sooner or later. This muck has been festering in your settlement for years.' The words hissed out hot and satisfying as a fart, before she could stop them.

Headman Kedric's eyes opened wide, then drew together narrower than before. 'This is a fine place – if you don't like it, get out! I'll take pleasure in driving you away myself. Be glad if it's only the butt of my spear on your shoulders.'

Hilda turned aside and drew cool air into her lungs to calm down.

Curious people gathered round, drawn by the raised voices. Meg slid close, her wide brow drawn into a frown. Seren passed by, carrying an earthenware jar, intent on not spilling a drop as she hurried to the elders' bothy and pushed through the leather curtain. *Tooth medicine; Edith must be in pain.*

A tangle of bodies and shouts broke into Hilda's worry. The scurry scrambled towards Hilda and slid in a heap at her feet.

'It's *my* stick – I made it! *I* want to dangle the king by his hair. Hilda, tell her to let me …' Roslinda held up a willow stick by its twigs and May made a grab for it.

'No, *I* want to! I'll show you how to do it.'

'Why don't you take turns?' Hilda felt her mouth twitch into a smile. 'That way you can make sure he's well dangled. Have you frightened him enough? Will he go home and ask everybody what women want?' They giggled, and passed the stick between them, swinging it wildly. Hilda leant down to them and suggested, 'Put on your rowanberry-red dresses, both of you!' May's open face was serious, drinking in every word. Roslinda's blue eyes opened round among the freckles. 'We need as many goddesses as we can get, to dance the land to life. Will you do it?'

They nodded in awe, took hands and whirled away, pulling their tunics downwards into imaginary skirts that kissed the grass. People smiled and clapped in time as the little ones danced.

Hilda stood upright again and let her own words sink into her. *I may feel like rattling Kedric's teeth in his skull, but … I've got to do what Breejsh did to bring the forest back to life. I must drum anger out through the soles of my feet. Drink love in from the heart of the earth. Open to life as it flows hot through me, sings in my blood, warms my tongue.* Fear slid off her shoulders like rain. *He's proud of this place.*

She turned back to Kedric. 'You've worked hard to make Wellstowe into a strong settlement.'

'Yes, and I'm not going to let you bring it to ruin with your whispering in corners.'

'You see women clustered together and you feel out in the cold?' Hilda guessed.

'I don't know what you're up to, maybe cooking up some plot to make me look a fool.'

She sprayed him with dew in her mind, like a goddess healing wounds, and felt its cool herself. 'If you feel they don't respect you, it must blister like a boot that rubs. We all need to trust the people we work with. When I get together with a group of women, we don't talk about you. I'm usually telling a story and they're chewing it over as they work.'

Women nodded agreement.

'But what are they for, these tales? What are you up to, Storyteller?' Kedric glowered.

Hilda sifted words. *What can I tell him? I'm not up to anything … But I am! I'm waking up women. That doesn't mean squashing men, though. Men would be happier if they didn't scrunch up their soft innards trying to look tough. This is not just for Headman Kedric, I've got a small audience now.*

'The myths I tell come from the deep past, when women and men worked together. They show us that we can recreate that friendship, if women claim back strength and men allow each other to feel …'

Elder Elfric's horn rang out, cutting through all talk. *Surely much too soon! A Doom requires careful wording, dignified sentences, well-crafted decisions. They can't have done all that by now!*

The crowd gathered to listen to the elders. Redwald stood beside their chairs. Elder Edith rapped her stick against a chair-leg. Elfric had to sound his horn again for silence.

Edith announced, 'We laid our foreheads against the cool grass of the barrow to listen to the ancestors. Their voices were hard to hear at first, like noises underwater. When we talked in our bothy, their meaning swam out from the depths of our minds, as clear as the moon when clouds float away. This is what we understood: it is our task, as elders, to have the final say, but those who are hurt in this dispute have to craft the agreement.

'Long ago, our clan mothers knew this way to weave peace. In the hurry and worry of moving across lands, rowing over the ocean and building settlements, our folk forgot much. Riders, fighters and oarsmen became our leaders; peacemakers were left to tend the children.'

Hilda stared at the ground. *Don't catch my eye; don't say anything about Varagan, or I'll be in that thorny hedge before the day's out …*

Edith continued, 'This dispute needs loving care, heartfelt listening, and fairness: the skills tended by mothers through generations. Our foremothers in the barrow guide us to make use of their ancient wisdom. We shall draw together those who carry bitterness, asking them to speak from their hearts and listen to each other. Only then will we see how to build the way forward.

'So this is not our final judgment, the Doom you're all waiting for. That must come later. Seren, wise woman of Wellstowe, reminded us that this old tradition is called the Ring to Create Justice. That is how we shall go forward …'

'Slaves taking charge now, eh?' Thane Roger cut in. 'Let me sort this out; we've had enough chatter. The girl Ursel clearly needs a husband; she'll be happier when she's got responsibilities. I'm telling you …'

'We are not asking you, Thane Roger.' Edith drew herself up to her full height and looked him in the eye.

What's in that tooth medicine? Strong stuff! Hilda thought.

'We will not tolerate your interruptions. This is not chatter. We are conveying the sacred guidance of the ancestors in this deep matter. It reaches far back into the past and away into a future beyond our seeing. It can't be resolved with shouting or arguing. You talk like a bully. Is that how you want people to think of you?'

Hilda couldn't help herself. The tune to 'Bully-boys and Braggarts, Beware of the Boggarts' slipped out of her elder pipe and set a few toes tapping.

Thane Roger shifted uncomfortably.

Meg covered her mouth, but her giggles overflowed.

Thane Roger snarled, 'I'm going to trade with Osric.' He swaggered off, but looked about him as if a bogle might be lurking in the shadows.

Edith's shoulders sagged. *Stay strong,* Hilda willed.

Elder Mildreth grimaced, saying, 'Kedric's stuck in the cart rut of having to be in charge. Ursel's bogged down in needing to stand up for herself because she's used to being squashed. Everybody's tired. Look, people are wandering off. I hear grumbles about how long all this is taking.'

Hilda played a rising chord on her harp, almost a fanfare. Edith took control again. 'The Ring to Create Justice! Whether this custom is British or Anglish, or if it comes from further away, we cannot say; that's lost in the rolling years. We'll sit in a ring, not the big circle. Drag some logs closer together. Ursel, Kedric and Elders, you may each choose a friend to sit with you. Everyone else, you're free to go and tend children, animals and cooking-fires. You may stay and watch if you're quiet.'

'I'm glad to get away. All this talk is battering my brains,' Oswynne said. 'Seren, how's the stew coming along?' She sent children to find green stuff to add to the pot.

Hilda licked her lips as Seren called for sorrel. A saunter round the shady margins of the beech wood sounded delightful.

'Hilda the Bard, you've seen many places, I choose you to help me. Come into the ring.'

Edith needs me. Hilda sighed and went to join the group.

Ursel asked for Winfrith; Kedric drew in Bertold; Lynna came to sit by Elder Mildreth; Elder Elfric called over the big-boned woman from Mereham whose name was Elwaru; Redwald asked Oswynne to help – she stamped back to the ring, rubbing her neck, and plonked Hubert on the grass. Meg stayed, quietly watching.

Hilda asked, 'Please explain what we're doing, Elder Edith, I'm not familiar with this Ring.'

'Each will tell what the anger between niece and uncle does to them. This may help us see our next steps towards agreement.' Edith held up the whetstone with the intricate handle: 'We only speak when we have the speaking-staff; we'll pass it round. I'll start.' She sighed. 'I remember how proud my sister Merewyn was of you, Kedric, her lovely boy. It hurts me to see you so roughened that you can be violent. Ursel, I feel an ache and sense a hole in your life where your father should be. Your uncle could fill that gap, so this dispute makes it hurt more.' She passed the staff on.

Elder Mildreth held it up. 'When one settlement is torn apart, it damages us all. We can't rely on you, our neighbours, to help us in time of trouble, if you're fighting amongst yourselves. You're our cousins. Our ancestors grumble in their graves when there's discord.'

Redwald was careful not to look at Ursel. 'I see two people who could support each other and work together in their settlement – both with talents. It's a waste for such courage to drain away into the mud.'

Elder Elfric took his turn. 'I've got to sort out the shocking behaviour of the Mereham Headman.' He rubbed his head. 'This dispute, on top of all that, gives me a headache.' He passed the speaking-staff to Ursel.

'You all saw my bruises.' Ursel seemed to shrink. 'The wounds inside hurt more. The names he called me made me feel like a clod to be kicked aside, of no value. My friends helped, but still I sometimes feel small.'

Hilda was glad to see Ursel nod to Meg, while grasping Winfrith's hand.

Ursel passed the staff to Kedric. He set his jaw firmly. 'If anybody can defy the rule of the headman – any headman – chaos could come. I have got to keep everybody safe, and the only way I can fulfill that responsibility is if everybody does as they are told. Smartly, no arguments.'

Bertold caught his eye and said, 'This dispute adds to your worries. Makes your job more difficult.'

Kedric grunted agreement.

Bertold thought for a moment, tugging on his long white-blond moustache. 'When you hit her that evening, what you wanted to beat out of her was the disobedience that threatens our settlement. You want to keep us working well, ready to face any danger together.'

Elder Edith said, 'Let's stay on the track of talking about how this affects each of us. What does it do to you, Bertold?'

Bertold looked at both Ursel and Kedric before replying, 'It makes my old friend Kedric look bad, but he's just trying to look after us all. Here he is getting riled with his niece. She's not a hungry bear or a bunch of invaders – that's what we should be worrying about more. And Ursel – I hated seeing those bruises and scabs.' He shook his bald head, looking at the ground.

'What does the dispute do to you, yourself?' Edith insisted.

'Curdles my guts, if you must know,' Bertold replied. 'Can't sleep well.'

Kedric's head jerked up. He looked around the ring, eyes narrowed, fists clenching. *What's he thinking?* Hilda wondered. *Is he getting ready to defend his friend from attack by the other men, for showing weakness?*

'Thank you for your honesty, Bertold,' Elder Edith said.

'It is heavy, this burden we carry when we look after a whole settlement,' Elder Elfric leaned forward to speak forcefully. 'Headman Kedric is lucky to have a friend who loses sleep out of concern for him. Kedric, how are you sleeping?'

Kedric harrumphed and looked at the ground again.

Elder Elfric went on, 'I know that churning gut, Bertold. It goes away when a fight's over – but when it keeps going all night, ugh.'

Kedric was sneaking a look around again. *Will there be mockery?* Hilda glanced around too.

Redwald's face was open. He nodded, serious. He took the speaking-staff. 'I'm not looking forward to that when I ... if I ... have responsibilities.' He coughed to cover embarrassment, and waved the speaking-staff to pass it on quickly.

Ursel took it. 'I see this is hard,' she ventured. 'I didn't know, Uncle Kedric.'

Kedric looked up again in surprise.

Elder Edith took the staff. 'Bertold, have you anything to add?'

He nodded. 'Talking about waste – the girl's a good tracker, we all know that. What was it you said about the old stag, Ursel?'

'I can lead you to him, if you'll trust my tracking skills.' Ursel replied. 'He's got flesh on him still that would make a good meal for many people. The herd doesn't need him now the young stags are grown.'

Kedric burst out with, 'So you do understand about the settlement needing meat!'

Ursel kept the speaking-staff. 'Of course, Uncle Kedric. That's another reason to protect the pregnant hinds, to make sure we have enough venison in the years to come.'

'You said that yourself, old man,' Bertold stated, 'you wouldn't normally go after a breeding female.'

'I know what I'm doing in field and forest and fen!' Headman Kedric snapped. 'Of course we look after the wild herds as well as our own flocks, that's good husbandry.'

'Ursel still has the speaking-staff,' Elder Mildreth interrupted. 'Ursel, do you want to say something?'

Ursel hesitated, trying not to catch Kedric's fierce eye. 'If … we agree not to target breeding hinds … If I was allowed to join the hunt …'

Elder Edith sat up straight. 'We have a suggestion, coming forth from the Ring! Headman Kedric and Ursel, will you hunt together, using all your skills for the benefit of the whole community?'

Hilda breathed deeply, relishing beauty and balance. *All will be well now, and we can move into the dancing and feasting, happy together …*

'You can't make me do that! She'll scare away the game, like she did before!' Kedric snarled.

'How do I know he won't hit me as soon as we're out of sight of the settlement?' Ursel held her arms in front of her body and shuddered.

Arguments broke out, shouts and swearing. Hubert wailed. Edith blanched and swayed.

Beauty and balance? Cluck cluck gabble gabble! When will you learn, Hilda, you can't make everything right with a story. Even if it's your best story and you tell it as well as you know how. If only I had my swan-bone flute! No, that wouldn't work either. Try something – anything!

Hilda played a ripple of notes on her harp. Elder Elfric took his lead from her and sounded his horn. 'We will take a short break,' he announced. 'Elder Edith needs to rest.'

Elder Mildreth wrapped an arm round Edith. 'Fetch her some bread and a drink to sop it in, and get Seren over here; we need her.' Her blue eyes seethed with fury. 'How dare those two disrupt the ancestors' custom? I feel like knocking their heads together to teach them sense! Ah, Seren, wise woman of Wellstowe, as Edith calls you, you know about the Ring; what can we do when they break it with their angry words?'

Meg dunked a crust in ale for Edith.

With many eyes on her, will Seren disappear into blankness? Hilda moved to Seren's side.

'Listen better. Listen deeper. Get to the roots,' Seren said. Her words left a silence as the elders thought.

'Pass my stick, Meg. A little blast on your horn, please, Elfric. Bring them back together.' Tension made her body look frail, but Edith was on her feet again. 'Advisors, ask your friends to delve deeper. Help them say more about their fears.'

Bertold's bald head moved closer to Kedric's dark one; Winfrith beckoned Lynna to join her and Ursel. The elders moved around to join each group, questioning, listening, nodding.

Elder Mildreth laid a hand on Ursel's shoulder. 'If they hunt together, Ursel is concerned about being trusted. If she tries to show Kedric signs in the undergrowth – a hair caught on a briar perhaps – will he ignore it, interrupt her, insist on going the wrong way, until it's dusk and they're exhausted? She fears that her skills will be ground under his heel, her knowledge shouted down, she'll feel less valued than a worm, crushed like a beetle in the dust.'

'I don't shout without good reason.' Kedric glowered.

'Can you understand the feeling of not being valued? Has that ever happened to you?' Elder Mildreth enquired, calm but insistent.

Bertold spoke for his friend. 'Of course he has, haven't you Kedric? Your brothers treated you like that – and when they went off without you, you were sunk.'

Elder Edith regarded Bertold with respect. 'You know everyone so well, Bertold. Your friendship with Headman Kedric is a – what did you call it, Hilda? – a rooftree for our settlement.'

Kedric looked down, his face closed.

Elder Elfric opened his arms wide. 'Headman Kedric sees the hunt like this: Ursel and he set out from the settlement and she's arguing every step of the way. He tries to show her how to move silently but she says she knows already. When they get near an animal, she shouts, it runs, she laughs at him.'

Ursel took the speaking-staff, 'Uncle Kedric, I would never do that.' Kedric looked up, surprised. Ursel met his the eye. 'You know why I saved the hind that one time. I was not laughing at you. If I could join the hunt, as an equal …' She choked.

Ursel really wants to do this! Hilda realised. *She wants her uncle to see her as an adult.*

Ursel went on '… I would work with you, carefully. You have brought meat home from the forest all of my life.'

'So, you do have some respect for me,' Kedric growled. 'I didn't want to bash the spirit out of you, girl. My brothers were harsh with me, so I do know what that's like, as Bertold says.' He checked the faces around them. Nobody was laughing at him.

Hilda held her breath. Kedric went on, 'Ursel, would you do as I say without questioning, in silence, and learn to move as part of one body of hunters?'

Ursel's voice trembled, 'Could I be sure you wouldn't bash me if a twig broke?'

They looked at each other doubtfully.

Hilda, breathing softly, wanted to help but didn't know how.

Redwald leaned over for the speaking-staff. 'May I bring a thought? Ursel has offered her skills in tracking. Headman Kedric, you have a particular skill in carving,' he held out the whetstone with its intertwined hounds. 'Could you use your artistry to build trust with Ursel?'

'Deer Mother.' The voice made them look up. It was Seren, bringing ale. She blushed, 'I meant to keep my words in my head, but they slid over my tongue.'

Edith took her gently by the arm and drew her into the ring. 'The ancestors have spoken through you, Seren. Tell us more.'

'A carving of Deer Mother is stepping through mist in my mind.'

'I could make one.' Kedric's hands shaped his vision in the air, 'The hooves would be tricky, they're so delicate. I could do the curve of her flanks with the calf inside her belly. How do they sniff the wind? There's something about the eye ...'

His cheeks are pink under the black beard! He's pleased to have his skill recognised. Hilda breathed out gently.

Ursel offered, 'I could lead you to a pregnant hind, if I can be sure you won't shoot, Uncle. You could see how she moves.'

'Would you do this, both of you?' Elder Edith was rapt. 'It is what the ancient ones of the barrow have given us, in the voice of our wise woman, Seren the healer.'

Swallows swooped over their heads and everyone looked up to welcome them back from who knows where. The elders withdrew again, to consider their Doom. Seren brought the elders ale and bread – a refill and another.

They're so weary now, Hilda thought, *can they manage it?*

CHAPTER 40

THE ELDERS DEEM THEIR DOOM

HILDA

Across the fen, sunset blazed across the sky. It glinted on the silver circlet that bound the cloud of Elder Mildreth's hair, and picked out bronze buckles on the strap of Elder Elfric's horn. He sounded a long note.

People gathered from their tasks, some carrying sleepy children. They fell silent as the elders raised their arms in prayer. Edith's voice floated over their heads. 'Ancient ones who rest in Wellstowe Barrow, you watch the stars wheel over generations, you track patterns of dark and spark. We listened for your voices beyond our own thoughts. Please accept our gifts, stay close.' She poured a cup of water on the barrow's slope among the daisies.

Elfric spoke: 'You steadied us as we walked a hard path with tongues and hearts, from the marshes of bitterness to firm ground.' He sprinkled drops of mead among the mosses.

Mildreth crumbled bread onto the grass. 'You squat in shadow behind tender leaves, hands full of blossom. Your eyes filled us with kindness.'

Edith spread her arms wide. 'We, the elders of this place, inherit the duty to say what shall be. We harkened to the voices in this word-wrangle and chewed over all the morsels: meat, bone and gristle. Thank you for the thoughts you stirred up and what you gave of yourselves, every one of you. Thank you, Kedric and Ursel, for your toil.'

She's found the full depth of her voice, Hilda thought.

Elder Mildreth stood up. 'Kedric, you have shown us that you put your shoulder into your responsibilities as headman. We look out from this high place …' Mildreth turned towards the sunset and swept her arm to draw their eyes to the shining fen, 'and see streams winding together to join the great river. You look around at what's happening and see settlements flowing together. You want Wellstowe to be part of the current, not stuck in a muddy backwater.'

Headman Kedric nodded.

Elder Elfric's deep tone rang out. 'Your devotion to your peoples' future dazzled you, Headman Kedric, and led you to make mistakes. It is always wrong to beat or mistreat a person you should look after; we have agreed that today. This applies to all of you, people of three settlements!' Elfric threw a sharp glance towards Osric, the Mereham Headman. *I shall always think of Osric as Pigface,* Hilda thought.

Elder Mildreth spoke again. 'Ursel, your cunning in the ways of the wild gives you a nose for the tangle of roots and growing. You look deep into causes and you want to put everything right.'

Elfric added, 'Your deep vision led you to disagree with your Headman. We understand there was no time when you saved the hind, but if something like this happens again, you must talk about it! Bring it up with your uncle beforehand, or at least afterwards. We are glad you have agreed not to defy Headman Kedric without good reason. This Moot is in accord that we follow the lead of our headman. We will all respect that custom, people of three settlements!' Heads nodded, people looked around, thoughtful.

Elder Edith announced, 'Kedric and Ursel: this is the first part of our Doom. Kedric, we remind you that a smack fires hate and leaches trust. We want you to give Ursel a boar piglet in recompense for the one you required her to give for the Feast of Hretha.'

Kedric's brows knitted together and his bottom lip thrust forward, but Edith left him no space to speak.

Hilda's mouth twitched as the elders turned their faces to Ursel. *They agreed that beforehand,* she thought. *Maybe they practised in the bothy behind the leather curtain.*

'Ursel, to remind you that a headman carries the lives of the people on his shoulders, and as a sign of respect for the hunt, we want you to use part of your pig's skin when it's slaughtered to make a quiver for your uncle.' Ursel chewed her lip.

Elder Edith spread her arms wide. Was that a wobble? Mildreth and Elfric stood close by to support her. 'Friends and neighbours, do you agree this is a sound beginning for our judgment today?' Cries of assent greeted her question. Ursel and Kedric shrugged and nodded their agreement. Seren thrust a steaming mug into Edith's hand – nettle tea by the smell of it, with a rosemary sprig for clarity of mind.

When the buzz of talk died down, Elder Mildreth spoke, 'The second part of our Doom is a long view. Both of you complainants must learn from each other.'

Elder Edith took up the theme. 'The ancestors brought to our minds an ancient pattern of wise leadership: where leaders and people work together as partners.'

Redwald was alert, watching faces, thinking.

Edith continued, 'Kedric, you can become a leader who walks alongside his people. Ask them to help you shoulder the weight of leadership. Look out for those who have a yearning to do more. You'll find them by what they throw your way, perhaps clumsily, as happened this time. Boys and young men may be keen to join in. If girls and young women are slow to step forward, don't be fooled – they have skills your settlement needs. We are beginning to tell young girls to hide half of who they are; we shame them if they stand tall. Any girl who breaks out of the cramped hen-coop of her life will be all beak and claws – until she finds her place to sing.'

She turned to Ursel. 'You can find out from Kedric what it feels like to be the one everybody relies on. He has been trained to carry this burden alone – we do this to our boys without thinking of the strain it puts on them. Sometimes it's heavy and their hearts ache. Our Headman has been told never to complain; there is no escape for him; that's when his fists fly. Look for Kedric the man, who was a boy, who will be old, with hopes and fears of his own and the great goddess shining within him. Use your tracking skills to sniff out the truth about people; you can use this wherever life takes you.

'Work together and listen warmly, both of you. It may take moons. You may prickle each other like holly. But don't give up; turn to your helpers and try again. When you're ready, both of you go out hunting, with your friends from Wellstowe, and bring back food for the settlement. This is the task we set before you.'

As the two complainants looked doubtful, Edith continued. 'Kedric, you will learn to recognise a deer from it's hoof-print in mud, what it's eaten by its droppings, and what that means for the health of the herd. You'll learn to understand the web of life, not just animals as prey. Ursel, you'll discover how to butcher a carcass, joint it and lug it home without spoiling; remember how much salt meat is left in the barrels and what more will be needed to feed a settlement through the hungry gap of spring.'

Elder Elfric used his loudest voice. 'We want to tell you, people of three settlements, how much these two have achieved today. They have agreed to kill only weak deer and always spare breeding females. They agree that nobody should defy their headman wilfully.'

Edith pushed herself up on the arms of her chair.

Hilda heard a soft grunt. *Pain?*

Elder Edith took no notice of it. 'This is the third and deepest part of our Doom. It welled up from the wisdom of the ancestors, speaking through three wise voices: Seren the healer, Bertold of Wellstowe, and Redwald of the Wuffings.'

She swept her gaze round to catch the attention of every person there, then went on: 'Kedric and Ursel, when you feel sure of each other, find a hind in calf. Go together in silence, without arrows or spears. Follow the spoor; listen. Watch how the hind moves, the curve of her belly, the strength of her flank. Notice what she eats, what scares her, the twitch of her ears when a twig snaps, how she can be alert and at peace in herself.

'When her eye meets yours, breathe softly. In the peat-brown deep of the pool of her gaze, you will each know yourself as a child of Deer Mother, the oldest of our ancestors. You will recognise the hind as your sister, since she too is a child of our ancient mother. You will shiver in awe at the new life growing in her womb, secret as a hazelnut. Life trembles on the edge of death, and roars back in glory every spring.

'Stay in silence and walk back to the settlement.

'Kedric, take your tools and carve her image – delicate and strong, fleet and still. Use your skill to show the calf in her belly.

'Ursel, help him remember the tilt of her head, the flick of her tail.

'Wellstowe hunters, make a place for the figure beside the path you follow when you set out to hunt, to remind you to protect the hinds. Make sure it's at a height the deer can nose as they go by; they will smell your reverence for Deer Mother. If she gives one of the herd to you in death to feed the people, lay an offering there in thanks – carrots or beans, whatever you have.

'This is the Doom we have wrought together, here at Wellstowe's sorrow-mound, in accord with the ways of our ancestors. People of three settlements, do you agree?'

There was silence. Hilda wiped a tear from her eye, and noticed others doing the same.

Then the cheering began, drums joined in and the noise built to a thunderstorm as Elder Edith proclaimed: 'The Moot is ended. Let the Beltane festival begin!'

Chapter 41

Spring Cleaning

Hilda

'A fair judgment?' Hilda asked Headman Kedric, breathing slowly to still the knock of her heart against her ribs. If he thought it was, she might stay. If he felt slighted, he would blame her. *I can almost feel the blunt end of his spear!*

Kedric looked at Hilda as if coming back from far away. 'I'm not sure my niece will be able to do what they say – follow my orders for the hunt.' He shook his head, frowning. 'At least they recognise my skill.' He patted his scabbard. *He gave his seax into the pile when he was cleansed for the Moot, like everybody else*, Hilda realised.

Breath eased out of Hilda's mouth. 'They recognised your concern for the settlement and everyone you're responsible for, as well,' she offered.

His chin lifted and he looked her in the eye. 'There'll be no more stories just for the women, none of that hole and corner giggling, or else …'

So I can stay – today. Boldness leapt up her spine and opened her throat. 'I delight in telling tales to nourish all your people.' She narrowed her eyes and looked into his, to be sure he heard her. 'I need to know they will be allowed time to listen.'

He nodded swiftly, as if closing a bargain, and said: 'For men, as well as women.' He strode off towards the bustle at the top of the slope. 'Bigger branches, lads; we want leaping flames tonight.'

Hilda sat on the turf with a bump. A bee buzzed away from the daisy she'd landed on.

Meg came and sat next to her, quiet. 'I saw you talking to Headman Kedric. What's happening, Hilda?'

'What have I just promised? I told Kedric I'd tell stories for men as well as women.'

'Is that hard?'

'Before I can even begin, I'll have to grab their attention – they'll be expecting battle-axes and heroes ankle-deep in blood; that's not what I tell.'

'Your stories are exciting. I can't wait to hear what happens next.'

'Yes, I can keep up the pace, plenty of action, that's not the problem. It's bigger than that,' Hilda sighed. 'It's so big I feel like that ant looking up at the mountain.'

'I remember,' Meg grinned, 'when you first came here and May didn't know what a mountain was.'

'This time the ant's got to climb up the mountain and it doesn't know the way.'

Meg drew her brows together. 'Are you the ant this time? Can I help you find the way?'

A rush of gratitude flooded Hilda. It came out as a chuckle.

'Last time I told for men and women all together, it was on the plain in the north, next to a big river. They threatened to chuck me in, after my story got out of hand – I couldn't help making the goat speak with the same self-important swagger as their headman. Everybody laughed – except him. He went purple. I had to scarper – didn't want my harp to get soaked. I think I've learned not to mock people now – well not so they notice, anyway.'

'So, that's what you don't want to do: make a wrong turn on the mountain. What do you want to do, little ant?'

As Meg joined in her word-game, bands loosened in Hilda's chest so she breathed deeper, searching inside. The rage that boiled up took her by surprise.

'I want to make it stop. Beatings, rapes, hate-words, starvation; all the ways they push us down and keep us down. Every time a woman gets attacked or threatened – like you were at the Feast, Meg – others watch and learn: keep your heads down, could be you next.

'I've always got this pot of rage seething inside. Usually when I tell the story of Peony Valley, I let it boil over. I call the men harsh names, the ones who invade that peaceful territory. I say they do bad things because they're nasty. Blame slips so soft and easy off my tongue! Like when women get together and we grumble about the things men do and call them daft, and laugh.

'But blame takes the cauldron off the fire! Blaming somebody is like throwing a ladleful of steaming food in their face – there's satisfaction in the splat of it, it's out of the pot, and the hungry person gets it; but they can't taste it or chew it. They've no idea what's in it and it doesn't do them any good. All they get is a sore feeling that quickly turns into anger. There's warmth and nourishment in the stew. I want to serve it up hot and tasty, so everybody gets a share.'

'Is the ant on the mountain making stew now?' Meg sounded so puzzled that Hilda grinned. The smile slid off her face and she thumped one hand on the other.

'This time when I tell the story of the invasion of the Queen's land, I want to stay warm and angry and loving. I want the men to feel what it's like to be a woman who's kept in her place by fear, and carry that in their lives every day, so they can see things through a woman's eyes.

'I want them to see how those men in the story got their brains scrambled badly enough to become bitter fighters – and let the story sink into their bones while they sleep, and wake up changed. I'll have to find out what happens to men. We all love our baby boys, but how do they get twisted into men who are capable of cruelty? I don't know, Meg! This is where the ant on the mountain feels the cold wind whistle. Does anybody know the well-springs of hate?'

'I'm sure you'll work it out,' Meg comforted her.

Hilda's shoulders twisted. 'I shrivel up when you reassure me. Let me have my despair. I need to feel it.'

Meg's eyes popped open. 'Oh, is this a time when I should stitch up my mouth and flap my ears and nod wisely?'

Her own words coming back at her tickled Hilda. 'You learn fast!' she smiled.

Meg nodded, wisely. 'You can't see how to do it?' she ventured.

'Right. I've never had to face up to this before. And, I don't want to! Why should I have to work out how boys get damaged and turned into men who can kill? Why can't the men figure it out – what hurts them and how to get better from it? Why does it always have to be a woman cleaning up their mess?' She stuck her hands in her hair and rubbed her scalp.

'But they get hurt too. Boys driven off to war, with glory on their tongues – coming back hacked and bloody, what they've seen and done dinning in their heads when they lie down to sleep … The ones who think they can never go home because of what they have become … It's not just the mothers wailing as they lay their lovely boys in the cold ground; it's the men keening for their own selves, their boyhood stolen, their manhood broken.'

Meg's face twisted.

Hilda's eyebrows stretched upward as a thought struck her. 'This is all woven together. Girls who go quiet and freeze when they should be shouting "Stop!" and boys who do hateful things because something inside them torments them. Men and women hurt each other and nobody knows why. It all twists together. Somebody's got to get to the bottom of this, before we can start to unpick it. Even if one person can't do it, we've got to do it, all together.'

'Could we ask somebody to help – Wulf might talk about when he was growing up, or Aikin?'

'Good idea. And there's wisdom in the story that could help. Thousands of tongues have told it down the years, and added in their own hearts' grace too. There are good men in Peony Valley who can show our fellows how to be heroes of peace, who struggle with being one of the brotherhood or who take a risk and stand alone against cruelty. I'll talk to Huldran the wise woman; she'll help me.'

Hilda noticed Meg's look of surprise. 'It's a good way to get deeper, when you're preparing a story,' Hilda explained. 'The people in it can always tell you more about themselves and each other. I'll ask Marelda and Snow Storm, her daughter, too.'

'Ooh, the baby who was born at the end – I can't wait to hear about her! What's she like?' Meg glowed.

'You'll have to wait,' Hilda teased. 'You should see what she does when she grows up!'

'I wish I had a powerful name like her.'

'But you do! Meg means "mighty". Didn't you know?'

'Mother never told me,' Meg pouted. 'Hilda, what have I done wrong with Mother? Why does she like Cafell more than me now? I thought Cafell was my friend, but now it's – I'll do this, I'll do that – trying to show she's better than me. How am I going to stand her butting in all the time?'

'Ah. I asked her to help out,' Hilda said. Meg jerked back. 'I wanted you to have some freedom to come with me and work on your story.'

'What story?'

'Whatever you want to tell by the fire tonight. I know it's not the Great Hall, but you'll have plenty of people to listen to you after we've eaten. You've got a wealth of stories that Seren's told you. Which will it be?'

A grin chased the scowl across Meg's face, hovered, and stayed. 'That's your job. You made a deal with Headman Kedric. Won't he want one of yours?'

'I want to help you grow into the fine storyteller that you are, Meg. You've got it all – imagination, heart and soul, a voice as true as a star – just waiting to unfurl like one of the ferns on the barrow. I don't know how long Headman Kedric will let me stay. We haven't got much time. You're more important to me than the hide of my backside, which has been tanned until it's leather already. Let's find a quiet place to practise. What about the deer-scrape?'

SEREN

Seren sniffed the stew and sprinkled in more thyme. The fat lamb from Thornthicket, butchered and chopped up this morning, bubbled in the huge iron pot along with peas and barley, nettles and carrot. Seren wiped sweat from her forehead with her sleeve and glanced over to the other cooking-fires. 'Ready?' she called.

Tegwen nodded and Cafell answered 'Yes.'

'Watch out with that trestle, Aikin; you're dragging it through the embers. Tell Headman's Wife Oswynne it's cooked.'

He grinned and left with the message.

There was no ceremony as eating started – famished, everyone stuffed themselves. Seren scraped the pot and ladled out the last morsels into the slaves' wooden bowls, licked her fingers and looked up. Wulf held out an empty platter for more bread. As she filled it from the basket, their fingers brushed. She took his hand in her own and felt the familiar callous on his thumb, the roughness of his palm, his warm grip.

Elder Edith called for silence and a rising cadence from Hilda's elder flute caught everyone's attention. Edith welcomed everyone to the feast; Elfric encouraged them to enjoy the last of the food and drink their fill.

Elder Mildreth announced: 'After we've feasted, the cooking-fires will be put out. We will honour the quiet before we light the new fire east of the barrow. You all know the dances. Touch the ground and each other lightly with each step.

'I will remind you of the custom and law of this Beltane festival: this is the night when Earth Mother chooses her Green Man and he works to give her joy. Like them, we women choose our partners for this holy night, saying: "I choose you to worship the Goddess with me tonight." It is the sacred duty of each chosen man to bring her to ecstasy, as often and as loud as she wants. There is no rush; we have until sunrise. If we make the greenwood cry out over and over, Earth Mother's womb will fill with abundant berries and seeds, calves and foals, in the coming year. If children come from these unions, they will be welcomed as warmly as every child and have the same share of all that's good. Do your best to please Earth Mother!'

Seren's eyes met Wulf's and her lips parted. 'Soon, love,' she whispered. She touched his mouth with her finger and ran it down the streak of grey in his beard. He smiled with his eyes full of softness, lingered a moment, then took the platter back to the table.

As Seren savoured the meat in her bowl, she imagined the night to come. *We'll steal away, hand in hand, through the thickets and find a place just for us. His voice will rumble in his chest as he asks how I am and which bit aches tonight? His warm hands rub my back. He talks about how hard I work, understanding how I take care of everybody. He murmurs how he loves that in me and worries about me. I'll ask him if his legs are tired and knead the knots so he sighs and relaxes. I guide his hand to my breast and melt against his body. I draw him down – must make sure to bring a cloak, the twigs are prickly – under an oak tree and we breathe together. I trace my fingers over his arms, pelted on the outside, tender in the elbow joint. He throbs with eagerness, but this night I can tell him: Wait, I say what we do, and when. A deep kiss while the owls call.* Already she felt the wet well up inside her, just thinking about it.

Back in the here and now, some chap from Mereham was asking for cheese. She pointed to where it lay in the cool grass. He looked surprised, then bobbed his head respectfully and hauled it up onto the table.

Where was I? She turned again to her fantasy among the oak roots. *I kiss his hand and slide it ... but something doesn't feel right!* Now, sitting eating, and in her dream of love – what was it that bothered her? Cafell's words echoed in her head about what the Mereham headman did to her. Seren shivered. *On an ordinary night, he might follow the old track and I might close my eyes and let him, and go far away inside myself. But this holy night, everything matters. Breejsh is with us. It must be done right.*

Wulf slid onto the bench next to her, his thigh along hers. 'You will choose me, won't you? I mean – will you choose me?' His face went long and serious.

She laughed and pulled his ear. 'You'd better be nice to me!'

'What would you like? I could make you a crown of may blossom or celandines ...'

A sob choked her.

'What's wrong?'

The look of concern in Wulf's eyes touched her deeply. She grabbed his hand. 'I didn't like it when I heard what happened to Cafell.'

He stroked her arm and soothed her like a mare in foal. 'It will never happen to you, honey-sweet. I'll look after you.'

'That's not the point. Just knowing that men do those things, and get away with it, makes my skin crawl. My insides curl up like a hedgehog, I'm all prickles.'

'What do you want me to do?'

'Forget the flowers. Go to Pigface-Osric, the Mereham headman, and tell him you don't like what he did to Cafell – it's wrong, and you don't want to hear about anything like that again, from him or anyone.' Seren was surprised to hear her own voice so definite. It felt good.

Wulf bit his lip. She didn't like to see the playfulness drain out of him – but his face matched how she felt. 'But ... he's the headman and I'm only ...'

'Are you ashamed of your mother, Wendreda? Because she was British – like me?'

'No, of course not, but I only know how to make tools and fence-posts. I don't know how to do clever talk.'

'It doesn't need to be clever, just clear. You're a fine man, Wulf. You're honest and kind and strong and you make beautiful things as well as fence posts, and I'm proud to be with you.'

'But ... you won't love me if I don't talk to him?'

She spoke close and warm. 'Don't talk daft. I will always love you. But when I think about ... what he did to Cafell, I freeze up.'

'I felt sick when I heard about it,' Wulf agreed.

'Tell him! He needs to hear what good men think of rape. This feels like dirt in our settlements. It needs cleaning up before we can celebrate a new spring.'

405

Wulf gulped. 'Have I got to talk to him tonight?'

'Talk to Elfric. He's upset about it. He was fidgeting and muttering when the elders were trying to talk about their judgment. Edith told him a few times to bring his mind back. Maybe some of the others will help. Pick me some flowers on your way back.' She gave him a little shove, and a kiss to sweeten it. The shakiness flowed out of her in a deep sigh.

Oswynne

Once the trestle tables were cleared and taken down, Oswynne felt her shoulders loosen. Hilda's harp music floated in the dusk and a bat fluttered by. Oswynne looked around for her husband.

He sat apart from the crowd, his back to them, facing west to catch the last glow of the sky. His small seax was in his hand and he whistled tunelessly – the way he did when he whittled. The form of a hind was emerging from the piece of beech in his hand, a trial piece. He smoothed the curve of the animal's neck.

So he is taking the elders' words seriously! If he makes the image for the deer, maybe he can also learn to work with Ursel and listen to what she knows. Can he be the leader they spoke of, bringing out the best in every person in the settlement?

When he carved, whether it was a peg to hold thatch in place, or a pattern to bless the threshold, Oswynne's heart softened for him. She smiled to herself.

Later, I will choose you, she thought. *You will listen to me and do the things I like, under green boughs.*

Ursel

Ursel borrowed Winfrith's scraper as they cleaned dishes.

Winfrith said, 'I'm looking forward to going hunting with you and the others. Do you think Kedric will really follow what you say?'

'That's the bit I'm not sure about. Will they listen to me the way you do? You always put down what you're doing when I need your ear. Can men do that?'

'They won't need to listen to you pouring out your heart – just about finding deer tracks and smelling scents. Talking about your heart, your boy over there's going to be looking for you, as soon as he's finished stacking trestles with the others. Are you going into the greenwood with him tonight?'

Ursel felt heat rush to her cheeks. She put down her spoon and drew her friend away from the others. The sun lingered on the horizon, and Winfrith's pale skin was lit with pink.

'I … think so. But Winfrith … what's it like? Does it hurt?'

'I told you all about it last year!'

'Yes, but I had that fever and I can't remember everything you said. You picked a man from Mereham with a soft beard and you really liked him – is he here today? Oh, Winfrith, I've been so wrapped up in what's happening for me, I forgot to ask you!'

'He hasn't come. I asked his sister and she said he's just had a baby with a girl from downriver and he's staying to look after them.'

'Oh, sorry to hear that. Are you sad? Will you choose another one?'

Winfrith shrugged. 'It was just Beltane night; no promises were made. It was good, I chose well! Elder Mildreth's grandson seems nice but I don't think I'll risk it tonight, I've got my clear stringy signs so I could get pregnant. I could get pennyroyal tea from Seren in the morning but that doesn't always work. I don't want to make a baby tonight. It did hurt a bit the first time. Tell him you haven't done it before, so he's gentle and doesn't get carried away.'

'Remember when we used to go round and listen to all the couples in the dark on Beltane nights?' They both giggled. 'Some of them made such a noise!'

'Sounded like pigs. Well, why not? Hedgehogs do, too.'

'I'm not going to make pig noises!'

'You don't know, you might! But I know this is serious for you. This is one you want to see again, isn't it?'

Ursel nodded, as sureness crashed through her. 'I want to be with him, all the time. If I can't, I don't know what I'll do.'

'He's coming over. But Ursel – before you go, I need to warn you: Redwald's part of the ruling family, they won't let him choose ...'

Ursel's ears heard her friend's words, but they bounced away from her. *There he is!* He reached out for her hand and she smiled over her shoulder for Winfrith as she walked away with Redwald. *Is that a wobble in my friend's answering smile? Is Winfrith being brave, does she feel left out?* Redwald squeezed Ursel's hand. *In all the world, there's only this warm palm against mine, this thump in my chest when our eyes meet.*

Ursel took a deep breath. She was sure – but it felt like jumping out of a boat into deep water. 'When it's time, I choose you to worship the Goddess with me this night,' she breathed in his ear.

She drew him to the back of the rows of people, cross-legged on the ground round a fire that sank into ash and embers. 'Oh, it's Meg telling the story, not Hilda. I didn't know she could tell for a big group. She must be nervous!' She leaned forward to hear.

CHAPTER 42

BELTANE FIRE

URSEL

'I'll tell you a story of the place where Mother grew up – and Headman's Wife Oswynne too,' Meg announced.

THE UGLY WORM OF THE MISTY SANDBANKS

Meg the storyteller stood at the edge of the fire-glow and swept them all in with her warmth.

Ursel was entranced, and when she glanced round, so was everyone else.

I've never seen the sea, but Mother says it's water, wider than the mere, stretching out as far as you can see, till it meets the sky. It shines some days; other days it's grey and ruffled like iron hammered in the forge. Mist rises up from it – they call it sea fret – so thick that if you're out in a boat, fishing, you can't see the land or hear the waves on the shore. Strange creatures with whiskers or fangs live in the deep; sometimes they get washed up on the shore or hauled aboard in nets.

Once there was a queen who lived near the sea with her husband, the King. They had two daughters, Cefin and Derin, and they grew up strong and brave. The Queen died, and they all mourned for her.

Cefin travelled far away over the seas to marry a prince, and Derin learned how to manage the settlement, the farms and the household. Her father trusted her and asked her advice every day.

After a while, the King married again. Some say Behoc cast spells on him with her green eyes and hair shiny like a raven's wing, but perhaps he was just lonely. When Behoc came to the Hall, Derin was there to welcome her and show her round the storerooms and work sheds, the granaries and orchards all dusted with snow.

Behoc thought: 'This girl knows everything! She has her father's heart in the palm of her hand. She's watching me for mistakes with her sea-grey eyes. She thinks I don't deserve to be with the King, to be happy.'

At the wedding feast, Derin poured mead for her father's friends, laughing and joking with them; she had known each one since she was a baby. They smiled and greeted her warmly – and looked with cautious eyes at the new queen.

Behoc felt a stab of jealousy. 'She's in my place! How can they ever learn to respect me when she's in my way? Her beauty shines so bright she makes me look ugly.' Behoc spied a farmer with a greasy chin and a raucous laugh, who pinched the bottoms of all the serving girls. 'He'll do for my plan,' she thought.

The next morning, the King sent for Derin as usual, to ask her advice about next year's planting.

Behoc thought: 'He loves her more than me. This is my chance – I want to be the King's advisor, not just a woman in the shadows. I'll have to get rid of her.'

Queen Behoc sent for Derin. 'My dear, I want to do your hair in a different way; here, let me plait it for you.' She twisted it so tight on top of Derin's head that it hurt. 'You must look your prettiest, well, as pretty as we can make you ...'

Ursel smiled as Meg made herself into the Queen and pretended to think her stepdaughter ugly and to want to make her beautiful.

'… Farmer Gifre is coming soon. Your Father has arranged for you to marry him. Didn't you know? You're lucky to get a husband at all, with your pudgy mouth and fat hips.'

Derin pulled away from her. 'It's not true! Father would never arrange a match without asking me. I'm not fat … am I?'

She ran to ask her father, but he was out hunting.

Behoc rubbed her hands together with glee.

That evening, Derin was pale and quiet.

'It's working,' Behoc thought.

But Derin asked the king, and he looked up from his chess game and said, 'What, hmm, you want to marry Gifre? Oh, you don't want to marry him? Well, that's alright then. Couldn't do without you round the place.'

So Behoc conjured magic. She brewed a storm in the night and with a roar of thunder and a glare of lightning, she turned Derin into a loathsome dragon.

Meg's hands slapped together and Ursel jumped as if it was real thunder. The listeners gasped.

In the morning, Derin was nowhere to be found and the people drove the dragon down into the freezing sea.

Dragon-Derin swam out to a sandbank and coiled herself up. Loneliness ached in her heart and she bellowed, the sound echoing through the sea fret. She hated herself and her hide grew scales, thick and hard. She hated Behoc and her claws grew spiky. She hated this world and she roared; fire came out of her mouth! She did it again – and again. The people on the shore shivered and kept their spears close to hand. The dragon paced around her frosty sandbank.

Ice crackled in the creeks and gripped the bends of the river as it made its way towards the sea, through saltmarsh and mudflat. If the people ventured out on it to make holes to fish through, it cracked with a rumble. The birds stayed away – so there were no nests for people to raid.

When Dragon-Derin tried to catch fish, they swam away. She slithered into the water, crossed the channel to the beach and roamed along it until she found a cow that had strayed from the herd, caught it and ate it.

After that, the people kept watch. If they filled a trough with milk every night, the dragon drank it and left the herds alone. Still, spring did not come.

After many months, news reached Cefin. She told it to the Prince, her husband: 'Derin has disappeared! A dragon is harrying the land. They think it must have devoured her.' So Cefin and her husband built a ship and set out to avenge her sister.

Behoc saw the ship approaching and her heart pounded in fear. She sent waves to wreck it. The ship overturned, and the tide washed Cefin and her husband onto the sandbank where her dragon-sister howled.

Cefin and her husband heard the fearful noise and went in search of the dragon, gripping swords and daggers. A huge shape reared up out of the mist. Flame scorched the sand around them. The Prince leaped out of the way and raised his blade to strike.

The golden eye of the dragon found Cefin and the great beast knelt down on her front legs and whimpered. Cefin grabbed her husband's sword-arm and dragged it down so that he dropped his blade. They drew back, but still held their daggers at the ready.

The dragon's tongue snaked out. They gasped in fear of poison. But it licked Cefin's face softly.

'What are you? Who are you?' Cefin breathed.

The dragon found her human voice, husky from not being used for so long. 'I am your sister, Derin,' she croaked. 'Kiss me three times on the nose.'

'Don't trust it!' the Prince shouted. But Cefin sheathed her knife and leant to kiss the great knobbly snout. The dragon's breath cooled as the world looked sunny to her again.

Her sister kissed her again and the dragon's claws clattered onto the pebbles.

The dragon sighed and growled, 'Behoc is just an unhappy woman.'

Cefin planted another kiss on the dragon's nose.

'I did what I could,' the dragon sighed, and all her scales fell glittering onto the sand. Derin stepped forward, herself again, laughing and crying at the same time.

The three swam back to the beach through the blue sea and ran, hand in hand and dripping, seaweed in their hair, to find the King. He was overjoyed to find both his lost daughters at once and to meet Cefin's husband. Bright sun blessed them. They told him over and over again what had happened, until at last he understood – and looked around for Behoc, who by that time had made a run for it.

They chased her through barns and byres, sheds and grain-stores, until at last they found her crouched in a stable.

'What are you going to do to me?' she asked, pale with fear.

The sisters stepped forward and kissed her on both cheeks.

Behoc wailed and cried so hard that she threw up – vomiting a giant toad.

The toad croaked, 'I'm ugly. I don't deserve happiness. Nobody can love me. There's no place for me in this world.'

The sisters grabbed for it, but it wriggled out of their hands and crawled away. They chased the toad round and round until at last they caught it and threw it down a well.

Behoc slid to the floor, pale and exhausted. She was ill for a long time.

Outside, blossom opened on the fruit trees, bees and butterflies visited, green shoots unfurled, and the air was full of birdsong and wings.

They nursed Behoc back to health and always after that she used her skills to heal and help. And they all lived happily together ...

But sometimes, you might hear something croaking: 'I'm disgusting, I don't deserve to be happy! Nobody will ever love me.'

If you find that thing shuffling round again – try kissing it on the nose three times and see if it changes. But if it still croaks, throw it down a well!

Everybody laughed.

Ursel was glad. 'She helped me before the Moot,' she told Redwald. 'She told me how to lay it all out clear for them.' It mattered that Redwald should understand. 'She's more than she looks.'

'I know. She terrified my foster-father – and me – last night, conjuring dragons out of the fen! I liked this dragon better, poor old monster, I could hear her groaning. I even felt sorry for the bad woman – how did Meg do that?'

Ursel feasted her eyes on this boy who was wrinkling his fair brow to understand her friend, her life and her world.

'Ursel, were you satisfied with the elders' judgment? Don't mash your beautiful lip!'

'I don't know if my uncle will really harken to me when we hunt together. I'm glad Winfrith and Bertold will be there to help. I like the idea of Uncle Kedric making a carving of a hind; that'll make him take notice – with his creative self. His hands will tell if he's truly looked into Deer Mother's eye.'

'I'm glad you like that.' Redwald looked shy as he smiled. 'Oh, what's Elder Elfric doing now?'

Ursel slid her hand into Redwald's to keep this precious closeness, as the blare of the horn broke into it.

'We have another matter to settle before we bring in the spring!' announced Elder Elfric. 'Our settlement of Mereham has been made murky by the transgression of our headman. We have spoken with Osric

– good men of three settlements agree – and he recognises what he did to the slave, Cafell, is wrong. Of course breeding with slaves is allowed – but forcing an unwilling woman, especially one so young, is not. She now has safety – but we need to make it clear to the gods and goddesses that we do not tolerate rape. When we get home, the folk of our settlement will go down to the mere's edge and make a song offering to the Mere-Wife, to ask her forgiveness for allowing this horror to happen. I have asked Osric to give up his position of headman. Osric, do you agree?'

Many voices rose in wonder. A line of men faced the Mereham headman, arms folded. Wulf, Bertold, Aikin and many Ursel didn't know. Not Thane Roger – she was not surprised. Not Kedric either. She nudged Redwald and raised an enquiring eyebrow. He squeezed her hand and went to join the line.

Osric-Pigface looked around, cornered. He took off his torc and handed it to the elder. Elfric held it aloft for all to see. 'As Elder of Mereham, it is my duty to confirm the next headman. I have consulted with family leaders and all agree: the best choice this time is a headwoman – Sunnifa.' So Pigface's wife got the torc around her neck along with Oswynne's amber beads.

'I'm not staying to be bossed around by a woman, especially my own wife,' Pigface growled. 'As soon as ploughing's finished, I'll be off to join Thane Roger's ditch-builders. We'll have more fun there, I reckon.'

Comment gabbled on every side. Ursel's eye reached out to Redwald – *don't get caught up in some argument!* He came back and sat with her.

At last, the elders formed a procession with their helpers and circled the barrow again, drums and pipes accompanying them. The last ash of the fire was scattered. Silence dropped. The first stars tingled in a dusky sky. Blackbirds still sang from the tops of the beeches.

Ursel felt the shiver of Earth's new life move up her spine and spread into her arms, her hands, the roots of her hair. It throbbed in the base of her body.

'Uncle Kedric's lighting the fire,' she whispered. Redwald nodded. *Of course he knows the ritual; it's the same everywhere,* she thought.

Kedric knelt over the wooden fire-bowl, his hands a blur of movement as he rubbed the stick between his palms. Everyone held their breath. A spark leapt onto the dry leaves in the bowl and made a flame, thin and blue, with a wisp of smoke. A gasp of relief could be heard; there would be firelight again this year. Kedric fed twigs into the bowl and carried it in his two hands up to the top of the rise. He gave the gift to the ready-built pile of sticks and birch logs and it burst into life with twists of red and sunset, forge-glow bronze and jay's-wing blue. Everybody cheered.

Drums started; the tree-trunk one that boomed through her gut and a dozen frame-drums that picked up her feet. Ursel pulled her man, laughing, into the line of dancers and they circled the fire. Arms punched the air, whoops leapt up with the sparks.

The line snaked down the slope to a flat place where two circles of people formed with men on the inside and women on the outside. She lost sight of Redwald as they whirled round, then landed in his arms to swing partners. Voices shrieked and hooted. Then partners changed, other arms caught her on the turn; different hands linked hers as they looped and swayed through the dance. She caught sight of Hilda playing the tune. Meg was breathless and pink-cheeked. She smiled encouragement as she passed by Ragnild; *Mother always likes the dance – but this is our first one without Father.* Winfrith seemed to have both May and Roslinda as her partners. Laughing hard, they moved on.

When the dancers stopped for breath, Ursel tugged at Redwald's hand. 'I know a quiet place,' she whispered. The dance thinned out as people slipped away.

'I choose you to worship Earth Mother with me tonight,' rang out in dozens of women's voices, some confident, some whispering. Each woman drew the man she wanted away from the firelight. Couples brushed past, hand in hand, into the dark wood. Under the leaves, Earth Mother worship flooded the women with desire; the air grew rich with cries of fulfillment.

Ursel took Redwald past the barrow along the track towards the settlement, until they found the slippery way down the chalk scarp to the spring. She leaned down and cupped her hands, giving him a drink of cold spring water. Her lips touched his hands as he did the same for her.

'This is a special place,' he said, quietly.

The half-moon trembled in the water between ash branches, as their own moon-shadows rippled among the reflections. She had her eye on a thicket just across the stream – but somebody had got there before them.

They were from Thornthicket. The old slave woman tended a small fire and Elder Mildreth was strewing sweet-smelling herbs into a cauldron. Lynna and Seren were singing over Cafell, who lay on a blanket.

May, holding Cafell's baby, came down to dip a little bucket in the spring. 'Oh, you made me jump!' she said as she saw Ursel. 'You'd better not bring your man down here. We're doing sacred bathing for Cafell. Won't be too long though. Mam's eager to get back to Wulf.'

'We'll go further down this side,' Ursel told her. They worked their way through undergrowth, round the bend of the stream out of sight of the spring, until they found a cluster of hawthorns. They ducked under a curtain of blossom. 'It's dry inside. Mind the thorns,' she said. They chuckled. At last – their own safe place.

This kind of kissing was new to her – the way they turned their mouths to make their tongues meet and slide deeper. She ran her hands through his hair and found the tender place at the base of his skull. Another kiss brought her body so close to him that his breath and hers mingled.

He stepped back, unpinned his cloak and laid it on the ground. 'Will you lie with me?'

She would.

There was laughter and playfulness and rising passion. When she was ready, she unclipped her brooches and let her overdress slip down. 'Be gentle. This is my first time.'

'I'm honoured.' He was not teasing now. 'Is there a chance we'll make a baby tonight – do you want that?'

'Not likely, I checked and this is my white time, it usually is at waxing half-moon. Full moon brings baby-making nights for me. Hilda's stories reminded me to ask my mother all about it.'

His hands were almost too gentle. 'That's a bit spidery, oh, not so heavy, stroke like this,' she told him.

'Are you ready to take off your shift? Let's wrap a fold of cloak around us,' he offered. Bare skin slid together and her hunger for him overwhelmed her.

Winfrith's words echoed in her ear – it's only Beltane night, no promises. Did she dare to trust him? She hesitated.

'What's wrong, sweetheart?'

'How many girls do you call sweetheart? How did you learn all this?'

He rested on an elbow. 'There's a kitchen-girl at Thaneshall who showed me what to do, but she has her own sweetheart.'

'Kitchen? Isn't that a special shed where they cook? I didn't know Thaneshall was so grand! Don't kitchens catch fire though?'

'When it did, I helped her get out – I think that's why she likes me!' He laughed and kissed Ursel on the nose. 'Sometimes my uncles try to get me interested in their friends' daughters – but there's nobody like you, Ursel. I've never felt this … warmth … in my heart before. I want to learn how to make you happy – how to truly worship the goddess with you.'

She remembered what she'd seen from the bushes every Beltane when she and Winfrith hid to watch the couples. She lay on her back – but twigs pricked her skin through the cloak. Side by side, they slid closer.

'Are you ready?' he asked.

'I don't know.'

'Tell me if this feels good.'

'Oh! Yes, no, too much, more, again, oh …' There was pain, and then it was gone.

He followed as she guided him. Wave after wave of ecstasy lifted her, surged and ebbed. Bliss washed over her, until at last they rested in each other's arms. Woven wool against her bare skin and his heartbeat slowing under her ear, she murmured, 'I love you.'

'I love you, too.'

In the bushes something rustled. 'What's that?' He reached for his dagger. Whatever it was giggled.

'It's just the little ones, learning how love is made. We used to go round the thickets on Beltane night, too, me and Winfrith. Go away, May and Roslinda! Go and find somebody else to annoy.' The rustling grew fainter. There was splashing, then silence, apart from the song of a nightingale. She lay back in Redwald's arms. 'Do you have to go, in the morning?'

'Don't think about that. We've got this night.'

'Is that all?'

'I want to be with you, all the time. But it's difficult. My uncles are lining up princesses for me to choose from in the Rhinemouth and the land of Kent. It's about joining up kingdoms and stopping wars, setting up trade routes and making allies. Sometimes I feel like a game piece on their board.'

'Play with me, not them!'

And so he did.

When Earth Mother had cried out in ecstasy many times with Ursel's voice, they rested. Sleepily, she asked, 'Are you going to be King?'

'I think so. They're doing the choosing soon and everybody says it will be me, not my brother, nor any of my half-brothers or cousins. I have to ride over to Rendlesham.'

'Surely kings can do what they like?'

'I will do everything in my power to have you beside me always, Ursel. You are my chosen one, my love. I will come back for you.'

MEG

As Meg got back to the fire from the barrow, people thanked her for her story. Brimming with joy, she sat down next to Hilda. The grass was chilly now but nothing could dampen her happiness.

'Everyone could hear you, even over the crackling of the fire,' said Hilda. 'You drew your breath up out of the earth, out of your soul. Where the prince fought the dragon, I couldn't breathe. Even though you told me the ending before, I still thought he might kill her. It was like that for you, too, wasn't it?'

Meg nodded.

'You created it new and fresh. Powerful work, Meg.'

Meg glowed. 'I never realised what it was about, until I told it just now. It's about everything dying and coming back to life when the sun gets warm again, in spring, isn't it? Or people dying and then – maybe – coming back into the world again somehow. I've heard it so many times in Mother's voice and never noticed, but when I told it, the sun shone through.'

'That's when you know you're on the right track,' Hilda said, 'when the story ripples over your tongue and shows you its slow pools as well as its waterfalls. Then you know the ancestors are walking with you, those who told that story long ago. Hold their hands and trust them to lead you into deep parts of yourself, and let the story carry you.'

'Like a leaf on a river.' Meg saw Hilda's words.

'Eh, eh, there you are,' Tegwen wheezed as she plumped herself down next to Meg. 'I've been looking everywhere for your Mam but she's nowhere to be found. I was taking the ale around, filling the leather mugs and the drinking-horns, and I heard them planning the wedding feast.'

'Who's planning what?' Meg asked, 'Whose wedding?'

'Headman Kedric and Thane Roger, I had to lean in close to catch it and spilled some ale on his lovely trousers, well they're Headman Kedric's second-best trousers really, aren't they, the yellow and red checked ones, didn't Thane borrow them when he got muddy?'

'Yes, that's right, but what were they saying?'

'I had to wipe him up with my cloth. They think I'm deaf so they just talked over me, see. I reckon your Mam's going to be baking again soon. They want the feast as soon as possible.' Loose flaps of skin in Tegwen's neck wobbled as she bobbed her head to mark her words.

'Who is getting married?' Meg asked, mouthing the words slowly.

For some reason, Hilda spluttered into her cup.

'Young Ursel, of course, and the Thane's son, what's his name, the one who makes the arrows, Grimbold is it? They've got it all worked out, the bride-gifts, the morning-gift, a fine horse Thane Roger offered, and Headman Kedric – he likes horses, doesn't he?'

'We'll tell Seren, when we see her,' Hilda said, flat and heavy now. 'Thank you, Tegwen.'

'That's not all! Elwaru from Mereham, the big-boned one who helped Elder Elfric in the talking – remember her? She came up and tapped Thane Roger on the shoulder and said: "I choose you!" He goes white and red and purple, tries to get out of it, "I've got to tend to the horses" or something, but she won't let him off. "There's a strength in your thighs I want to feel," says she. So off he went with her into the woods and I'd love to be a hedgehog and see what she makes him do!'

'Can't bear to think about it.' Meg snorted. 'Ask May and Roslinda!'

Tegwen chuckled and went to look for them.

Meg chewed her bottom lip. 'Should we find Ursel and tell her about the wedding plan?'

'I think, not tonight,' said Hilda gently. 'This trouble is coming with the dawn. It is not now. But perhaps we should tell Elder Edith. Where is she?'

'I don't think we can talk to her tonight, either. I helped her round to the west side of the barrow and brought her blankets, and a hot flint from the fire wrapped in wool – and the old masks and headdresses from her chest. She's staying there under the stars to listen for the voices of the ancestors. She's alone. The other elders were too tired. Edith will touch hands with the ancestors and ask them about our antler dance, who should lead it now she's getting creaky and Kenelm is gone. It's the ancestors' choice because the man and woman they think can carry the teaching will become joined to the creatures of the forest for a time, to guide the young people on their journey in the spirit-world. She's asking them who should be Elder after her too.'

'Why the west side of the barrow?' Hilda's eyes were wide, drinking Meg's words.

'That's where we open the entrance for the sun to shine into, at sunset on the shortest day of the year. It's a long needle of light that shines right into the inside of the tomb, where the bones are. Edith told me about it; she goes in to talk to the Old Ones on that day, so she's seen the colour – like the heart of a fire, she said. It wakes them and they warm their hands, and she asks their advice about things in the settlement, until at last she says, "Shush now, go back to sleep".'

HILDA

Hilda wrapped a blanket around Meg, pulled her old cloak round her shoulders, and sat close to her. 'I have walked the length and breadth of this land searching for one like you, Meg. You are the one I've been looking for, my chosen apprentice who has the deep pools of understanding and the running joy of creativity. Never mind if trouble comes with the dawn. We can take turns telling stories for any who will listen, as long as this night lasts.'

Meg turned, mouth open. 'I said it in the punt when we watched the cranes – don't go. I can't come with you if you have to leave. I'm un-free.'

Visions wracked Hilda of Meg being traded away to some other settlement – *not to Thane Roger, please gods!* She shivered. 'Is there any way you could get away? I'm a storyteller. I'll never have enough to trade for your freedom.' Hilda grimaced.

Meg snuggled closer to Hilda. 'Teach me everything you know,' she whispered. 'Don't let them push you out – I need to hear about Snow Storm. Does she go to Huldran's Cave of Dreams?'

'And I need you to help me find out how King Bors got to be such a mess. I'm not hungry for thorns in my backside, dear apprentice. I'll try to stay!'

The waxing half-moon hung high over their heads. An ice rainbow circled it, as it had that first night when Hilda listened to her own words rolling off Meg's tongue. When Meg talked softly about the stories that lived in both of them, the doorway of Hilda's heart creaked open. Like sunset on the darkest day, a needle of warmth the colour of fire pierced her loneliness. The shaft of hope lit the hollow between her ribs.

Hilda woke with Meg shaking her shoulder and whispering in her ear, 'Something – somebody is coming down from the barrow. It's Deer Mother!'

Hilda rubbed her eyes with her dew-drenched cloak. Stepping towards them through the dawn came a figure crowned with antlers. As a wreath of mist blew away, Meg hissed again, 'It's Elder Edith, wearing the antler mask.' They both watched in awe as the elder raised her arm, seeming to command thrushes and blackbirds to start their chorus.

Hilda noticed the elder sway a little. 'Bring her carved chair quickly, Meg,' Hilda asked, 'I'll wake everybody.'

My harp strings are damp. I'll play a tune on my elder wood pipe. The sound is too thin! I must get Elder Elfric.

Hilda hurried to the elders' bothy and spoke urgently to wake the old man. 'Please blow your horn!'

It took a long note, repeated many times, to gather the folk of three settlements. Bleary-eyed, some stumbled out of the beech wood holding hands. Others roused themselves from around the embers of the Beltane fire.

Tegwen coaxed a cooking fire into life. 'Pale as a bone she is, poor old thing. Take her this.' She pushed a mug of hot feverfew tea into Meg's hand, for Elder Edith.

The rim of the sun lit the tallest trees first. Elder Edith commanded silence by raising the whetstone speaking-staff to catch a gleam of light.

'Last night, I sat with my ear against the turf of the barrow. In deep meditation, I asked the ancestors within: "Should we revive the antler dance?" A great roar drew me into the warmth of their assent. In spirit, I stepped inside the sorrow-mound and greeted my sister Merewyn, Kenelm who left us at Yule, and so many dear ones.

'"Choose who shall be Elder of Wellstowe after me. Who will lead the antler dance? Who will sit in my carved chair at moots?" I asked them. Their murmurs grew louder. At last their voices spoke together, clear as the tone of the horn. "There shall be two Elders! We choose Seren, wise woman of Wellstowe. She will lead the antler dance. Let her man Wulf help her. With Seren, we choose Bertold as Elder!" They faded back into the dark and I journeyed back from the other world. Stand forward, Seren, Wulf and Bertold!'

Elder Edith stood, took off the horned headdress and laid it on Seren's dark hair. Wulf bent down so that she could put a circlet of carved oak leaves on his head. She turned to Bertold. He bowed to her and she handed him the Wellstowe speaking-staff. 'Serve the people well, for many years to come!' she called.

Ragged cheering broke out. Grumbles, talk and questions were heard.

Elder Elfric blew his horn for the May morning dancing to begin.

Seren pushed the mask aside and rushed to catch Elder Edith as she collapsed onto the wet grass.

LIST OF CHARACTERS IN THE SWAN-BONE FLUTE

Pronounce names how they are written. Most are based on Anglo-Saxon and Celtic names that may be spelled differently.

Adults are in their 30s or 40s unless stated otherwise.

BERTOLD'S HALL

Bertold, Kedric's friend. (Bertold's wife, Emma, died ten years ago.)

Winfrith (16), Bertold's daughter, Ursel's best friend.

Evrard (19), married to **Keenbur** (20, originally from Thornthicket), with a baby on the way.

Gaufrid (22), married to **Nelda** (19, originally from Thornthicket), with their children **Leofric** (2) and **Elvie** (8 months). **Roslinda** (8), Gaufrid's daughter from a previous marriage. Nelda is her stepmother.

ELDER EDITH'S HALL

Elder **Edith** (60), aunt of Kedric and Ragnild. (Edith's sister, Merewyn, mother of Ragnild and Kedric, died many years ago.)

Ragnild, sister of Kedric, mother of **Ursel** (16) and **Otred** (9). (Ragnild's husband Kenelm died last Yule.)

Wulf, Kenelm's twin brother, blacksmith and bone-carver, father of May. (Wendreda, mother of Wulf and Kenelm, lived on Eel Island, died nine years ago.)

HEADMAN KEDRIC'S HALL

Kedric, Headman and Farmer of Wellstowe, nephew of Edith, brother of Ragnild.

Oswynne, wife of Kedric, mother of their children **Edgar** (13), **Adela** (10, nickname Puffin), **Elstan** (8) and **Hubert** (2).

Seren, British slave of Oswynne, and her daughters, **Meg** (14) and **May** (8). (Seren's hand-fasted man Drem, Meg's father, died when Meg was a baby.) Wulf is Seren's lover and father of May.

Hilda, travelling storyteller.

Thane Roger.

Grimbold (19), Thane Roger's son.

Redwald (18), Thane Roger's foster-son, and son of the Wuffing royal family, lives (temporarily) with Thane Roger and family.

Brother Michael, Christian missionary, originally from Ireland.

Elder **Mildreth** (59) and her granddaughter **Lynna** (17).

Tola, Nelda's mother.

Tegwen (49), slave, and her son **Madoc** (20).

Elder **Elfric** (58).

Osric (also known as Pigface), Headman of Mereham, married to **Sunnifa**.

Cafell (15), slave of Sunnifa and Osric, mother of baby Cariad.

Elwaru helps Elder Elfric during the Moot.

Marelda – in her twenties, queen of Peony Valley.

Huldran – wise woman who lives at Raven Crag. She's old, in her fifties.

Bors – King of Peony Valley, Marelda's husband.

Piroshka – Marelda's former nurse and servant, friend of Huldran.

Varagan – leads the plains nomads, invader then King of Peony Valley, father of Bors.

Daros – a boy from Peony Valley.

(**Velika** – Marelda's mother, died in the invasion of Peony Valley.)

Marn – Huldran's son.

Ziske – will be queen of the Mountain People.

Olgor – friend and advisor to King Bors.

Author's Notes

On Herbs, Family Planning, Nettles, Three Muds, History and Herstory, Mothering and Parenting, Where Do Hilda's Stories Come From?, Shamanism, Did Anglo-Saxons Use Talking Sticks? Religions, and The Moot.

Herbs

If you want the power and delight of herbal medicine, see a qualified herbal practitioner.

DO NOT USE THE HERBAL REMEDIES THAT YOU FIND IN THIS BOOK.

DO NOT EAT ANY PART OF ANY PLANT IF YOU'RE NOT SURE WHAT IT IS.

DO NOT EAT PEONY SEEDS IN LABOUR OR AT ANY OTHER TIME.

I have based Seren's remedies on a mix of written sources, general information and guesswork.

It has been fascinating to delve into *Leechcraft, Early English Charms, Plantlore and Healing* by Stephen Pollington. I have enjoyed chasing the thoughts of early healers through meadows and heath, woods and water's edge. The rich and varied ecosystems that formed the healers' world have vanished with modern industrial cultivation methods. Our nature reserves and wild patches connect us with animals and birds – and also with the textures, scents and sights of the leaves and roots our bodies crave. Plants were our ancestors' friends and family.

If you go foraging, go with an expert guide, or use a reliable guidebook (such as Richard Mabey's *Food for Free*).

Peony plants are very different now from European Bronze Age peonies. Usage in the story is based on Greek myth and folk remedies. If anyone is doing scientific research on peonies, please let me know your conclusions.

Family Planning

If you wish to use Huldran's knowledge to plan or avoid conceptions, please also consult your registered healthcare professionals. You will also need a more comprehensive source of information, such as *Taking Charge of Your Fertility: The Definitive Guide to Natural Birth Control, Pregnancy Achievement and Reproductive Health* by Toni Weschler.

Would You Like to Try British nettles?

British nettles are edible. Other countries may have different nettles. Please check before picking!

NEW ZEALAND NETTLES CAN CAUSE SERIOUS ILLNESS, EVEN DEATH (urtica ferox, ongaonga)

You'll need a patch of clean edible British-type stinging nettles *(urtica dioica)* free from sprays. The top crown of leaves is the most tender, especially if picked before they flower. An easy way to pick them is with scissors and a colander. (How Seren would have loved to have cooking scissors and a colander!) Wash the leaves thoroughly, snip them up, and tip them into your vegetable stir-fry towards the end – they need to wilt down and heat through well. Or cook your nettles like spinach with butter.

Three Muds – Geography

When I go for a walk, I crunch over chalk, slither on clay, squelch through peat, or encounter all three in the same afternoon. The same three muds smear the bare feet or boots of the Wellstowe characters, who live on the fen edge as I do. The fen is a ghost of itself now, with acres of sugar beet stretching between regimented rivers. When Seren and Oswynne travelled upstream from the coast it was a wilderness, except for the remains of some Roman attempts at drainage.

You won't find Wellstowe on a modern map. You may catch sight of it out of the corner of your eye … I have exaggerated some features of the landscape. Postholes show archaeologists where Anglo-Saxon dwellings stood; many have been found in fen edge communities. Ploughed-out round barrows are marked on old maps. The ARCHI UK website is a trove of detail which reveals the tools and skills of those who left their footprints on our trackways.[1]

---

[1] ARCHI UK Archaeology website: http://www.archiuk.com/

Traders brought ideas and stories, along with their goods, from far countries. Near Stockholm, a small bronze figure of Buddha, with silver eyes to show enlightenment, was found in an excavation. It was brought from India about the time of our story. (*Hammer of the North, Myths and Heroes of the Viking Age*, Magnus Magnusson.)

History and Herstory

This novel is set in 598 CE/AD, when the Romans were long gone. Written records start a hundred years later (in England), written by monks such as the Venerable Bede in Northumbria. The Book of Kells was written around two hundred years after the time of this novel.

Women's rights were changing at this time. Christine Fell guides us through this confusing time, before and after laws were written, in *Women in Anglo-Saxon England*. In *Peace-weavers and Shield-Maidens, Women in Early English Society*, Kathleen Herbert gives fascinating glimpses of a war-like princess who claims her husband, and roving women who seek out their lovers … as well as detailing laws and events. Within a couple of centuries, women's freedom contracted to the mediaeval level, and has not yet fully recovered.

I have been exhilarated, heart-broken and inspired by Manda Scott's Boudica series of historical novels: *Dreaming the Eagle, Dreaming the Bull, Dreaming the Hound* and *Dreaming the Serpent Spear*. Our Celtic ancestors come alive through the power of her voice.[2]

Jean Markale in *Women of the Celts* gives us an inspiring picture of our ancestors, perhaps not historically accurate. He understands myths and legends in depth.

Was there ever a 'golden age' when women and men lived in equality and harmony, with social justice and no extremes of wealth and poverty? The archaeologist Marija Gimbutas found evidence of such cultures in 'old' Europe – the Balkan peninsula.[3] Her digs unearthed figurines of

---

[2] https://mandascott.co.uk

[3] The countries that now cover Old Europe, as excavated and described by Marija Gimbutas, are as follows: parts of the Czech Republic, Austria, Slovakia, Ukraine, Slovenia, Hungary, Romania, Moldova, Croatia, Bosnia and

goddesses amongst unfortified settlements, where dwellings of similar sizes revealed a more equitable society. Her conclusions are in her books: *Goddesses and Gods of Old Europe*, *The Civilization of the Goddess* and many more. She found evidence of invasions by horse-riding nomads from the steppes, which wiped out these peaceful societies and swept through Europe, changing cultures in ways we do not yet fully understand.

Marija Gimbutas was disbelieved and put down by established archaeology in her lifetime; her conclusions were considered much too feminist! Recently, DNA studies have backed up her arguments, and conventional archaeology has recognised she was right. Colin Renfrew lays out the evidence in his lecture, *Marija Rediviva: DNA and Indo-European origins*, which can be seen on Youtube.[4]

A thorough defence of Gimbutas and explanation of her ideas was written by Max Dashu, director of the Suppressed Histories Archive.[5]

The story of Varagan's invasion of Peony Valley may be more historically accurate than Hilda knew!

Stephen O Glosecki, academic researcher into early English, found echoes of a matrilinear society in Beowulf and in Anglo-Saxon laws.[6] Perhaps the clan mothers from before the Crossing are smiling on us!

Herstory, or women's history, often relies on cross-cultural comparisons, insight and hunches to make sense of the gaps. Men's writing covered what they considered interesting and important, and what they had access to; women's lives often slipped through the net of history.

Valuable information about women's lives can be found in *Anglo-Saxon Food and Drink, Production, Processing, Distribution and Consumption* by Ann Hagen. Evidence about daily life also comes from *The Earliest English* by Samantha Glasswell.

Herzegovina, Montenegro, Serbia, Bulgaria, Albania, Macedonia, Greece.

[4] Lord Colin Renfrew 'Marija Rediviva: DNA and Indo-European Origins.' www.youtube.com/watch?v=pmv3J55bdZc

[5] Suppressed Histories Archive article on Marija Gimbutas: http://www. suppressedhistories.net/articles/strawdolls.html

[6] http://www.heroicage.org/issues/5/Glosecki1.html

The various tribes of Celtic peoples were not native to Britain, of course. Waves of migration and cultural change brought them to Britain long before. The Anglo-Saxons were newcomers from areas that are now in Denmark and Germany.

In the rite of Glory-Dawn, the earth blessing is inspired by an Anglo-Saxon field remedy. I owe the beauty of the wording to those who sang it long ago.

Redwald is a historical figure. No spoilers for forthcoming books in this trilogy! Sam Newton can be relied on for detail and ongoing discoveries about him.[7]

Ola is also a historical queen of Essex, documented as Ricola. Ric means queen: compare Glasgow Queen Street rail station, and the Morrigan, great goddess of Ireland (formidable when furious; not one to mess with!)

Queen Ola most probably did not own thigh-length white patent boots, or any of the fashions depicted in tv shows that poke fun at modern women of Essex. Read more about Ola in Books 2 and 3 of The Storytellers Trilogy: *The Antler Mask* and *The Dolphin-Rib Harp*. Join my mailing list for news.[8]

I have attempted to stay within the boundaries of history when it's known, and riffed on these themes free-form when history has neglected to supply useful facts. This is not a history book! Fiction with a dash of fantasy can be more interesting than history, as a way to explore big questions.

Mothering and Parenting

I am interested in why some societies are patriarchal, and what types of parenting techniques create the unease in children that leads to social injustice in adults. Erik H Erikson's *Childhood and Society* first got me thinking about this, as part of a university course in Childhood Development. No children were involved in that course …

---

[7] www.wuffings.co.uk

[8] https://racheloleary.co.uk

During three decades of helping mothers and babies learn to breastfeed, I have discovered more about the ways we get oppressed by a kyriarchal society that disrespects mothering. Mothers and other parents heroically battle to stop passing on their own hang-ups to their children. It's a daily struggle to remember our own self-worth and re-create it in our children, while the big world dismisses us as unimportant, lazy etc. Anyone nurturing a child is investing energy in the next generation, a vital task for our survival.

Gabrielle Palmer takes us 'from the stone age to steam engines: a gallop through history' in *The Politics of Breastfeeding*. This vision-changing book covers many aspects of infant feeding, including how mothers support each other when permitted by our cultures. Read *Why the Politics of Breastfeeding Matters* by the same author, but don't miss the longer book.

How can women and parents support each other around birth and breastfeeding, in defiance of systems set up to process our bodies like meat? Maddie McMahon finds rays of hope in her books *Why Doulas Matter* and *Why Mothering Matters*.

Several charities exist to facilitate support for breastfeeding. Don't wait until you have a problem to get in touch! Learn, make friends, support others, build a community, at any time in your parenting journey.[9]

Where Do Hilda's Stories Come From?

If you think you hear echoes in these tales of ones you tell your children from books of 'fairy tales', that's because they do link up. There's nothing like reading the same story ten times a night to start a brain thinking about meanings and variations ...

There's little left in Western Europe of the dark forest of the Grimms' *Household Tales*. The Woodland Trust and local Wildlife Trusts take care of areas of old-growth woodland in the UK, a precious resource for all wildlife, including humans. You may find stories lurking in the undergrowth, jumping out of clearings, lazing under logs ... The

---

[9] www.laleche.org.uk and www.llli.org

mountains, forests and plains of Old Europe are still lurking at the corners of our imagination, rich in folk tales and traditions.

The riddles Hilda tells are simplified versions of genuine Anglo-Saxon riddles. See *Anglo-Saxon Riddles* by John Porter.

Meg's story *The Buried (or Dead) Moon* comes from the Lincolnshire carrs. It was told by her grandmother to a nine-year-old disabled girl, probably Agnes Brattan, who told it to the collector Marie Balfour. Agnes apparently relished the gruesome details and fairly made the flesh creep with her words and gestures. MC Balfour published it in 1891. It appears in folk tale collections, most recently *Lincolnshire Folk Tales* by Maureen James.[10]

When Meg tells the traditional northern story *The Laidly Worm of Spindlestone Heugh*, it is set in Seren's home country by the shore. Stories travel!

If you are seeking British folk tales, browse the History Press series by counties, for adults and for children.[11]

Shamanic Practices

For clues about shamanic practices, *The Way of Wyrd* by Brian Bates is inspiring. Mircea Eliade on *Shamanism* sparked my imagination. Joan Halifax in *Shamanic Voices* brought these experiences closer to our time and understanding.

Did Anglo-Saxons Use Talking Sticks?

I have borrowed the concept of the talking stick (speaking-staff) from Native American traditions. Many thanks to these tradition-keepers for such a simple, elegant, and powerful tool, now in use worldwide. If you are from a Native American culture, and my usage seems like cultural appropriation to you, please contact me so I can learn and do better.

The Garboldisham macehead could have been a speaking-staff – we do not know how it was used.[12] The Sutton Hoo sceptre is in the form of

---

[10] http://www.tellinghistory.co.uk

[11] www.thehistorypress.co.uk/local-history/storytelling/

[12] https://prehistories.wordpress.com/tag/garboldisham-macehead/

a whetstone but was never used for sharpening weapons or tools.[13] Could this have been a speaking-staff?

Religions

Seren and Hilda are moved by goddesses of Celtic origin. The Anglo-Saxons brought their own gods and goddesses to Britain. They hide in place names and days of the week.

Carved figures like the Breejsh stone that Seren adores can be found all over the British Isles, Ireland and continental Europe, now integrated into churches. They are known as Sheela Na Gigs; there is ongoing discussion of their meanings and origins.[14]

Christianity came to these islands with the Romans, then disappeared when they left. At the time of this book it is making a new entrance, with Celtic monks like Brother Michael, and, further south, St Augustine's mission to Kent.

As Christianity tagged along with the language and structures of feudalism, kings, crowns, princes and lordship became welded into it. The two structures strengthened each other – and conspired to relegate female sexuality to the realms of sin and social horror.

Seren and Meg notice how the stories told by the missionary put women down. He denies the existence of their goddesses, and their experience of being cared for by earth, water and fire. We can guess how successful the early missionaries were by the frequent letters from popes, admonishing people for worshipping at wells, stones, and trees ... They did better when they absorbed pagan holy places into church buildings.[15]

The shortage of speaking parts for females in Christianity bites, in the run-up to every nativity play, as young girls discover they can be Mary, the Angel (of questionable gender) or ... nobody. Meanwhile, unlimited numbers of their brothers can wear the inevitable tea towel to

---

[13] http://www.britishmuseum.org/research/collection_online/collection_object_details.aspx?objectId=88895&partId=1

[14] http://www.sheelanagig.org/wordpress

[15] http://www.oxfordreference.com/view/10.1093/oi/authority.20110803100337215

play shepherds, three don dressing gowns and crowns, Joseph and the innkeeper have lines to remember. Even the ox is a boy.

Nowadays Christians do much good work within their communities and worldwide, with initiatives for fair trade and social justice, in charities and co-operatives. It seems that an understanding of compassion as central to the message is re-emerging.

The Moot

The moot was certainly a historical folkway. Many moot-hills survive in English place names. How were moots organised? We do not know. Echoes of the methods in Edith's tradition can be found in some practices of the Society of Friends (Quakers), in AS Neill's *Summerhill*, in the restorative justice movement, and in some Native American wisdom.[16]

Open source technology is already using this ethos to develop software.

Let's create more new traditions based on these wisdoms!

---

[16] https://upliftconnect.com/peacemaking-the-navajo-way

Acknowledgements

I am grateful to my Mum for reading to me, doing the voices, and sharing her love of stories with me.

Thank you to my children, who wanted stories 'again, again' and sometimes a story 'without a book'.

I'd like to thank my husband, Martin, for sharing his scientific observations of birds over many years. His understanding of the ecology of fen and forest brings the beat of wings into *The Swan-Bone Flute*, and enriches my life.

Dido Dunlop has worked in a creative peer supervisor relationship with me throughout the writing process of *The Swan-Bone Flute*. Her insights and challenges helped me to bring out the depth and power of Hilda's stories and to explore the Anglo-Saxon and Celtic characters. With similar research interests, we have crawled into Neolithic barrows together, hunted goddesses through the British Museum, and shared knowledge and skills. Our Skype sessions often began in desperate stuck places and ended in laughter and renewed creativity. Dido's book, *Storm Weathering, A Workbook for our Inner and Outer Climate*, provides pathways into the inner changes we need to help us counteract environmental and social damage.[17]

Many thanks to the artist and illustrator, Katherine Soutar for capturing the spirit of the book in her beautiful cover art and drawings in the text. I danced round the kitchen when she said she 'rather loved' the book! It's been a delight to work with her because of the deep connection she forms with the stories she illustrates, as well as her skill and patience.[18]

Caroline Barden proofread the text with a sparrowhawk eye for detail, and improved the clarity of the writing. She pounced on stray hyphens with kindness and rigour. Thank you![19]

---

[17] Dido Dunlop: http://www.wisebirds.org

[18] Katherine Soutar, artist: https://katherinesoutarillustration.com

[19] Caroline Barden, proofreader: http://www.cbproofreader.com

Amy Corzine suggested many improvements to the text. Thank you for engaging with the story so creatively. I am grateful for your editing skill and knowledge.[20]

Alan Wilkie wrangled the design angle by laying out the text, covers and illustrations, and assisted with the process of publication. Thank you for your care, artistry and skill, attention to every detail, endless patience, kindness and humour, even when being climbed over by your grandchildren while working.

Miss Jackson taught me to read and write. I never thanked her enough. Barbara Wilson gave me a thirst for history and opened out the possibility that people were different in times gone by.

Many thanks to all who taught my university courses in history, and social and political sciences. It's not your fault!

I proudly claim any mistakes in this book as my own.

Many thanks to Jem Dick for details of swan-bone flutes. With amazing synchronicity, he found a swan wing in a fox's earth and made a swan-bone flute from it. The music he plays on it sends shivers down the spine. I am glad I met you, long after putting those details in the text. Thank you for the music.

The late Hilda Ellis Davidson read an early draft and challenged Hilda Hedgebackwards to make more of a difference. 'She could do more! Have more effect!' she charged me at her Folklore Society meetings, while her labrador snaffled pink wafer biscuits from a low coffee table. I hope Hilda ED would have liked the effect she had on the story.

Sal Hunter, scientist and artist, thank you for seeing what I wanted to do and holding me to it, with warmth and humour.

My friend, Brighid Simpkin, has trodden the storytelling path with me from the first, 'Why don't we meet up and just tell stories?' Let's share many more fireside miles and tales!

---

[20] Amy Corzine: https://www.amycorzine.com

My friends from Cambridge Storytellers have nurtured me as a listener and storyteller, and brought wonderful tellers to our area.[21] Our patron Hugh Lupton is a constant source of inspiration.[22]

Thank you to Cath Little[23] and Shonaleigh Cumbers.[24] Both these professional storytellers send roots deep into their different cultures to draw up stories that nourish and sustain the women of today.

I have enjoyed and learned from workshops and courses led by Michael Harvey and Hazel Bradley, Sharon Jacksties, and Richard Neville (original owner of the eyebrows, thanks for the loan!)

The Company of Storytellers revived storytelling as an art in Britain. Hearing them made my jaw drop in astonishment at the beauty and power of old tales well told. I started chasing chances to learn, tell, and listen to myths, legends and folk tales after those early performances. Thank you Hugh Lupton, Sally Pomme Clayton and Ben Haggarty.

West Stow Anglo-Saxon Village and Country Park is where I go to step back into the early Middle Ages. Thank you to all involved in building it: experimental archaeologists, wood carvers, carpenters and thatchers. Thanks to all who care for it, develop it, fund it, administrate it, fight for it in committees, and help us enjoy and learn from this amazing place.[25]

Various re-enactment groups have answered endless questions, demonstrated craftwork, and not minded me hanging around and watching everything. Thank you all!

The workshop led by Stephanie Hale that I attended was very helpful in shaping this book and the rest of the trilogy (forthcoming!). I appreciated her follow-up phone call.

I learned the life-changing potential of women sharing personal stories from La Leche League breastfeeding support organisation. I'd like

[21] Cambridge Storytellers: cambridgestorytellers.com

[22] Hugh Lupton, storyteller: www.angelfire.com/folk/hughlupton/index.html

[23] Cath Little, storyteller: www.cathlittle.co.uk

[24] Shonaleigh, storyteller: http://www.shonaleigh.uk

[25] West Stow Anglo-Saxon Village: http://www.weststow.org

to thank everyone who attends groups or writes for LLL magazines – and my sensitive colleagues who facilitate honest, heart-felt sharing in a safe environment.

Some of Huldran's wisdom comes from Re-evaluation Counselling (co-counselling). I'd like to thank the friends who taught me how to 'ride the river of tears and laughter' to wash away hurt (see Chapter 10). Thank you to all those who continue to use it to free people from oppressions, so we can change the world.[26]

The movements taught by the spirit-swan derive from Dru Yoga.[27] Many thanks to all my yoga teachers, in their various traditions.

Doulas' fierce compassion for families in the childbearing year is a well of hope for the world. The organisers, workshop leaders, and participants in Doula UK Retreat have enabled me to work with these stories to unleash the power in them.[28]

I would like to thank the members of the Matriarchy Research and Reclaim Network for opening doors in hearts and minds. I picked up the magazine a few decades ago in a wholefood co-op among the dates and lentils – and your definition of matriarchy as 'mothering first' changed my life.

Thank you, Sisters of Gaia, for all the loving energy we raised and sent out to the earth, from muddy woods and dusty community halls. Stay merry!

Thank you to my book club friends, for sharing enjoyment of books, and fun.

Many friends have encouraged me during the writing and publishing process. I have appreciated every kind word. You know who you are … thank you!

Rachel O'Leary, Spring 2019

---

[26] Re-evaluation Counselling (co-counselling): http://www.rc.org
[27] Dru Yoga: https://druyoga.com
[28] Doula UK: https://doula.org.uk

Book Club Questions
About The Swan-Bone Flute

About the story ...

- Which character do you identify most with in *The Swan-Bone Flute*? What would you like to say to her or him? How does this character develop during the story?

- What was your favourite fairy tale when you were younger? What did you like about it? What effect did it have in your life?

- There are different kinds of stories in *The Swan-Bone Flute*: personal stories recounted by various characters from their own experiences; mythical stories told by Hilda and Meg; and the adventures of the characters in the plot. Which type of story did you enjoy most? Which resonated most with you?

- A hero's journey is sometimes described as a rocky road of trials; a heroine's journey as spirals going ever deeper. How does this apply to the characters in this book? Do you think your life is more like one or the other, or both pathways?

About our environment ...

- Where does the water come from, where you live? How do you get it?

- What birds have you seen or heard today? What plants have you touched today? When did you last have your hands in earth or compost? What stops us being in touch with our environment?

- Ursel is passionate about protecting the deer, and all the life of the forest. What threatens our environment now? How do you contribute to work to protect the planet? What makes it hard for you to take action? How can we support each other in care for our world?

- When did you last see the moon? What energy changes do you notice as the moon waxes and wanes?

- What do you know about the history of your local area? How could you find out more?

About women's lives …

- If Hilda dropped by into your community, how would she 'wake up the women'? If the women of your community woke up, what would they do? What forces make women's lives difficult? What stops women from making our or their lives better? (Inside the self, or outside, or both?) What similarities or differences are there for transwomen?

- The story, *The Rowanberry Dress*, derives from a mediaeval ballad, and a version is told by the Wife of Bath in Chaucer's *Canterbury Tales*. It is sometimes called 'What Women Want'. What do you want? What do you need? Practice saying: 'I Want … I Need …' out loud! All together? Encourage each other, everybody!

- Have you used decision-making processes like those at the Moot? How did it go? Could you try them in your work or with your family?

- In what ways do you feel like a slave in your life, and when do you feel like a slave-owner? Who benefits from your work? Who picks your tea?

- Our attitudes towards others sometimes change when we hear more about their lives. Have you got any experiences of this that you would like to share?

- If you could rebuild your community based on mothering values, what would it be like? What would you hear, smell, taste, feel, see?

Get in touch

If you would like …

- Rachel to come and tell stories for your group
- or if you'd like Rachel to lead a workshop for your women's group, environmental group, co-op or community
- or if you prefer to work with Rachel to create your own workshop based on stories from *The Swan-Bone Flute*
- and you have some ideas about funding to make it happen!

One workshop leader said:

'I held survivors' group tonight and read the story you sent me (The Rowanberry Dress) and we all did the task and it was really emotional and empowering, the women loved it, we did more a shout what we need to let out, some anger and frustration, and the atmosphere was amazing.'

Ms Kelly Collins

(Thank you for permission to use this quote.)

Storytellers, if you would like to tell stories from this book, in paid or unpaid settings, please get in touch at the planning stage so we can work together.

racheloleary.co.uk

Rachel O'Leary ... telling a story

The character in this story is hamming up her stomach ache, to swindle her brother ... Eventually she claims her power and stands up for herself; they resolve their conflict and feast on pies and cider (with the giants and the dogs).

As a storyteller, I like myths where feisty females do zappy things, like the ice giantess who skis down a mountain with her wolves to grab herself a husband, because the gods owe her one. (I won't reveal how she got the wrong one, or what they had to do to make her laugh; that would spoil it for you ...)

I love stories where a small act of kindness is rewarded with Mother Nature's astonishing generosity.

When I'm helping parents and babies learn to breastfeed, that resounding response often happens when the little one gazes into her mother's eyes and milk flows. I see it again when that mother or nursing parent turns to the next family and encourages them, and a friendship develops. This is how communities grow.

It's not all cooing at babies; part of my work is to support breastfeeding organisations, and stand up for the rights of parents to make their decisions free from commercial exploitation. You meet good people that way!

When I'm not working or telling stories, I like to walk over the landscape where I live and where *The Swan-Bone Flute* is set. I make a habit of swimming in any water deep enough: mountain tarns, rivers, lakes, and the sea of course. *Photo: Paul Jackson*

443

Rachel O'Leary ... writing

Rachel's articles, poems and stories have been published in the following:

Journals and newsletters

- La Leche League GB Newsletter
- Breastfeeding Matters Magazine
- Feedback
- Leaven
- Treasure Chest (Lactation Consultants GB journal)
- Cambridge UK Birth Centre Newsletter
- Association of Radical Midwives Journal
- Women for Life on Earth magazine
- AIMS Journal (Association for Improvements in the Maternity Services)
- Childbirth Alternatives Quarterly

Books

- *Pregnancy and birth: in support of autonomy,*   Lisa Fannen, ed. (Brighton Women's Health Information Collective, 2004)
- *A Woman's Place,* Veronica Hannon, ed. (Poetry Now, 1993)
- *Musings on Mothering,* Teika Bellamy, ed. (Mother's Milk Books 2012)

Lightning Source UK Ltd.
Milton Keynes UK
UKHW021021250919
350431UK00009B/301/P